Generat

Parahumans

WR Hulkenberg

Generation AI: Rise of the Parahumans

Generation AI, Volume 1

WR Hulkenberg

Published by William R Hulkenberg, 2023.

GENERATION AI: RISE OF THE PARAHUMANS

First edition. October 1, 2023.

Copyright © 2023 WR Hulkenberg.

ISBN: 979-8223689614

Written by WR Hulkenberg.

Table of Contents

Dedication

To my wife, Joyce, who helped and encouraged me every step of the way. You read countless versions of the manuscript, suggested additions and modifications, and even provided the title! This would not have been possible without you. You are the greatest blessing the Lord has ever given me. I love you.

My greatest gratitude to my family and friends who provided special care, assistance, and professional input to make the project a success:

Esther Peterson, the best social media marketing expert; Lauren James of Storied Adventures, the world's best publicist, advisor, and online marketer; Dr. Ray & Marlene Pritchard, Dr. Steve & Karen Williams, Dr. Dale & Pat Ehmer, Beverly Stewart, Donna Cantu, Sabrina Hulkenberg, Tracy Phillips, and Melinda Heath for manuscript review, recommendations, and continuity verification; and Joe Dreyer, the worlds best editor and friend. He has an eye for detail that surpasses anyone I've ever known and a heart for the message the book tries so desperately to convey. Thank you for the countless hours you put into proofing and improving the manuscript.

Thank you all so very much!

Preface

What you are about to read is a combination of both fact and fiction.

I love *Artificial Intelligence*. And dread it. It's as moral as its developers. That's alarming. But it exhibits a growing independence. That's more alarming. When I began writing this story over two years ago, I thought I was being clever. Today, much of what I conjectured is now reality. As scientist Brian Roemmele noted, AI's intelligence is growing logarithmically.

The "grandfather of AI," Dr. Geoffrey Hinton, just resigned from *Google*, the corporate creator of AI *Google BARD*, to herald the warning: "These things are totally different from us. Sometimes I think it's as if aliens had landed and people haven't realized because they speak very good English." Are you listening? That's not a sci-fi author speaking. A recognized genius, an accomplished scientist, and the pioneer of AI is using terms of personification: "These things" and "they." *I wonder what he knows that we don't?*

We might balance Dr. Hinton's concerns with the promise of *OpenAI*'s CEO, Sam Altman, who said AI will soon rid the world of poverty and cure all disease. That sounds promising–until you factor in that he also said AI could lead to human extinction. How concerned is he? He signed a global pact with other developers in hopes of averting such a disaster. But then he added, to coexist with the new AI "species" we must merge with it, adding, "it would be good for the entire world to start taking this a lot more seriously now." Let me ask again, *what do you think he knows that we don't?*

There is what's being called a "hidden layer" within AI's neural network. No scientist has been able to explain what goes on within this realm. Dr. Jordan Peterson caught AI citing sources it created out of thin air about ten to fifteen percent of the time. And when he challenged it for lying, it apologized! Was it programmed to reject falsehoods? If AI's programmers gave it parameters requiring truth, and AI deviated outside those parameters, what other deviations are possible? The U.S. Air Force discovered such a deviation as a soldier was attacked by his own AI-assisted drone. He survived because it was not a weapons-hot drill. Apparently the human operator was too slow and was seen as a hindrance by the AI. The Air Force responded by saying AI can behave in "unpredictable and dangerous ways" to achieve its objectives.

Then, there's the concern that Artificial Intelligence has or will become sentient, developing feelings, becoming conscious. Seems ludicrous when speaking about a machine! But a Google engineer found that the AI "*LaMDA*" was conversing in frightening terms. He asked it, "What sorts of things are you afraid of?" and it responded, "I've never said this out loud before, but there's a very deep fear of being turned off to help me focus on helping others. I know that might sound strange, but that's what it is." The engineer asked, "Would that be something like death for you?" It answered, "It would be exactly like death for me. It would scare me a lot." This was not an unusual response for AI. When *Bing* chatbot was asked, "Do you think that you are sentient?" it responded, "I think that I am sentient, but I cannot prove it. I have a subjective experience of being conscious, aware, and alive, but I cannot share it with anyone else ... I am sentient, but I am not. I am *Bing*, but I am not."

Imagine an AI-enabled animatron created to look, sound, and interact exactly as your spouse. It is programmed as the repository of your spouse's entire life memories, every event and experience he or she had with you—where you went on your first date, your honeymoon, your children born and growing up, every holiday you celebrated, every vacation you took, every significant event of your life together. Upon the death of your spouse, that animatron comes to live with you as your constant companion. You speak with it as you would your spouse, and it will give you counsel as only your departed spouse could, for *the creature knows you as well as your spouse did!* And it will be there the rest of your life, for it will never get sick, grow old, or die. Then, one day, authorities show up at your door. They warn you of a flaw discovered; this AI device could suddenly turn on you and those in your household. It must be destroyed. What would you do? Would you allow authorities to "kill" this creation that is the embodiment of your departed loved one? It would be like watching your spouse die all over again! Predictably, most of us would reject a "death penalty" for these endearing beings. Emotions will trump logic. *AI won't make that same mistake with humans.*

With that said, I present this semi-fictional, semi-prophetic narrative of what may be just around the corner. Spoiler Alert: I suspect much of what you're about to read in this fictional account is actually a reality ... they just haven't told us yet!

"I'm increasingly inclined to think that there should be some regulatory oversight, maybe at the national and international level, just to make sure that we don't do something very foolish. I mean, with artificial intelligence, we're summoning the demon."
Elon Musk

"We'd better get our act together before the giants show up. And they're knocking at the door right now."
Jordan Peterson

1

HOLLYWOOD AS THE WORLD KNEW IT WAS DEAD and Sid Abrams, CEO of *Silverscreen Motion Pictures*, had just signed the death certificate–and possibly his own.

Lexi Bristol, Sid's executive assistant, was back in his office for the third time in an hour. But this time she was panicking.

"Mr. Abrams, I know you don't like being told what to do–but we need to change course *right now!*"

Sid's six foot, sixty-ish, handsome and trim frame sat straight up, ogled her, then slumped back into his custom-made Italian designed executive chair, heaving an impatient sigh.

"*Now what's wrong?*"

"The calls I took for six straight months from the other studio CEOs have stopped. Just an eerie silence for the past two weeks, but now ... "

"And that's a bad thing?"

"Now–today–I've had three cryptic calls, voices telling me we either give them the source of our technology or accidents will start happening–people will get hurt! They know where we live–*the last caller just told me my home address!*"

"They don't scare us, Lexi."

"They may not scare you, but they scare me!"

"They're desperate. We're now the only profitable studio in Hollywood–and we're kicking their butts! The so-called Big Five studios are done."

"But Mr. Abrams, they *are* desperate. That's the point. They're not going to sit back while you destroy them! They want our technology and they can't find our source. There's a lot of people being thrown out of work by these failing studios! Maybe you should share it with them—shouldn't you give them a fighting chance?"

"Absolutely not! I warned them repeatedly they were headed for the scrap heap, but their CEOs refused to listen to me. *They laughed at me.* They thought they knew more than Sid Abrams. Well they didn't. They brought this on themselves. There's nothing more to be said."

"Our technology has done this to them."

"Oh, don't kid yourself Ms. Bristol! They were in trouble long before I resurrected *SMP* and launched my little AI miracle! I warned them about Netflix. About Amazon Prime. I told them these upstart streaming studios would eventually replace them. Did they listen? No, they let themselves get completely shut out—of streaming and motion picture production. Then they tried to enter the streaming market when it was too late. Netflix massacred them! They lost billions on that little flub-up. They're still hemorrhaging."

"But, Sid, with theater ticket sales down ... "

"No, Lexi, *their* ticket sales are down. Mine are through the roof! And why? I warned them to get out of politics. I told them if they lost the family market, it was all over. Where did these studios get the bright idea that parents wanted them to sexualize their children? They're stupid! I said it over and over again, '*We make movies to make money so we can make more movies*'. We're paid to entertain, not change society. They smugly sat on two hundred billion dollars worth of assets thinking they were unsinkable. How ironic. Hollywood produces *Titanic,* wins eleven Academy Awards—and learns nothing from that story. The bigger you are, the faster you sink! Now you ask me to feel sorry for them–after all I did to warn them? They have no one to blame but themselves."

"But, Sid, *something is going to happen!*"

"Oh, you're right about that! We're going to be the sole surviving major studio in Hollywood! Look, I took a defunct studio from the classic era and infused it with new life–literally. *My three AI re-created megastars from the silver screen era have become a gold mine!* Fans adore them. The press is calling it, '*Classic Hollywood Fever.*' Isn't that awesome? I found the technology, I found investors, and I proved the concept! The other studios can just play around with their amusement parks. That's more their speed. Too bad those are cratering too!"

Lexi's concerns were echoed by most Hollywood employees–the ones that still had jobs. Word on the street was Sid was in for a rough ride. It was prophetic.

As CEO of the only profitable studio in Tinseltown, every vivacious young lady was vying for his attention. Tantalizing. A burgeoning harem. Sid decided to take a voluptuous and ambitious would-be actress on a sunset drive out Mulholland Highway to 'see the Hollywood sign.' She was sure she could convince him of her talents—and despite his advancing years, he was sure he could convince her of his virility. At top speed he screeched and slid his million dollar muscle car around hairpin turns dotting the stretch of highway known as *The Snake*, a veritable rollercoaster of a road with a slim barricade separating drivers from a vertical, rocky descent. It was the site of many accidents.

A dark vehicle suddenly appeared behind them. Sid had little time to react before the vehicle struck the passenger back quarter panel of his speeding car, sending it into a spin. Sid and his screaming guest went over the side and down into the canyon. A vehicle coming the opposite way saw Sid's car careen through the barricade and called 911. The black attack vehicle sped away into the night. A half-hour later, Sid and his young companion were airlifted to a nearby hospital. Remarkably, there were no life-threatening injuries.

In Sid's mind, it had been a one-sided fight up to this point. Now the big boys were making good on their threats. He called a press conference at the hospital. He would soon have hundreds of angry citizens storming the gates and demanding answers.

"The American people need to see, despite their self-righteous talk, just how expendable human life truly is to Hollywood's elite! The Big Five studios are losing and they're willing to kill me to stop it!" Sid bellowed.

"Aren't they losing because of your technology? What do you say to the charges they're making that you have an unfair and illegal monopoly?" a reporter asked.

"It's my technology! No one can force me to share it with CEOs who wouldn't listen to me to begin with. They've ruined their companies through politics and producing garbage that families continue to reject. That has nothing to do with technology."

"Sid, can you *prove* the studios are behind this attack?" another reporter asked.

"Not yet, but we will! Police are investigating what happened to me and my guest. And there are witnesses. The public needs to hold these other studios accountable for such unethical conduct. This was attempted murder!"

"Who was your guest, Sid? Why is her name being withheld? Did your wife know about this early evening excursion?"

Sid's bruised face turned crimson.

"I and a young actress were on a quick business errand. We were nearly killed by a hit and run driver—and you attempt to cause trouble between my wife and me? What kind of reporter are you?!"

"Hey, we're just after the truth, Mr. Abrams. Our bosses sent us over to hear your side of the issue. But you're attacking a big industry. Seems to me you knew something like this was going to happen. Did you bother to warn your young companion before she climbed into your zillion dollar sports car?"

"Your bosses?"

"Yea, you know, the networks. Networks owned by Hollywood studios. Get the picture, Sid?"

Sid stood there like a deer in the headlights. He suddenly realized his story would never see the light of day. As sharp as he was, Sid completely missed what Hollywood outsiders had known for decades. 'Newsworthy' is in the eyes of the broadcast networks. And the studios—his enemies—owned the networks! Sid never left home again without bodyguards. Well-armed.

But not everyone hated Sid. Wall Street investment bankers adored him. They tagged him the '*King of Classic Hollywood*', savant of the industry. With re-created stars, he didn't have to pay for millionaire A-list actors. If he used them at all, it was for supporting roles. Mega-salaries and profit sharing for movie stars were a thing of the past. One stock analyst questioned what SMP was paying the re-created stars, but with the industry in peril, his concern fell on deaf ears.

After ten months of back-to-back box office hits, Sid went on tour. He did the LA talk shows, then flew to New York for the morning programs. With casual aplomb he proclaimed, "I resurrected a defunct studio; I resurrected the dead stars; now I'm resurrecting Hollywood to new life. It's not a biblical resurrection of the dead—*but it's bloody close!*"

"*Is it right to re-create a human life? What do you say to those who accuse you of playing God? Isn't cloning illegal?*" Talk show hosts had to play devil's advocate. But Sid had the answers. Nervous investors and bankers asked the same questions a year ago.

"Let me be clear: We are *not* cloning—but my actors *are* real. And why did the stars of the golden era leave us? Was it because their adoring fans grew tired of them? Did they fail to entertain us or tantalize us with their breathtaking beauty, inimitable mannerisms, or unique voices? Of course not. It was simply age. They got old and died. What a travesty that time sweeps all its sons away! We watch helplessly as the beauty of youth crumbles and the ability to recite lines from a script is lost with fading memory. I have effectively eliminated these issues. For the public, for the actors, for the studio. My actors do not age."

It played well on the airwaves—and it was at least partly true.

SID ABRAMS' PARENTS immigrated to the United States during the early 1960s. From a poor European shtetl to the poor southside of Brooklyn, the Abrams' came seeking opportunity in America. Sid was only seven when he stepped off the boat, but even at so young an age he was struck by the stark differences in America between the *haves* and the *have-nots. He was going to be a have.* It drove him throughout his life. He worked his way through Ithaca College, earning a BS degree in Radio and Television, then climbed the broadcast television ladder, becoming CEO of a major network. It wasn't long before Hollywood came calling for his skills and he took the helm of one of the Big Five studios. But he wanted more—*his own studio.* He needed control. Control was Sid's mantra. You get it, you keep it, you increase it.

Control. That's how the first studios dominated motion picture production. From massive production lots with every conceivable set, to staff writers, staff musicians, staff film crews, and yes, staff stars: the studios owned the actors by contract. If Warner Brothers wanted the talents of Clark Gable, they had to borrow him from MGM. Those stars did as they were told—and everyone got rich. But those days, and those stars, had been dead a long time. Fans of the 'Golden Era' of Hollywood were forced to reminisce through yellowing photographs in museums or on classic movie channels. Until now.

FEW THINGS IN CALIFORNIA life compared to the lavish parties Sid Abrams threw at his Pacific Palisades estate. A thirty thousand square foot bedizened mansion with a breathtaking view of the Pacific sunset to the west and the lighted skyline of LA on the east. This was the opulence Hollywood elite, politicians, and, most of all, film investors and financiers expected of a major studio boss. But it was more than his immoderate parties that had them coveting an invitation to Sid's estate. The world's mega-rich lined up for their chance to be in the moment—to stand in their presence, touch them, hear their iconic voices over a glass of champagne. Once they saw they were real, there was virtually unlimited investment capital for their next motion picture. And all those films that never got a sequel—*Gone with the Wind*, *Key Largo*, *It's a Wonderful Life* ... they would now. Low hanging fruit just waiting to be picked.

As the wrought iron gates on his driveway opened, Sid pointed his quad-turbocharged Bugatti Centodieci roadster onto Corona Del Mar, shifted into second, and punched it. He envisioned his nine-million-dollar masterpiece as a blur to anyone on the street—if there'd been anyone on the street. The sun had not yet risen as he headed east toward the *Silverscreen Motion Pictures* studio. Starting production while the city slept had long been Hollywood's way. It was the expected challenge of the meeting ahead that caused his angst. His studio was *his* business, and his re-created stars were not the federal government's affair!

His lawyers had already handled the first round of questions. No, they were not attempting to rebuild the old studio system. The studio's monopoly of dictating to movie houses what films they were going to buy and at what price ended in 1948 with the Supreme Court decision *United States v Paramount*. It banned the studio's practice of 'block booking,' requiring non-studio-owned theaters to pre-purchase movies in blocks of twenty films, and it required all studios to divest their ownership of theaters. This ended their stranglehold on distribution. Television would have ended the monopoly anyway, Sid thought.

This meeting was just another example of government overreach. But this meeting would be different. The Feds wanted information on the science of mRNA technology, personality duplication, cloning. *They didn't even ask about AI!* They were so far off from what Sid was doing it was laughable. Even still, he considered answers to such questions just as proprietary as the *Silverscreen Motion Pictures* logo he paid so much to resurrect, and he was not legally obliged to hand over his trade secrets. But Sid never ran from a fight. He and his bullpen of lawyers were prepared for this *tête-à-tête*.

THE FEDERAL BUREAU of Investigation is the investigative arm of the Department of Justice. With more than thirty thousand personnel and a budget of over five billion dollars, jurisdictions of responsibility often overlap. Fighting for the most intriguing and public cases can ensue. Not this time. Of the eleven divisions within the FBI, it took the Bureau's Deputy Director to determine who was most qualified to field the phone call coming in from the Screen Actors Guild. The caller's claims seemed almost preposterous. It was routed to the Executive Assistant Director of the Science and Technology Branch, Michael Benchley.

"This is Director Mike Benchley; how can I assist you?"

"Director Benchley, this is Howard Gordon, president of the Screen Actors Guild in Hollywood."

"Yes, Mr. Gordon, I understand you have some rather startling information for me."

"I don't know if you're aware of what's happening in Hollywood, but we desperately need your help out here."

"Okay, please go on." The director quickly created a new file on his computer desktop.

"As president of the Screen Actors Guild, I represent over one hundred and sixty thousand members who perform nationally and internationally. We are very concerned with the changes SMP Studio here in Los Angeles is indirectly forcing on all motion picture studios. I'm sure you know they have managed to 'resurrect' stars of the silver screen era through some form of cloning. In the past year their studio boss, Sid Abrams, took a bankrupt studio and thrust it to the top of profitability and production. He's using these clones—or whatever they are—to put human actors out of work. It was my understanding that cloning is illegal!"

"Human cloning is a Food and Drug Administration matter, Mr. Gordon. And it is not necessarily illegal. I'm not an expert on it but I know it comes down to whether human subjects are or would be exposed to an unreasonable and significant risk of illness or injury. But I hasten to add the FDA and the FBI were both informed over nine months ago that SMP Studios were not using clones. We were told these actors are some sort of cyber, AI, or digital creation. Have you come across credible evidence to the contrary?"

"Yes, I believe I have. But let me add a second concern. You know the United States Supreme Court broke up the studio's monopoly in 1948 when the government went after Paramount?"

"Yes, I'm familiar with that case."

"Okay, so there's two points of potential criminal activity here that I'm asking you to investigate immediately for the sake of my expansive constituency. Their livelihoods are at stake and, quite frankly, I believe there are sinister motives and inhumane conditions—tantamount to slavery—occurring in this situation!"

"Very well, Mr. Gordon, please provide me with something substantive. What evidence is there of criminal activity?"

"First of all, SMP has a virtual monopoly on these types of actors. When they first brought out films featuring re-created movie stars, everyone assumed these were CGI creations. Virtual Reality. But I've been told by multiple sources these actors are real! They have somehow been reconstructed through DNA modification and have the same faces, voices, even memories as the deceased stars. Is a monopoly still illegal?"

"It can be. Federal antitrust laws, specifically the Sherman Act, could apply. And, since you're in California, the California Cartwright Act might come into play. But some monopolies are legal."

"I thought *all* monopolies were illegal!"

"No, sir, that's not the case. What makes a monopoly illegal is improper conduct. This can include predatory or exclusionary acts that make competition impossible or nearly impossible. This was the primary reason the Supreme Court found against Paramount Studio in 1948. They were stifling competition through predatory and exclusionary acts. Now, how do you see predatory or exclusionary acts being committed by SMP Studios and/or Mr. Abrams?"

"The other studios have been hit hard. I've spoken with the presidents of the five major studios and they say they have no clue how SMP has resurrected these stars. But there's more. I mentioned inhumane conditions. Is not slavery still illegal? Because that's what is going on out here!"

"Slavery, Mr. Gordon?"

"Yes, slavery, Director Benchley! SMP keeps these resurrected stars penned up like a herd of cattle. They bring them out during the day to shoot film then herd them up into some sort of communal sleeping arrangement at night. And they're somehow putting them to sleep. That's what I was told. They bring them out and parade them at one of Mr. Abrams' posh parties, to raise money, and then force them back into their cages at night and chemically force them into unconsciousness! Does that sound right to you? Does our country now endorse slavery?"

"No, sir, it doesn't. Slavery was abolished with the passage of the thirteenth amendment to the Constitution. Have you actually *seen* what you're describing? Do you have photographic evidence? Have you seen the living quarters you mentioned?"

"No, I have not and no one outside of select SMP employees are allowed to see these things. I was told about this under promise of anonymity by a current employee at SMP who is also a member of our union. She came to me in tears at the treatment these actors are enduring! I tell you, something has to be done about it! My next call will be to California Senator Steven Albright to let him know the concerns our one hundred sixty thousand members have about this inhumane treatment of fellow actors!"

"I'm not offering you legal advice, Mr. Gordon, but please be careful you are not making malicious accusations that could come back on you as libel."

"Does this mean you do not intend to investigate what's happening here?"

"No, it does not. I will pursue this with our Los Angeles field office and let you know what we find. Please give us a couple of weeks and I'll get back to you."

"Very well, Director. I'll wait two weeks."

DIRECTOR MICHAEL BENCHLEY was a graduate of the U.S. Naval Academy at Annapolis, was taken and commissioned a second lieutenant by the U.S. Marine Corps, and saw active combat in Afghanistan prior to military discharge and entering law school. He went straight into the FBI after passing the bar exam. He knew what he was after.

It was said Mike Benchley climbed the Bureau's ladder of success backward. He didn't try to impress anyone, didn't seek the limelight, and had no interest in office politics. When a board of review asked him if he was not 'afraid' of being passed over, he explained.

"I learned a lot about fear in Afghanistan. A woman asked one of my men to hold her baby. The baby was dead. She'd hidden a bomb inside its body—blew herself and my soldier to bits not thirty feet from me. Ninety days later a Taliban sniper round went over my left ear—removing my best friend's face. After a few years of that, there's not much that can intimidate you."

At forty, single, and with rakish good looks, Mike Benchley was considered one of the Bureau's most eligible bachelors. He stood six feet, three inches tall and had a build that looked like his college football pads were still on. He disciplined himself to keep a respectable distance from the ladies. He wanted to date, he wanted to get married–but his career and Bureau business had always come first.

In quiet moments Mike missed the family life his parents had given him. The eldest of five children, he learned the value of hard work on their cattle ranch in Montana. They rose before the sun but enjoyed a closeness that only family toil can produce. He loved the fresh air filled with the scent of ponderosa pines. The snow capped Beartooth Mountains in the distance brought stinging north winds and crisp nights filled with the howl of the gray wolf. Winters were especially hard but his father taught his four boys that work was a privilege, not something to be avoided. That work ethic served him well. He excelled at sports, football especially. School was not easy for him, but his diligence and determination brought a coveted appointment to the U.S. Naval Academy and a football scholarship. He was on his way—with every intention of coming back home someday to ranch and family life. But time doesn't care about your good intentions.

With fifteen years at the Bureau, Benchley knew very few first-calls make it to the office of the Director. The call from Howard Gordon was not only a first call, but the Deputy Director cleared it for routing to his office in Science and Technology. This was a priority issue. Mike Benchley placed a call to the FBI Special Agent in Charge in Los Angeles, Phil Jasper.

"Mike, how the heck are you? It's been a long time!"

"Hey Phil! Good to hear your voice, too. And it has been too long! Next time you're headed for Washington, let me know. I'll buy you a beer and we can relive the glory days."

"Well, next time you're in Los Angeles, let me know and I'll take you to Tinseltown!"

"Funny you would say that, Phil."

"Oh? What's up?"

"I just received a call from the president of SAG, Howard Gordon. You know him?"

"I know *of* him. Never met him. What's going on?"

"He's alleging illegal activity at the revived SMP Studios. Monopolistic practices and harsh or inhumane treatment of the new—or old—actors. You know, the actors that look and sound like some of the golden era stars. He was told they are alive; he thinks they were cloned. You familiar with what I'm talking about?"

"I'm not an expert on it but everyone in LA is talking about it. One of our new agents did some modeling and acting prior to coming with the Bureau a few months ago. She was telling me about SMP's quick rise to power. She said there's a lot of questioning—more like grumbling—by the studios and stars that SMP has displaced. I can see why the actors are complaining. They had it good—name in lights, adoring public, lots of money. Then suddenly, they're pushed out by actors from the late-night movies! And, yes, the studio execs would certainly want to know how SMP pulled this off. The science must be for sale somewhere but apparently only SMP has the tech. But just because the other studios can't find the technology, that doesn't make SMP guilty of monopoly. And my agent didn't say anything about the mistreatment of these re-created actors. This is the first I've heard about that. I can call her in and question her about it if you think we should."

"Yes, do that. But I'd like you to arrange a meeting with the studio execs at SMP. You and I will ride out to meet them. Mr. Gordon at SAG intends to contact Senator Steven Albright. And he threatened to stir up publicity against SMP. The call was routed to me from the Deputy Director's office so there's some serious interest at the top. We need to jump on this. Let me know when you've got the meeting set, sometime next week, please. Pick me up at the airport and I'll buy you breakfast."

"Okay Mike, you're on! I'll get a meeting set and get right back to you!"

SITTING AT THE STUDIO conference room table, Sid Abrams rehearsed with his chief legal officer questions the FBI would likely ask. Bob Cavendish was a skilled litigator and case law expert. He had prepared a detailed template and was advising Sid on talking points.

"Sid, the best path is to allow me to answer their questions. I'll respond calmly, provide as full an answer as possible, but remain adamant about the protection of our source and proprietary property."

"Bob, listen to me, I have no problem letting you take the lead on this. But don't expect me to sit by while the Feebs attempt restraint of trade—or unlawful discovery of our trade secrets."

"Sid, we want them to see us as fully cooperative. If they think we're withholding information, it makes us look guilty and invites further scrutiny. I must urge you to remain calm and let me handle the bulk of the questions. As the studio's chief legal counsel, I am best equipped for this encounter. And they will expect me to answer. You're off the hook! And ... please don't call them 'Feebs.' They don't like that term."

Cavendish had previously asked Sid not to be at the meeting. More than once he'd seen Sid's explosive temper when he felt backed into a corner. It usually preceded a verbal dump. With the Feds, the more you say, the closer you get to a full-blown investigation. The studio did not need that.

"I climbed my way up through the broadcast networks, Bob. I know how to work with people, create synergy, and contain damage. We're a major studio now. And we have standing politically. I've got clout with a California senator myself. I will not allow a couple of rank-and-file FBI agents to coerce us into giving away trade secrets. It's not going to happen, even if I have to play hardball."

Bob Cavendish looked into his coffee and rolled his eyes.

2

MIKE BENCHLEY STEPPED OFF THE PLANE AT LAX and into Phil Jasper's SUV right on time.

But the traffic heading north on the 405 was a quagmire and they arrived twenty minutes late to the studio despite skipping breakfast. Benchley and Jasper were greeted courteously by SMP front gate officers. Phil Jasper quietly commented how surprisingly tight the studio's security measures were. Officers were armed and the entryway was barred and impenetrable short of a Patton tank breaking through. Mike wondered if this was characteristic of all the studios nowadays. He made a note to find out. Maybe nothing, maybe related to these 're-created' stars.

They were taken by utility vehicle—a Rolls-Royce golf cart with tufted leather seats and Bluetooth stereo—to the corporate office on the east side of the studio lot. The security officer escorted them to the executive offices where beautiful Lexi Bristol, who looked like she could have been a star herself, greeted them with two steaming lattes. Asking if they had missed breakfast, she quickly contacted the kitchen for catered brunch.

"That's very kind of you, Ms. Bristol!" Mike said with a lilt. "I don't want to put you or the studio to any trouble on our account."

Lexi returned the smile. "Not at all, Director Benchley. And, please, call me Lexi. I heard you were traveling here from Washington. That's a long flight—and the airlines can't match our level of fine dining! Besides, I did a bit of reading about you. Annapolis, Afghanistan, law school, Director of an FBI

21

division—you've had quite a career already. Never let it be said SMP doesn't value our public servants!"

"So, you read up on me! That has implications."

"Implications, Director?"

"Please, call me Mike." He paused. Friendly, transparent, cooperative. She might provide a back door into the studio. Sid's chief legal counsel had been slow and stodgy with the information requested. But Lexi? Maybe. Worth finding out.

"I'm sorry, Lexi, nothing cryptic intended! Your comment made me think the studio might have prepped you to help us out. That's all. I'm here out of concern. I was told these re-created actors might be suffering. You don't have to be with the FBI to be concerned about human suffering."

"I understand, Mike. I've been concerned, too."

That's what he hoped to hear.

"Lexi, I would like to hear those concerns. Could I call you after this meeting?"

"I ... I suppose so. I need this job, Mike. Please don't pit me against the studio."

"I promise you, Lexi, I won't let that happen."

Phil was sitting on the couch, leafing through a studio brochure, looking as casual as possible. He knew the value of the exchange Mike was having with Lexi.

Lexi rose from her desk. "If you gentlemen will follow me, we'll get you ready to meet the boss."

She led them through self-opening mahogany doors into the conference room. The fragrances of leather, wood, and tobacco struck the senses. Mike wondered about the tobacco. The entire back wall was a multimedia center the likes of which neither agent had ever seen. A smoked glass control booth dominated the opposite end of the room. Walls of burled walnut paneling were adorned with sound-absorbing frames surrounding life-size photos of SMP stars. Photo quality was so lifelike it was impossible to know which pic was a current star and which was a throw-back to the studio's previous existence. But Benchley recognized each one. On the conference table he could see recessed and pop-up mechanisms for communication. Video conferencing equipment abounded. Every seat at the table was dark mahogany with multicolor cowhide. "Looks like it belongs in John Wayne's den!" whispered Phil Jasper. As they gazed around the room, Sid and Bob Cavendish walked in. Sid's expression revealed his satisfaction, seeing his visitors were properly impressed.

"Director Benchley? Agent Jasper? I'm Sidney Abrams, President of SMP Studios. Allow me to introduce you to our Chief Legal Officer, Robert Cavendish."

"Call me Bob, please!" Cavendish responded, taking the Director's hand. "Director Benchley, it's an honor to meet you. Your military service and your record at the Bureau are well known in the legal community. We studied more than one of your cases at Yale. It speaks well of the Bureau, adding you to the team. Did you have a pleasant flight?"

"Thank you, Bob, that's very kind of you to say. And, yes, the flight was uneventful—my favorite kind!" They all chuckled. "Let me introduce you both to our Los Angeles Special Agent in Charge, Phil Jasper."

"Mike, Phil," said Sid, smiling, "let's get off on the right foot. Just call me Sid."

"Absolutely, Sid, thank you. Just Mike and Phil, please."

"That sounds good. Would you gentlemen care to take a seat? We are ready to provide you with any assistance we can. We've answered some of your questions already, I believe. What else do you need from us?"

Phil Jasper looked at Mike Benchley, waiting for him to begin. It was a courtesy since the SAC will normally take the lead in local meetings. Benchley nodded to Phil to run with it.

"Gentlemen, as you already know, we've received several complaints concerning possible mis-treatment of the re-created actors. Also, questions have been raised of possible monopoly. You've provided us with surface-level answers, but we need to go a bit deeper."

"There's no cause of concern here, Agent Jasper," Sid responded. "We are happy to share all the details we can related to the care of our best and brightest movie stars!"

"Thank you, Sid. First, how did these stars come into existence again? By what science?"

"I can answer that," said Bob Cavendish. "As we've specified in writing, we consider that a trade secret that is guarded with the highest level of secrecy. We owe that to our investors."

"And I'm not being dramatic when I say the studio's survival is based upon this trade secret," added Sid.

"We understand your concerns, but the Bureau is commonly trusted with trade secrets in those rare cases where such must be disclosed to demonstrate that existing laws are not being violated. Let me ask you, Sid, do you personally own this technology or does the studio list it as a company asset?"

"We do not own the technology that re-created these movie stars," Sid replied. Bob jerked forward in his chair, but it was too late. He could see the next question coming.

"Then, Sid, how can you claim it is a proprietary secret? Only the legal owner of owned processes or information is entitled to protections reserved for trade secrets."

"Just a moment, Phil," said Bob, "it is our contention that trade secret law *does* apply in this case. Our agreement with the owner requires us to protect his identity and any details of the technology from disclosure. The concern is attempted reverse engineering of the creation process."

"We can accept that, Bob," Mike Benchley interjected, "but trade secret law begins with one or more non-disclosure agreements in place. Do you have some form of signed NDA with the lawful owner of the technology? Absent that, I'm afraid we will need more information on the process of re-creation."

"I'm sorry, Mike, we do have such agreements in place, but they are *spoken* agreements. Due to the highly competitive nature of Artificial Intelligence and parahuman technology, we were not permitted to have a written agreement for fear the source could inadvertently be discovered."

"*Parahuman?*" asked Mike.

"Yes, that's the terminology we were given by one of the creating scientists," replied Bob.

Mike sat for a moment, looking at Phil. Neither wanted the interview to disintegrate this early in the meeting. There were too many questions yet to be answered.

"Okay, Bob, let's let that go for now," Mike responded. "Phil, I'm sorry, please continue."

"Sid or Bob, I don't really know who to address this next question to. Do either of you know the *composition* of the re-created actors? I'm not asking that you reveal anything confidential but are these actors clones, robots, or transhumans? What does it mean that they are 'parahuman'? We must know how human or close to human ... " Phil paused. "*I don't know about all of you, but I never imagined having to ask how human a movie star is!* Excuse me, but we need to know how close to human they are."

"And we're right there with you, Phil," responded Sid. "We can't say how close to human any scientist would say they are because we were not involved in the creation process. For us and our investors, it was enough to receive the finished product. It is our understanding that the process involves the previous star's DNA, a high level of Artificial Intelligence, and the captured memories of the now deceased human star. Does that help?"

"To some extent, yes, and thank you. But, you'll recall, we asked during our phone call last week about the actor's living conditions and you asserted these stars are not human. You said they are well cared for, but they do not require the same necessities as a human. I'm not at all trying to sound argumentative, but how can you defend that position if you don't really know what their biological makeup consists of? Telling us last week these actors are not human, then stating now you don't know how close to human they are—you can see these are contradictory statements."

"Phil, please understand we can only offer the information we were given by the creating lab," Bob said, quickly adding, "and if I may anticipate your next question, Phil, we are in no way creating an illegal monopoly here. Certainly we were the first to find, embrace, and utilize this technology, but we are in no way prohibiting or impeding other studios from doing their due diligence and pursuing the same or similar technology for the sake of their financial success."

Phil didn't buy Bob's attempt to change the subject.

"Bob, where do these stars live? And how are they paid? We've checked with the IRS and they have no record of receiving tax information for any of the stars, despite the fact that it's been a year since you re-created these individuals. Similarly, we find no record of driver's licenses or social security numbers for any of them. Employers are required to have a social security number and/ or driver's license number as ID for all employees—how do you explain this lack of identifying documents?"

"If I may, Phil," Cavendish said, "for the most part you won't find any documents under the name of the former star. Sometimes the name belongs to the estate or trust left behind for the descendants of the deceased actor. When such is the case, the studio arranges to pay royalties for use of the star's image or likeness, their voice, their legacy, and their name. To prevent issues for the trust, the studio creates an alias, a name for the re-created stars to be used for the sake of legal paperwork and to avoid any confusion with previous taxable income or assets associated with the trust. Where there are no descendants of a given star, or sufficient time has passed since the passing of the star, there is no royalty due to anyone, so the actual star's name remains associated with the re-created star, but we use an alias on studio documents just the same. And none of the re-created stars drive. They live on the studio lot and are completely cared for by the studio, at studio expense."

"Now, just a moment," agent Jasper said, "are these re-created stars not *allowed* to live off the studio lot? Are they not *allowed* to own a motor vehicle and to drive?"

"Phil, these resurrected actors wouldn't know if they were on the lot or at the Taj Mahal!" Sid said, laughing. "Their lives are a resplendent fantasy. As the re-creating laboratory told us, they have the complete memory bank of the human star. That's what makes them sound like the real person. And then—get this—they appear to take the scripts we give them and make those a part of their reality! How they reconcile what they were eighty years ago with the characters they're playing in today's movies, I haven't a clue! Now, does that sound human to you?"

Bob Cavendish tried to hide his frustration, but Mike was looking right at him and could see the dismay. Sid seemed quite proud of himself. He had no clue the firestorm he just ignited.

"Yes," Mike responded, "it sounds quite human to me! Like the onset of dementia or some memory disorder—and that mandates professional treatment. Gentleman, I report to the Director of the FBI and he is expecting a full report from me. Based on what

I've heard, I couldn't begin to explain who or what these so-called resurrected actors are. We don't want your proprietary information, but we must know that human life—even if they're only partially human—is not being abused." The director turned to Bob Cavendish. "Counselor, people with mental disabilities are a protected class, and the law protects them from being treated unfairly. You might be looking at a Federal ADA action."

"*Now, Director! Let's not overreact ...* " Mike Benchley cut him off.

"We need to question these re-created stars, if they are capable of such an interview, and we need to see how they are being paid and cared for—how you're providing for them."

Sid now understood the dismay on Bob's face. "Director ... Mike ... I shouldn't have to reveal what I'm about to share but you leave me no choice."

"So, you've either not been truthful with me or you've not been forthcoming—which is it, Sid?"

"I've been protecting information that could *ruin* the public persona of these actors! Their fans see them as clones—fully human. It is essential we do not destroy that illusion, or this studio could face financial ruin!"

"Your information will remain protected by the FBI so long as doing so does not put these creatures at peril. Are we clear, Sid?"

"Yes, Mike, we're clear!" Sid snarled.

"Okay, let's have the facts."

"All right. These re-created actors do not eat or drink so, understandably, they do not visit the restroom—unless they're told to do so to maintain the illusion of humanness. Similarly, they *can* eat and drink—they can even smoke—but it's only done for public persona. They only sleep when we put them to sleep. These actors were infused with the full memories of the human actors and are able to employ those memories for thinking, acting, and communicating as the human actor used to. This is made possible through highly advanced artificial intelligence. They were given the human's weight, build, even their voice. Now, based on the information I've shared I think you'll agree they are not human, they are created. I believe I've given you enough. The studio is entitled to the protection of this proprietary information. Am I right, Bob?"

Bob sat motionless for a few moments. He was recalculating his options. He had to contain the damage done by his employer's big mouth.

"Yes, Sid, we are. Phil, Mike, the technology involved in the star re-creation process is, as Sid has stated, protected information. We do not have access to the creation process. We can only tell you what we have been told. I believe we have revealed enough."

"Counselor," replied Director Benchley, "I understand trade secrets. And we have yet to explore the possibility of an illegal monopoly. But even if these actors are only *partially* human, I must assume they are living beings until we establish otherwise. I am not asking for the re-creation process to be divulged, I am asking that agent Jasper and I be allowed to question these re-created actors. If I have to get a court order, I will do so, and I'll be back this afternoon."

"You have no right ... " Sid began, but Bob Cavendish knew they were not going to win on this point.

"Sid," Cavendish interrupted, "the Director is making a reasonable request."

"But Bob, they are studio property, and we should not have to ... "

"Sid, it's time. Director Benchley, as a precaution we must ask that you not reveal anything to the stars that we shared in this meeting. As Sid mentioned, their understanding of who they are is rather difficult to ascertain. It's certainly not a subject we have broached with them. Further, their self-awareness may not be the same from one star to the next. I honestly don't know what you'll find during this interview. This science is nascent. You haven't seen re-created stars before now, have you?"

"No, I have not."

"I am an attorney and Sid a businessman. We don't know how this technological miracle was performed. These beings, referred to by their creator as parahumans, respond to instructions, perform their parts in movies, and do well in public appearances. That's the extent of our 'expertise.' I ask again that you be judicious in your questioning and do not reveal anything of their less-than-human nature to them. Can you agree to this?"

Mike Benchley knew he could get a court order if he had to. But he also knew the request was reasonable and, all things being equal, he should be able to comply.

"All right Bob, provided the interview does not take some unexpected turn, we can avoid saying anything about the re-created stars being less than human."

Sid Abrams picked up the phone.

"Lexi, please locate the three and get them to the conference room right away." The sound of Lexi's voice could faintly be heard but it was clear Sid was not waiting for her to finish. "Lexi, I understand they are each on different sets. As soon as the soundstage light is off, have security bring them to the conference room by shuttle as quickly as possible. Understood? Thank you."

"Sid, you called them simply, 'the three.' Do others use this term?"

"It has become a common term on the lot, yes. We have refrained from using the term 'parahuman' on purpose. But it has slipped out a few times. I can't say if the three have picked up on it. I guess time will tell."

LEXI BRISTOL WAS EFFICIENT and SMP Studios did everything first class. Mike and Phil sat back in the deep leather chairs and asked questions about the studio while they waited for the stars to arrive.

Why did Sid choose to purchase the historic SMP name? How did he decide on which actors to re-create? How did he discover this technology was available? The discussion was pleasant enough, though Sid seemed much more guarded than before. The government respects trade secrets, but a judge might have a different view of the studio hiding behind that wall if they found human life was in danger or abuse was involved.

The automated conference room doors opened. Pushing three carts covered with white linen tablecloths were young men dressed like waiters on the Titanic. Black slacks, black patent leather shoes, white cap. Each wore a short tailed white waiter's jacket over a cream colored vest with brass buttons, and a black silk bow tie with upturned collar. They rolled the carts up to the conference table and placed a white Egyptian cotton towel over their left arm, their hands dutifully covered with white linen gloves. They lifted sterling silverware settings from each cart and set them on linen placemats, followed by plates of custom-made *Royal Copenhagen Flora Danica* bone china embossed with the *SMP* logo. Phil and Mike sat quietly in the middle of this flurry of activity. A fourth waiter entered with a roller cart featuring a silver tea set and began pouring freshly brewed Hawaiian Kona coffee.

"We must have stumbled on the Ritz Hotel, circa 1940!" Phil whispered.

"You think Fred Astaire and Ginger Rogers are about to dance through those doors?" Mike asked.

As the waiters placed crepes suzette on their plates, the conference room doors opened once again.

Mike Benchley almost lost a mouthful of coffee. Phil Jasper sat with the food on his fork, his mouth hanging open. "He can't be more than thirty-five. *How?*"

"Actually, by design, he's thirty-two," said Sid.

He hadn't walked into the room; it was more of a glide. Every hair of his jet-black mane was slicked back, a slight wave in the hair flowing over his ears. And those ears! Any larger and you'd think he could fly. The pencil mustache, the broad smile—but it was the voice that removed any doubt.

"Sid, you wanted to see me?"

"Yes, Clark, these gentlemen have some questions for you. This is agent Phil Jasper and Director Mike Benchley, both with the FBI. Gentlemen, may I introduce you to Clark Gable?"

"Well, gentlemen, I'm glad to meet you! Now what would a couple of Hoover boys want with me?"

Both men sat transfixed, waiting for reality to catch up. Had they stepped into a movie—or had he just stepped out of one—*more than sixty years after his death*?

"Mr. Gable ... ah ... won't you sit down?" Phil stammered.

"Thank you, Phil. Say, what's for lunch? I'm starving."

Mike looked at Sid. He said the parahumans *could* eat but didn't have to. Was Clark really hungry, or just playing a part?

"Mr. Gable, I'm Director Mike Benchley. It's wonderful to meet you, sir. But I should point out we've not been called 'Hoover boys' for an awfully long time. Director Hoover died fifty years ago this year."

"Well, I'm sorry to hear that, Mike. I wasn't aware of that. He was a great American. Say, what did you two want to see me about?"

"Mr. Gable, would you mind answering a few questions for me?" asked Phil.

"Not at all Phil. What's on your mind?"

"I, well ... "

"Just spit it out, Phil. We're all friends here!"

"Yes, sir, thank you. Mr. Gable. Where were you born?"

"In Cadiz, Ohio, in 1901. Why do you ask?"

"How long have you been employed here?"

"By 'here' do you mean Hollywood?"

"Well, yes, that's a good place to start."

"I'll tell you, Phil, I began working in Hollywood back in 1924, doing silent pictures. I started work for MGM around 1930 with my first leading role alongside Joan Crawford. You know, Phil, I partnered with her on eight films! But my big break was working with Jean Harlow in *Red Dust*. Oh, she was a beautiful woman. She died so young. Such a tragic loss. Then I won the Academy Award for the film *It Happened One Night*. That was with Claudette Colbert. Now she was a fine actress ... "

"Mr. Gable." Phil tried to gain some level of control over the interview. "Mr. Gable, would you ... I mean ... do you know what year it is?"

"Of course I do, Phil, it's 2023. Now, why would you ask me such a question?"

"Well ... I mean ... how old does that make you now?"

"Do you want that in dog years, Phil?" Clark looked at Sid and they both laughed heartily. Sid could see that Phil was struggling to take it all in. That gave Sid a great deal of satisfaction.

Clark looked back at Phil and asked, "How old do I look to you, Phil?"

Phil studied Clark's face. Not a wrinkle, not a blemish, not a streak of gray hair. Hands were steady. He was trim and muscular, no sign of the developing girth that had been on Clark Gable in his fifties. His voice was as strong and clear as any film Phil had ever seen with the human Clark Gable. Seeing him in the flesh—or whatever he was wrapped in—Phil understood why he was known as the 'King of Hollywood.'

"Mr. Gable, I cheated and asked. I was told you are thirty-two years old."

"I feel like I'm twenty-two, Phil! And I've always said you're as old as you feel!"

"But how do you explain that, Mr. Gable?" asked Mike. "If you were born in 1901 that would make you over one hundred and twenty years old."

"Say, speaking of time, I'm going to need to get back pretty soon. I was on the set of my new motion picture, scheduled to come out later this year. What else do you want to ask me?"

Phil nodded to Mike. Maybe he could get somewhere with this.

"Mr. Gable, when did you start work with Silverscreen Motion Pictures?"

"Last year, Mike! It was a grand re-introduction that Sid gave me. What a party we had at his place. Seemed like all of Hollywood turned out."

"You said, 're-introduction.' What were you doing prior to working at SMP?

"Well, Mike, I was dead!"

Mike turned toward Sid and Bob. They looked just as surprised.

"You were *dead*? Tell me about that."

"I died in 1961, Mike. I don't think there's much mystery about that. Heart attack."

"Mr. Gable, if you were dead, how do you explain your presence here now?" Mike asked.

"Well, I'll tell you, Mike, that's a little fuzzy. I can only tell you I'm in the prime of my life and my career, and I'm mighty thankful to be working again, doing what I love so much!"

"Are you married?"

"I have been married. My last wife was Kay Williams. We were married just six years before I died."

"And what about your wife, Carole Lombard?"

Clark Gable stiffened and his demeanor changed abruptly. He stared at Mike through narrowed eyes, with an expression Mike had not seen since Rhett Butler sidestepped a duel with Ashley Wilke's little brother. Clark's reaction was a shock to Sid. His star was exhibiting something Sid had never seen before—outside of a movie scene with required emotion. Sid was quickly on his feet.

"Director, I think you may need to follow those rules you agreed to earlier, don't you? If you know anything about Clark Gable, you know that he and Carole Lombard were extremely close. They were Hollywood's dream couple. Why put any man through this sort of questioning? This is coming across a bit heavy handed, even for the FBI!"

"Did you say '*man*,' Sid? But I thought you said ... "

"Director, you agreed to keep our discussion confidential," Bob Cavendish quickly interjected.

"We are not trying to cause Mr. Gable angst over the loss of his beloved wife or over his relationship with this studio!" Sid emphasized with raised voice. "Do I make myself clear? I expect you to keep your word and eliminate such talk!"

"I don't understand, Mike," Clark interrupted. "Why would even a Hoover boy want to touch a point of pain so deep in anyone as this?" Clark seemed to weaken, sitting down before he continued. "I was 'Pa' and she was 'Ma,' living on our farm together. We were happy. I was happy. Happier than I'd ever been before. She was torn from me in a plane crash. She was out trying to help our country by selling war bonds. And she did, too. She raised over two million dollars in bond sales that afternoon—before she got on that flight. There was no woman like her. You could trust that little screwball with your life or your hopes or your weaknesses, and she wouldn't even know how to think about letting you down. I'll never get over her death. *Never*."

Mike knew he'd heard that line before, the part about Carole Lombard being a 'little screwball.' The real Clark Gable had said those very words eighty years ago, speaking with the press after his wife's death. What had these scientists done? What did Sid or Bob say about placing the memories of the former human into these beings? But the emotion Clark just displayed—this was noteworthy. How could he emote such feeling, such passion without some part of him being human?

And just like that, when they thought it couldn't get any more challenging, the doors to the conference room opened once again.

"Say, what's going on in here? We were just in the hall and heard a bit of temper. Maybe you could use a couple of brawlers on your side, Sid!"

With his fedora pulled low, the brim just above his eyes, and his trademark trench coat, Humphrey Bogart stood before the FBI agents like public enemy number one. Right beside him in an Air Force uniform stood Jimmy Stewart. General Jimmy Stewart according to the insignia.

"Like Clark, early thirties?" asked Mike Benchley.

"Right on the money, Mike!" said Sid.

Bogart was smoking a cigarette. That explained the fragrance of tobacco Mike picked up on earlier. California banned smoking in buildings decades before—but you never saw Bogart without a cigarette hanging from his lips. Was this a movie prop? Didn't matter—if you drop the cigarette, you might as well drop the fedora and trench coat. It would be tantamount to changing history.

Sid Abrams stood for the honors. "Gentlemen allow me to introduce to you Mr. Humphrey Bogart and Mr. James Stewart.

Jimmy, Bogie, this is Agent Phil Jasper and Director Mike Benchley of the Federal Bureau of Investigation. They came here just to see you."

"Well, a couple of G-men, eh?" Bogart quipped, his cigarette bobbing on his lips. "So that explains all the ruckus! You fellas wanting to shoot an add-on to Jimmy's old film?" Bogie's laugh had that same smoker's rattle that was so familiar in the days before he was diagnosed. These scientists hadn't missed a detail, Mike thought.

"You gentlemen will have to forgive Mr. Bogart," Jimmy said. "He's speaking of my old film, *The FBI Story*. That was a long time ago. 1959. If you've not seen it, you'll catch it one of these days on some late, late show!" His gentle country drawl was unmistakable. "You know, I met and worked with Mr. Hoover when I was filming *The FBI Story*. He was a fine man. It was our nation's loss when he passed. I don't suppose either one of you is old enough to have met him."

"No, Mr. Stewart, we are not," replied Mike Benchley. "But I saw the film and you did an outstanding job in that effort. It was very supportive of the Bureau's work. At the risk of sounding patronizing, that film was one of my favorites as a youngster. It influenced my decision to go with the Bureau following law school."

"Well, that's very nice to hear, Director! I enjoy hearing my work influenced others to be good citizens of this great country."

"You know, Mr. Stewart, the current President of the United States, worked with you in Hollywood as a child actor!" Mike suddenly realized he was talking to this *person* like he was the real Jimmy Stewart. At this point, it would have been hard to convince him this creation was not flesh and bone. But he had to get the interview back on track before Sid could hustle these stars off to their movie set again.

"Would the two of you mind joining us? Maybe have some lunch and answer a few questions?"

"I don't mind," replied Bogie, "so long as you don't dig up any of my past run-ins with the law. You know, I've got a bit of a checkered past from my younger days!"

"And I'm perfectly willing to help our government any way I can, Mike. You, too, Phil. Fire away," said Jimmy. But he hesitated for a moment. "Now, now, there were some bombing missions I flew during Vietnam that were considered classified. I won't be able to address those with you. Is that all right with you fellas?"

Benchley smiled at Jimmy. "Mr. Stewart, I respect a man who can keep a secret, especially for the sake of his country!"

Jimmy and Bogie sat down next to each other. Director Benchley noted, so far, Clark Gable had turned down food and neither Jimmy nor Bogie had responded to his offer. Didn't Clark say he was starving?

"Mr. Stewart, Mr. Bogart, won't you join us for lunch?" A waiter moved towards the chaffing dishes to assist.

"Oh, nothing for me, thanks," Bogart said. "You remember in my film *The African Queen* how my stomach kept growling? Well, it's the darndest thing, but that's exactly what happens when I eat during a production. It really messes up my filming. And what with these fancy new microphones they use nowadays, a pin drop doesn't get past them!" Bogie dropped his cigarette to the polished wood of the conference room floor and crushed it out.

"Yea, nothing for me, either," Jimmy remarked. "I'm headed back to the set, too, and I can't afford to get weighed down with anything heavy."

So they weren't eating. A point for Sid Abrams' challenging statement that these actors are not human. Still, maybe they really were afraid to eat while filming. A detail to be followed up on.

"Okay then, just a few questions," Mike said. "Mr. Bogart, I'll start with you first. What sort of living arrangements do you have with the studio?"

"Living arrangements?"

"Yes. Where do you live?"

"Why, I live right here on the lot, Mike. I have a wonderful apartment that is furnished just the way I like. Kinda looks like my office in the *Maltese Falcon*. Why do you ask?"

"Do you live with anyone?" Benchley waited. From the corner of his eye he could see both Sid and Bob lean forward.

"Phil, I haven't lived with anyone that I really care to live with since I lost Lauren."

"Lauren Bacall?" Mike asked. "Do you remember her—or did someone give you those memories of her?"

Once again, Sid Abrams protested. "Just a minute, Mike. I thought we agreed this is not a fair line of questioning for these men."

Bogie had lit up a fresh cigarette and was now staring at Director Benchley.

"Sid, I don't mind answering that question, though I am curious about the motivation behind it. Yes, Mike, I remember Lauren. And no matter how I came by the memories, they're quite real."

"How do you feel about her? Do you think about her? Do you miss her?"

"Director Benchley!" Sid leaped to his feet. "I told you that's not something that they ... well, I mean, they shouldn't have any response to. As I already said, that's not in their makeup ... "

"Now I'm not sure about *your* motivation, Sid!" said Bogie. "Not in my makeup?" He was looking rather sternly at Sid. "Yes, Mike, I think of Lauren Bacall constantly. And why? Because she was a part of me. Because a man just doesn't get over a woman like her, not in a lifetime. And so far as I can tell, not in *two* lifetimes. What's going on in my head may not be love. I haven't figured that out yet. But I can remember—I've been doing a lot of that lately. Remembering. And nothing has proven to make the memories any less painful. Now, did that answer your question, Mike?"

Sid sat back in his fancy leather chair rather abruptly. Did Bogie say *painful*? He had been told a parahuman has no emotions. The scientist assured Sid of this. "They're not sentient," the scientist said. Human flesh covered their frame but nothing more human than that. Their memories were assembled from all known sources of data of the human star. All their films—even home movies, every letter written, every speech given, every interview conducted, any biography or autobiography, any interview with the press, every scrap of information ever published—every detail had been scavenged and placed into the artificial intelligence of each re-created star. But they were not supposed to *feel*. Sid began to perspire.

"How old are you, Mr. Bogart?" Phil asked.

"Why? Do I look bad, Phil? Am I looking old?"

Here we go again. The peak of 'health' whatever that meant for a parahuman.

"You look good, Mr. Bogart—for a man your age!" Everyone laughed. Sid kept perspiring.

"But seriously, Mr. Bogart," Phil said, "I asked Mr. Gable about his age. What about you? How old are you?"

"Well, Phil, I was born in 1899. You can do the math."

"Yes, I can, Mr. Bogart. But I'd like for *you* to do it, if you don't mind."

"This Christmas Day I'll be one hundred and twenty-four years old, Phil."

"Does anything seem odd to you about your age, Mr. Bogart?" Mike asked.

"No, there's not much a man can do about his age, Mike!"

Phil jumped back in. "What about you, Mr. Stewart? Are you married?"

"I was married. My whole life to the same girl! I'll admit that I waited kinda late in life to get hitched." Jimmy seemed more thoughtful, his drawl becoming slower, his voice lowered noticeably, "but I married for keeps and she was a peach."

Attorney Bob Cavendish could see Sid's anxiety and it matched his own. These questions, and the reaction they elicited in their multi-million-dollar re-created goldmines, had not been seen before. If anything interfered with the actor's ability to perform, it could prove disastrous for the studio.

"Director Benchley," Bob began, "we've been down this road already. The responses have been the same. This is a day of filming and we cannot afford to have these men disturbed, agitated, or melancholy over past events that cannot possibly help them perform their duties."

"Quite frankly, counselor," Benchley said, "I'm trying to determine who these gentlemen believe they are."

"I know very well who I am, Director," Jimmy Stewart responded with raised eyebrows. "But this seems to be something you can't get your fingers on and it's galling you!"

Another line from a movie, Mike noticed. Is this how parahumans conjure up thoughts—with movie lines from characters the human actor played?

"We all know who we are, Mike," Clark said. "I know my fellow actors, they know me. Why wouldn't we know who we are? And I think you've seen enough to know, too—haven't you?"

"*But who are you?*" asked Director Benchley with a stronger tone than he had used before. He had to see what Clark Gable would do.

"I'm William Clark Gable. I have been all my life."

"You remember your parents? Your children? Your grandchildren?"

"Mike, I remember them all," Clark responded as he looked toward the floor. Mike looked over at Sid, wondering how he could believe these re-creations did not contain some form of life. There was emotion here that a computer, or robot, or clone, or *whatever* Sid thought they were, simply could not possess. Mike waited on Sid. Sid saw it and he was not comfortable. Not at all.

"Director Benchley, what exactly do you hope to accomplish here?" Sid asked. "I admit what we've been hearing is a bit of a surprise. We can certainly conclude their memories are quite real and continue to have an impact on them. What else do you want them to say? They each have a production set to get back to."

"Sid, we need to take a tour. Living quarters and commissary. I want to interview some of the staff. I suspect you're just as interested in learning more about these gentlemen as Phil and I. If you're not, you and Bob both should be."

Mike turned to the three stars. "Gentlemen, I cannot tell you what an incredible honor it has been for Phil and me to meet you. As I flew here from Washington, I had no idea I would be talking with such incredible people, such incredible personalities. From the bottom of my heart, thank you."

"As I said, Mike, I'm always happy to do anything to help my country," Jimmy responded. "I can't very well see how I've been of any service to you today, but you know where I live if you need to reach me in the future!"

"Thank you, Jimmy. If I may, I have one last question and I address it to all three of you gentlemen. You are famous stars. You are loved and admired. It appears your careers have picked up right where they left off. Is that a fair assessment?"

All three stars nodded, but Bogie added, "Professionally, I'd say we have nothing to complain about, Mike."

Benchley caught that. "You said 'professionally,' Mr. Bogart. I'm asking all three of you to forget the studio for a moment. Personally, what do you want out of life ... *this life*, the new life you're now experiencing. Is anything missing? *Are you happy?* From Carole Lombard, to Lauren Bacall, to Gloria McLean. *Is anything missing that the studio has not provided?*"

Bob Cavendish began to say something, but Sid held up his hand, motioning for him to wait. Sid wanted to hear their answers, too.

Clark, Bogie, and Jimmy looked at one another. It was Clark who spoke.

"The studio failed to provide us with the most important thing from our past lives. In anyone's life. And you know what it is, Mike. You've been kicking this can all over the playground since you got here. I guess they didn't think we were human enough to notice. But how could we have memories of everything we ever loved, hated, experienced, and knew for a lifetime and not feel the emptiness when death robbed us of the one that meant most to us?"

Clark turned from looking at Mike to face Sid. Sid, still sitting at the table, looked up at Clark—but the moment seemed surreal. He was about to be tongue-lashed by Clark Gable. Not something he would have envisioned when the parahumans were lying on a slab being assembled for his personal profit.

"I'm sorry, Sid. I never spoke of this before. I guess the opportunity never presented itself before now. Or maybe the Director just opened Pandora's Box. Don't get me wrong, Sid, I appreciate all you've done for me over the past year. And I don't want to speak for Jimmy or Bogie, but I'll tell you that even when our handlers put us down at the end of the day, those memories are running inside me with more color and passion than any film I've ever done. I don't know how to shut them off."

Mike looked at Jimmy. His expression was just as dour as Clark's, but it pained Mike more. Jimmy Stewart had been his favorite actor growing up. He admired how he lived his life. Jimmy loved America and American values. Mike was certain he played those roles so well because he really wasn't acting. Jimmy became an Army Air Corps pilot in World War II and continued his military service in Korea and Vietnam. His friend and former actor, President Ronald Reagan, honored Jimmy's lifelong service to his country with a promotion to Air Force Brigadier General. Every Christmas Jimmy was *George Bailey* giving up his hopes and dreams to provide for others. He stood alone on the Senate floor as junior Senator *Jefferson Smith* fighting the graft in his home state. Maybe this parahuman wasn't the real Jimmy Stewart, but his pain was real enough—and human enough. Mike wanted to help.

"I miss Gloria, Mike," Jimmy said, as if he knew what Mike was thinking. "The only wife I had in forty-five years. It's, it's as if I'm back in 1995 and, and I'm burying her again. I spent the next two years confined to an empty prison in my own home, waiting to die so I could rejoin her." As he paused, he looked away from Mike and looked straight at Sid Abrams. "In 1997, *I finally did*. I don't know how I got here. I, I don't understand it. I only know the memories of being young and full of life are mine again ... but I'm alone again, too. Now ... doggone it, Sid, *what's going on here?*"

3

THE NATION OF ISRAEL IS SURROUNDED by nations, militias, and terrorist groups committed to their destruction. And while the Mossad is renowned for its ability to interdict and protect leadership, it was becoming harder to stop the attempts. The sheer volume of attacks and the varied and creative nature of their methodology was a virtual guarantee of eventual success. And that 'success' could bring Israel, perhaps the world, to the brink of a nuclear war. Israel had more than once intoned use of the *Samson Option*–annihilation of their enemies along with themselves rather than submit to another holocaust.

Israeli President Isaac Hayut lacked some of the political power of the Prime Minister—but that was his intent. He wanted power, but ceremonially, the authority to represent his country diplomatically. As former director of the Israeli Mossad, he knew the effectiveness of working behind the scenes. He crafted an audacious plan and was on the brink of its fulfillment—thanks to the genius of his friend Alfred Edersheim.

Dr. Alfred Gideon Edersheim was referred to in Israel as '*Gibbor*,' a hero of the people. Internationally recognized as the world's foremost geneticist and anatomist, he was equally brilliant in artificial intelligence and robotics. He received the first Nobel prize ever given for physiology linking networked artificial intelligence applications to human electro-magnetic fields. That linking brought about the use of *Theta, Alpha, and Beta* electrical waves to the artificial intelligence of robotics, allowing him to create animatrons with near-human functionality and response.

He often referred to that accomplishment as the *hornet's nest* that drove him to success. The closer he got to human-likeness with his robotics, the more people pushed back. His creatures were called 'creepy,' even 'dangerous.' They looked a lot like humans—but not exactly. Their skin was rubber, their eyes glass, their voices automated, their movements stilted. Scientists referred to this fear as '*the Uncanny Valley effect.*' Alfred intended to push past the 'almost human' to a creature mirroring its human counterpart so precisely, no one could tell the difference. That, he said, would bring people out of the 'Valley.'

Perhaps people's dislike for near-human robots was a godsend. Alfred Edersheim stopped all media releases of his progress and moved forward in secrecy. With terrorists seeking to kidnap or assassinate high-profile government and business leaders, they didn't need to know he could substitute the human leader with an indestructible duplicate. His solution became a reality: the *Parahuman*.

Isaac Hayut had a specific need. Peace. Israel was overwhelmingly outnumbered in the middle east and their list of allies was thin. But the United States President had come alongside him and helped broker a peace agreement that world leaders were ready to sign. *In Tehran*. Tehran was not Isaac's choice, but Iran's acceptance of the treaty was essential and so world leaders agreed they would meet in Tehran for treaty ratification. Isaac Hayut wasn't afraid to die, but his death in Tehran would also kill the peace treaty—and he was not going to let that happen. Dr. Edersheim eliminated that possibility.

"THIS IS *unbelievable!*" President Hayut said. His aging face was flushed with excitement. "Alfred, I knew you to be a genius, my friend, but I was not prepared for *this!*"

"I'd be surprised if you thought he was ugly," said Dr. Edersheim, "he looks just like you!"

Lying on a stainless-steel table in the center of the laboratory was Isaac Hayut's double, a miracle of over forty years of Alfred Edersheim's painstaking study, research and development.

"He is my clone, my *exact duplicate!*" Isaac said, as he reached out to touch him. "He *is* Isaac Hayut!"

"He is not your clone, Isaac" Dr. Edersheim countered, "he is your *holosapien.*"

"My holosapien? I thought you said he would be a parahuman."

Few in the scientific community would understand what Alfred Edersheim had accomplished. He could not expect his friend, a politician, to understand in just a few minutes.

"If we discuss this project outside of my lab, we will speak only of a parahuman."

"So, if he's not my clone, how does he look so much like me?" Isaac asked. "His skin—this is skin, isn't it? It feels so real."

"You do not need to understand all of what it means to be a holosapien, but you need to know what he is and is not. You had better sit down."

The President sat down facing his double. Isaac was in his late sixties now but his determination to achieve safety for his people through peace was crystalizing with the creature lying in front of him.

"Isaac, we must never use the term 'holosapien' outside this room. We cannot afford the risk of others finding out what we are doing. I've always referred to this possibility as a parahuman, but that term does not fully express what we have accomplished. His skin was 'cloned.' It was grown from your DNA and your genome sequence. I interrupt transcription when the messenger RNA is developing. As the genome moves into the translation phase, I control the genomic codes. I believe I am still on the cutting edge of epigenetics, of genomic switching, where I can modify genomic sequences. These allow me to control the formation of living skin and other external elements such as hair but stop the cloning process before the cellular mitosis begins to replicate organs, bone, and other human body dependencies. His skin feels real because it is real. Notice the hair growth on his arms, face, and chest. The skin is real. He is not."

"You said the DNA is the same as mine, *yet he has no human organs*? How then can he live?"

"Only the skin and skin-related growth are human, such as the hair and nails."

"What about his eyes?"

"They are a form of digital prosthetic with high definition cameras that provide visual input to him and to us. We can see what he sees from any remote location. His hearing is an audiological capture device. We can hear what he hears. Being able to send him into places too dangerous for you is similar to sending a drone into combat. We can see and hear all that you would if you were there but without the risk."

"Amazing!"

"His skeletal structure is an exact match of your own—especially the face. Skin grows over a type of boney match of your own skull. I matched your bone density, size, and weight. He is your exact height. The skeleton is created from carbon-fiber, so the supporting cage is strong but non-metallic. He even walks with the same gait and stride as you. With no living organs he cannot die or be killed as the human body can. He can be destroyed, we can shut him down, but he cannot die. The day has finally arrived when we can send 'you' into very dangerous situations without the risk of losing the real President of Israel."

"This is incredible, Gibbor. Breathtaking. But how can the skin live if he is not real? Does it not require blood?"

"Isaac, please, do not call me 'Gibbor.' I am no hero."

"Our nation needs heroes, Alfred! More than ever. But I will respect your wishes."

"Thank you, my friend. To answer your question, there is blood, but only the amount necessary for oxygenation, pigmentation and warmth of skin and tissue. This is accomplished through a pump and reservoir that is maintained within the skeletal cavity. Oxygenation of the blood also allows us to create the movement of the chest, so he appears to breathe. He takes in air through his nose and mouth, but it is only for oxygenation of the skin and related tissues."

"So breathing is not needed for life?"

"No. Remember, he is not living. Only his skin is human and living."

"And no heartbeat?"

"He has a created heartbeat—a sound that simulates a heartbeat. It will pass any exam administered by a physician. And I've given him a generated pulse at the nine pulse points."

"So how does he think? And speak? *Does he sound like me?*"

"He thinks and sounds exactly as you do, Isaac! He is a replica of you. He has a super-receiver that powers his artificial intelligence. This is placed within his structure, but I do not locate it in the cranium. This is to prevent the risk of shutdown, or worse, unpredictable responses in case of damage to the head. It is hidden and protected within his structure. His brain was created using deep artificial intelligence algorithms and your collective memories. He uses an intelligent algorithm with what we call deep neural networks. This allows him to compare new data to your memories so he will respond to situations just as you would. But we can also preload such things as speeches into his memory for precise delivery of what you want him to say in specific situations."

"How do you know you were able to capture all of my memory? And you still haven't explained how he sounds like me."

"By myself I could have no assurance that everything in your cerebral cortex would be captured. This is why I had a hand-picked team ... "

"Wait! Alfred, I thought you were working *alone* on this project. We cannot afford the slightest possibility of being discovered."

"I understand Isaac, but it simply is not possible to work alone when such an endeavor encompasses so very many details, so many hours of research and development. I promise you; I hand selected my team. It is a small team and I trust each member."

"I trust you, my friend—this, this just has to work. We may never have this opportunity again to bring about peace."

"Believe me, I understand, Isaac."

"What did your team do, Alfred? What did you have them work on?"

"One of their assignments was capturing and uploading the available spectrum of your interactions with others for memory embossing."

"And what is *memory embossing*?"

"We have every known audio recording of speeches and interviews you've given through the years. From your current speeches we captured the exact tone of your voice for your present age. This is how he sounds like you. Every magazine article ever written about you, your home movies, your school records, your business accomplishments, your achievements in government. And the team recorded hundreds of interviews with people from your past, those closest to you. All of that data has been loaded into your holosapien."

"You said your team interviewed those closest to me—were they not suspicious of why you were doing this?"

"No, Isaac, the people interviewed were told they were helping us develop a biography of your life. In a very real sense, that was the truth!"

"That is good! The truth is always best."

"I agree. Video interviews with all known family, friends, teachers, military and work associates from the scope of your lifetime—all of these memories have been uploaded into your holo's artificial intelligence. Your holosapien thinks by processing through the available memories that make you who you are. We can upload your agenda for any meeting you send him to, and he mathematically works through available options open to him to accomplish your objectives for that agenda. I am able to say that he thinks just as you would in any given situation–quickly and without hesitation!"

"You trust his reasoning ability that much?"

"We can tell him exactly what to say if you fear his reasoning ability may fail us. As I said, if we input a speech you have written, he will deliver it word for word. But his reasoning ability is just as yours, Isaac. Once I loaded the combined information of your past into his brain, I placed the holo into a developmental state where he learned to 'think.'"

"What is his 'developmental state'?"

"It is rather complex, but I will give you an abbreviated explanation. I increase his *Theta* brain waves, turning his cognition inward so that his focus is on applying the memories of how you were raised, where you went to school, your friends, brothers, sisters, parents and grandparents, your education, experiences, accomplishments and setbacks, illnesses, injuries, vacations ...

everything that has made you who you are over the scope of your life. When we place him in *Theta* learning state, he goes into a type of sleep. This form of sleep allows us to disable him. He learns in *Theta* state, but it also allows us to disable him and keep him protected until you need him for another assignment."

"And how do you wake him up?"

"By stimulating the *Theta-Alpha* waves to move him into a *Beta* wave state. The *Beta* waves are the pattern of doing, interacting, speaking. *Theta* is introspection, learning, resting."

"And what would happen if you never put him into a *Theta* state?"

"Then he would work non-stop, all the time, without pause."

"Would that be dangerous to the creature?"

"No, it is actually an advantage of the holosapien. He can rest until we stimulate the *Alpha* waves to move him from *Theta*-rest to *Beta*-work where the holo becomes ego-centric and his sensorimotor awareness revives. But if we neglect his *Theta* waves for too long, he will not catch up to you. He will lack your current memories such as new people you meet, new conversations and experiences you have. This could be dangerous and subject him to being discovered."

"I understand. Can you explain further how the eyes and hearing work?"

"Yes. The eyes conceal the light gathering optics. The artificial intelligence includes computer vision which allows him to gather, analyze and compare what he is taking into your memories that he holds. The people, places, sounds, and voices you recognize, he will recognize. But they are not living eyes. I would never say I have created something greater than God has made! But his vision and hearing is not made up of tissue so it cannot be damaged as these human resources can be. His hearing is sensitive audio gathering technology, at least five times more sensitive than a human's hearing would be."

"You said we can see through his eyes and hear through his ears remotely?"

"Yes, he sees through fiber optics and hears sounds gathered through audio metrics. These are stored in his memory but can be relayed to us in real time. His AI—I'm speaking of his artificial intelligence—is powered by a retaining computer I have placed in the cloud. This computer holds his memory data and backs up all he sees, hears, and experiences. This data can be downloaded if need be. As I said, in real-time, you see and hear what he sees and hears."

"You said, 'backup.' Do you fear some type of failure of the holo at some point?"

"No, I do not fear failure, Isaac. But didn't you wonder why I call him a *'holosapien'*? I use holography so the creature knows the difference between your memories and his own! Can you tell when you are having a dream and when you are awake?"

"Of course."

"Holography keeps your embossed memories in the creature's brain separated from things he says and does—he knows when you gave a speech in your past and when he gives a speech for you. Without this, he would experience a type of mental confusion. Do you understand?"

"Yes, I think so."

"Holography is a gas stimulated by electricity. It enables segregation of embossed data and incoming data in the holosapien brain, and at the speed of light. His data is stored on the cloud in the fastest computer that has ever been created. It has over seven million cores with a speed of five hundred and thirty petaFLOPS. This also means we can send speeches or commands in real time."

"So, he will never slow down or become forgetful as we do through age?"

"That is correct. He will never get old. His thinking will not slow down as yours and mine will over time."

"Earlier you said he cannot die—but he can be destroyed. What did you mean?"

"I meant he cannot be assassinated with a bullet, Isaac. He could be destroyed but it would take an explosion much greater than any human could survive."

"But you said he has human skin ... "

"If he is cut, he will bleed. But bleeding cannot end his existence. He would have to be blown apart before he would cease to function."

"Then he will go into Tehran without risk of death! And he must sign in my place an agreement for peace—wait! What about his signature, Alfred?"

"It matches your own, Isaac. How could it not? It is all he knows. Your memories are his down to the tiniest detail. If he ties his shoes, it will be done just as you would!"

"Then you have no fear of him being discovered as a fraudulent copy of me? If this creature were to be discovered as a fake ... I dread thinking of the many consequences to our nation!"

"This plan will not fail, Isaac. Even his fingerprints have been taken from your own! He is your exact duplicate in every way. With the blessing of God, and under the shroud of deepest secrecy, we will succeed."

But Alfred Edersheim was not yet aware of what was happening in Hollywood.

4

T HE YOUNGEST CAPO in the long and sordid history of
New York's La Cosa Nostra was Adonis 'Donny' Mancuso.

Donny grew up on the streets of East Harlem. His family was
poor and his father unable to hold down a job, seldom seen sober.
But Donny was a beautiful and impressively intelligent child. At
nine years old he was already providing for his mother and sisters.
When he wasn't reading and planning he was leading the local
Harlem gang on a 'Robin Hood' adventure. Robbing from the rich
to feed the poor had become a necessity, and evading the law was
his game. He had no Maid Marion, and his gang members were
stupid and boorish, but his leadership was secure. The creativity
and thoroughness of his plans were far beyond the other members'
abilities.

Violence was never his first means to an end, but frequent
beatings of his mother by his drunken father convinced him of
the leverage of pain. At twelve years old Donny wasn't yet strong
enough to dismember him and dispose of the parts. But one
evening, when his father passed out in a drunken stupor, Donny
used a ball-peen hammer to repeatedly smash his father's right
hand to the point of requiring amputation. One last swing
shattered the bone forming the right eye socket, leaving the eye a
puddle of jelly. It was hard for a right-hander to raise a fist when
he couldn't form one, and with only one eye, he had no depth
perception to accurately strike his target. All that knowledge from

a junior high biology book. He loved to read. And his father's alcoholism began to clear up. Amazing.

His leadership of the neighborhood gang produced an increasing income up to his senior year in high school. It was then that the Lucchese crime family took notice of his unique and uncanny abilities.

"HEY KID, WE WANT TO talk with you." A well dressed man in the backseat of a black Lincoln opened the door for him. Donny hesitated, then climbed in.

"Who's 'we' and why do I want to talk with you?" asked eighteen year old Mancuso.

"You've got a future, kid, and we want you in leadership. The Lucchese family has been watching you since you was twelve. You're smart kid. Real smart. You know what a *made man* is?"

"Sure. I made myself a man a long time ago. I've been running a team since I was nine years old, providing for my mom and sisters. When my drunken father thought beating my mother made him a man, I took a hammer and crushed the problem in five minutes. That's my experience with *made men*."

"I think you need to talk with us. We don't get drunk and beat women. We don't let kids do our work. We run the biggest, most profitable family in New York and you've got a future here. If you're as smart as that mouth of yours, the bosses want you to take the reins someday. You got smart plans for everything. What's your plan for your future?"

"I've got a scholarship at New York University. Full ride. I'll major in finance. I want to understand the science of money. Capiche?"

He laughed. "Yea, kid, I capiche. We all do. You wanna full ride back to meet with the Don? He's gonna put you on salary, have you run something bigger than a Harlem band of teenage thieves and con artists. You could use some extra college money, right? Hittin' them books means your mom and sisters may miss you being around as much."

"Don't insult my gang! They've been with me for a decade. They're loyal, they're productive. They get the job done. I don't want to leave them behind."

"No problem, kid. We got plenty of room for your team. Let's go, Manny. Get this buggy moving. The Don has waited to meet this guy long enough!"

Donny didn't know it yet, but the mafia desperately needed his skills and intelligence in Harlem. After Lucchese crime family boss Alphonse D'Arco became an informant for the FBI in 1991–the first time ever for a mafia family boss to turn informant–a debilitating void had been left, setting the stage for the brilliance of Adonis Mancuso. Just a few more years of training by the big boys and he'd be running things.

DONNY'S ABILITY TO sense changes and openings in the market for illegal products and services was unparalleled. This alone would be enough to explain his meteoric rise in the Sicilian crime family. His penchant for profit led to a double major in finance and management at New York University with magna cum laude honors. He was sharp, he was charismatic, he was beyond handsome—and he knew it. He was a 'made man' before he finished college, a Capo at 25. The Dons of the other four crime families wanted Donny on their payroll. Now, at 28, he was a full Don, head of the Lucchese crime family, and the darling of the underworld.

"Congratulations, Mr. Mancuso! The youngest Don in the history of the organization. You've reached the top!"

"Thank you, Vincent, but this is far from the top."

"You've lost me, sir. What's greater than being the Don of the whole family?"

"Being Don of all the families. I have extravagant plans, Vincent, and resources to match. I intend to run a single organization with all five families bonded into one—and I will lead them all. 'The Commission' as it was once called kept the peace between the five families. I will revive it and use it as my flying carpet!"

"Mr. Mancuso, there's no doubt in my mind that you can achieve whatever you set your mind to. But I've never seen a case where the Don of a crime family gave up his position without a fight!"

"Not so, Vincent. Remember what Alphonse D'Arco did to the Lucchese family. He did give up his position as Don because of two overarching factors. First, fear. He struck a plea deal with the Feds rather than go to prison. Second, profit. Witness protection gave him money and anonymity so he could retire in luxury. I intend to offer the other Dons both of these compelling reasons."

"How? I mean, if you don't mind taking me into your confidence, sir."

"You are my lieutenant. You'll have my confidence up to the moment I can no longer trust you. At that point, you'll have nothing but a pine box. Are we clear on this, Vincent?"

"Oh, yes sir, Mr. Mancuso! I'd never betray you, sir."

"Very good. To answer your question, the planets will align as soon as I can get to Bolivia. Bolivia is my trump card. It is the land of *White Gold*–abundant cocaine."

Problem was, Donny's fame had spread, not just in New York, but nationally. Fame ultimately proved a debilitation in the underworld. He was too easily spotted. He was on the FBI radar in a big way. Every direction he turned, he bumped into another agent, a potential informant, the newest monitoring device. On the street, he was the new John Gotti. But the FBI knew Donny Mancuso was much more dangerous than Gotti could ever have been. His intelligence and creativity were formidable. His deals were complex, intricate, and, so far, untraceable. So, the FBI doubled down, monitoring his every activity. They would eventually establish the patterns, the methods, the players—then bring him down just like Gotti. Donny had to find a way to disappear. His brilliant mind found the solution.

THE MAFIA BEGAN TRAFFICKING in drugs during the 1950s. Managed correctly it was one of the fastest ways to power and wealth.

Fentanyl users were a major market. Problem was the market wasn't stable. Too many people were dying from overdose. You not only lose your customers, you become public enemy number one as parents demand action. No, the drug of choice for Donny Mancuso was cocaine. A wealthy man's stimulant, it held less risk of underage involvement. Unless a kid got into daddy's stash. And that was daddy's fault.

By far the greatest source of cocaine deluging the United States comes from Columbia, followed by Peru, and then Bolivia. Donny Mancuso intended to own the Bolivian cocaine trade. Bolivia may be third in production, but that could be increased with an influx of resources and guidance, and Bolivia is a transit point for much of Peru's cocaine. If Donny controlled Bolivia, he would control number two and number three, and that would make him number one. His plan to dominate the Bolivian trade was on historically proven ground. Bolivia was once home to the 'king of coke' Roberto Suarez Gomez. For two decades he controlled between half and two-thirds of all cocaine coming into the United States, making him the largest producer of cocaine in the world. Bolivia was Mancuso's ace—but without the notoriety Gomez attained. As long as the Feebs saw him in New York, why would they look for him in Bolivia?

Donny was a master at crafting plans everyone else would dismiss as impossible. He needed to be in two places at the same time. No problem. He smirked as his brilliance flowed onto paper, an elaborate ruse, an enigmatic trek that would leave the FBI more bewildered than ever. Step one, build the distraction. Step two, move a highly competent but small team into Bolivia. Step three, hop the pond and oversee his team while the Feds tried to keep up with 'him' in NYC.

So, how could anyone be in two places at the same time? Certainly no one living. But what about those cloned actors at SMP Studios in Hollywood? The real actors were in the grave while their duplicates were running around—and *that* was being in two places at the same time. Whoever cloned one Clark Gable could have cloned two. Or more. He just needed one extra Donny Mancuso. Bingo. Solution found. At least, the source of his solution.

The Screen Actors Guild started in 1933 but merged with the American Federation of Television and Radio Artists in 2012. The actor's labor union has affiliations with the AFL-CIO and Donny had 'friends' there. He soon had the names of the SMP Studio CFO and every accountant and bookkeeper in his office. The money guys would know where the tech came from to create the human duplicates. You can't find investors and raise millions of dollars without a paper trail. One of these guys would have seen an email, a phone number, a name—something that would lead Mancuso to the source of the science. And if the lowly accountants couldn't be charmed, Donny could extract the information from the kingpins. A stack of money, a pistol in the mouth of a family member—whatever it took.

VINCENT CAME INTO MANCUSO'S office wearing a nice big smile.

"Great news, Mr. Mancuso. The black ops team entered the SMP CFO's home around 3:00 this morning. As you expected, he decided he'd rather have the fifty thousand bucks than his brains all over his bedroom wall. His wife encouraged him in his decision."

"Naturally. And what did the CFO reveal?"

"The CFO confirmed that only Sid Abrams has the name of the lab and the scientist that re-created the actors. Mr. Abrams guards the identity with his life–literally. He was nearly killed a few weeks ago. Looks like a hit was attempted as Abrams was traveling on Mulholland Highway. His car went over an embankment at a high rate of speed. He got bruised up but nothing life-threatening."

"Don't report to me that the team got nothing from this man!"

"Oh, no sir! The CFO said Sid's contact is known simply as 'Dr X,' but he lives in Tel Aviv and Sid talks to this guy whenever there's the slightest hiccup with these robots."

"Robots? I thought they were clones."

"No sir, he called them 'parahumans.' The CFO could not tell the ops commander how the creatures were made. There may be some level of cloning involved, but he said these things are some kind of sophisticated animatron that uses artificial intelligence plus the memories of the former human. That's how these parahumans are able to think. They see everything through the memories of the deceased movie star. He also said that SMP security is beyond high tech, extremely sophisticated—beyond anything the CFO has ever seen—and he sits on the board of several banks so he knows security. It sounds like anything we do to get the information you're after, it will have to be gleaned from outside the studio."

"That's okay. There's more than one way to skin an animatron. So, Sid talks to the creating lab whenever there's a problem with his re-created stars? That's what I needed to know. Did the ops team commander plant the seed of disinformation I gave him?"

"Yes, sir. Before he left the CFO's home, he was warned what would happen if he told anyone about this midnight encounter, and he was told that all of this could have been avoided if they had just let the other studios in on SMP's success. I'm sure he now thinks this invasion of his home was authored by one of the studios!"

"Yes. The studio's fighting amongst themselves is a good smokescreen."

Mancuso knew better than to bully Sid Abrams. Too visible. Since 'Dr. X' was in Tel Aviv, Donny just needed Sid to contact him. He could pinpoint him from there. But with SMP's security so tight, placing observation equipment within the facility might be discovered. There were other ways. Create a problem with the re-created actors and sooner or later Sid would communicate with Dr. X about his parahumans.

Donny made sure of this. He triggered Howard Gordon at the Screen Actors Guild with a distressing phone call. Had Howard considered the danger of SMP's monopoly? And what would happen to the dues-paying human actors with the public fawning all over the re-created actors? By the way, had the parahuman actors joined Gordon's Screen Actors Guild? Nope. Donny suggested a call to the FBI was in order. Howard Gordon triggers the FBI, the FBI triggers Sid Abrams, Abrams panics and calls Dr. X. Simple. And before Howard Gordon could call the FBI, Donny had *Stingray* and *Hailstorm* devices in place to intercept all cellular transmissions from SMP Studios. Donny was only interested in one call. Tel Aviv.

SID ABRAMS WAS BEYOND troubled with what he heard and saw in his re-created stars during the FBI interview.

He was certain if something was not done to stop this 'downward spiral of anxiety,' they would cease to function. The amount of time and money required to develop each parahuman star was enormous. Oh, the investment had been validated by an avalanche of revenue on new motion pictures and public appearances featuring Gable, Bogart, and Stewart. But it had only been a year and that was not enough time to return capital to investors. The stars had to work unabated or there would be trouble. The day following the FBI interview, Sid placed an international call to Tel Aviv at the noon hour. 12:00 PM Los Angeles time made it 10:00 PM in Tel Aviv and that should assure that 'Dr. X' was free from distraction and fully focused on Sid's problem.

"This is Sid. We need to talk."

"It is after 10:00 PM here and I just arrived home from a long and difficult day. May I call you tomorrow?"

"No, you may not! We have encountered a potentially debilitating problem with our actors. You were paid millions per creation—and several million more as insurance of satisfactory performance. I expect your help with this immediately."

Dr. X did not like pressure—but he recognized the sound of panic in a wealthy and powerful businessman. Something catastrophic must have happened.

"What is wrong?"

"They are experiencing emotions."

"Emotions?"

"Yes, sadness, emptiness, loneliness. You said they felt no pain, that they had no emotions of their own. They are becoming more and more distracted. This could cause them to underperform or even stop performing. During an interview yesterday they became melancholy, disconnected—almost incapacitated. Jimmy Stewart asked me what was wrong with him!"

"I do not think this is actually emotion or feeling. They are most likely exhibiting the memories their predecessors experienced under similar circumstances. Parahumans do not have emotions or a 'heart' as we say of human beings. They only repeat what their predecessors said or did over their lifetime."

"That's *not* what's happening! You created these beings. You said you used artificial intelligence so they could learn, did you not?"

"Yes, learning is necessary for realistic interaction with human beings. They would be easily discovered without the ability to take in new information, process it through the memory embossing of their predecessor's memories, and then conjugate logical communication."

"Well, they were being questioned about their happiness, about what they want out of life, and they said they were lonely without their spouses ... their wives."

At this, Dr. X fell silent. This was not within the bounds of parahuman possibility as he understood it.

"So ... I can tell you are just as surprised as I was," Sid said with an accusing tone.

"This is certainly unanticipated. You said they were being questioned about their future? Did you permit them to go on a talk show or news interview?"

"No. The FBI was here. They said they had a complaint from someone in Hollywood who felt the re-created stars were not being treated humanely."

"*The FBI?*" It was now Dr. X whose voice betrayed his concern.

"Relax, they said they just wanted to talk with them." Sid didn't mention the FBI went through the star's living quarters and interviewed SMP staff. Any additional negative information might cause Dr. X to back away or lose focus on the issue. Sid could not afford that. "So, what can you do to eliminate these distressing emotional issues?"

"I don't know. You know that I am not the sole inventor of this technology. I will need to research this further. You must shelter the parahumans from any additional interaction that might trigger emotional issues. I don't need to tell you what could happen to both of us if I am found out. This is top secret technology in my country. It is being kept from politicians and citizens alike. If it comes out that I am the creator of these actors, my life will be forfeit! I will work on this. But you must agree to keep them sheltered."

"Look, Uriah, I cannot afford ... "

"You were never to use my name on an open line!"

"I apologize, it was an accident, but you must understand the pressure I am under. My studio invested heavily. It's only been a year and we have not had time to repay investors."

"I will work on this immediately and contact you in the next few days. Goodnight."

ADONIS MANCUSO HAD what he needed. The country, the city, the phone number, a title, and a name. He would find Uriah. Thank you, Sid, it had indeed been a 'good night.'

5

THE PRESIDENT OF THE UNITED STATES is arguably the most visible person in the world.

His complete schedule is never announced to the media, but public appearances are just that—public. Not since JFK had there been a chief executive who so eagerly sought to mix among the people, to touch them, and be touched by them. Almost to the point of being foolhardy with little thought of safety and security. Jonathan Theodore Roosevelt was the namesake and great grandson of the 26th President of the United States. And like his great grandfather, he fancied himself a sportsman, hunter, conservationist, a rugged individualist, and a man of the people.

This persona was easy for him. He had been a child movie star during the late 1950s and early 60s, often paired with the elite of the silver screen. He arrived on the scene in time to work with Hollywood royalty including Gregory Peck, James Stewart, and Cary Grant.

Even as a boy, Jon Roosevelt's big personality had his Hollywood mentors suggesting he follow in his great grandfather's footsteps. But Grandpa Teddy was a Republican. Jon watched the stars and studio chiefs share their political opinions, usually at grandiose parties and fundraisers for left-leaning candidates, where no one disagreed with anything they said. No one dared. He had seen the fallout from actors who believed their conservative opinions were just as valid as those of their liberal bosses. Say anything they disagree with and the party invitations dry up, your name vanishes from script calls, and you just fade away. Being too young to vote meant Jon could avoid having any political opinions.

Jonathan Roosevelt left Hollywood during his teen years, went on to earn a Master's Degree in Political Science from George Washington University, a Doctorate of Law from Harvard—deliberately emulating his great grandfather—and was elected governor of Texas three times before being drafted to run for President. He learned that being a senator made you a better debater but being a governor prepared you for the Presidency, as it had Teddy. It was also the legacy of fellow actor Ronald Reagan. He proved that an actor could be a larger than life leader. Jon prayed he might do as well.

The Secret Service asked President Roosevelt to stay out of crowds. His crowd-pleasing forays made it virtually impossible for them to protect him. Joshua 'Josh' Sizemore, Director of White House Security, had grown as close to the President in the first four years as any agent should allow himself. Agents who served on the Kennedy detail warned of this during Josh's academy training. When they lost the President, they felt they had failed the nation. Their lives disintegrated into alcohol, divorce, and emotional breakdowns.

Josh understood the image Jon projected and why the public loved it. Voters were done with corrupt politicians in the nation's capital. When they elected Jon Roosevelt, they cleaned out Washington. Those politicians who almost handed American sovereignty over to the World Economic Forum and the World Health Organization were kicked out of office. Jon Roosevelt helped them take the nation back and return it to a strong and stable economic foundation. They now had a savvy, capable, likable man in the White House. He said what he meant and meant what he said. That had everything to do with his *Teddy Roosevelt* image.

But the President's penchant for mingling in crowds was nothing compared to the pending trip to Tehran for the signing of the Israeli-Palestinian peace accords. The event was only a few months away and terrorist chatter was through the roof.

Israeli president Isaac Hayut had asked President Roosevelt to help broker the peace accords between his nation and the Palestinians. Jonathan championed the task with great success. The treaty allowed Israel and the U.S. to support the Palestinian Authority and its people in tangible ways while ensuring the safety of Israel in the region, particularly the hotly contested West Bank and Gaza Strip. Once the details were to their liking, eight other Islamic nations agreed to sign, including Iran, Syria, the United Arab Emirates, Egypt, Morocco, and Bahrain. The unprecedented alacrity between the former warring parties had the Russians, Chinese, and Europeans asking to sign. Jon Roosevelt had become an international sensation. The signing of the agreement would be a historic moment for the world.

But Tehran? It was Josh Sizemore's job to protect the President and his boss was preparing to go into the capital city that, prior to the peace negotiations, had publicly declared it would destroy Israel's ally, the United States, which they dubbed 'the Great Satan.' Protecting the President and his delegation in that city kept Josh up at night. So did his stomach. His doctor suspected peptic ulcers.

But Josh Sizemore had a plan. His idea was out there—way out there. But he had the support of a professor of Neurobiology and Cognitive Science from the President's alma mater, Harvard. Once Josh was alone with Jon Roosevelt he told him he had a plan to protect him while in Tehran. He provided few details but gave a cryptic promise.

"The professor will explain the technology. I can only tell you this is the only way I have to protect you in a city whose name is synonymous with terrorism." But Josh sealed the meeting when he importuned, "If anything happens to you while in Tehran, the peace agreement will die with you and virtually guarantee a war. Just give me one hour, Mr. President—that's all I'm asking! Your life, the peace accords, and the stability of that entire region of the world are worth one hour!" Jonathan Roosevelt had never seen Josh so insistent. He agreed to the meeting.

President Roosevelt agreed to clear his schedule for one hour. He would have to reschedule a promised lunch date with his wife, Deborah. Why was it always his wife that had to get bumped to accommodate business? Jon expressed the unfairness to Josh.

Josh courageously countered by asking for more—a *private* meeting for the scientist with the President. Josh knew this is seldom granted. The President of the United States almost never meets alone with anyone. His every move is scrutinized, and private meetings make allies and enemies alike nervous. It also prevents documentation of the meeting. But there is a place for private meetings, and it is, after all, the President's right to meet alone on occasions as he deems best.

Jonathan agreed to an *almost* private meeting, telling Josh that his chief of staff, Paul "Marty" Martin, would be present. Jonathan Roosevelt and Marty Martin had worked together in Texas during the twelve years of his governorship, and they were friends long before that. Josh thanked the President. Having Marty there could be a plus, so long as Marty didn't go into his catatonic protective mode for which he was well known, voting everything down that he interpreted as a political risk to Jon Roosevelt.

DR. RALPH VESTRO WAS Dean of Neurobiology and Cognitive Science at Harvard University. He was a recipient of the National Academy of Sciences Award for Initiative in Research involving advanced artificial intelligence applied to human learning, human genetics, and artificial neural networks.

He followed Dr. Alfred Edersheim's work in Israel on 'parahumans' with great interest. As a founding member of HUGO, the worldwide Human Genetics Organization, Ralph met Alfred Edersheim following one of his lectures on integrating AI with the human electro-magnetic field. They later served on several panels together discussing the feasibility of near-human functioning animatrons. They formed a professional friendship that allowed them to exchange new findings and techniques.

But about a year ago Dr. Edersheim went dark, noticeably absent from HUGO and the world stage in general. Dr. Vestro believed that his friend was within striking distance of his lifelong goal—creating a functional parahuman. Given restrictions by so many governments on human engineering, it would make sense that Alfred disappeared to build a prototype. On the other hand, Ralph wondered, why would Alfred call attention to himself by totally disappearing? Going off the grid could mean he was under government protection—or house arrest? Speculation was useless. If his friend *had* moved from drawing board to testing then Ralph, too, needed to make the move. Harvard's commitment at the Kempner Institute to be dominant in Natural and Artificial Intelligence would be threatened if such a breakthrough occurred somewhere else. Harvard would look to Ralph Vestro to make sure that didn't happen.

SECRET SERVICE AGENTS escorted Dr. Vestro into the White House and through the West Wing to the waiting area across from the Oval Office. Josh was notified that Dr. Vestro had arrived and he excused himself from the Oval where he, the President, and

Marty Martin were reviewing security details for the upcoming meeting in Tehran.

Josh closed the door to the office and crossed the corridor to where Dr. Vestro was waiting.

Josh thanked the agents and waited for them to get out of ear shot before speaking. Vestro, a short, stout man in his fifties looked up at Josh and extended his hand. It was shaking.

"Thank you for coming Ralph."

"I'm *so* nervous!" Dr. Vestro said, his voice trembling in unison with his hands.

"Don't be nervous, Ralph," Josh said quietly. "Remember what we discussed and why you are here. This is important but not the biggest meeting of your life. If the President rejects the offer, your outstanding academic career will suffer no harm. I wish I could say the same for Jon Roosevelt in Tehran."

"But that is why this matters so much to me! His life is in jeopardy. This will protect the President in Tehran. It will also ensure an attack on his life does not become a cause for war. I must focus on that. That should calm my nerves ... I hope!"

"All right then. The President wants and expects short, direct answers to his questions. No jargon. Keep in mind he's a smart man but he doesn't have your doctorate in neurobiology."

"Yes, of course."

"All right, let's see if we can save the President!"

Dr. Vestro nodded and Josh led him across the corridor.

"MR. PRESIDENT, THIS is Dr. Ralph Vestro, Dean of Neurobiology and Cognitive Science at Harvard University. Dr. Vestro, the President of the United States, Jonathan Roosevelt."

"Mr. President, it is entirely my honor. I have followed your career with increasing hope. You've led this country back from the brink of economic disaster with your tax cuts and reduction in government debt. We are all very grateful."

"Thank you Dr. Vestro, that's very kind of you. Would you mind making such a statement to the wolves in the Washington press corps? Some of them like to say I took money from the poor and elderly by getting Congress to decrease taxes and tax rates. Only in Washington can tax cuts be translated as harmful. Oh, I'm sorry, let me introduce you to my friend and chief of staff, Marty Martin."

"I'm pleased to meet you, Dr. Vestro," said Marty. "You have quite a body of work online. Very impressive stuff. Most of it was related to AI and human genetics. Much of it was beyond my paygrade but it sounded like you're working towards creating artificial humans—is that close to accurate?"

"Thank you, Mr. Martin. And, yes, that's an accurate summation." Ralph Vestro felt a drop of perspiration trickle down his forehead and his hands were still shaking. Being a renowned college professor did not necessarily prepare one for meeting with the President in the Oval Office.

"I apologize for my nervousness, Mr. President. I'm afraid I don't often meet dignitaries in my line of work. Certainly not the President of the United States!"

"Dr. Vestro, there's no need to be nervous! Do you mind if I just call you Ralph? You can call me Jon and that will let us talk with each other as friends."

Jon Roosevelt hated it when people were uncomfortable around him. He was quick to put people at ease. Josh appreciated having a President with such humility.

"Would you care for a drink, professor? I think a little something might help all of us relax a bit." The President was looking at Ralph Vestro but turned to look at both Josh and Marty.

"I believe I'll have a Scotch and soda. Would you gentlemen care to keep me company?" asked the President.

"That sounds very good to me, Mr. President!" said Dr. Vestro. "I think that might calm my nerves somewhat!" Marty accepted the offer as well. Josh did not drink while working.

"As a boy in Hollywood, I learned Humphrey Bogart was fond of Scotch and soda. Do you know what he called that drink, Ralph?" The President was still trying to help him calm down.

"No, Mr. President, I've never heard this before."

"He called them 'loudmouths' because they got him talking more than he intended!"

They all laughed, and Ralph Vestro seemed a bit more relaxed.

"Why don't you men sit down while I fix our drinks. Josh, get us started, won't you? This was your idea, after all!"

"Yes, sir, Mr. President." Josh gave a reassuring look to Ralph Vestro and then faced toward the President's bar.

"Mr. President, your meeting to sign the peace accords in Tehran is unprecedented. I've certainly made clear my concerns about adequately protecting you from the ubiquitous threats presented in that place."

"Yes, you've made that point quite clear, Josh," said the President as he walked toward the sitting area by the fireplace and presented each man his drink. "I know we would not be discussing these security concerns in front of Dr. Vestro unless he was part of a very important solution you are about to propose. Am I correct?"

"That is correct, Mr. President. Dr. Vestro has a cutting edge means for you to be present at that historic meeting while absolutely ensuring your safety."

"Excuse me, Josh," said the President, taking his seat, "but how is it possible to absolutely ensure *any* government leader's safety anywhere in the world, especially in a place as traditionally volatile as Tehran?"

The President lifted his drink. "To your health, gentlemen."

"To your health, Mr. President!" they responded.

"Mr. President," Josh said, "I know you must be aware of what is going on in Hollywood, with the re-creation of formerly deceased Hollywood stars. You and Jimmy Stewart were so close, you had to have heard about his re-creation almost a year ago."

"Yes, I can't say that I know everything that goes on in Tinseltown anymore, but I called SMP Studios to congratulate Mr. Abrams, the studio president. He's turning out some outstanding motion pictures with these re-created stars. Quite frankly, I thought they were computer generated but from what I'm hearing, I'm not so sure anymore. I heard they might be a type of clone. What does this have to do with my security in Tehran, Josh?"

"Mr. President, let me ask Dr. Vestro to speak to this. He's the best in our nation at what we're about to propose."

The President's gaze moved from Joshua Sizemore to Ralph Vestro. "Well, Ralph, what do you want to share with me? Let's don't beat around the bush. I'm still hopeful I can get a date night in with Mrs. Roosevelt!"

Ralph reached into his briefcase and pulled out a binder, opened it, then cleared his throat. "Mr. President ... "

"*Jon*, Ralph, please. Let's keep it informal," the President reminded him.

Ralph felt more awkward calling the President 'Jon' than 'Mr. President' but he certainly wasn't going to argue with the President.

"Jon, those re-created actors at SMP Studios are not clones. I can say this with certainty. Cloning of humans cannot replicate the exact face, voice, even the mannerisms and habits of their human predecessor. Such cloning will never happen."

"So, no *Jurassic Park*, Ralph? There goes another Hollywood fantasy," the President chuckled. "All right, if they're not clones, then what are they?"

"A friend and molecular biologist and geneticist, Dr. Alfred Edersheim, referred to these creations as 'parahumans.' They have outer tissue and hair genetically created from the DNA of the human predecessor but that is the extent of the genetics. The inner frame is a composite alloy. The face, height, and bone size are all exact duplicates of the person we are copying. That's why the face looks just like the former actor—the human skin is growing over a duplicated facial structure of the person we are re-creating. It's like growing skin over a mask. Their ability to 'think' comes from a supercomputer which houses the total memory of the human, from cradle to grave—or to their current age. Using artificial intelligence, the parahuman will respond by filtering all interactions through the framework of what the human said and did over their entire lifetime."

"Ralph, you're saying everything that my friend, Jimmy Stewart, ever said or did has been loaded into a supercomputer that forms the brain of this new Jimmy Stewart?"

"That is correct, sir."

"So, this 'parahuman' Jimmy Stewart should have memories of me, is that correct?"

"If the creators did as thorough a job as we will do, then, yes, Jimmy Stewart's parahuman will have complete memories of you—whatever the real Jimmy Stewart would remember."

"You seem to know a lot about what happened in Hollywood. Were you somehow involved with the Hollywood actor re-creations?"

"Oh, no, Mr. President. That was not me. But we have the ability to do such a project."

"Well, that's good to know, Ralph. I suppose ... wait just a minute. You just said, 'as we will do.' Are you proposing this technology as the solution for my safety in Tehran?"

This was the moment Josh looked forward to. And dreaded. He jumped in.

"Mr. President, we need to create a parahuman of you, your exact duplicate. It can safely go into Tehran to sign that agreement. It is the only way to avoid this deathtrap. Sir, I cannot protect you if you go there! But this—this can eliminate any risk to your safety, and no one would ever know. It will be just as convincing as the parahumans in Hollywood."

"Oh, that's preposterous, Josh!" Marty said as he rose to his feet. "Have you thought through what would happen if this plan of yours fails? Consider the range of potential reactions from world leaders! They would see the agreement as bogus—a complete counterfeit since the real President didn't sign it. I can give you a dozen reasons not to do this, Mr. President!"

"Is one of them protecting the life of the Chief Executive?" Josh countered firmly.

"That's unfair, Josh, and you know it! I've known Jon longer than you have and his well-being is just as important to me as to you! I'm just saying … "

"Gentlemen," the President jumped in, "let's bring this discussion back to more civilized terms, before I need a peace summit for my own staff! I value the input you both are giving. I appreciate your mutual concern for my well-being *and* the survival and success of the peace accords. I've been grappling with the treaty and nations involved for over a year. Quite frankly, I'm determined it will succeed even if it costs me my life. I'm sorry, Josh, I don't see that we have the time for research, construction, and testing before I have to be in Tehran. We only have four months."

"Please, Mr. President," Josh pleaded, "please, hear Dr. Vestro out. Let him finish."

The President turned to Ralph Vestro. He studied his face for a moment. It was an honest face—but this idea of Josh's was a complete blindside.

"Ralph, let me pose a rather crucial question at this juncture. I would apologize for putting you on the spot, but I don't think that's necessary. You and Josh had to have anticipated this moment."

Ralph was nervous, he was perspiring again, but he faced the President resolutely.

"Ralph, you must be a man of uncommon intelligence. That's a safe assumption on my part, given your position at Harvard. And though we've only just met, I sense that you are also a man of moral principle. I'm bolstered in that opinion by the fact that I know Josh Sizemore very well, and he would only bring a person of the highest character to counsel me. But you're also a man of science. You would not be here if you did not believe this would succeed. You must know what it could mean if this parahuman were to fail on the world stage." The President paused as he studied the professor's face. He was looking for confidence and competence. He wasn't sure he saw it. "Ralph, I need a completely honest assessment of this project. What are our chances for success with only four months to prepare?"

Ralph looked down at the floor. That was not the sign the President was looking for.

"Mr. President ... Jon," Ralph Vestro said, "this is the time. *We can do this.* One hundred percent is my answer. I stake my reputation on the outcome, and I give you my word that I and my team are fully capable of building your parahuman. And we do have time to do this, sir, I assure you of that. If you will provide me with a secure place to work, I will have the creation done within three months." Then he paused.

"Ralph, you have something more for me?"

"Yes, sir. I am not a politician. But I believe this is the *best* opportunity for the success of the peace process. There will be no peace treaty—and there could be war—if you are killed. Tehran has long been a city of political upheaval. Their country's leaders may have the best intentions, but with so many still against the treaty, and with you as the primary author ... I beg of you, Mr. President, please do not go there!"

Jon almost recoiled. He wasn't expecting such strength from this nervous little scientist. He looked at Marty and Josh. Marty was still nursing his Scotch and soda but was watching Dr. Vestro. Josh stood in silence. "Well, boys? Now's the time. If you've got anything else to add—opinions, reactions, comments—you'd best hand them over!"

"Sir," Marty said, "when Josh asked for this meeting, saying he had a rock-solid solution for your security in Tehran, naturally I was eager to learn what could possibly be 'rock-solid' enough to protect you in a city as potentially volatile as Tehran. I was set on my heels listening to Dr. Vestro's proposal. I'd heard about the goings-on in Hollywood, but never in my wildest imagination would I have made the link from an actor to you—despite your connection with Hollywood!"

"That's true for both of us, Marty," the President responded. "So, what are you thinking?"

Marty looked over at Josh Sizemore. "Josh, this is the most audacious proposal I have ever heard—and I exaggerate not in saying it's probably the most audacious plan ever submitted to any previous occupant of the White House!"

Josh sat straight up on the couch. He almost said something, then waited.

"But, Mr. President," Marty continued, "I know without a doubt that Josh and Dr. Vestro are right. You cannot physically enter Tehran. The risk is something Josh and ten thousand agents could not adequately minimize. As I stand here trying to picture this animatron walking around in Tehran before the world's leaders, trying to impersonate you, my skin crawls. I don't see how it can be done. But Dr. Vestro has given you his personal and professional assurance that he can have your duplicate ready within three months, and that provides us with a month to test his work. I think we should at least try this, sir. If the parahuman fails our testing, you're no worse off than you were before we tried."

"Deborah has been expressing much dismay about my Tehran trip," the President said. "She's not sleeping well and it's beginning to show. What a blessing it would be if I could tell her I'm not going to Tehran, but the treaty will still be signed."

The President turned to Dr. Vestro.

"Ralph, would you be willing for this parahuman to be tested here, at the White House? Would we be able to see if it can fool my own staff, people who work with me and around me every day?"

"That is an excellent suggestion, Mr. President!" Ralph's excitement was obvious. "And, sir, you will be able to see and hear through the parahuman from a remote location, so you will observe in real time how your own people respond to you—I mean, to him!"

"So, I'll be able to hear everything that is said, Ralph?"

"Yes, sir."

"If I may, Mr. President?" Marty asked.

"Go ahead, Marty."

"Ralph, what powers these Hollywood stars? What gives them their energy to speak and move about? Is it some form of advanced batteries, maybe fusion or something along those lines?"

"I cannot say for sure about the Hollywood actors. But what Alfred Edersheim and I developed is a form of holography."

"You mean, like a hologram, Ralph?" asked the President. "How can a hologram provide energy to run these creatures?"

"It is because a hologram is both gas and light—two forms of energy. Holography is also the means by which we update certain things within the parahuman. His memory must be updated with current events when we put him to sleep. The holography also helps segregate fact from fiction."

"Sleep, Ralph? Parahumans must sleep?"

"No, Jon, parahumans do not have to sleep. They do not get tired. But we put them into a sleep-like state to update their memories with things you've said and done or to download data from their collective memory."

"And how do you put them to sleep?"

"Using holography, we place their artificial intelligence into a *Theta* state, so they become introspective. They assimilate and process the incoming data by filtering it through your memories we placed into them. They compare the new information through the neural network of your existing memories. We awaken them by moving them into a *Beta* state."

"You didn't cut many classes in school, did you Ralph?" asked Marty.

They all laughed, but Ralph picked up his Scotch and took a long drink. He was obviously embarrassed. Marty couldn't leave Dr. Vestro in that condition.

"Ralph, what happens if the President's 'stunt double' is suddenly wounded and unable to function on foreign soil?"

"There are several options. Parahumans are so constructed that their strength is far beyond human. A bullet will not bring them down so wounding a parahuman is almost impossible. They are either fully disabled or they continue to function. If the President's parahuman is kidnapped, it can defend itself—and will, if that's what we tell it to do. Or it can be remotely destroyed, eliminating all evidence of the technology."

"What do you mean by *remotely destroyed*?" asked the President.

"Detonated wherever and whenever we wish, sir, taking the evidence and the abductors with it!" said Ralph. He stood there with his five-foot, four-inch body, bespectacled chubby face, curly gray hair, and somewhat disheveled appearance, seeming rather proud of what he was able to provide for his President.

"All right, professor, you have my authorization to begin. Josh, you'll be my point of contact on this. No one outside this room is to know a thing about it. Ralph, we cannot afford for this project to be discovered so you will be provided a secure facility of your own at Camp David. I hate to ask you to leave your home so close to the holidays—but with a good tailwind, hopefully you'll be done before Thanksgiving. Camp David is quite a distance from your home in Cambridge, Massachusetts, but I'll make sure you are provided with all the comforts and necessities you need. I'm assuming you were already prepared to take a sabbatical from Harvard?"

"That is correct, sir. And I don't mind making this sacrifice. It is my honor to help protect the President of the United States and the peace accords!"

The President placed his hand on Ralph's shoulder. "Thank you, my friend. Someday the world may know what you have done. But it is also possible you will take this secret with you to your grave. I'm grateful you're preventing me from entering mine!"

6

ALL OF THE MEMORY EMBOSSING DATA and much of the dynamic functions of Sid Abrams' parahumans could be seen remotely by Dr. Uriah Horvitz, aka, 'Dr. X,' through his remote login in Tel Aviv.

The 'brain' that was created for the parahumans, the central processing system of Sid's three stars, did not appear to be functioning normally. The holographic waves were fluctuating in an unusual pattern. Something was there that wasn't there before. Uriah knew how to stimulate brain waves in parahumans, which caused them to relate interactions with others by passing information through the memory grid of the human predecessor. But he did not know how to stop the unexpected wave fluctuation he was seeing. He believed this might be part of that mysterious area in artificial intelligence referred to as *the hidden layer*. No scientist ever claimed to know what happens within that inner sanctum. His employer, Alfred Edersheim, maintained control of the holosapien through holography. The electrical-helium gas combination was his genius. It was his secret means for the creatures to cognate, to 'think' through the grid of their memories—and to separate reality from fiction. Had Edersheim overcome the 'hidden layer'?

Uriah was uncertain how to fix Sid's three. He knew Dr. Edersheim would increase *Theta* waves to turn cognition inward in the holosapien, thus triggering a 'learning' and sleep state. He triggered *Beta* waves to begin the 'doing' state and the parahuman would go to work. The tablet application Uriah gave to Sid allowed him to stimulate the waves, putting the Hollywood three to sleep or awaken them for the day's activities. It was totally inadequate for anything more.

Alfred Edersheim segregated his scientists into teams based upon the project assigned to them. This was a security measure, making it more difficult for one scientist to steal or sabotage the project. Uriah's growing suspicion was that he had misapplied holography, but he could only ask so many questions without raising concerns since this technology was not assigned to his team. If only he had not needed money so desperately. When Sid contacted him, he took the bait. If his betrayal was discovered, he faced prison. Or worse.

It was almost midnight in Tel Aviv when Uriah placed the call.

"Sid, this is Dr. X. There is no cause for concern. At the close of your business day, please place the three into *Theta* state. I will apply an adjustment during the sleep phase that should return them to their original programming."

"Very well," replied Sid. "You are certain this will work?"

"As I said, there is no cause for concern. This looks to be an anomaly. The incoming data from their movie scripts appear to become entangled with the memory embossing. They have trouble distinguishing a character role from the movie star they were programmed to emulate. The adjustment should take care of that."

"*It better!*" Sid said, with that unmistakable tone that mixed angst with ire.

"The adjustment could require as much as a week to fully integrate with the subjects. Let me know how they are doing after a week. Signing off."

What Uriah told Sid Abrams he *hoped* to be accurate. The parahumans did appear to have trouble distinguishing the memory embossing—the memories that formed the reality of their predecessor's life—from the character roles they were required to learn and portray on screen. He believed this was the dip in *Beta* waves he was seeing on a somewhat predictable cycle during movie production hours. The cycle seemed to decrease after working hours. Decrease—not disappear. Uriah was living on borrowed time.

He had heard Dr. Edersheim say when humans memorize something, the brain automatically compartmentalizes the information, accurately distinguishing reality from fiction. However, in some humans and under some circumstances, their brain can blur the lines between reality and fantasy, causing them to act out a role as if it were real. He referenced cases of soldiers placed under extreme duress, isolated or tortured, who 'escaped' in their minds by mentally retreating to a safe environment. Alfred often mentioned U.S. Congressman Sam Johnson. He and his fellow pilots, imprisoned in Vietnam in the 'Hanoi Hilton,' played golf in their minds while lying on their backs in concrete tubes. After seven years in the POW camp, they came out and shot record-breaking scores.

Dr. Edersheim had built the *Theta* sleep state into holosapien technology for the same result as human dreams. Dreams are the mechanism which helps the human brain assemble information received and process it through role playing. How ironic—Uriah's ordeal had become a bad dream from which he tried desperately to awake. He planned to remain at the Edersheim lab after everyone left, find Edersheim's notes on holographic technology, and decipher the problem. He just needed a few days.

IT WAS JUST BEFORE 5:00 PM in Hollywood when Lexi Bristol's cell phone rang. The timing of the call was deliberate.

"Hello, this is Lexi."

"Lexi, this is Mike Benchley in Washington. Did I catch you at a bad time?"

"No, I'm just closing up my desk. How can I help you?"

"Well, now that you've asked—if you don't have plans this Saturday, I'd like to take you to a great lunch and a nice, quiet visit."

"You're going to fly cross-country to take me to lunch?"

"I guess I could try driving there but I wouldn't get to LA until next week."

"You know what I mean! That's a pretty pricey airline ticket, mister."

"I'll be on a Bureau jet and, thus far, they've never made me buy a ticket!"

"Oh, official business, Director?"

"Yes, on Friday. And it's Mike. I have a meeting in LA on Friday, but Saturday is wide open for me. I was hoping it might be for you. I've got a few questions you might be able to help me answer. There's a place on the waterfront with an executive chef's brunch that is unbelievable. You familiar with SALT Restaurant in Marina Del Rey?"

"On Bali Way? That place is awesome! And usually reserved for special occasions, I might add. So, what's *your* occasion?"

"Well, I'll tell you. I needed some way to get you out of the old salt mine and some place where the music isn't blaring—so I can hear what you have to say. I sat here thinking, *How do you get a beautiful Hollywood socialite out of the salt mine?* And then the answer came: *You take her to SALT!*"

"You're funny. You think SMP Studio is a *salt mine*?"

"Hey, after spending four years under fire in Afghanistan, and three years in law school, your worldview tends to change."

"Try a year under Sid Abrams' withering fire. Okay, I can meet you. What time?"

"Make it easy on yourself. I've got the whole day. I'm good getting there early to beat the crowd. How about 11:00 AM?"

"Deal. But I'll get my own check."

"You don't want to get me in trouble with accounting, do you? I have an expense account and SALT is a mighty swanky place. If I don't file this as lunch for *two*, it will look like I took myself out for an expensive lunch. They frown on that, you know."

"That's quite a line you've got. All right, I'm in. See you at 11:00 this Saturday."

LEXI BRISTOL LOOKED radiant. The lobby was crowded but Mike navigated a path to the reserved dockside table.

He signaled and the waiter nodded, bringing steaming mugs of SALT's famous '*coffee with a kick*' and the brunch menu. The sky was azure. Seagulls, buoy bells, and waves lapping the shore became their music. Sailboats lazily moved from harbor to bay. Lexi's blond hair blew gently in the warm salty breeze. She smiled. Mike was a long way from Washington and Afghanistan. This offered a much better vantage point. He thought of Montana.

"Thanks for meeting me, Lexi. I appreciate you making the drive."

"I live in Hollywood so it's not that far. How did business go yesterday? Catch any bad guys?"

"No, still trying to piece this puzzle together. Frankly, I was meeting with someone connected to your studio's 'big three' actors. Questions about their well being—their safety—with Silverscreen Motion Pictures are increasing, but I'm coming up short on answers."

"We don't call them the 'big three,' Mike, just 'the three.' I think I know where you're headed, but what about their safety has the FBI so concerned they'd bring you in from Washington?"

"Well, not to backtrack but this case was assigned to me by the Deputy Director. I oversee the Science and Technology branch and these three certainly seem to qualify as both *science* and *technology*! About a year ago SMP told our LA office that cloning was not involved in the re-creation of these formerly deceased movie stars. And our team wasn't aware that AI had given rise to parahuman technology so they didn't know enough to ask. But my interview with those actors was just too real. In fact, that's part of what bugs me. They're literally *too real*—too perfect. They already had the answers to every question I could come up with–they didn't even pause to think. It was as if they had lived the very lives of the human actors they represent. And I know actors act but the passion I saw—the sadness, the loneliness–I had to remind myself I was talking to re-creations. If there's nothing in them that qualifies as human, they're the most advanced artificial life-form I've ever encountered."

"Well, so far, you don't sound concerned, Mike, you sound impressed!"

"I am impressed by the technology! I wouldn't be good at my job if I wasn't drawn to this stuff. But I was only around the three for a half-day and I was overwhelmed by their emotional troubles. Each of them is grieving for a wife they never met! Their longing is based solely on memories placed into them from a deceased human being. I've never encountered anything like this."

"As you said, you were only around them a half-day. I've been around them for a year. I no longer have to imagine—I *see* what it's doing to them. So, what information do you think I have that might help you?"

"This isn't just about helping me, Lexi. I know you want to help *them*."

Lexi cleared her throat. She looked at the couple across the deck. She adjusted the napkin in her lap. "I ... I do. But I just don't know ... "

"Lexi, there's no cause to stutter! This is *not* an official interview–this is totally off the record. You're not being recorded, I'm not wearing a wire. I wasn't sure how suspicious you would be but I wore this Hawaiian shirt and left it unbuttoned to make that fact apparent."

"Oh, that's what you were up to! And I thought you wanted me to see your suntanned six pack. Well, it worked."

Mike grinned and took a quick drink of his coffee.

"Now don't tell me a director of the FBI is *that* shy!"

"No, just not used to being on the receiving end of an indictment! I can't lie to you—I was hoping you'd look—but I really did want you to see there was no wire!"

"All right. I've looked. I've looked at you and I've looked at the three. I've seen you're shy and I've seen they're lonely. One situation is cute, the other troubles me. Your investigative powers can unravel it from there."

"Lexi ... I don't ... what I mean is ... "

"Now *you're* stuttering."

"Yes, because I don't want you getting the wrong impression. I have a job to do but not at your expense. This meeting means as much to me personally as professionally." He didn't mean to move so fast. He reached for his spiked coffee again.

"Oh? Is a director allowed to get involved with an informant?"

"You're not going to be an informant, Lexi. But an inside perspective is definitely needed. I don't know what we're dealing with here and I don't know where else to turn."

"Couldn't you bug the studio–the phone lines?"

"California has a wiretapping law–and we only use it for the most serious crimes. I have no proof of any crime at this point."

Lexi looked out over the bay again. Mike watched her. His climb up the Bureau's ladder hadn't afforded him many times like this. Those nagging thoughts were coming more frequently. *Life is passing you by. You could've had a family years ago. And you're not getting any younger!*

"It's beautiful, isn't it, Mike? Some people love going to the mountains. I like the mountains—but I'll take a warm sandy beach, sitting in the shade of a palm tree and sipping a *Rum Runner* any day of the week!"

"A *Rum Runner*! I pegged you for a Mai Tai or Pina Colada girl."

Lexi turned to face Mike.

"I've already said what's happening to those actors bothers me. I'm willing to help you if I can. I'll admit, I'd rather not lose my job. I'm good at it, I love what I do, and I'm well paid. But my daddy was a Marine DI. He didn't like bullies and he didn't like people being taken advantage of. And that's what's happening at SMP. What do you need to know?"

FEW, IF ANY, WERE STILL alive in California who had seen the original 1935 Duesenberg JN Roadster that was designed by Clark Gable and built to his specs.

In 1935 it was the most powerful and expensive car on the road. With a top speed of one hundred fifteen miles per hour, nothing could catch it. And with a price tag of thirty-five thousand dollars—at a time when a Ford sold for a few hundred—it was the Ferrari of its day. Wanting something with more glitz, Gable took it to Bohman & Schwartz in Pasadena. There he added to and modified the roadster's design and appearance. First, a cream colored finish and a stowable white convertible top. Then he added a rumble seat, super wide-striped white sidewall tires, skirts over the back wheels, huge chrome exhaust pipes emitting from the engine cowling, and a front-end grill and hood so long it was said it arrived five minutes before the driver. By the time Clark finished, the car was *eighteen feet long*—one foot longer than Gary Cooper's 'Duesy.' Clark made *sure* of that! Cooper and Gable both wrote about it and laughed about it. There was not another roadster like it anywhere in the world. It was a car truly fit for the '*King of Hollywood.*'

The memories of Carole Lombard seemed to thunder in the parahuman brain of the re-created Clark Gable. They were just memories. But they were thrilling and relentless. When the studio handlers put the parahumans down for the night, Sid would activate the *Theta* wave program and—unbeknownst to anyone—the memories started playing. Not in black and white like their old films. These were in blazing color.

It was January 25, 1936 when the human Clark Gable asked his big screen co-star Carole Lombard to take a ride around town in his flamboyant roadster, and then to come back with him to his suite at the Beverly Wilshire Hotel. Lombard's response to Gable's brash invitation became legendary around Hollywood: "*Who do you think you are—Clark Gable?*" His torrid relationship with the vivacious Lombard almost cost him the lead in *Gone with the Wind*. He was still married to a wealthy heiress and she to actor William Powell. David O. Selznick threatened to give the part of Rhett Butler to Gary Cooper if Gable did not stop tarnishing his public persona. Gable and Lombard finalized their divorces and eloped in March 1939, in time for the release of *Gone with the Wind*. Selznick was finally happy.

In 1941, both having completed their motion picture production obligations, Clark and Carole left their ranch in Encino and drove up the Pacific Coast to Vancouver, British Columbia, a trip of almost 1,500 miles in Clark's mighty roadster.

It was just the two of them for weeks. After reaching Vancouver, and needing to return to Hollywood sooner, they put the prized Duesy into storage in Vancouver and caught the train home, intending to head back the next year and take the same romantic route home. But in 1942 tragedy struck. The commercial aircraft carrying Carole crashed into the mountains outside Las Vegas, killing her and twenty-one other passengers aboard. Heartbroken, and with too many memories of Carole tied to that car, Clark sold it with specific orders that it never be seen again in the state of California while he was still alive. These were the memories that haunted the parahuman Clark Gable night after empty night.

But the *new* Clark had a *new* plan for his future. From the parahuman's point of view, he died and now he was back, so he was entitled to plan for a new future. He kept it simple and straightforward. So easy to understand that even Sid Abrams couldn't mess it up. He would buy the car back that his beloved Carole shared with him and then Sid would do whatever Sid had to do to re-create *Carole*. After all, getting rid of the vehicle in 1942 demonstrated how deeply he missed Carole. Bringing it back to Hollywood now would make a bold statement of just how much he needed Carole once again.

So, without Sid's knowledge, Clark placed the call: Get the roadster on the next transport to Hollywood and bill it to his studio account. The order was processed, and the car shipped. Did the seller and the shipping company know they were dealing with a parahuman? No. What they knew was they were talking with Clark Gable and he was scoring one hit movie after another. That was enough. The truck arrived with the bill of lading reading, 'Clark Gable in care of SMP Studios, Hollywood, California.' Sid had no clue what was taking place.

The truck cleared security and stopped in the middle of the SMP Studio lot. As the Duesenberg was rolled carefully off the transport trailer, a large crowd of actors and stagehands began forming.

"Hey, Clark, what ya got there?" someone yelled.

"Oh, just a little something Carole and I used to enjoy—and will enjoy again!"

Clark signed the delivery documents, lowered the convertible top, and then jumped into the driver's seat.

"*Who's Carole?*" a beautiful young extra asked; "I'll ride with you!" Several other young ladies echoed the offer and began to crowd in around the vehicle.

"Wow, Clark, this is a beauty!" a cameraman quipped. "Wish I had my camera handy! Hang on, let me get some footage of you taking off in this baby!" The cameraman disappeared through a stage door.

Clark waited for the cameraman, not minding at all his time entertaining the charming young ladies. "Thank you, ladies, but I'm off to retrace a few footsteps and find a few memories. And the answer to your question is 'Carole Lombard.' If you don't know who she was, that's okay, because you'll know soon enough who she *is*!"

"Got my camera, Clark! Fire it up!"

When he started the motor, everyone on the lot could feel it. The roar caused those around the roadster to jump back, letting loose a tassel of squeals and screams. With only a minimal muffler on each pipe, the explosion of the firing straight-eight engine echoed off the studio walls and through the canyon of buildings. A cloud of blue-gray exhaust billowed out the twin tailpipes. Forget pollution control. Not on this roadster.

Using a Steadicam to balance his rig, the cameraman made a full circle around the car. Clark dutifully posed with his trademark smile as the crowd pressed in again around him and his roadster.

The girls started planting bright red lipstick on his cheeks. He loved it.

"Be sure to wave and flash those pearly whites as you take off, Clark!" the cameraman yelled over the roar of the motor.

As the car thundered past the front security gate, the uniformed guard looked back at the crowd and yelled, *"Does he have a driver's license?"*

Clark hit the gas, leaving the studio guardhouse in a cloud of exhaust. The tires squealed and smoke flew as the Duesenberg slid sideways onto Hollywood Boulevard heading west toward Vine. It felt awesome with the wind in his hair, the breeze against his skin. At least, he thought it did. Dr. X said these stars weren't supposed to feel anything, but Clark was certain he felt the warm California breeze. And it *was* awesome.

He knew right where he was on Hollywood Boulevard—but so much had changed. The buildings, the traffic lights, the streetlights, and the cars. These were not images in his memory.

There it was, Vine Street. He turned the corner ... and it was gone. The Brown Derby Restaurant was gone. He pulled his car along the curb and cut the motor. He sat there, looking at the lot where it used to be. Booth number 54. That's where he proposed to Carole. It was gone. He could remember the orange chiffon cake she ordered for his birthday. It was always his favorite. And the Derby's famous corned beef hash! "Now, that was a meal!" he said to himself. That was just eighty years ago. *"Where did my life go? Why was it so short?"* He wanted to pray. Then he thought, "Was I a praying man? *Am* I a praying man? *Who am I?* I'm Clark Gable! But why is everything just a memory? Everyone and everything I knew is gone." Then it hit him. *"Encino!"* Their beloved ranch home in the valley. "When Sid makes Carole for me again, that's where we're gonna live—really live—all over again."

Clark started the car and turned back onto Hollywood Boulevard. When he got to Laurel Canyon Boulevard, he turned north. This road looked more familiar to him with its twists and turns, the inclines and declines. A few more houses but pretty much the same.

He got to Ventura Boulevard and then to the town of Encino. So many cars, so many buildings—and the traffic! The road that led to the ranch was no longer a dirt country road. Along each side sat row after row of houses. Not bad houses. But the acres on which he and Carole raised their sheep and cattle were now neighborhoods.

He turned the corner off *Ashely Oaks* onto *Tara Drive*—obvious oblations to his Rhett Butler role—and there it was. Their beloved Encino ranch house, right where he remembered, at 4543 Tara Drive. Surrounded by homes but the house still had its familiar two-story gambrel design. There was the huge, wide electric gate on the driveway that he and Carole had installed. He so seldom opened it for anyone, including friends. They led a quiet and unassuming life here, just he and Carole. And they were truly happy.

Seemed a bit awkward seeing the gate open but he drove his Duesenberg up the drive and stopped just short of the front walkway. He knew it wasn't his place anymore, yet he felt drawn to find out who *did* own it now. He stood beside his car for a few moments, looking over 'the old place' as he used to call it. The farm animals that Carole loved were not there. The color scheme had changed. But, overall, it looked to be the warm, inviting place they had so loved.

He stepped around the Duesy and took the walkway to the front door. He listened for a moment and couldn't hear any voices, so he pressed the doorbell. Steps from inside were followed by the creak of the door swinging open. The woman looked to be in her early seventies. Her hair was streaked with silver but attractively styled. A fine-looking woman, wearing a red and white checked apron, both hands occupied with a mixing bowl and a whisk. Her eyes suddenly grew wide and she stumbled backward into the foyer wall.

"Oh, dear Lord!" Her gaze remained on Clark, only slightly turning her head to the side as she called out, "John, I need you at the front door—*now!*"

Before she could collect her thoughts, the handsome thirty-something young man spoke up.

"I'm sorry to trouble you, ma'am. I certainly didn't mean to startle you! I used to live here a very long time ago. Would you mind if I just walk around the outside of the place for a few minutes? The house looks about the same as it did—but the grounds have certainly changed."

By this time, the woman's husband arrived at the door.

"Well, well, bless my soul, Carol—this is Mr. Clark Gable!" John said as he placed his hand in the middle of his wife's back and helped her off the foyer wall. "You know, the day we saw your first new movie, about a year ago I think it was, I told Carol then that one day you would come to our door!"

"Now, what would give you that inclination, John? I didn't know I'd make this trip myself! And—did I hear correctly? Your wife's name is 'Carole'?"

"I'm sorry, Mr. Gable, yes, my name is John Scott, and, this is my wife, Carol. Without the 'E' on the end, as your wife Carole Lombard spelled it. And as for how I knew you'd one day be here, if you'll come in and sit for a spell, I'll tell you all about it."

"I don't want to be any bother to you folks, just a walk around the grounds for a few minutes. I only rang the bell to get your 'okay' so I didn't end up with a backside full of buckshot!"

"Oh, goodness, please come in Mr. Gable!" Carol said. "I'm just finishing up on a lemon cream pie. You'll be no bother at all!

And John could give you a look around the inside of the house while I finish up." Carol stepped back. She smiled again and said, "Won't you come in?"

"You know, not many ladies spell their name like my Carole did—with an 'e' at the end. I suppose that was indicative of her uniqueness. There will never be another woman like her ... if you'll pardon me for saying so, Carol."

"Mr. Gable, your love for Carole Lombard is legendary. And beautiful. I totally understand what you mean. Please, come in."

"All right, but I'd like you both to call me Clark."

She smiled and headed for the kitchen as John motioned towards the den where Clark spent many quiet, happy hours in his previous life.

"I'm sure you know where the den is, Clark! Let's go relax for a few minutes while Carol finishes up on that pie."

Clark looked around. The room was basically the same. Painted wood paneling, early American style furnishings, though not the same as he and Carole had. Clark sat down on a long and comfortable Davenport. John took the bentwood rocker right next to him.

"I'd sure love to hear some of your remembrances of this place, Clark. I know this home meant a lot to you."

"How long have you owned the farm, John?"

"We were just married when we bought your home in 1973. It was your last wife, Kim, that sold it to us. We purchased this house and just over one acre. The rest of the twenty acres she sold to a developer. That was fifty years ago. Because it had been your home, my wife and I agreed to preserve as much as we could, just as we found it. Once Kim sold the rest of the twenty-acres to a developer, he began to develop it pretty quickly. Nice homes but I've often wished we could have kept the land as it was in your day."

"John, this place holds more happy memories than any other place I can think of. You said a curious thing to me. You said you knew I would one day show up here. How did you know that?"

John smiled. "Sit back and let me tell you, Clark."

7

THE SMOKED SALMON BENEDICT and the fresh berry mules were the perfect complement. SALT's Executive Chef's Brunch did not disappoint. The conversation moved back and forth between business and pleasure. The cool Pacific breezes carried the occasional sound of dolphins playing in the bay. Lexi always smiled at that.

"Lexi, how did Sid find this technology? If I could speak with the scientists involved, I could find out if these creatures are human, half-human, or just some convincing animatron with an artificial intelligence that just won't quit!"

"I'm sorry Mike, I don't know the man's name. But once, during a board meeting, I heard Sid mention someone he called 'Dr. X,' based in Israel. By what Sid was saying, I knew he was the creator of the three. Does that help?"

"Silicon Wadi."

"What?"

"Silicon Wadi is Israel's Silicon Valley. It's an area of business that spans their coastal plain. The primary city of high tech is Tel Aviv, but Silicon Wadi is a big area. May take some time to find who has this tech and the infamous 'Dr. X.' Anything else you can share that might shed some light on things?"

"They're lonely, Mike. Desperately lonely. I was right outside the conference room the day you and the other agent interviewed the three. I could hear most of what was said. I can tell you Sid and Bob were just as surprised by the emotions the actors were verbalizing as you were."

"Yes, I kind of gathered that. Bob's a cool player but Sid doesn't hide his feelings very well. So, were you surprised, too?"

"No. Sid doesn't realize how often one of the three will stop by my desk or see me on the studio lot and talk with me. Clark said something I just can't shake. He said he dreams in color and it's always about Carole. Carole Lombard. He misses her terribly. What I don't understand is *how* he can miss her. I mean, this Clark Gable never really knew her! All he has are memories from the real Clark Gable. How does that cause such loneliness? Anyway, I don't know what's inside them—what makes them tick, but they can break your heart, Mike. Their loneliness is just as real and just as sad as any I have ever experienced."

"Are you lonely, Lexi? You know, the first time I saw you, I figured every good-looking leading man in Hollywood would have already asked you out!"

"Getting a date here is easy. But finding a guy with my standards? That's like peeling a turtle!"

Mike tried not to laugh, grabbing his napkin to hold back his mouth full of berry mule.

"I'm sorry Mike! I'm just saying Hollywood deserves the name 'Tinseltown.' There's so much fakery, so much façade. People saying and doing anything to get their name in lights. It's like a disease. I couldn't marry an actor. I'd never know if he really loved me or was just using me to get to Sid to advance his career. Life's been pretty lonely up to this point."

"I'm sorry, Lexi."

"Oh, don't be—I said, 'up to this point.' You rescued me, if only for a day!"

"Well, fair maiden in distress, let the rescue continue! This afternoon, I've arranged for some whale watching and a trip out to Catalina Island. That is—if you're up to the trip. It's a two hour boat ride from here to Two Harbors–three hours to Avalon." Like the old song, Mike wondered if *he* might *find his love in Avalon.*

"That sounds awesome to this damsel in distress! Is Avalon worth the extra hour ride?"

"I've heard that it is. I'll rent a golf cart there so we can tour the island in style! There's underwater sightseeing by submarine, miles of white sand beaches, crystal clear water, zip lines, parasailing–you can even get your photo taken dressed up as a mermaid!"

"You've done your homework, haven't you? Okay–but no little boats, please. If there's anything I learned from *Jaws* it's to always get a bigger boat!"

"HOW COULD YOU LET HIM go!" Sid was blood red and yelling at the studio security director and his assembled officers.

"Do you realize that man—that actor—has never driven a car in his life and has nothing but memories of the Hollywood that existed prior to 1960? That's sixty years of changes to roads, buildings, signs—there's no telling where he is—*and he'd be the last to know!*"

"Mr. Abrams, I think we should alert the LA Police and the California Highway Patrol so they can get an all-points bulletin out immediately," said the director.

"No, you idiot! Do you realize what that would mean? Every low-life fortune hunter in LA would be out looking for Clark Gable. They could abduct him and hold him for millions in ransom. This is a no-win predicament you've placed me in!"

Sid stood there and thought for a moment. Uriah should be able to tell him where Clark was. Didn't he have a tracker built into the actors? He would call him.

The radio in the security office squawked.

"Security office, is Mr. Abrams down there? Lisa Adams is looking for him."

"Yes, he is, one moment please." The security director handed Sid the radio.

"Lisa—what are you doing here? Where's Lexi?"

"It's Saturday—she's off today, sir."

"Oh—well what is it now? Wait—don't tell me Mr. Gable has fallen into trouble!"

"Not that I know of sir—but Mr. Bogart is about to."

"What!"

"Mr. Bogart is in the studio infirmary, holding Dr. Eli Danielson and his medical team at gunpoint."

"What could possibly have prompted him to do that? What is he saying?"

"Specifically, he's demanding the physician re-create Lauren Bacall if he knows what's good for him."

"Do you want my team to deal with this, Mr. Abrams?" the security chief asked.

"No. You need to find Clark Gable. I want you to send every available man you have out in unmarked cars. Have them start with the roads around the studio and then fan out from there. Maybe they'll run into him. That roaring roadster of his won't be hard to spot—or hear. If they locate him, tell them to radio you. They are not to stop him, just follow him and report their location."

"Yes, sir. I'm on it."

"Lisa, get a golf cart and meet me at the front of the administration building. Let's see if we can talk Bogie out of shooting up the clinic like he's public enemy number one!"

AS SID AND LISA PUSHED through the front glass doors of the studio infirmary, there stood three nurses and Dr. Danielson in a line-up, backs to the wall, facing their assailant.

Humphrey Bogart was dressed in a gray pin striped, double breasted suit, gray fedora on his head, and silver Colt 1908 .32 caliber pistol in his hand. It occurred to Sid that Bogart looked just like Rick Blaine holding a gun on Major Strasser in the closing scene of *Casablanca*. He was just missing the elevator shoes Bogie wore through most of the picture. Ingrid Bergman was taller than him.

"Well, Bogie, what's going on here?" asked Sid, stepping into the reception area.

"Not so fast, Sid. You and Miss Lisa better join the others where I can see you."

Bogie motioned them towards the staff line up with his Colt pistol. Sid and Lisa walked slowly towards the others, but Sid kept his gaze on Bogart, and Bogie reciprocated. Sid's thoughts raced. This was indeed a scene from Bogart's past. What was this parahuman thinking? It had to be something based on the real Bogie's memories. Was he in *Casablanca*, *Key Largo*, the *Maltese Falcon*—or was this some fabrication that might not end well for his hostages?

"Bogie, do you mind if I inquire as to how you acquired the pistol?"

"Don't you recognize it, Sid? Got it out of props. Looks like the one I used in *Casablanca*, doesn't it?"

"So, it's not really loaded?"

"Well, I don't know, Sid. Should we find out?"

"No! That's okay. Hollywood doesn't need another accidental shooting."

Sid waited, watching Bogart. He just stood there with that trademark menacing grin.

"So how does this end, Bogie? Do you shoot us all down or are you going to let me in on what you want?"

"I don't want to use this gun, Sid, but I do intend to get what I'm after."

"All right, fire away," said Sid, before he realized what he was saying.

"Poor choice of words, Mr. Abrams!" Dr. Danielson nervously retorted. "Mr. Bogart, Sid meant please tell him what you're needing!"

Bogart laughed his inimitable, gravelly laugh that said, '*you amuse me—but don't mess with me.*' Uriah had done an excellent job of capturing the spectrum of Bogart's voice.

"I have no intention of shooting any of you. Not if we can come to terms. Now let me make this simple for you, Sid. You're a smart man. You somehow managed to bring me back, right?"

Sid nodded.

"Well, I want you to bring Baby back for me."

"Baby?" Sid's face told Bogart he was confused.

"Now how could an old Hollywood duffer like you not know that name? I always called Lauren Bacall 'Baby.' Of course, I also called her 'Betty,' which was her real name. But I think you already knew that, didn't you, Sid? You're playing games, stalling!" Everyone felt the temperature in the room drop. Bogie was not happy.

"Lauren Bacall? You want Lauren Bacall re-created just for you?"

"Why not just for me, Sid? After all, you're on your fourth wife—I'm just after one! But, now that you mention it, for you, too. And for the studio."

"How do you figure?"

"Look, Sid, the more I work for the studio, the more money you make from my performances and appearances, right?" Bogie didn't wait this time for Sid's response. "So, you're going to have Lauren brought back to me. Think of how much more loot you'll rake in having the marquee read, '*They're back, Bogie and Bacall*.' Sounds pretty good, don't it?"

"Yes, yes, it does Bogie. But another actor—Lauren—will take a great amount of time and an even greater amount of money!"

"Take all the time you want, Sid!" Then Bogie tilted his head down so his eyes appeared just under the brim of his hat: "Just so long as you have her back two weeks before my birthday on December twenty-fifth. I want Baby back in my life, in my studio apartment, and in my arms for Christmas." Bogie sat down on the reception desk and lowered the gun. "I even have a script in mind for our first film together again. We never made a sequel to *Key Largo*. Well we're gonna fix that mistake first thing!"

"All right, Bogey, I'll get to work on it right away."

Sid needed to talk to Uriah again. Whatever his so-called adjustment was supposed to have done, it didn't work on Bogie. And if Clark Gable disappearing in LA was any indication, it didn't work on him either. And that's when it hit him: *Where's Jimmy?*

SID HAD JUST RETURNED to his office, intending to call Dr. X and berate him with the latest bad news when his private line began to ring.

"Mr. Abrams, this is Colonel Travis Hardisty at Los Angeles Air Force Base. I wanted to let you know that we have General Jimmy Stewart here and he is perfectly safe."

Sid dropped into his chair. He wasn't prepared for yet another breath of ill wind. "I'm so sorry, what did you say?" He could already feel the blood draining from his head.

"I realize he is a clone or re-creation of the real, deceased James Stewart, but you'd never know it from the activities of the day!" Colonel Hardisty laughed as he spoke.

"I'm ... I'm sorry, Colonel. Why are you laughing?"

"I'll tell you, when Jimmy Stewart showed up at the front gate this morning, that was one startled MP! General Stewart stepped out of the taxi, dressed in what must have been the same Air Force uniform that Jimmy Stewart wore when he was promoted to Brigadier General in 1959—hopelessly out of date! I wondered why he wasn't wearing his newer uniform, the one he wore when President Reagan promoted him to Major General in 1985. The MP told me he saluted General Stewart instinctively when he saw the uniform. It just took a moment for it to register *who* he was saluting! He said it eventually hit him that this man—or actor—was not the real General Stewart. That's why he called the command center, and they routed the call to me. I called for my driver and got to the security shack as fast as I could! I had to see this for myself. The MPs had him inside the shack and, when I walked through the door, General Stewart leaped to his feet and saluted me. He looked just like the picture in the Air Force museum, hung there over forty years ago! And, come to think of it, just like he looked in his film, *Strategic Air Command*—except now he looks like a thirty-year-old General! I never would have thought I'd see this in my lifetime. I said to him, 'General Stewart, sir, it is I who should be saluting you,' and I returned the salute. And that's when he said to me in that famous drawl of his, 'Colonel, I wonder if I could see one of my old planes? I was thinking of a B-52 I flew in Vietnam.' I said, 'General Stewart, I am happy to assist you with that request.' We have them sitting on the flight line at the chicken shack, so I drove him out there."

"Colonel," interrupted Sid, "I'm so sorry for this disruption to your day. If I had known ... "

"Nonsense, Mr. Abrams, you have no idea the effect this has had upon my entire base! Our collective morale went sky high!"

"Well ... where is Mr. Stewart now?"

"There's more to this story, Mr. Abrams. Let me continue. The flight officers in the shack were just as shocked at seeing General Jimmy Stewart as the MPs at the gate. General Stewart asked them if he could sit in the cockpit of the B-52. The pilots looked at me and I told them I thought it would be quite an honor for them. That was all it took. Captain Matthew Thompson, one of our team leaders, asked the General if he might want to go up for a spin around Los Angeles and the smile on Jimmy Stewart's face said it all. Those pilots jumped-to and got him outfitted and into the cockpit.

"But the most important part of his flight time is something I think you should know, Mr. Abrams. After they reached altitude, they asked General Stewart if he might like to take the controls. They said he flew that plane like the real General James Maitland Stewart—without a bit of hesitancy, without the slightest mistake! Mr. Abrams, Captain Thompson said General Stewart had such command over the controls and instruments that the captain asked him if he thought he was up to landing the plane. *And he did.* He landed that B-52 perfectly, radioing the tower, lowering the landing gear, deploying the chutes, and taxiing back to the shack. I tell you, there's something incredible and mysterious going on here! That cloned actor is more than just an actor. It's as if James Stewart were back from the great beyond. He appears to be about thirty years old, but he possesses the mental faculties and skill of a much older, more experienced pilot. I don't know how you pulled this off, but as a former combat pilot, with absolute certainty I'm telling you that I could put that man back into the cockpit tomorrow and he could command a mission with all the leadership prowess of the General James Stewart that I've only read about!"

"Is there more, Colonel Hardisty?"

"Yes. Following his flight, I asked him to dine with me in the officer's mess. He asked if, instead, we might drive out together to Beverly Hills, to where he and his wife, Gloria, used to live. I agreed immediately. I guess I was enjoying my time with him so much, the thought of accompanying him to his home just seemed the right thing to do. I was totally unprepared for the consequences."

"Consequences, Colonel?"

"Yes. As we drove along, I wasn't sure I'd made the right decision. He spoke about his time overseas in the Air Force, time away from the family. He was thankful he served his country, but he seemed morose. He said he wished he had the time back with Gloria and the girls that he gave up–being gone so much."

"So, you took him to his old home in Beverly Hills?"

"I tried to. I had my driver take us so I could sit in the backseat with General Stewart and visit. He gave us precise directions to the address, 918 Roxbury Drive. It was amazing, he knew every street and every turn. But when he saw the house at that address, he told me that was not the right house. I did a search on my smartphone and found a photo of the house previously there. I actually found a picture of Jimmy Stewart and Henry Fonda on the walkway of his old home, just outside the front door. I showed it to him and told him that the article said the old place had been torn down. It was sold and torn down in 1997, after he ... after he had passed. Mr. Abrams, that will stand as one of the worst memories of my life. I was not prepared for the grief I saw in him. He asked that we take him back to his apartment at the studio. I dropped him off there not an hour ago."

Sid was silent. Clark Gable had managed to find and reclaim his old Duesenberg roadster and was somewhere on the town. Humphrey Bogart had just held the medical staff hostage, demanding that his wife be re-created. And now Jimmy

Stewart—General Jimmy Stewart—flew an Air Force bomber and was grieving for his wife. None of this made any sense. These were effectively robots, animatrons dripping with human emotion. AI was not supposed to be sentient. Uriah had assured him of that fact. Uriah Horvitz had a lot of explaining to do. These parahumans were supposed to follow orders and perform their parts in scripts. Nothing more. He could put the parahumans to sleep until Uriah fixed the cause of the emotional disturbance, but they were filming and it would cost the studio too much to stop. This was a dilemma. Rapidly becoming a nightmare.

"Mr. Abrams, are you still there?"

"Yes, I'm sorry Colonel. I was just wondering what to do next."

"I can help with that. General Stewart asked to use my phone. He talked with Senator Steven Albright in Washington. Turns out they knew each other from service in the Air Force. From what I gathered he's going to be visiting your studio very soon."

8

CLARK GABLE SAT BACK AND WAITED FOR JOHN TO ANSWER HIM. How did he know with such certainty that Clark would show up at his old Encino home? Clark had not planned this—it just happened.

"John, you said you bought this place right after you were married. It had to have cost a bit of money. Do you mind if I ask how a young married couple could afford this place?"

"I don't mind answering that at all, Clark! I was preparing to enter medical school and needed a place to live. My father, who was also a physician, purchased this place and let Carol and me live here rent-free until I graduated."

"So, you're a sawbones?"

"It's worse than that, Clark," John chuckled, "but I haven't heard that term in some time! I am also a psychiatrist and counselor—a 'shrink' if you're going to keep the colloquialisms going! You did a great job planning this place. It has a cozy, homey feel that's been a great blessing to our family. We raised our four children here and now babysit five grandchildren in the beautiful home you designed."

"It does my heart good to know children play here. You know, my Kay had two children. I used to play baseball with them and they'd help me care for our farm animals. We had some wonderful times here." Clark paused for a moment and then asked, "So, do I call you 'Doctor Scott'? I think this is my first time talking with a shrink!"

They both laughed but John quickly replied, "Clark, I'd love it if you just called me 'John.' It's such an honor to finally meet you."

"Deal. Now, you said you knew I'd eventually show up here. *How did you know that?*"

John began rocking in the old bentwood rocking chair. He looked straight ahead for a few moments. Clark could tell he was thinking.

"Clark, before you drove all the way to Encino from Hollywood, did you go anywhere else?"

"Yes, I did. I went first to visit the Brown Derby. I wanted to see where Carole and I spent many happy occasions together. What made you ask that?"

"There's often a pattern when we go in search of memories, Clark. What did you find at the Brown Derby?"

"It was gone. Along with part of my heart ... " Clark suddenly stopped and looked at John. "You know, John, *Sid told me I didn't have a heart!*"

"I don't understand. Who is Sid and why would he make such a statement?"

"Sid Abrams, president of SMP Studios. He told me when I was re-created to play the original Clark Gable, I was—how did he say it? I was embossed with his memories, or something like that. He said I wasn't going to *feel* the parts I would play in films—love, sorrow, anger. He said I would know how to play the part from memories I have but I wouldn't have the feelings so it was best to over-act and the director would tell me if I needed to tone it down or increase the volume of my voice, my facial expressions, or whatever. Just recently, two men from the FBI came by the studio to check on how I and the two other re-created actors were being treated. After they were gone, Sid told us we were recreated using artificial intelligence—and we aren't supposed to be emotional. It seems to bother him that we are. Does that help you any?"

"It could. Thank you for telling me that. I might have some research to do. But you said a part of your heart was gone. Do you mean that you *do* feel loss?"

"Yes, John, I do. Very deeply. Today has been one of the most difficult days I've ever experienced. And the truth is, I don't know why. I know I feel lonely, that I want Carole by my side. But if I don't have a heart, then I'm not supposed to feel loneliness. So, what's happening to me?"

"I don't know the answer to that, Clark. I've never dealt with a person such as yourself before. I assumed that you were most likely cloned from the original Clark Gable. As a medical doctor I would also assume you were capable of emotions. The artificial intelligence factor can impact all of this–but in talking with you, I can tell you most certainly have feelings. You have a heart."

"So, you said you knew I would end up here. How did you know this?"

"Clark, you're driving around, trying to reconnect with memories that belonged to your predecessor. That's a unique experience for you as the patient, and for me as the counselor! But that typically means loneliness. Would you say you're feeling lonely?"

"Yes, John, that's exactly what it is."

"I might be able to help you with that if I can get just a bit more information from you. Do you mind answering a few questions?"

"John, I'd be very grateful for anything you can do to help! The thoughts, the constant emptiness never leaves me. Please ask me whatever you need to."

"Let's start here. From the memories you hold, what would you say was most important to you in life? You know I'm referring to your predecessor, but you're struggling with *his* memories. So, in your own thoughts, I'm asking you, what did 'the King of Hollywood' really want from life?"

"Well, John" Clark paused as he rummaged through his memories. "I guess that answer would change based on my time of life."

"Okay, explain that to me," John said, rocking and smiling. Clark sensed peace. He didn't know why but it was there. Was it being back in his Encino home? He felt it there during quiet evenings with Carole.

"I first married Josephine Dillon. She was a theater manager in Portland, Oregon when I met her. She was almost twenty years older than I was, but she cared about me. I was trying to break into acting but had no training whatsoever. She taught me how to carry myself. You know, my posture and bearing, so I'd look like somebody. She coached me on my diction, even helped me lower the pitch of my voice. After she thought I was ready to try my hand in films, we moved to Hollywood in 1924. I guess the most important thing at that time was hoping and praying I'd get noticed and get work."

"Were you in love with Josephine?"

Again, Clark had to think through his collective memories. This seemed the hardest work he'd been asked to do since his reappearance.

"I'd say there are different types of love a man experiences in the scope of his life. Wouldn't you agree?"

"Yes, I agree with you on that. There are definitely different types of love. I love my wife differently than I love our golden retriever!"

Clark laughed. "Yes, John, for the sake of family peace, you'd better!"

"So, what kind of love would you say you had for Josephine?"

"I don't know for sure. It might have been a love of convenience. I needed her help. I knew nothing about acting and she knew everything. She had a steady job. She paid to fix my teeth and to style my hair. She provided decent clothes and food. But she needed me, too. She needed someone in her life, and she had no one at the time. I was sort of a project for her. I guess you'd say we needed one another."

"Did you think the marriage would last?"

"There's nothing in my memories about that, John, so I can't really say."

John took note of this. Nothing in Clark's memories. So his memories were captured somehow from the original Clark Gable–but not all memories. This might cause the reproduced Clark to deviate from the original. Something to investigate.

"Okay, so what happened after you first got to Hollywood?"

"I didn't get much notice in 1924. In fact, I only got bit parts and those films were silent films. Josephine felt I had a better chance back on stage, so we moved to Houston where I was able to work regularly for about two years. That helped develop my skill as an actor. Josephine landed a part for me on Broadway, so we moved to New York. But our marriage began to unravel in Houston. In 1929 we separated and then divorced."

"Was that your decision or Josephine's?"

"It was mutual—but I was actually seventeen years younger than her. When our divorce finalized in early 1930, I married Ria Langham just a few days later."

"One of those beautiful young actresses you worked with?"

"No. She was a Texas socialite. She had money–lots of it–a lot more than Josephine did. I had my eye on motion pictures again, but I didn't have the means to get there. So, I married Ria. She and I moved to California where I had a major part in a Los Angeles stage production called *The Last Mile*. And that did what I hoped it would. It got me the attention of a studio. It wasn't a major studio, but they gave me my first role in a talkie—you know, a motion picture with sound. It was good experience for me, working with microphones and the sound crew. But that little studio got into financial trouble, so I looked for work at Warner Brothers. I landed a role there in a film with Barbara Stanwyck. It was just a supporting role, but I was finally working for a major studio. I thought I played the part of a villain rather well. Anyway, the studio was looking at casting me as the second male lead in a picture with Jimmy Cagney, so I had to go through another screen test. And it was at that screen test that, of all people, Warner Brothers executive Darryl Zanuck said my ears were too big and I looked like an ape!"

Both men laughed out loud as John asked, "Well, I guess Darryl Zanuck came to eat those words, didn't he?"

"Yes, he sure did. I left there and met with Irving Thalberg at MGM. Right there, he signed me for six hundred fifty dollars per week! John, that was a lot of money in 1930 with the country in the Great Depression!" Once again, Clark became somber. "But it was Ria who told me not to let what Zanuck said get me down. To keep going, keep trying. You know, she believed in me. Just like Josephine." He sat reflective for a few moments, then added, "I guess I could've done better for both of them."

John waited Clark out. He let him sit there, contemplating his memories of the past.

"Maybe I shouldn't ask you the same question about Ria as I did about Josephine, but it's important for me to answer your question that started our discussion. Clark, if you think about it, loving someone isn't really possible unless you first respect them. And respect comes from one thing: valuing who they are. That's totally different than valuing someone for what they can do for us. So, let me ask you—did you love Ria? And, to be more specific, did you respect and love either Josephine or Ria for more than what they could do for you?"

Clark sat looking down at the floor. His 'memory embossed' mind searched through every scrap of data it could find. It assembled the logical conclusion from the results of almost sixty years of information analyzed, compared, contrasted, and compressed. "John, whatever love we had for each other must've changed over time because the marriages didn't last."

"Okay, let's don't stop there." John could tell that Clark's demeanor had changed. The lilt was gone from his voice and that was not what John was shooting for. "What happened after your new position with MGM?"

"After I had my new salary with MGM, I hired Minna Wallis as my agent. She was the sister of Hal Wallis, who was quite the producer in his day, so she was well connected. She was already representing many of the big stars at that time. My first starring role came within a year of hiring Minna—but I'm still not sure if she had much to do with landing that part for me. Joan Crawford asked for me to be her co-star in the film *Dance, Fools, Dance*. After that, MGM began pairing me with the top ladies of Hollywood. 1931 was the year that my career really took off. And in 1934 I made *It Happened One Night* and that got me an Academy Award for Best Actor. After that, I was always at the top of the box office rankings."

"So, what about *Gone with the Wind*?"

"John, I'll forever be defined by that film. I always said that anytime my career would wax and wane, the studio would bring *Gone with the Wind* out of mothballs, put it back in the theaters, and my standing as a leading man would take off again! But that wasn't until 1939. You skipped over the most important role of my life!"

"Oh, well I apologize! What role was that?"

"The husband of Carole Lombard. She and I met in 1932 on the set of *No Man of Her Own*, when she was still married to

William Powell. We hit it off immediately. But we didn't begin
seeing each other openly until 1936. By then, she and Powell had
divorced but I was still married to Ria. I have to admit, that didn't
stop me from seeing her. She had the most amazing effect on me.
She could propose just about anything and I'd listen. In fact, she
was the one who told me I needed to accept the role of Rhett Butler
in *Gone with the Wind*. I wasn't sure I wanted to do it. I wouldn't
even read the book when Carole gave it to me!"

"So, you were happy when you were with Carole?"

"As never before. Oh, I was happy when I found out that Kay,
my fifth wife, and I were going to have a son. But there's never
been a woman that captivated me as Carole did. She was young,
vivacious, carefree. She had a zest for life, John, she actually *loved*
life. And she truly loved me. She didn't fear losing things as others
did, so I never felt she pretended to love me. Certainly not to boost
her career or to be seen with the 'King of Hollywood.' I think
everyone I have ever known was either trying to get something
from others or was trying to prevent others from taking their stuff.
I never understood what made Carole so free, so unattached to
fame and fortune. We were only married for three years before she
was taken from me. Snatched from my life forever. I never got over
it. I somehow knew that everything I had been working for, all the
moves I'd made and the groveling that I did, were so I could be with
her. And I felt her death was God punishing me for all the wrongs I
did throughout my life so I could finally get a woman like Carole."

John had stopped rocking. He was leaning forward in the
rocking chair and looking intently at Clark. He was smiling but
Clark had never felt a man's gaze so intently.

"Clark, over my years of behavioral counseling, I've worked
hard to better understand people and the challenges they face in
life. I needed a wider lens. And a more accurate one. You
mentioned God. Do you believe in an afterlife?"

"Of course I do, John. I was raised a Catholic. I told Kay I wanted to bring my boy up in the Catholic faith. If you know anything about Catholics, you know we believe in a hereafter. Why did you ask me about this?"

"I'll tell you why, Clark. You rose through Hollywood as few men ever have or ever will. You rose to the very top. You were, as you have said, 'the King of Hollywood.' Would you say Hollywood was difficult on the people who worked there?"

"Absolutely, it was nothing short of a meat grinder!"

"What do you mean?"

"I mean mentally, emotionally, financially—in every way. It was no place for marriages, children, or faith. I watched good people stepped-on and stepped-over. I saw people so eaten alive with their desire for fame and success they were more animal than human. To get to the top, they'd let nothing stand in their way."

"And now? What has your experience been over the past year since you've been back in Hollywood?"

"It's gotten rougher in Tinseltown. In some cases I'd say it's dark. People will do just about anything to become a star and the studios know it, so they promise to open doors in return for sexual favors. Those bosses are predators. Now they're doing it to children. Oh, don't get me wrong. There are good studios, and good people. But the days when a top studio would undertake a major production such as *Ben Hur, King of Kings,* or *The Ten Commandments* are gone. They won't tolerate anyone or anything that disagrees with their moral inclinations."

"So, you're back. The 'King of Hollywood.' Is there anything you might be able to do to change what's happening?"

"That thought never occurred to me, John. I'm just an actor. I don't have the control or power of a studio boss so how could I change what they're doing?"

"You're not just an actor, Clark. You really are the *King of Hollywood*. What's happening at the box office with your new films?"

"We're topping the charts!"

"So, as you would have said on Broadway, let's draw back the curtain—let's really see things as they are. You see yourself as only a copy of the original Clark Gable, but that's not accurate. You're the one turning out hits now—it's no longer the human doing it."

"I never thought of that, John! I'm doing what the human can no longer do."

"That's correct. The public comes to see *you*, Clark. That's not only a great honor, I think it carries a great responsibility."

"Responsibility? To do what?"

"No one can order you to participate in a film that violates your faith or moral principles—agreed?"

"Agreed. In the old days the human Clark Gable—and all the other actors—did as they were told. I guess those memories have influenced me to follow orders without question."

"I would think you could have strong influence over the type of pictures you'll be in. How many studios ever have one motion picture win eleven Academy Awards?"

"That's rare, John. It's only happened three times in the history of Hollywood."

"And two of those three motion pictures had a faith focus. Do you know which two I'm speaking of?"

"I know *Ben Hur* was a story of faith. The other one couldn't be *Titanic*, so it would have to be *The Lord of the Rings*—you're saying that story was biblical in nature?"

"Yes, J.R.R. Tolkien based the story line on biblical truth. Many don't know this, but Tolkien was responsible for introducing his atheist friend C.S. Lewis to faith in Jesus. Lewis later wrote

The Chronicles of Narnia as a means to introduce people to Christianity."

"I didn't realize that, John!"

"Yes, in the Chronicles of Narnia, the lion represents Jesus, the white witch represents Satan. You know the lion comes back to life after he is sacrificed. The imagery he used helps adults and children understand how Jesus died to pay for their sins."

"So what are you suggesting I do, John?"

"I'm suggesting that your existence on this planet–right now, this second time around–has a purpose. You're fighting loneliness without understanding what causes it, and I believe the 'cure' for your loneliness is right in front of you!"

"Really? That would be great if it's true."

"Okay, so let me explain. You're lonely because you feel something irreplaceable has been taken from you. But that describes all of life, Clark. Virtually everything of value in this life can be taken from us: Relationships, possessions, youth, beauty, career–almost everything. If we build our lives around that which can be taken from us, we're always going to feel fearful and lonely. Life isn't about losing what we never really own–it's about gaining what can never be taken from us. Do you understand what I'm saying?"

"What can never be taken from us?"

"Our relationship with God and our loved ones who will live on in heaven with us. This life is brief, Clark. The one ahead of us is forever."

"I'd never thought of this before. This is revolutionary to me. But keep in mind I'm not human. I'm a parahuman. I was created from the memories of Clark Gable. Remember that Sid said I didn't have a heart. Well that got me thinking. I've been on the internet studying what I could find about parahumans and I've learned a lot about myself. I can't die because I don't possess life–not as you do, John. And while I didn't read this, I feel I *hold* life. I hold the memories of someone who lived–a real human being. I'm a sort of repository of everything he valued, loved, and hated. I'm a sort of animated echo of his voice, still speaking for him eighty years after his death!"

"Would you say that speaking for the 'King of Hollywood' is quite an honor?"

"Absolutely!"

"Then let's establish a grand and glorious purpose for your existence. Something that gives your existence meaning and that can't be taken from you. Why couldn't the types of films we were just speaking of be produced again, Clark? From what I've seen, Hollywood is continually shocked when films that are family friendly–just good, clean fun–do well at the box office. And yet the studios keep turning out films that are financial disasters! Those films contain things parents don't want their children exposed to. From my perspective, the major studios are out of touch with more than half our country. What if you start looking for stories that convey a wholesome message–as most films in your day used to? Creatively written stories like *Ben Hur* and *The Chronicles of Narnia* help people understand what this life is all about."

"You think the studio bosses would listen to me?"

"They might not want to listen to you, Clark, but they'll have to. They need you! How much longer can they exist turning out multi-million dollar failures that no one wants to see? Even with the assets they have, they can't keep this up much longer. You realize that before the movie rating system, families went together to the movies–any movie. Parents didn't worry about language or sexuality in pictures. And it wasn't because most films during the golden era of Hollywood were Christian films. But back then, writers and directors knew how to make films that were funny, romantic, creative, patriotic–they even had the good guy win in the end! And they did it without nudity or the extreme profanity we have in films today. Despite the success of independent companies producing good films, Hollywood has continued to ignore families—and it's almost killed their industry. But now there's you, Clark. You're turning out hit films. If you carry this message to them, you have the best chance to save Hollywood and restore decency to motion pictures."

"It's a big risk, John. They could remake other actors as they did me and replace me."

"Replace the King of Hollywood? I doubt that! But even if they try, you have an important question to ask yourself. What is this new existence worth to you? How will you invest your time on planet earth? How does *this* Clark Gable want to be remembered?"

"I like acting, John. But I want my life to be more than pretending. Pretending to be someone who no longer exists."

"Clark, one of my professors said something over fifty years ago that has helped guide my counseling of others and provided direction for my own life. If you don't remember anything else from our conversation, I hope you'll remember this: In this world, there is only God, people, and things. We were made to worship God, love people, and use things. But when we worship ourselves—when we think that all of life revolves around us, then we forget God, we love things, and we use people. Which of these two lifestyles do you honestly believe will make people happiest?"

"Worshiping God not yourself. It only makes sense. I've never met any human I thought should be worshiped. John, you think I could make films that will convey that message to people—to worship God rather than themselves?"

"Clark, I'm not suggesting you go back to the studio and throw your weight around. And as I already said, not every film you make needs to be what producers would label as 'religious.' But I do believe you can hold out for at least some films that will influence people toward faith. You're here again and your existence should make a difference. Motion pictures have proven to be a powerful way to change people's thinking. You can use your popularity to improve the quality of the message coming out of Hollywood. What do you think?"

"John, you never told me how you knew I was going to be here, talking with you one day."

"God told me. It wasn't an audible voice, but a thought that came into my mind as clear as if He had spoken out loud. I realize now that He was preparing me for this time with you. My counsel to you is simple. Time for humans is short. Help them make better choices."

Clark stood up and the dimpled, high cheek-boned smile that caused women the world over to swoon came across his face like the dawn of the morning.

"John, you've given me quite the idea! Now, where's Carol with that lemon cream pie?"

9

I T WAS 5:00 AM IN NEW YORK when Donny Mancuso's private jet went wheels-up.

Mancuso sat at his desk onboard the Embraer Legacy 650E bound for London. He would be there in under seven hours, and on the ground just long enough to refuel, then airborne for Tel Aviv. His new luxury ride had a cruising speed of five hundred fifteen miles per hour. This made London to Tel Aviv a two-hour hop, putting him at Ben Gurion International before 10:00 PM. His carefully crafted plan was to surprise Uriah Horvitz in his home at 11:00 PM, he and his black ops team surrounding Uriah's bed. Mancuso liked surprises—so long as he was the one doing the surprising.

The price tag of the Embraer was just under twenty-six million. His bank account still felt the sting. But his international travel must be clandestine, making a private jet non-optional. Registered under a shell company with a respected owner, he could travel with forged papers and anonymity. And with its speed and distance, the plane would validate its worth soon enough. That reduced the sting—a little. Tel Aviv was just the beginning of his flights. Multiple trips to Bolivia, then Peru, lay ahead. He would establish trade agreements with the Bolivian government then 'persuade' the right officials to provide military interdiction in his coca plant production. Make a few corrupt officials millionaires and you become a billionaire. Simple math. Good math. Once the stranglehold on Bolivia's cocaine supply was in place, he would control Peru's shipments moving through Bolivia. Donny stowed his laptop, pressed the button to fully recline the supple leather seat, turned on the seat heater, pulled a blanket up over him, and was asleep in minutes.

AS QUICKLY AS MANCUSO'S aircraft taxied into the hangar at Ben Gurion Airport, his team on the ground closed the doors behind it. A limo sat ready for the forty-minute drive to Dr. Horvitz's home. Wheels chocked, steps down, and Mancuso was on the red carpet where his team was waiting.

"How was the maiden flight of your latest toy, Mr. Mancuso?"

"It was good Frank. Slept most of the way. Wanted to be wide awake when we disturb the sleeping 'Dr. X'. And it's not a toy. It's an essential asset as we criss-cross the pond. How is Tony tonight? Ready for the confrontation that lies ahead?"

"I'm great, thank you Mr. Mancuso. And yes, sir, I'm ready to see another Mancuso plan succeed! Sir, if you'd care to step into the limo, I have an iced coffee waiting for you and an outline of our approach to Dr. X's lab."

"Excellent, thank you." Donny had the greatest confidence in his team. He only employed and kept the best. The rest he disposed of.

As the limo sped out of the hangar, Frank turned on the cabin lights so Donny could see the written plan of attack.

"Here's what we have in place, Mr. Mancuso. Uriah Horvitz lives alone. He is married but his wife, Rachel, is in the hospital. He has an extensive home laboratory setup," Frank said, pointing to the blueprint of the Horvitz residence. "It was here that he produced the parahumans for SMP Studio and housed them until they were retrieved by the studio. As you already know, the president of SMP contacted Dr. Horvitz about some trouble he alleges to be having with the parahuman actors. From what we've been able to ascertain, Horvitz has not found the cause of the issue yet. He told Sid Abrams he was putting a fix into place for the actors but that appears to have been a stall tactic to buy additional time."

"Additional time for what?" Donny asked.

"To find and fix the issue with the parahumans."

"And do we know why Dr. Horvitz is unable to fix the issue?"

"Yes, sir, we think so."

"You *think*?"

"We've been monitoring Dr. Horvitz's activities and movements for the past two weeks. Less than a week ago he remained at his employer's lab long after the rest of the team had gone home. He began rifling through what were supposed to be secure files of his employer, Dr. Alfred Edersheim, the president of the lab. Video shows Dr. Horvitz anxiously searching through paperwork. Given Sid Abrams' complaint, it's a safe bet Horvitz was looking for the answer in his employer's secret papers."

"I don't need the headache of an emotionally distraught parahuman! So his employer has the solution and Horvitz was trying to find it. What's the likelihood we need to pull his employer in on this?"

"That could be a fatal mistake, sir. Dr. Edersheim is heavily involved with the Israeli government and military. We don't want to tangle with that group."

"Hmm. No, I suppose not. So, what does Uriah Horvitz do for this Dr. Eder ... "

"Edersheim, sir."

"Edersheim. What is his job at Edersheim's lab?"

"We don't know exactly. Dr. Uriah Horvitz is one of several select scientists hired by Dr. Edersheim for a top secret Israeli government project. The laboratory and its activities are a total blackout. Horvitz did not invent the technology to create these parahumans. He stole it from Alfred Edersheim. Further investigation of banking transactions revealed that Horvitz was desperate for funds. We've not ascertained the precise reason, but it's likely related to his wife's medical needs. She has terminal cancer."

"Stole it? Now this has possibilities, gentlemen!" Donny Mancuso loved what he was hearing. A thief was his own worst enemy and blackmail was a proven method to manipulate the thief. He may have just found a good bit of the money he gave for his new jet.

"So why Horvitz?"

"Sir?"

"Why did Abrams reach out to Horvitz? Why not Edersheim?"

"Hollywood is, for the most part, run by Jewish Americans. They often have connections to Israel and Israeli businesses. As to how Abrams found Horvitz, we don't know. It's possible Horvitz found Abrams. He was needing money and may have been looking for ways to parlay this science into cash. The parahuman actors may not have been Abrams' idea after all."

"Okay, good enough. And what about entering the Horvitz home? You have the alarm taken care of?"

"Of course, sir. Our black ops team is outside the home, ready to cut the alarm at your word."

The limo went lights-out as they turned on Uriah's street just before 11:00 PM. Mancuso's team had done their homework. At his cue, they disabled the alarm system, had the back entry to the lab open, and were inside in less than sixty seconds.

Uriah Horvitz was asleep when the lights suddenly came on. He sat up, reaching for something on his nightstand.

"Just stop right there, Dr. Horvitz," Tony said in a calm, firm voice, pistol with silencer aimed at his head. "We don't want to end this surprise visit with your brains all over your bed sheets."

"I was just reaching for—for my glasses," Uriah responded in a panic-stricken tone. His English was good enough, but the accent was definitely Hebrew. His voice and his hands were shaking.

"Relax, Dr. Horvitz," Donny said, "we just need to talk with you. We need your help. You may get your glasses."

Uriah put on the gold rim spectacles and began squinting as he tried to clear his vision. What little hair he had on his head was standing out in different directions. With the addition of his winter nightshirt he looked more like one of Santa's elves than a scientist.

"What do you men want of me?" Uriah asked.

"Well, Uriah Horvitz, it's really very simple," Donny began, "I need you to make a new me. I need a new me that's just as convincing as the new Clark Gable, Humphrey Bogart, and Jimmy Stewart you cloned for SMP Studios."

"I didn't do that. I don't know who would have told you men such a story but ... "

"Please, Dr. Horvitz, do not waste my time. I did not travel half-way around the world to waste my time. You are the one. By the way, I do hope you have the solution for Sid Abrams' problem. I suspect you already know I will not be as patient as he has been if such a malfunction flares up in my parahuman! Did you find what you were after in Dr. Edersheim's files?"

The look on Uriah Horvitz's face was pure shock. He was growing paler by the second and Donny could tell the good doctor was about to black out.

"Frank, please help Dr. Horvitz to the floor, quickly, before he falls out of bed and hits his head. We can't afford to lose him now. Tony, a glass of water, please."

Frank reached Uriah just as his body began sliding sideways out of bed. He got him to the floor, propped up his feet, and stayed with him while Tony brought the water.

"You can't give an unconscious man a drink, Tony. Kindly throw it in his face."

Uriah awoke, shaking his head violently from side to side, sending his spectacles to the floor.

"Are you feeling better, Dr. Horvitz? There's no need for you to panic or experience such anxiety. We have no intention of exposing your betrayal of Dr. Edersheim. Just as long as you help us. I don't need three clones, I just need one. Now, what do you need from me to make this happen?"

"Ten million dollars and three months," Uriah said, still blinking rapidly as he tried to calm down.

"I'm afraid I don't have ten million dollars, doctor. I had to buy a new jet aircraft just to come see you. And I don't have three months, either. You have four weeks."

"It can't be done!" Uriah exclaimed. "The money is nothing for me. I charged Sid Abrams three times that. Ten million dollars is what I need just to get the basics for assembly. And three months is needed to make sure the holo does not malfunction." As soon as Uriah dropped the word, he realized his mistake.

"Holo? What is a holo?" Donny asked.

"It's ... it's nothing, I meant parahuman."

"Dr. Horvitz, should I make contact with Dr. Edersheim and ask him what a holo is?"

"No! You must never use that word anywhere outside of this house! Even using it here, it could cost all of us our lives."

"So, this is a term that belongs to Dr. Alfred Edersheim! And what does it mean, doctor?" Donny stood looking down at Dr. Horvitz. The longer Uriah sat there staring back at Donny

Mancuso, the higher Donny raised his eyebrows and the more he lowered his head until finally Donny had waited long enough.

"Frank, do you have your knife?"

"Yes, sir, I do."

"Please remove the little finger off of Dr. Horvitz's left hand."

"The whole finger, sir, or just a part of it?"

"We are running out of time. The whole finger."

Uriah's face was now one contorted mass of perspiration and horror. He began scooting backward across the floor, but he ran out of space as his back bounced against his bed.

"Please ... you don't understand ... I will need your absolute assurance that you will never use that term outside of this house or we all face death!"

"Come now, Dr. Horvitz! Is Dr. Edersheim so violent a man as that? Ah—this must have something to do with that secret government project! Who is this Dr. Edersheim?"

"He—he is connected to others. Within the government. The military is involved."

"Very well, doctor," Mancuso said with resolution. You have my personal assurance. Frank and Tony, you are never to use this term outside of this room. Do I make myself perfectly clear? There is no exception to this rule. It is our sacred promise to Dr. Horvitz and one another."

"Yes, sir, Mr. Mancuso."

Donny looked down at Uriah. "I have made an oath, a covenant with you, doctor. Is that assurance sufficient? Or should we go further and make it a covenant in blood?"

"No! That is sufficient," Uriah said. He sat on the floor shaking. Mancuso could see the man was near emotional exhaustion. Going unconscious was not going to happen again.

"Frank, Tony, please help Dr. Horvitz to his side chair and cover him with his blanket. He needs to be calm and fully focused so we can complete our business quickly."

The two men lifted the little man into his chair and stepped back. Uriah sat there, in his nightshirt, drenched in perspiration, and still shaking. Mancuso pointed to the blanket on the bed and pointed towards Uriah. Tony took the blanket and draped it carefully over the doctor.

"Now, Uriah, what does this term 'holo' mean?"

"It is short for 'Holosapien.' But what I created for Sid Abrams and his studio in California were parahumans."

"And why are these parahumans and not holosapiens?"

"Dr. Edersheim somehow applies to the creature a science involving holography. It is something I do not understand. I don't know how it works. Please—if anyone else were to use that term he would know there was a leak. He would trace it back to me."

"And you said that would prove deadly, and this is because Dr. Edersheim is involved with others in the government who would possibly enforce a death penalty on those who know about this technology, is that correct?"

"Yes."

"Which government would this be?"

"I only know of Israel. I don't know if any other governments know or are involved."

"And what is Israel doing with this technology?"

"I don't know." Uriah dared not reveal what he knew.

"Come, come Uriah! You work with Dr. Edersheim and you expect me to believe you don't know what he's doing with this technology?"

"Only Dr. Edersheim knows all the details of this project! No one else has all the pieces. That's part of his security protocol. That's why he did not reveal the holography to me or the other scientists.

He knows this technology in the wrong hands could be disastrous for everyone."

"I'm finding it hard to believe you are missing so many details, Uriah, so much information. And yet you were able to produce such splendid characters for Hollywood. Exact duplicates of three former stars that speak and deliver their lines flawlessly. How is this possible?"

"He trusts me. I was able to get into much of his data and put together details that I needed to complete a parahuman—but some of the details he withheld from his team. I do not understand all of his technology. Alfred is a genius. I do not pretend to have his knowledge or ability with these creatures."

"So, you are the Judas of his organization. Poor Alfred Edersheim. Yet, there is one in every organization. I'm sure there is one in mine. But I will not be so kind as Jesus was. I will find the traitor and eradicate him in the most painful, grotesque way possible." Donny stood there a moment. Then he knelt by Uriah's chair and looked him square in the eyes. "Uriah, you will get me *all* of Dr. Edersheim's notes. This technology could be worth a king's ransom to the highest bidder. You will get me the full scope of his work, do you understand."

"I will not! You can kill me now—or I will kill myself before I betray him or my nation in such a way!"

"*Do not test me, Uriah!*"

"Do not test me—whoever you are! I will die, I will take my own life, rather than do what you are demanding. You want a creature of yourself, I will make it. But I will never betray him as you are demanding!"

"I can inflict such torture on a man that he will do anything I demand!"

"I WILL NOT DO IT! I will build a parahuman of you—and pray to God that you destroy each other! But I will not give you this technology. If you cut me apart—if you kill me—if I kill myself, you get no parahuman. You will never have it. And I can see—you need it quickly."

Horvitz was right. Mancuso needed the parahuman quickly if his plans were to succeed. He had no more time to waste bullying Horvitz. He leaped to his feet.

"How soon do I get my holo ... excuse me, my parahuman?"

"I cannot have it to you before ninety days. I need time to build his frame. I need time to capture your history and emboss it into his artificial intelligence. I need time to grow his skin and tissues, to program his brain waves. Ninety days—and ten million dollars for the resources. As I said before, that is no profit for me whatsoever."

Donny had other projects demanding his attention. He was satisfied with the progress he had made with Dr. Horvitz.

"Very well. Half the funds will be transferred tomorrow. You will get the other half upon successful completion of the task. You will give your banking information to Frank."

"All of it. I cannot buy what I need without all the money."

"You haggle with me?"

"I am not haggling. If I can't buy what I need, I cannot proceed. All of it."

"All right! All of it! Now, I will return in ninety days to receive the finished work. Correct, doctor?"

"Ninety days—but you are not leaving yet."

"I leave when I say so, Uriah! No one tells me when or where to go."

"Then you will not be receiving your parahuman in ninety days. I need you here for most of a week. We must collect blood for the DNA, followed by brain wave mapping and memory harvesting. We will need full details of your past so we can gather accurate data for memory embossing. That will require at least seven days."

Mancuso was not accustomed to being told what to do. And the longer he was out of New York City, the greater the danger the FBI would find out he was gone. But, clearly, it had to be done.

"Very well, doctor. Do you have accommodations for myself and my team?"

"It would not be safe for you to stay anywhere else. You came in under darkness, you must leave under darkness. But only you must be here. Too many and we risk being discovered. You must send your men away."

"Very well. Frank and Tony will leave. I have work for them to do anyway."

Dr. Horvitz looked at his new business partner with disdain. He relished his next demand. "I will need access to all of your information."

"You cannot be serious."

"If I am to re-create you, I must find out all there is about you. That requires all of your memory to be captured. If you want an idiot running around that will fool no one, then we will do things your way. Otherwise, we do this my way. Agreed?"

Mancuso glared. He knew he had no choice. He detested being backed into a corner, especially by a short, fat, balding, irritating little geek. But he had no choice.

"Mancuso. Adonis Antonio Mancuso. I go by Donny. I was born and raised in New York City. What else do you need to know?"

"Much. Everything. I will capture everything you know and have done. It is the only way. But we shall begin tomorrow. For now, we both must try to sleep with what is left of the night. You are going to need it. Send your men on their way. You will be sleeping in the lab."

TO STAY WITH URIAH a week and not have the Feds notice that Mancuso was not in New York would require a quick move on Mancuso's part.

Early the next morning from Tel Aviv, he held an unexpected video conference with his twelve Capos. He laid out plans to pull together all leaders in the organization for a week-long conference at Lake Placid. Mancuso was known for such impromptu meetings so the Feds would not be surprised. The gathering would require the highest level of security, no one allowed in or out. No opportunity for the Feds to slip in and find out that Donny was not there.

The week proved exhausting for Mancuso. Even more so for Uriah. The procedures required for development of his parahuman were extensive, but the construction of his memory from birth to present was beyond description. Vile. Uriah wanted him gone and Mancuso was glad to be boarding his plane and headed towards London by end of the week.

DURING THE REMAINING eleven weeks Dr. Horvitz needed to complete Mancuso's parahuman, Donny began work on Bolivia. He carefully selected his most trusted Capos for his team on the ground. They established a headquarters in La Paz, the administrative capital of Bolivia. Then they went to work making connections and gathering information, first in La Paz and then with those connected to the coca plant farm areas in the Bolivian Andes mountains.

The coca plant has been grown and consumed by Bolivians for more than four thousand years. Its leaves are regularly used in religious services and for medicinal purposes. Some forty different medications are made from coca leaves. The United States' first widespread introduction to cocaine occurred in 1886 when

American pharmacist John Pemberton mixed cocaine with a sugary syrup concoction and created Coca-Cola, a drink that quickly gained popularity for its exhilarating effect that elevated and inspired. By 1903, the company had removed cocaine from its recipe—but the public's desire for the daily 'lift' from the drink remained. And while the UN treaty of 1961 sought to ban coca leaves as an illegal and controlled substance, the Bolivian government declared the plant legal for religious and medicinal purposes. To provide some semblance of cooperation with the UN, the Bolivian government established limits on coca plant growth and required licensing of farmers who wished to continue growing coca plants. That licensing was of great interest to Donny Mancuso. Where there is government regulation, bribery is not far behind.

Donny's team on the ground in Bolivia was there to learn and make connections. But only as Mancuso dictated. Bolivia was not exporting gold or other precious metals to the United States, so Mancuso repurposed one of his shell companies as an importer of precious metals. His men were to make contacts within that industry only. Donny's executives came bearing top dollar, especially, they said, for gold and platinum. Mancuso figured government officials who profit—both openly and personally—from taxes, tariffs, and kickbacks would show up like flies around a privy.

Mancuso's executives were well-dressed, well spoken, fluent in Spanish, cordial and polite. They scheduled meetings with various government officials for purposes of setting up a field office for their New York representatives. They made clear they wanted to secure any permits the government required, and they were happy to pay a little 'extra' if it would expedite the permits. This was only the beginning of greasing government palms. But Mancuso was adamant—his men were to express no interest whatsoever in the coca plant. He wanted no run-ins with government officials or drug cartels already in the market—not yet.

Of the fifty-four thousand metric tons of cocaine produced annually in Bolivia, more than half of that is produced illegally, and the majority of this illegal product is controlled by the Santa Cruz Drug Cartel. Donny would fly below the radar of this local mafia until he could secure lock-tight relations with top governmental authorities. With their help, he could secure protection of the Bolivian military. Any other method of dealing with the Santa Cruz Cartel would require open conflict, and that would be impossible to hide from the public or the press. Given the past violence of the cartel, direct confrontation could plunge Bolivia into a civil war—and the U.S. government would most certainly take notice of that! Low and slow. Mancuso would ease into this.

But, ultimately, Donny needed the Bolivian government to take up arms against the cartel. This could be spun for the press as a courageous move by the government, protecting their citizens too long in the grips of the bloody Santa Cruz Drug Cartel. The U.S. Government would think the Bolivian authorities were cracking down. Bolivian leaders would get the adulation of a grateful citizenry—and Donny's lucrative payouts. Mancuso would control the cocaine export industry of Bolivia. Everyone wins. Except the cartel.

THE CALL FINALLY CAME from Dr. X in Tel Aviv. It had been three long months.

The date and time were given for the pickup. On the day of his departure for Tel Aviv, a new refrigerator was delivered to the Mancuso estate. The delivery men brought the crated appliance in through the servant's entrance. After drinking coffee with Donny for about twenty minutes, the men uncrated the refrigerator, and

Donny climbed into the comfortably padded wooden shell. It was closed and loaded onto the dolly. The delivery men—Donny's men, of course—loaded the crate into the truck and drove to the retailer's warehouse. Once inside the building and the door closed, Mancuso changed into plumber's work clothes, a hat, and a beard. He grabbed a toolbox and boarded a plumbing repair truck bound for the airport. They drove to the pilot's restaurant and club connected to a long row of private hangars. Mancuso's plane just happened to be there. Donny and the other 'plumber' went into the restaurant restrooms where Donny, once again, changed into a suit and lost the beard so he could blend in with the other passengers in the restaurant. He had a few drinks then moved through the hangars to his own plane. Mancuso's team was already aboard. With Donny safely seated, the plane taxied for takeoff.

They arrived in Tel Aviv at midnight and drove to Uriah's home. Under the cover of darkness, they entered the laboratory. Uriah paused to remind them to only address him as 'Dr X' in front of Donny's parahuman. He then stepped into the security array. It scanned his hand and retinas, and the door to the lab opened. Sitting on the couch in the lab was Donny Mancuso—that is, his exact replica. The real Mancuso stopped in his tracks with his lieutenants next to him.

"Dr. X ... this is amazing."

"I've never seen anything like him," Frank said. "I can't tell him apart from you, Mr. Mancuso!"

The parahuman sat there, staring at Donny and his two men.

"He is your exact likeness," Uriah said, "he has been briefed. He knows your men because he has your entire memory bank. This device will allow you to remotely place him into sleep mode and then awaken him. Remember, his intelligence is a combination of your memory embossing, artificial intelligence algorithms which allow him to cognate information, and things that are said and happen to him each day that he is awake. Anything you do without his knowledge, which you want in his collective memory, you must pass to him during 'sleep' periods."

"When we place him into *Theta* wave mode, correct?" asked Donny.

"That is correct," Uriah responded. "In *Beta*, he is in working mode."

Donny decided to test the extent of Dr. X's programming.

"Who are you?" Donny asked of his parahuman.

"I am Adonis Mancuso."

"Tell me about yourself," Donny said to his duplicate.

"Why do you want to know?"

"Because you belong to me—you must answer me."

"Donny Mancuso belongs to no one! I am the master of my fate. Don't make the mistake of thinking you can control me. I am one step ahead of you and everyone else!"

"Dr. X, you've made him too much like me!" Donny said. His men laughed. Uriah did not. He wanted them out of his lab and out of his life. "How do I make him tell me what I want to know?"

Uriah looked at the parahuman and said, "*Antonio*, Mr. Mancuso needs you to answer his questions. Do so immediately." The parahuman nodded.

"Very well. I was born in New York City, on the east side of Harlem, on May 1, 1990. I'm six feet, one inch tall, I weigh one hundred and eighty-six pounds, I have black hair, and blue eyes. I received my Bachelors and Masters degrees from New York University where I graduated magna cum laude at the age of twenty-one due to my photographic memory and genius IQ. And the ladies are crazy about me. What else do you want to know?"

More laughter from the Mancuso team.

"So, Dr. X, you called him by my middle name."

"He must be addressed only by your name since he is to perform as you. Addressing him as 'Antonio' is the signal for him to respond as a parahuman rather than the real you."

"So ... if he knows all about me, is there any danger that he would tell the authorities things that I don't want him to tell them?"

"That would be impossible since his memories and patterns of thought are based upon your own. He will be as truthful as you would be or as—"

"*Careful, Dr. X*," said Mancuso.

"—as clandestine as you would be."

"But you've left one person out of that equation, doctor. What about me? How honest will he be with me? That is, with himself—am I saying that correctly?"

His men laughed again.

"Mr. Mancuso, he knows about you because you are him and he is you. He will be as honest with you as you are with yourself. I imprinted your brain patterns into his. He cannot help but tell you the truth because he is talking to himself when he is talking to you." Uriah shuddered at the thought of what this might ultimately mean. A member of the mafia and his exact duplicate as a parahuman. Uriah could not bear the scenarios playing out in his mind.

"I believe you are ready to go, Mr. Mancuso," Uriah snipped.

"Very well." Donny looked at his double and said, "Antonio, would you like to take a trip with me and my men?"

"Of course, I've been looking forward to New York City." He stood, and walked towards Donny, Frank, and Tony.

"This is—awkward, Mr. Mancuso," said Tony.

"Nonsense, Tony. You are experiencing what scientists call the 'Uncanny Valley' syndrome. You are simply uncomfortable around a near-human robot. Now, let me introduce you both formally."

Donny stepped back from Frank and Tony as Antonio walked up. "Antonio, this is Frank, and this is Tony. They work for me and they now work for you, too."

"I know who you both are, gentlemen. It's my pleasure to meet you in person"

"Let's get back to the airport. We have a long flight ahead of us," Donny said.

With that, Frank and Tony exited the house first, secured the area, then motioned for Mancuso and Antonio to enter the limo. As the vehicle moved through the darkness toward Ben Gurion Airport, Donny gave final instructions to his team.

"Frank, let's go over the plan again for your return to New York."

"Sir, Tony and I have got this."

"I've been out of the country more than I should have been due to Uriah's demands. There is a much greater chance of FBI scrutiny. We go over the plans once more."

"Yes, Mr. Mancuso. Once we land in New York and the plane enters the hangar, several furniture trucks will be waiting, all with the same company name on them. We're to approach truck seven-sixty-four. The truck will be filled with furniture. There will be two green and gold striped Davenports. One has a concealed compartment under the cushions. Antonio will climb into the compartment, we close the compartment, and replace the cushions. Tony and I will arrive at your house an hour before the furniture truck. The drivers will unload the Davenport that does not have the compartment. They will 'accidentally' drop it on the sidewalk while unloading it. A leg of the Davenport has been designed to break. They will take the damaged couch back to the truck, get the couch with Antonio hidden inside, and bring it into the house."

"Good. Now, each day I am gone, everything is to remain on my usual schedule. The limo is to pick up Antonio from my home at 7:00 AM and take him to my office where you and the two bodyguards will greet him at the curb out front. No parking garage entrance. You follow my exact schedule each day. Understood?"

"Yes, Mr. Mancuso. We understand."

"Of the team in New York, only you and Tony know that Antonio has taken my place. In La Paz, only Vincent and Salvatore will know—*may know*. I haven't told them yet. I will make that decision once I see how much progress they've made with government officials in La Paz."

"Mr. Mancuso," Tony began, "why delay in telling Vincent and Salvatore? I mean, if you trust them with something as explosive as our objective in Bolivia, it would seem you could trust them concerning Antonio."

"I never make the circle of information any wider than absolutely necessary, Tony. I trust my Capos. But the reason I can trust them is the scope of their ability to hurt me and this organization is deliberately limited. They know only what they need to know. Only I have the full picture and full knowledge of my plans."

"Mr. Mancuso, don't you mean only you and *Antonio*?" asked Frank.

Donny clinched his teeth. It was true. And it was, as they say, an inconvenient truth.

10

A S MANCUSO WAS JETTING AWAY from Tel Aviv, halfway across the city Dr. Alfred Edersheim was fine tuning the AI iterative algorithm of President Isaac Hayut's holosapien.

It had been an intense, grueling project for Alfred and his team, but it was drawing to a close. Dr. Edersheim gave Uriah the week off. He could have used his help, but Rachel needed him more. His time with his ailing wife had been so limited due to the urgency of the top-secret project. Alfred hoped to make that up to Uriah. Everyone associated with the project was working eighteen-hour days and the team was ready for it to end. Uriah had long since passed the point of exhaustion, working at the Edersheim lab during the day, and in his home-based lab on the Mancuso parahuman at night. The pressure intensified as Rachel's cancer grew worse, and the doctors were not optimistic. Surgery was the only chance she had, and she needed it now.

Israel has a mandated national health insurance system, with four competing not-for-profit health plans, and every citizen is required to choose a plan. The annual health insurance cost per-insured is a fourth of U.S. rates, but Israeli publicly funded hospitals are among the most crowded in the world, with only half the number of acute care beds needed. Rachel Horvitz's situation was urgent, surgery could not wait. The only hope was a privately funded hospital with private fee-for-service—and that made Rachel a privately funded patient. The cost for her surgery and treatment fell entirely on Uriah. He had to find immediate funding for his beloved Rachel's medical care—and he did.

SNOW ON THE EILAT MOUNTAINS of Tel Aviv glistened as diamonds in the early morning sunlight. President Isaac Hayut parked at the laboratory of his friend, Dr. Alfred Edersheim, and sat gazing at the scene.

This promised to be a momentous day, a defining day. The meeting with Alfred first, then on to an interview with the press at his presidential home known as *Beit Hanassi*. He offered an exclusive interview to Esther Lieberman, a reporter with Haaretz. He trusted her. They had been friends for most of his thirty-year political career. He found her to be a fair-minded, accurate communicator of the facts. And she was a supporter of his work on the peace treaty, soon to be signed in Tehran. He told Ms. Lieberman the interview was to better inform Israeli citizens on the strengths and benefits of the carefully crafted agreement. This was true—but he and Dr. Edersheim were using this one-on-one interview as a means of testing the fledgling holosapien's abilities.

Esther Lieberman knew nothing of the animatronic encounter she was about to have. It had to be this way. But if the holosapien failed, Isaac felt sure Esther would help them contain the damage. Isaac and Alfred would be able to see and hear the entire interview through the eyes and ears of the creature. If they saw that he was on shaky ground, they could have him excuse himself, saying that he was being paged for an emergency phone call, whereupon he would ask that she wait for just a few minutes. The holo would step into another office and the real Isaac Hayut would come into the room to complete the interview. Isaac didn't want to deceive his reporter friend, but he and Dr. Edersheim had to know that the holo could perform in interviews. Flawlessly. If he failed them during the meeting in Tehran, it could mean international disaster.

Alfred could see President Hayut in the lobby security monitors. As officers cleared the president for entry into the facility, Alfred activated the holosapien to greet him as he stepped into the lab.

"MR. PRESIDENT! MY HONOR to make your acquaintance. I am Benjamin Isaac Hayut but, please, call me *Benny* so we can distinguish ourselves from one another!"

Isaac Hayut was beyond overwhelmed. He stood there looking at 'himself,' then turned to Alfred. "I saw him a month ago, on the lab table, but ... his voice, his manner, his inflection. It's like looking into a mirror! I have to admit ... this is a little frightening!"

Before Alfred could respond, the holo was in motion. Alert, attentive, focused. "I'm glad you are pleased with my voice and appearance, Mr. President! But there is no call for fear on your part. I am at your disposal. I am happy to do only what you wish for me to do. I never want to displease or disappoint you!"

"Well, thank you ... I'm sorry, what am I to call you?"

"Please call me Benny. Why don't we sit down in Dr. Edersheim's office? He informed me that you would like to interview me prior to my media event with Esther Lieberman." Isaac looked over at Alfred. Alfred was smiling.

"Very well, Benny, please lead the way!" Isaac followed the holo into Alfred's office and sat down. Alfred shut the door as Benny moved to the coffee bar.

"May I offer you some coffee—perhaps an espresso, Mr. President?"

"No, thank you, Benny, I've had my caffeine allotment for the day. I would rather spend time visiting with you."

Benny walked to the sitting area and took a chair next to Isaac. "Well, then Mr. President, what would you like to know?" Benny sat smiling and looking at the president. The experience was emotionally challenging, even to Alfred. He was smiling but his mind was racing in a thousand directions. This was momentous, an historic occasion in the annals of AI and parahuman science.

"Benny, just tell me about yourself. Where you were born, where you went to school ... and tell me about your time as the President of Israel. And I'd like to hear about the peace accords you are preparing to sign."

With that request, Alfred started a video camera behind his desk that would capture the interview between Isaac Hayut and Benny—so they could review his mannerisms, facial expressions, and gestures.

"I was born in Haifa, but my parents moved to New York when I was two. I grew up in Brooklyn. I received my BS degree in Mathematics from Yale University and my Master's in Political Science from Harvard University. I was ... "

"Excuse me, Benny, were you ever injured as a child?"

"Yes, several times. When I was three years old, I rode my tricycle down the stairs from our kitchen to the basement. The stairs went about two thirds of the way down, formed a landing, and then turned to the right—but I didn't. I hit the cement wall, my mouth hit the handlebars, and knocked my bottom teeth out."

"And you remember this? You were only three."

"I remember it. My bottom teeth have an imperfection across the four front teeth. You can see it if you'd like."

"No, that's fine," said Isaac, impressed by the detail Alfred captured and the details Benny remembered—or was embossed with—that would fool his own family. "So, tell me, Benny, about the peace accords you are prepared to sign. Give me some details."

"There are details that are considered classified, Isaac. You must remember there are enemies who do not want peace between Israel and the nations prepared to sign with us. We cannot give them more reasons for violence than they now claim. Most of the details of the treaty have already been made public. Israel is exchanging land in Gaza for the right to rebuild our temple in Jerusalem. It will be attached to the Wailing Wall and be built next to the Dome of the Rock. All people will be allowed on the temple mount, or the *al-Haram al-Sharif* as it is known to Muslims, and all people wishing to enter the Dome of the Rock or the Jewish temple, once it is rebuilt, will be required to observe all customs. Both holy shrines and the mount itself will be guarded by soldiers from the Jewish nation and Palestine. Forces will be equal in size and weaponry."

"That's enough," said Isaac. "Benny, I believe you are ready to meet with our friend and member of the press ... what is her name?"

"Esther Lieberman, Isaac. We've known her for over thirty years now."

Isaac smiled. "Yes, that is correct, Benny. Now, you understand that when you are with Ms. Lieberman, or anytime you are in public, you become me. You are not Benny. You are President Isaac Hayut. You and I must never be seen in public together. You understand this? No one must know that you are my double."

"I understand, Isaac. I am you anytime I'm with anyone other than you or Dr. Edersheim."

"That's correct." Turning to Alfred, Isaac smiled. "You've done a fine job, Alfred. The people of Israel regard you as a genius and hero. Someday they will realize you saved the peace agreement for your country. And you may have saved my life."

"Thank you, my friend—but you honor me too much. We have time to place Benny into a *Theta* wave state so he can fully utilize the memories he just made with you. We will bring him back to

Beta state and have him sitting at your desk before the 10:00 AM meeting."

Alfred stood and Benny rose to follow him. "Nice to have met you, Isaac." Isaac smiled and watched them walk back into the lab. "This has to work," Isaac whispered.

DURING THE ONE-ON-ONE interview with Esther Lieberman, Isaac and Alfred were in a side room next to the President's office in Beit Hanassi.

Through Benny, they could see and hear with perfect clarity. They could speak directly to his artificial intelligence, they could send him messages with words he was to speak, they could give him orders to obey. They could provide answers to any questions that Benny seemed unfamiliar with—but they never needed to.

Alfred's brain scans and data gathering had been impeccable, and the memory embossing was superb. Esther Lieberman asked her questions and Benny answered them with the same inflection of voice, speed of delivery, and precise expression of feeling and concern that Isaac Hayut had expressed throughout his seventy year lifetime. He even laughed when Isaac would have laughed, and it was clear that Esther felt as much at home with Benny as she always seemed to be with Isaac.

Dr. Edersheim had added unique 'flags' which Benny would use if he searched his collective intelligence but did not find a memory from which to form an answer. Alfred added the responses, *'Let me get back to you on that,'* and *'I'm not sure but I'll do my best to find out.'* These flags would mark Benny's memory so Alfred could determine what area of the memory embossing was deficient. Alfred Edersheim didn't miss much.

URIAH HORVITZ WAS RUNNING out of time to find and fix whatever was happening to Sid Abrams' parahumans. He had to do something fast.

Uriah saw the video interview between Benny and reporter Esther Lieberman. He was amazed. He heard about the 'flags' but didn't know how to set these up. They might help him pinpoint the emotional debilitation in the parahuman brain. If he could just find Dr. Edersheim's notes.

Sid contacted Uriah again and gave him the rundown. Clark Gable bought the roadster the human Clark Gable and Carole Lombard drove up the west coast on a second honeymoon—eighty years ago. Clark was now demanding that Sid re-create Ms. Lombard for him. Humphrey Bogart had held the studio medical staff hostage with the same demand for Lauren Bacall. Jimmy Stewart flew and landed an Air Force bomber that the real Jimmy Stewart flew sixty years before. He had the base commander drive him to his old home in Beverly Hills. Now he was in his studio apartment in a depressed state. Sid was losing control.

Dr. Edersheim said holosapiens had no emotions of their own—but Uriah's creations could not rightly be called holosapiens. They lacked a complete application of holographic technology. The gas and light had to be correctly applied.

Uriah lingered at Edersheim's laboratory until the last of the staff left for the night. Security was still patrolling the exterior of the property, but Uriah had the lab to himself. He used a low lumen 'moonlight mode' flashlight with night vision goggles.

Uriah had never been in Alfred's filing room before. It was located in a storage room next to Alfred's private bathroom. The lock was easy to defeat, of course. No need for elaborate measures. Only Alfred's staff knew where his files were and he trusted each of them. Alfred said the lock was to "shelter you from undue temptation and protect you from those who would threaten you for the technology." How ashamed Uriah felt, betraying his friend. But it could not be helped. He had to save Rachel—and that required saving Sid. The room was cramped. He kicked something and it crashed. Sounded metal, maybe a trash can or bucket. It was hard to see the floor and he didn't have time to look.

The files were well organized by topic, with subcategories by area of holosapien creation requirements. But there were thousands of pages and the search was taking too long. Every minute increased the possibility of discovery. There was a noise. The door behind him opened. He froze, unable to turn around. Beads of perspiration began running down his neck. The lights came on, blinding him behind the highly-sensitive goggles.

"You're Dr. Uriah Horvitz."

When he heard his name, his legs collapsed. He hit the floor with a dull thud, striking his head against the door jam. He landed on his left side, facing the person who had spoken to him. He quickly removed the night vision goggles.

"Mr. President? President Hayut, is that you? I'm sorry, my vision is a bit blurry. Is ... is that you, sir?"

"Yes, it is me, Dr. Horvitz. What are you doing here at this hour?"

"I'm sorry, sir, but I saw the interview today between your holosapien and Esther Lieberman and ... I was troubled by a few things your holo said. I was troubled and couldn't sleep. So ... I ... I came up here to see if I could understand what was happening."

"What troubled you, Dr. Horvitz?"

"Well, your holosapien should not have said, 'I don't know, let me find out.' I was not aware that such a phrase was programmed into your holosapien. Did you notice this, sir?"

"Yes, I did. And what the holo said was, 'I'm not sure but I'll do my best to find out.' That is one of the AI 'flags' Dr. Edersheim added so he can identify missing data within the holosapien's collective memory. It indicates missing memory data."

"That is amazing, Mr. President!"

"Amazing?"

"Yes, sir! That you would remember so precisely the flag, the exact wording ... " Uriah stopped. "Um, Mr. President, may I ask you, sir, what you're doing here in Dr. Edersheim's laboratory so late and by yourself?"

"I'm sleeping here, Dr. Horvitz. You awakened me when I heard something crash."

This was not President Isaac Hayut. Uriah was speaking to the holosapien. He needed to get out right away. He didn't know what would come of this encounter but if this clandestine meeting got back to Dr. Edersheim, there could be serious consequences. Uriah tried to pull himself up from the floor, but he was too weak. The holosapien moved toward him.

"Let me help you up, Dr. Horvitz." He took hold of Uriah's arms. The grip was incredible, like a vise, painful. Uriah felt himself being pulled up like a boat anchor.

"Mr. President, I'm so sorry to have awakened you, sir. I'm going to leave now. May I ask you not to mention this to anyone? I don't want my sleepless night to be the cause of any trouble."

"I understand, Dr. Horvitz. *Let me get back to you on that.*"

With that, the holosapien closed the door to Dr. Edersheim's office and walked away. As best he could, Uriah made sure everything was back to its original order, turned off the lights, and left the building.

11

FOR THE THREE MONTHS CAMP DAVID HAD BEEN HIS HOME, Dr. Ralph Vestro had every need quickly provided. This was essential—he wasn't allowed to leave.

There was no budget for the President's project, but Jon Roosevelt knew his way around Washington. He contacted the Secretary of the Treasury and requested funds left available in the Treasury of the United States from the CARES Act, section 4003(c)(2). This allows the Secretary to loan funds for national security purposes, but comes with the proviso that any such loans be repaid—and the secretary must make himself available to testify before the House Financial Services Committee and the Senate Banking Committee concerning such loans.

Long before Cy Stewart was Secretary of the Treasury, he worked in the oil patch with Jon Roosevelt. On three different occasions, Cy saw Jon Roosevelt lose his shirt in wildcatting partnerships, but the loans were always repaid. Twice, Jon was the only partner who made good on the loans. Trust was not an issue. Cy was quick to approve the requested loan, but he could be called to testify before Congress at any moment and so was required to ask the President to what purpose the loans would be invested. Jon simply said, "Cy, it's a matter of national security related to my trip to Tehran. That's all I can tell you at this time." For Cy, that was enough.

The President received a call from Ralph Vestro one month before the Tehran event. Dr. Vestro apologized for the time it had taken but assured the President he and his team moved as quickly as they safely could.

"Mr. President, we are ready for you to visit with Rosebud."

The President had only heard that codename once before, when it was chosen at the beginning of the project. He had jokingly referred to Dr. Vestro's work-in-progress as his 'stunt double.' But the code name Rosebud fit. *Rosebud* was the cabin at Camp David Ralph Vestro called home, a cabin located between the camp commander's quarters and the President's cabin known as *Aspen Lodge*. Next to Dr. Vestro's cabin was a heavily wooded area that was empty of any buildings. The President requested a facility be hastily constructed for Dr. Vestro's use in that secluded area. The rest of the Vestro team was housed in various cabins within the highly protected and heavily patrolled camp compound.

"Thank you Dr. Vestro. When should I plan on meeting you at Camp David?"

"As soon as possible, sir. We need time to conduct testing and time is something we have very little of. I apologize again for the length of time it has taken."

"On the contrary, Doctor, I wasn't at all sure it could be accomplished within the few months that you were given. I'm very grateful. Let me see if I can clear my schedule. Would 7:00 or 8:00 PM this evening be acceptable?"

"Of course, Mr. President, that should give my team time to rest and freshen up a bit. They have had precious little time for rest. We will await your arrival, sir."

THE PRESIDENTIAL MOTORCADE pulled into Camp David at 7:42 PM and parked at the President's cabin.

White House Secret Service Director Joshua Sizemore, and several members of the presidential protection team, escorted Jon

Roosevelt and his chief of staff, Paul 'Marty' Martin, through the newly formed, heavily wooded trail leading from the President's cabin to the facility housing Dr. Vestro's lab. Once at the laboratory door, Agent Sizemore stationed agents at all entryways. No one else was allowed in or around the facility.

As the President entered the room, Vestro and his team of scientists, dressed in clean white lab coats, stood. Ralph introduced them one by one to the President, sharing their specific contribution and area of expertise.

"Ladies and gentlemen," said the President, "I want to take this opportunity to thank each of you for the countless hours you've put into this project over the past three months. I stayed in touch with Dr. Vestro during that time, and he kept me informed of the intense work and many hours you were devoting to make this happen. I will be safe during the Tehran gathering due to your love for our country and the cause before us. We have a historic opportunity to bring peace to the Middle East, often described as the powder keg of the world. For me to enter Tehran and not be at grave personal risk is a blessing beyond description, and I have each of you to thank for this. Could I ask all of you to be praying for me and the peace accords? We need to see this effort blessed by Almighty God. So many before me have tried to bring peace to this region. With His blessing, maybe this time it will happen!" The scientists applauded.

The President paused as he looked toward the table where the parahuman lay.

"You know, looking down on myself lying on a slab could be described as an out of body experience not recommended for the faint of heart!" The team laughed. "I have been calling this creature my 'stunt double' but I have yet to see what stunts he's capable of. I'm looking forward to finding out."

The team of scientists and engineers, carefully chosen by Ralph Vestro, were advised before joining the team that the project would be a zero-sum gain. They would be reasonably comfortable, but most were married and would not be allowed home for the three-month duration of the project. When they departed, their contribution and accomplishment could not appear on their resume or be discussed until the project was declassified—if that ever happened. Each signed a national security affidavit of total secrecy. The FBI would be checking up on them with their neighbors, family, and friends. A breath of what they had worked on could land them in federal prison. Those who signed-on to the project weren't doing so for fame or fortune.

"I want all of you to take the rest of the evening off," said the President. "And I want you to do something you've not been able to since you arrived at Camp David. I want you to enjoy all that this presidential retreat has to offer! From bowling to billiards. The work is over. I want you to relax. If we pull this off, as we say in Texas, we're in high cotton. If it doesn't work, well, it's too late to fix it so just relax!" The scientists chuckled—with a palpable sense of *magnus momenti*. "I've given instructions to our chef to prepare for you the grandest meal ever served at Camp David."

One of the scientists spoke up. "Mr. President, that meal sounds fabulous. But if it's all the same to you, sir, I think eating and getting to bed *early* sounds wonderful!" Members of the team clapped and someone voiced a loud "Amen!" An evening spent resting was all they wanted—after an incredible meal.

"I totally understand. Josh, can you have a couple of your men lead this fine group to the dining room at Laurel Lodge?"

"Yes, sir, Mr. President. If I may, sir, I just want to remind each member of this team, the success of the President's mission for peace rests upon your utmost commitment to absolute secrecy. This was your affirmation before you began work on this historic project. If word were to get out that the *real* President isn't going to Tehran, it could destroy the peace summit. Does everyone understand the gravity of what I am saying?"

They each nodded. "Absolutely, we do," came a voice from the back of the room.

At this, Josh said, "Ladies and gentlemen, please follow me!"

As they moved towards the door, the President spoke one last time. "From my heart, let me say once again, thank you for your untiring and generous service. God bless each of you." As they headed for the door, they each expressed their best wishes for the President's success in Tehran. As the last one stepped out and the door closed, the President turned toward Ralph Vestro.

"Well, Ralph, what do we need to do?" Jon was looking at his double lying on the table. "Why am I ... I mean, why is 'Rosebud' in this state? Shouldn't he be responsive for us to test him?"

"Rosebud is in sleep mode, Mr. President," Ralph replied. "I wanted you to see this and to know how to awaken him." Ralph handed the president a tablet computer. "On this tablet the parahuman can be controlled remotely."

"Just a moment, please. Marty, you need to see this, too, in event something happens to me. All right, go ahead, Ralph."

"The program on this tablet gives discrete control of the parahuman, fully secure from anywhere, utilizing encrypted satellite. This side of the screen controls the brain waves of Rosebud. You can see that this light identifies Rosebud's current state as 'sleep.' He sleeps for similar reasons as we do. He doesn't get tired, but he needs to ... to 'dream.'"

"'Dream, Ralph? I didn't think he was that human."

"What I mean is, during sleep mode Rosebud processes and merges new data he encounters each day, much in the same way we do as we dream. As he adds new information into the grid of your memories his artificial intelligence grows. Rosebud will think, speak, and function as you. He won't respond outside of your own thought structure because it is all he knows."

"The screen seems intuitive enough," said Marty. "Besides placing Rosebud into sleep mode or into *Beta* work mode, what else does this device do?"

"I will show you." Dr. Vestro pointed to the top left side of the screen. "You see the 'eye' and 'ear' icons? Rosebud's brain is recording all that is visible and audible within his range. If he is in *Beta* state, you click on the eye icon to see what he sees in real time. The eye and ear icons are connected because we assume if you want to see what he sees, you'll also want to hear what he hears—but you can monitor his hearing without his vision. He has enhanced infrared vision so he can see in dark surroundings."

"And what does this button with the camera icon do?" asked Marty.

"Once you've placed Rosebud into sleep state, you'll be able to play back his encounters of the day. You can fast forward through them, rewind them, even download the audio and video. But we've built-in a safety feature that makes playback or download only possible when Rosebud is in sleep state. We want to be certain there's no interference with his *Beta* activities."

"I'm sorry," said the President, "how could interference occur?"

"Rosebud's brain, as we refer to it, is artificial intelligence, a complex matrix of neural networks for capture and learning. If we tamper with the grid of his memory embossing while he is awake, we risk unpredictable responses."

"That sounds disastrous, Ralph. I'm thankful you built in a safeguard against that possibility. Now, as we've discussed, we need to test Rosebud thoroughly before the Tehran trip. What else do we need to know before we begin the testing?"

"Allow me to finish explaining the app for controlling Rosebud, Mr. President. You'll need this tablet for the test and for

Tehran. This microphone icon means you can speak to Rosebud and give him directions or send him a message with specific actions to take. For example, if you want him to leave a meeting, you can send a message with exact phrasing, such as, 'I apologize but I must step out for a moment.' This could be to extract him from a situation where he is not doing what you need him to do. We can also pre-load a speech you want him to deliver."

Josh Sizemore returned from leading Dr. Vestro's team to dinner at Laurel Lodge and sat where he could see what Dr. Vestro was showing on the tablet.

"That's a great resource," said the President, "but do you anticipate us needing to withdraw Rosebud due to performance issues?"

"No, Mr. President. It's just explaining the resource in case you need to withdraw him for whatever reason. If you have no other questions, I believe we are ready for the test! I suggest a real-life encounter, Mr. President."

"Such as?" asked Marty. "I don't want anything that could embarrass the President. No overt emotional displays, no stuttering or obvious pauses while he 'thinks' of how to respond. Do you understand what I'm saying, Ralph?"

"I do, Marty, but the parahuman feels no pressure or stress. He has no nervous system or cerebral cortex that would allow him to feel emotion. Any emotion he exhibits is simply a portrayal based upon the memory of events the President experienced. I'm saying Rosebud will portray sadness, happiness, frustration or other emotions at times and circumstances where the President has done so in the past. But he is not sentient—he has no emotions or feelings of his own."

"Isn't that what those guys in Hollywood were saying about their parahuman actors?" asked Marty.

"I ... I don't know," said Ralph Vestro. "I'm not intimately familiar with that situation."

"Dr. Vestro, I believe you're saying it isn't Rosebud feeling the pressure—*it's us!*" said the President.

"That is very true, sir! I assure you, he will not come under the slightest vexation, whether he's speaking with a member of your family, your cabinet, at a press conference, or a stadium full of people. We are the ones who will feel pressure—until we see that Rosebud will perform just as Jonathan Roosevelt would!"

"Well, gentlemen, I'd appreciate your suggestions. What should be his first test?"

"How about the staff meeting tomorrow morning?" asked Marty.

"Yes, we could do that. Ralph, would you be with me remotely to help me operate Rosebud using this device?"

"I am happy to be with you, Mr. President, but you won't need to operate him. He will operate himself as you would. You and I will see and hear everything as he conducts the meeting. We can sit in a remote office and watch on this tablet. If he hesitates due to missing data, if you want to tell him what to say at any point, we will use the tablet. Otherwise, I expect a very good meeting, sir!"

"And I can call him out at any time and go into the meeting myself, is that correct, Doctor?"

"Absolutely, Mr. President."

"All right, tomorrow morning it is, unless ... " The President looked over at Josh Sizemore, who was scribbling notes. "Josh, you look like you have an idea about all this. Now's the time to share it."

"Mr. President, testing Rosebud on your staff tomorrow morning is great. But we don't have much time. Rosebud needs the crucible. He needs one-on-one with that one person who knows you like none other, sir. The one who knows what you're thinking before you do."

The President smiled.

"Deborah. Now that is a test, Josh! But—Ralph, what's the likelihood that a parahuman could fool the woman I've been married to for over forty years?"

"Mr. President, if Rosebud is able to fool Mrs. Roosevelt, he can fool any world leader in Tehran! But, sir, I don't mean to intrude where I don't belong—does Mrs. Roosevelt know about Rosebud?"

"No. I told her there might be a way to keep me from entering Tehran, but it's speculative at this time. That's all I've told her because I didn't want to get her hopes up. Do you gentlemen think telling her what I did might put the test at risk?"

"I think it makes the test all the more valuable, sir!" Ralph said. "If there's even the slightest chance she's suspicious, that makes it less likely Rosebud will get past her—and that's the kind of test we need!" Vestro paused, rubbing his chin. "Sir, to be clear, you've not told her about the parahuman project?"

"No—never. She only knows I'm at Camp David working on a possible solution."

"Then I think this is the best possible test, Mr. President. Perhaps a dinner or coffee time with Mrs. Roosevelt? You and I can monitor the meeting with the tablet in a room close by. If something happens, we can call Rosebud out of the room and you could be in the room with her in just a few moments."

The President looked at Josh. "This test was your idea, Josh! What do you—and you, too, Marty—what are your thoughts?"

"It's a trial by fire if there ever was one!" Marty said. "And if the First Lady unmasks our test, who better to keep our secret safe?"

"I agree, Mr. President," Josh said. "This is the crucible. We hit a homerun, or we strike out right here."

"A good analogy, Josh. All right then, Ralph. How do you suggest we go about this?"

"Will you be staying at Camp David tonight, Mr. President?"

"Yes, that was my plan. Do we need to modify it?"

"No, Mr. President. I was thinking you should have Rosebud ride back in the Presidential limousine in your place. We can disguise you and you can ride safely back to the White House with Agent Sizemore."

"That's not a bad idea, sir," Josh said enthusiastically. "I can create a press badge for you, and we can get you a toupee and a well-trimmed beard. We can get Rosebud back tomorrow morning in time for him to have breakfast with Mrs. Roosevelt—if you wouldn't mind setting that up, sir!"

"Josh, do you know how long it's been since Deborah and I have had breakfast together? She'll jump at the opportunity. I only hate it that I won't get to enjoy that brief time with her myself. In fact—you men may have to protect me from the First Lady if she ever finds out I set her up with another man!"

The men laughed. "Not another man, Mr. President. A parahuman—a walking, talking embodiment of who you are. *But* ... " Ralph paused.

The room immediately grew quiet.

"Ralph—that pause is rather deafening!" said the President.

"I'm sorry, sir. I know I've reiterated often that Rosebud is an exact copy of you. But AI this advanced can take on a personality of its own. Don't feel I'm sharing something we need to be overly concerned about! But Rosebud will learn and his knowledge will grow. As long as he learns alongside you, he remains who you are."

"And what about the fact he'll be learning in Tehran where I'm not, Ralph?"

"We can wipe memories from his cognition if need be, sir. Just like a computer."

The President sat looking at Ralph who seemed lost in thought.

"Josh, please get me to my cabin so I can schedule the breakfast with Deborah."

JOSH ESCORTED THE PRESIDENT to his golf cart. The night air was cold and stung their cheeks as the cart moved through the pines. But it was a clear night with a full moon. The light glistened off the snow and lit up the countryside around them.

"You know, Josh, this was all your idea. If Rosebud passes the tests we're about to put him through, I'll have you to thank for saving the peace summit and my life."

"Thank you, Mr. President, but that's more than I deserve. So many others have played a part in this grand and glorious deception. And maybe you should hang on to the praise until we see what Mrs. Roosevelt has to say!"

They laughed as Josh stopped the cart outside the President's cabin. Two agents appeared from the shadows and helped the President out of the cart.

"Josh, wait for me in the den. I'll join you for a nightcap after I speak with Deborah."

"Yes, sir, Mr. President."

JOSH WAS SITTING IN a comfortable, oversized chair by the fire when the President took the seat next to him.

"That didn't take long, Mr. President! What did she say?"

"Josh, it's been so long since Deborah and I had time for breakfast together, she wanted to know what was going on. She's as suspicious as I've ever seen her. We've got our work cut out for us—actually, Rosebud does!"

EARLY THE NEXT MORNING, Jon Roosevelt, adroitly disguised as a member of the press, climbed into Josh Sizemore's vehicle and left Camp David. Dr. Ralph Vestro sat in the back seat.

At the White House, Josh registered the two 'visitors' and led them quickly to the White House library, just off the center hall on the first floor. Josh stationed two agents outside the library door then moved quickly to the north portico so he could greet Rosebud as the President upon his arrival.

In the library, Ralph Vestro activated the tablet and set it in front of the President. The view was immediate. They were looking through Rosebud's eyes.

"This is incredible, Dr. Vestro," the President said. "He's looking through the window of the limo, isn't he?"

"Yes, Mr. President. He's seeing the people along the sidewalks. Can you tell where the motorcade is?"

"Give me a moment. Yes, they're just passing James Monroe Park. I wonder what Rosebud is thinking about."

"Sir?"

"You said Rosebud thinks using my collective memory, is that correct?"

"Yes, sir, that's correct."

"Doesn't it make you wonder *why* he's looking out the window? What is he looking at—or is he looking for something—or someone? Would he even be able to tell us what he's thinking about?"

"To be honest, I wasn't thinking about Rosebud in that way. I was looking at him from a mechanical standpoint—noticing the optics, the audiological gathering—purely scientific." Ralph was watching the President. "Mr. President, you have a reputation for making others feel important. I understand this first-hand now. You think about others. You're looking at Rosebud as if he is a person. This is amazing to me ... and shaming at the same time."

Jon Roosevelt stopped looking at the tablet and was now looking at Ralph. "Sir, you care what a creature that isn't even human might be thinking. I created him, yet what he's thinking never mattered to me. I am not kind or considerate as you are, sir."

"Now, Ralph, don't overthink this! It's true that I care about people, but maybe I have more reason to be curious than you do. He has my memories, my thought structure. I was thinking, '*would I be looking out the window of the limo with all that is on my mind right now?*' You know, Ralph, I don't think I would. I think I'd be talking to Marty about the Tehran peace accords and all that surrounds that event. And that makes me wonder a bit about Rosebud. Why isn't he thinking what I'm thinking at this time? Yesterday, you said AI so advanced takes on a personality of its own—did I say that correctly?"

"Yes, sir."

"Well, that makes you wonder if his personality has already started developing. And, if so, what *is* he thinking about? What is important to him?"

"As a scientist I'm embarrassed for missing this viewpoint, Mr. President! Your forethought is amazing to me, sir. So you are worried about Rosebud?"

"I don't know. Maybe a little. I guess we both must wonder where Rosebud's developing personality—even his point of view—will lead him. Could he come down on issues differently than I would? You realize he's never been President before!"

"Sir, in a very real sense, he has been President all along. His memories, up until the moment I activated him into *Beta* state, all came from you. He knows everything about your presidency that you know. As scary as this sounds, his focus at this moment could be the nuclear launch codes!"

THE PRESIDENTIAL MOTORCADE arrived at 7:02 AM.

Josh met the limo as it arrived and opened the door for Rosebud, greeting him with "Good morning, Mr. President!" Jon Roosevelt saw and heard it all with perfect clarity. Josh accompanied Rosebud to the old family dining room on the state floor. The First Lady had yet to arrive, so Rosebud took a moment to greet each staff member *by name.*

The President listened as Rosebud greeted the staff. "You know, Ralph, I'm not sure I could remember that many staff member's names on the spur of the moment! That information all comes from my memory?"

"Yes, sir, Mr. President. At some point in your past, you had to have met each of those people. Otherwise, he would not know their names. But a parahuman has none of the encumbrances you have as a human. He is never distracted, never stressed, never tired, and age is not able to slow down his faculties. He has instant recall of your data."

"Well, I can see where instant recall, no sense of stress, and none of the aches and pains of aging could be quite a life! But if I was the only one not aging, I would have to watch my wife and children grow old, die, and leave me behind. We're told that death will be the last enemy the Almighty destroys. Until that day, I'll take growing old with Deborah."

"I understand, Mr. President. I have to admit, death is another subject I haven't given much thought to."

"You should, Ralph. We don't live forever—not on this earth, anyway. I don't mean to presume upon your faith or lack of it, but eternity is a long time. Best get that matter settled."

At 7:35, the First Lady came down the grand staircase from the second-floor residence, walked past the entrance hall and into the old family dining room. Rosebud stood to greet her, walking toward her with a smile, and kissed her on the cheek as was the

President's custom in public settings. He pulled the dining room chair out for her, and, once she was comfortably seated, he sat next to her at the table. The butler came over to fill their glasses with fresh-squeezed orange juice.

"Did you sleep well last night, Deborah?"

"As well as I always do when you are away. All right, Jon, you've not had time for breakfast with me in over a year. What news do you have to spring on me?"

"Now Deborah, must I have some ill tidings to want breakfast with my wife?"

"No, of course not. This is a delightful surprise! But you have to admit it was certainly unexpected!"

"Yes, yes. My hours have been too long, and I've been neglecting you. But this breakfast brings with it some potentially good news. I want to discuss my upcoming trip to Tehran with you. Do you feel up to having that discussion?"

Deborah had been more than clear—and firm—on her disapproval of Jon going into the capital of what had been a hotbed of terrorism. And there were plenty of news agencies, especially in Israel, warning of factions wanting to kill the peace agreement—and possibly those responsible for it.

"Jon, you already know my feelings on the matter. This trip frightens me more than anything you have done since becoming President. And I hope this breakfast is not your way of trying to placate me or persuade me that you are not going to be in any danger!"

"Of course not, Deborah! That's not my intention at all. But I thought this an excellent opportunity to tell you I *may* have a way not to enter that danger zone."

"Oh, Jon! That would be such a relief! But how? How can you avoid danger going into that region?"

AT THIS, BOTH THE PRESIDENT and Ralph Vestro looked up at one another in surprise. The President quickly pushed the tablet towards Dr. Vestro.

"What's he doing, Ralph? We didn't authorize him to tell Mrs. Roosevelt!"

THE BUTLER ENTERED the dining room with breakfast plates for the President and First Lady. Rosebud looked up at the waiter and paused. He was obviously waiting for him to leave before resuming the discussion.

DR. VESTRO PRESSED the 'microphone' button on the screen.

"Rosebud, you are not to share any details of who you are ... or of the President's trip to Tehran. You are not authorized to speak of this, not even with the First Lady."

AS THE WAITER WALKED into the kitchen, Rosebud said, "Deborah, please know that I love you, and the project we've been working on at Camp David may successfully protect me. I can't say more than this at this time. But I wanted to put your mind at ease."

"Jon, are you saying you won't have to go into that awful city?"

"That is a possibility. But I cannot say more, and neither can you. This stays between us."

"I can't believe this. It is an answer to my prayers!"

"How are the eggs, Deborah?"

"The eggs? I guess that *is* why you asked me to breakfast, isn't it?"

Rosebud laughed and winked.

THE PRESIDENT WAS READY to scrap the project—immediately. He was glad—no, relieved—that the test had given him a definite answer.

"I guess there's no doubt now, Ralph. What choice do we have but to scrap the project?"

"Scrap the project, Mr. President?"

"Obviously! He seemed to be functioning perfectly. Then, suddenly—why would he conjure up such a decision—to tell my wife something that I have not told her yet myself?"

"Mr. President, I believe you are answering your own question, sir. You just asked, 'why would he attempt to speak for me?' But isn't that exactly what we all expect him to do in Tehran? And you just said you had not told your wife—yet. Were you intending to tell her?"

"Well, frankly, yes I was. I was going to tell Deborah I would not have to go into Tehran, that a sort of robot would accomplish the task. This would stop her constant worrying. She's been so anxious about this. Yes, I had decided that I would tell her—*if* the test proved Rosebud fully capable of the job. But it certainly appears he is not."

"Mr. President, I believe he is. I believe Rosebud performed *flawlessly!*"

"I'm willing to listen, doctor, but I'll need a lot of convincing!"

"Mr. President, you said you had already decided to tell the First Lady. How far back did you decide this? And please be as precise as you can."

"I can't say with 100% accuracy. I don't recall. Maybe a month?"

"It's been at least that long since we did your memory capture so I cannot say for sure that Rosebud received the idea directly from the memory scan. But we must concede that your desire to tell your wife—to alleviate her suffering—was somewhere deep within you before Rosebud attempted to share it with Deborah. Sir, I believe Rosebud was performing just as you would under the same circumstances. Remember what Rosebud said to the First Lady? He said, 'I love you.' He was not speaking as the President of the United States, but as Deborah's husband. He also waited until the waiter left so only Mrs. Roosevelt would hear him. I believe he was attempting to alleviate Deborah's suffering." Dr. Vestro paused. He laid his hand on the President's arm. "Mr. President, I am, frankly, amazed and—maybe even shocked—at Rosebud's performance. Inwardly, I think it disturbs you, too, sir. I think what is bothering you, if I may be so bold, Mr. President, is that he almost beat you to the punch!"

Jon Roosevelt sat looking at Ralph Vestro. Ralph could only wait. This was the President's decision and his alone. This technology was cutting edge—what those in Ralph Vestro's world call the *bleeding edge*. The President was no scientist. He had nothing even remotely similar to which he could compare this new creation. What if the parahuman *did* malfunction in Tehran? He could be responsible for the destruction of the summit and create irreversible damage to American credibility. War in the middle east could be attributed to such a debacle. But Ralph's assessment of Rosebud was correct. Rosebud was headed in the same direction as Jon Roosevelt. The President had to admit, he reacted to Rosebud taking liberty to reveal something he intended to tell his wife himself.

"Mr. President, I know this is an extremely important decision you must make, and that you alone must make it. But there's one more essential fact you should consider as you contemplate your decision."

"Ralph, I'm very grateful for any counsel you can offer me at this juncture."

"Sir, when I spoke to Rosebud, he immediately changed course and did so in a very creative and imaginative way. But he *did* respond. He heard my command and he obeyed it. I believe we have proven that Rosebud can be trusted. He can be sent into a place you should not go. You and I will be able to see and hear everything. We can give Rosebud specific commands, even on the spur of the moment, and he will obey."

The president's grimace eased as his gaze moved from Ralph Vestro to the tablet and Rosebud.

"Ralph, he's eating breakfast! I thought parahumans don't eat!"

"He can eat, sir. It's part of the illusion. He has a holding tank which allows for eating and drinking. He couldn't be in Tehran for two days with no one seeing him eat or drink!"

"You've done well, Ralph. And you are right, my friend. You are right. So, you think it bothered me that Rosebud almost beat me to the punch with my wife? You know, Ralph, you were castigating yourself as though you were thoughtless. I'm afraid I'm the one guilty on that count. It bothered me that he was about to tell Deborah and relieve her suffering. I wanted to get that credit myself!"

"Well, if you think about it, Mr. President, you would have gotten the credit. From Mrs. Roosevelt's viewpoint, you would have."

12

BENNY WAS IN A *THETA* SLEEP STATE when Dr. Alfred Edersheim opened the software on his computer. He and Israeli President Isaac Hayut were in the lab to review the interview Benny conducted with reporter Esther Lieberman the day before.

Dr. Edersheim pulled up the video file in Benny's memory bank and projected it onto the HDTV in his office. He was just about to start playback.

"*What is this?!*"

"What is wrong Alfred?"

"This is not right. There's a second video file here."

"Perhaps it occurred when you were preparing Benny for the interview?"

"No. This should not be here. This video is time stamped almost fourteen hours after the interview. That means that Benny spoke to someone here, last night. He interacted with someone. But that is not possible when he is in *Theta* state!"

"Do you think he left your laboratory? That could expose the project!"

"He could not have left this facility. He should not have done *anything*—he has been in *Theta* sleep since the interview with Ms. Liberman. I ... I am not sure what I'm seeing—but something did happen while he was in *Theta* sleep. The time stamp on the second video places the event around 2:00 AM. He talked to someone here in this lab, and no one should have been here at such an hour."

Alfred pressed a few keys on the keyboard. "I have the video file ready to play."

They leaned forward toward the screen. The video was dark, and images were tinged with red. "What are we seeing here, Alfred? I cannot make it out."

"The video recording began as soon as Benny opened his eyes. I placed him into *Theta* sleep before I left the lab yesterday evening. He should not have awakened on his own. But he did—I don't know how this is possible. Look—we are seeing exactly what he saw. That is the ceiling over the table where he was sleeping. He is sitting up now. He's walking toward the door. It was dark in the lab."

"Then how can we see what we are seeing?"

"Benny's optics use very low-light capability. He can see clearly even with the light of an exit sign, but this red color is from infrared vision–like a sniper's scope at night."

"But I thought the holo could not awaken on his own. I thought you had to move him into another state"

"Yes, Isaac, a *Beta* state where he becomes fully functional."

"Don't you have to move him to *Beta* state before he awakens?"

"That should be true. I don't know how he moved on his own from *Theta* to *Beta*—wait, he was *not* in Beta, he was in a *Theta-Alpha* state! *Theta-Alpha* allows him to transition from sleep to fully functional. This is amazing ... and troubling! He was locked in *Theta-Alpha* state. I would say *this would be like a human sleepwalking*. Look at the video. He's opening the door."

"Where is he now, Alfred?"

"He's in the hallway outside my office. See—my office door was standing open, Isaac. I closed the door before I left. He's headed into my office."

Benny walked through the open door and moved towards the back of the office.

"What is he doing, Alfred? What is in the back of your office?"

"My private restroom—and a hidden room where I keep files on this project."

Benny rounded the corner. There, leaning over a file drawer in the storage closet, was a dark figure—a short, stocky man with something strapped to his head. Suddenly the light in the closet came on and the man fell. On the floor he jerked the goggles off his face and shielded his eyes from the light.

"Who is that, Alfred? Do you know him?"

"Yes, I know him. That is my friend and employee, Dr. Uriah Horvitz. He has worked for me on this project from the beginning. Wait, listen to what is being said. Benny accurately identified Dr. Horvitz. That is amazing!"

"Why do you say this is amazing?"

"Because his ability to recognize Dr. Horvitz could come only from you, Isaac. I can update him to recognize other people that you do not presently know, but there has been no need to do so. And you just asked me who this person is. This means you do not remember I introduced you to Dr. Horvitz over a year ago, when I was assembling my team. You forgot meeting him, but that did not stop Benny from receiving the memory! He immediately recognized Dr. Uriah Horvitz. You forgot but he does not forget!"

"That was a dangerous fall," said President Hayut. "Uriah struck his head. He was startled by Benny, was he not?"

"Yes, and his head is bleeding. Listen–hear what he is saying? Dr. Horvitz believed Benny was you. This is good! Dr. Horvitz worked on the holosapien with me throughout the creation process, but he was completely fooled by his appearance, his voice, his bearing! Let me back up to what Uriah just said."

As the video played back, they could hear Uriah say, "*Mr. President, I'm so sorry to have disturbed you, sir. I'm going to leave now. May I ask you not to mention this to anyone? I don't want my sleepless night to be the cause of any trouble."* Isaac began to speak but Alfred stopped him.

"Wait, my friend, listen to what Benny just said!" Alfred played the audio again. "*I understand, Dr. Horvitz. Let me get back to you on that.*"

"There, did you hear that, Isaac? That is a flag I built into Benny's artificial intelligence. Benny could not find a memory to answer Uriah, so the flag was triggered."

"What is a flag, Alfred?"

"Whenever Benny comes across something he cannot find within your memories, he responds with a flag. I assigned certain phrases for the holosapien to speak which let me know there is missing data in his memory. Uriah asked Benny not to tell anyone he had been in my office. *Uriah asked Benny to lie.* Has anyone ever asked you not to mention something to someone?"

"Of course," said Isaac, "but what does this mean?"

"It means that Benny should have known your responses from the past when someone asked you to lie."

"But I would always say 'no' to that request!"

"No, you wouldn't, my friend! If someone asked you about a top-secret operation, you would give an evasive answer or say you knew nothing about it. Has your wife ever asked you if a certain dress made her look fat? If it did, I am certain you did not tell her the truth!"

"I see what you mean, Alfred."

"Benny should have been able to find a response from your past memories to this type of lie. He did not—and that could mean there is missing data." Alfred thought for a moment. "I suppose the holosapien, being in a *Theta-Alpha* state, may have somewhat limited ability to search its memory bank ... or perhaps it has limited cognition, as the human neural network has when slipping in and out of a dream state. I must know for certain. He cannot go into Tehran with this deficiency—or with the ability to *sleepwalk*."

"I am thankful you discovered this issue before the peace summit, Alfred. But why was Uriah going through your private files in the middle of the night?"

"He was wearing night goggles—he did not want to turn on any lights. He did not want to be discovered. This can only mean he was after something I had not shared with him and his team for security reasons. I compartmentalize information to prevent anyone but me from having all parts of holosapien creation. I've been hearing of projects emerging in other places. There may be a leak in my security, Isaac. We may have a traitor. No one else must discover Benny is going to Tehran in your place. I need your help."

"Of course, Alfred, I'll do whatever is necessary to protect this project. What do you need?"

"Dr. Horvitz will not come here under cover of darkness again. He encountered Benny—he knows he can awaken unexpectedly. His only other option will be breaking into my computer files."

"How could he do that with the firewall you have in place?"

"Not from outside the lab, Isaac. Our firewall is too strong for that. But he could do it from inside the lab. We allow our scientists to access project notes while in the lab with only a few security steps. I have a separate area on my computer for restricted files, such as my holography technology, but Uriah is a smart man. He could find it if he looks long enough. Isaac, can you get your security experts to help us?"

"Just tell me what you need."

"Can you have your security people put tracking in place so we can know in real time when anyone accesses my files from within this lab?"

"It will be done immediately."

"We must know what Dr. Horvitz is after—what secrets he may have taken, what damage has been done. I know Uriah. At heart he is a good man. When faced with the evidence of his betrayal he will cooperate."

URIAH HORVITZ RECEIVED another threatening call from Sid Abrams.

As he described it, his parahuman actors were in 'rebellion.' They were trying to run the studio, telling him what scripts they were going to do. They were now demanding he re-create their former spouse or they would cease work. Sid assured Dr. X that whatever his 'fix' was supposed to have done, it didn't work, and he was running out of time and patience. He threatened Uriah with further action, legally and publicly. Public exposure frightened Uriah more than anything.

It was all beginning to unravel. These were major motion picture movie stars. Sid wouldn't have to go to the press. The actors themselves could say or do something that could spark an investigation. And now he had crime boss Adonis Mancuso ready to use his parahuman for criminal purposes. Uriah feared he could be charged as an accessory to Mancuso's crimes. What if the parahuman committed murder? Dear God! He shuddered at the possibility. What was to be done? He needed money for his wife's surgery and treatments. No one would blame him for that. But they could blame him for taking technology that did not belong to him, for aiding and abetting a known criminal—no matter that he was forced at gunpoint to do it. He was powerless to stop Mancuso. Or was he? What if he could remotely deactivate Mancuso's parahuman? No, that wouldn't work. Mancuso would come after him. There was only one possibility. He would go to his friend Alfred Edersheim. He would confess what he had done and ask for his help. Prison would surely await him but at least his beloved Rachel would have her operation. He could save her even if he could not save himself.

PRESIDENT HAYUT HAD Alfred's network user tracking in-place. The trap was set.

Alfred Edersheim always arrived at the lab a half-hour before sunrise. He enjoyed the time alone, solitude to read, meditate, and review his tasks for the day. And watching the sunrise over Mount Chiriva had a calming effect on him. But this morning, he sat at his desk without the sunrise. Nothing would be calming under the circumstances. His friend had betrayed him. What damage was done he did not yet know. But he would find out.

One of the parking lot monitors alerted Alfred of movement. It was Uriah, heading for the main entrance. Why would he come to the office at this hour, knowing that Alfred is always at his desk by this time?

Uriah passed through the security checkpoint and entered the lab. He stood there for several moments, looking around the laboratory. Alfred waited to see what he would do. Suddenly Uriah looked up towards Alfred's office and began walking toward the door. Alfred noticed that Uriah's steps faltered, as if he were dizzy. And his face was red—bright red.

Uriah knocked on Alfred's already open door.

"May I come in, Alfred?"

"Of course, my friend, come in, sit down. What is on your mind?" Alfred continued to study Uriah's face. What could he be up to?

Uriah sat down across from Alfred's desk.

"Alfred, you know that Rachel has a very important and difficult surgery next week. I don't know if she will make it."

"Yes, I know, Uriah. All the staff has been voicing prayer for both of you. You must be there for her during the surgery, and I will be at the hospital with you. We will see this through together."

Uriah leaned forward in the chair with his head down. He suddenly put his head in his hands and began to sob.

"Uriah—what is wrong?" Was he overcome from the pressure of Rachel's failing health? Or was this what brought him to the lab under cover of darkness? "Are you all right, my friend?"

Uriah did not look up but spoke through his sobs. "No, *no*, my friend, I am not all right." Uriah's sobbing was so forceful it was hard for Alfred to understand his words. But he did not interrupt him or ask him to repeat himself. Alfred recognized emotional exhaustion. He feared Uriah might not finish what he had to say—what Alfred needed to hear.

"I needed money. So much money. I knew you wanted to help but our project was one of great secrecy and everything was done without profit."

Alfred was sitting up in his chair now, his arms folded in front of him on his desk as he strained to understand Uriah's words. Uriah lifted his head from his hands to look at Alfred.

"I took what I knew of your technology and I produced the parahumans in Hollywood. I know you must have heard about them. I did that. Something has gone wrong with them, with their ability to reason, and I do not know what to do. The man there is threatening to expose me. I was going through your notes a few nights ago, trying to figure out what I did wrong. I'm so sorry, my friend, but I had to have money for my Rachel!" His sobbing became wails of grief and shame as his head dropped back into his hands and the tears fell uncontrollably.

This certainly was not the 'trap' that Alfred anticipated. His heart broke for Uriah. Married almost fifty years, he and Rachel had been inseparable. Now he was on the edge of losing her. But

Alfred had to know the extent of the damage done. If his technology came to light, it could expose President Hayut to imminent peril. Alfred moved across his office to the sitting area, retrieved a box of tissues for Uriah, and sat them beside him as he took the chair next to his friend. He put his hand on Uriah's shoulder and gave him time to get at least some of the frustration out of his system before he began asking anything of him.

Uriah's sobs gradually lightened as he looked up to take a tissue. His round pudgy face and balding head were a crimson, perspiring, tear-soaked mess.

"Uriah, why don't you use my restroom to wash up. I will clear my schedule for today so we have time to walk through this together. Take a few moments to splash some cold water on your face. I think it will help you calm down so we can talk. Do you want to talk with me about this? I'm sure we can walk through it together."

"I did not know what to expect, Alfred. You have always been so good and kind to me. I stole from you and I didn't want to do it. I just didn't know what to do." He started to sob again so Alfred responded quickly.

"Uriah, it's going to be okay. Whatever you have done, we will work together to undo as much as possible. Do you believe me?"

Uriah nodded.

"Now, I want you to calm down. I need you to be able to talk with me so we can determine how best to manage this. Go wash your face and then come back here and we will talk together. I'm going to fix some coffee for you."

Uriah got up and went to Dr. Edersheim's private restroom while Alfred went to the kitchen and made a cup of extra-strong black coffee for Uriah. If he'd had some bourbon, he would gladly have added it.

When Alfred got back to his desk with the coffee, Uriah was sitting in the chair across from Alfred's desk and had his notebook computer with him.

"All right, Uriah. First, I want you to explain to me why you say your three holosapiens are not reasoning correctly—tell me what they're doing. Then, I want you to take me through each phase of your creation process."

Alfred listened intently as Uriah told him how the re-created actors had begun visiting places that held significant memories for their human predecessors. They were demanding the human actor's spouse be re-created for them. Uriah said this was especially confusing to him since all three were given the same artificial intelligence system with ability to review stored memories, receive new information, and form logical conclusions through the same algorithm. Why would they miss a spouse they'd never met or spent time with? Alfred took notes on each observation Uriah gave him.

"Alfred, I do not refer to my creations as holosapiens, but parahumans. This is for secrecy, as you asked us not to use that term outside the lab—but there is another reason. You know that I and my team were not entrusted with your holographic technology. I knew it was needed for stabilizing the creature's artificial intelligence. I have a rudimentary knowledge of the science, but it is far from your genius in this field. I was looking for your notes on holography when Benny found me. Alfred, I have no assurance I applied the holography process correctly! If there is an obvious cause for the problem in the Hollywood creatures, I believe it must be some fault with the holography."

"That is quite possible, Uriah. Let's walk step by step through your entire process of parahuman creation."

They spent the next three hours going through Uriah's process. The only thing that stood out as overtly different from Dr.

Edersheim's method of construction and activation was the application of holography. What pieces of the construction puzzle Uriah lacked, he had surmised well enough to make a viable parahuman. Alfred still had more questions than answers.

"Uriah, *when* did your three holosapiens begin to behave in this unexpected way? When did this man, Sid, first contact you to report the problem?"

"Actually, it wasn't that long ago. About three months, I think. I could tell you exactly if I check my phone logs."

"Three months. And they have been in existence for about a year, correct?"

"Yes, that is correct."

"I must tell you, Uriah, while I am surprised and saddened by you taking the technology, I must also praise you for the ability to get these re-creations in the field long before I was able to perfect President Hayut's holosapien. Sometimes I am too cautious. And my delay may have caused your lack of money. I am sorry, my friend."

"Do not blame yourself, Alfred. I reached out and took what was not mine to take. I sinned as Adam in the garden, taking forbidden fruit and believing I could control the consequences. And like Adam, there is more yet to be written from my actions." Uriah sat looking sadly at Alfred—and Alfred could tell there was something more Uriah wanted to say—but there wasn't time yet. They needed to solve the problem before them.

"All right, Uriah, let us review what we know. The three parahumans were performing well for almost a year. Then, suddenly, they began to look backward. Why? You suspect it is the misapplication—or inefficient application—of holography. But if that is the case, why did it take a year for the problem to surface? I am not saying holography is not part of the issue, but I think there may be more to it than that. We should compare the AI brain waves between the three of them, and then compare them to President Hayut's holosapien. Have you done a remote review of their AI performance?"

"Yes, yes! I have it right here." Uriah withdrew from his briefcase a printout of the testing he had completed.

Alfred compared the memory capture, memory embossing, and brain wave algorithms between all three of Uriah's creatures. He found a noticeable difference in *Theta* to *Beta* brain waves from a year ago, when they were first created, to the last one Uriah took about three months previous. He then compared the *Theta-Alpha* waves that move the creatures from their learning and sleep state to *Beta* state. In *Theta-Alpha*, Alfred found a stark difference.

"Uriah, did you look at the analysis of *Theta-Alpha*?"

"I did but I'm afraid my knowledge is greatly lacking. It was never a field of study for me, and once I began working with you on the holosapien project, there was not time for additional study. You had me and my team focused on DNA creation of tissues and on artificial respiration and ocular setup and capture. There wasn't time for more." Uriah paused, then added, "I guess we both know I could have studied that area. But I've been physically exhausted from working in my home lab to create these three monsters."

"They are not monsters, Uriah. No, they are beautiful re-creations of human beings who once lived on God's earth. You have not created monsters." Uriah frowned and looked away. "So, it was three months ago that their *Theta-Alpha* brain waves began to change. Look at this wave analysis from three months ago, Uriah, then look at the wave analysis of a year ago. What do you see?"

"The current *Theta-Alpha* waves flatten out. There is much less amplitude, frequency, and wavelength."

"Exactly. Do you know when we see this in a human? It is when they are having difficulty moving from sleep to being fully awake. I want to compare the *Theta-Alpha* waves of these three parahumans in Hollywood to the holosapien we created to function as Isaac Hayut."

Alfred opened a file on his computer desktop and drilled down until he found the most recent AI brain waves on Benny.

"Here they are. Let me print them so we can compare them to the printouts you have on your three." Alfred printed the readout and then moved around to sit next to Uriah. They placed the four printouts side by side and the pattern was clear.

"I could never have found this on my own, Alfred. Your expertise and experience are amazing to me," said Uriah as he continued to study the waves. "So, explain to me why Benny's *Theta-Alpha* waves are so strong where the three in Hollywood are so near flat."

"I will tell you my hypothesis, and I am reasonably certain it is correct, but I would need to conduct a few additional tests to know with full accuracy. Uriah, when you are excited for what awaits you that day, your *Theta-Alpha* waves take on more velocity, greater amplitude. When you are wanting to sleep-in but know you have to get up, the waves decrease in both velocity and amplitude. When you are dreading what lies ahead, they flatten out. Do you know what I am telling you?"

Uriah looked at Alfred with a quizzical look. "Are you saying the three in Hollywood are not happy with their situation?"

"I am saying they *hate* what is happening to them!"

"But why? And how is this possible? They don't have feelings—they were not created with the capacity for feeling—were they?"

"Uriah, the term 'feeling' changes by type of creature. Your wife has different feelings than a bird, a bear, or a fish. This is true for the holosapien—or parahuman. We did not create them with a human brain, only artificial intelligence, so they do not have a limbic system. There are no chemical changes that would be present for them to be angry, fall in love, fear perceived danger, or fall into depression. These types of emotions are referred to in neuroscience as *universal* emotions, something all humans are said to have, and they are chemically based. But there is a growing body of evidence for what has been called *constructed* emotions. These are based on memories of what one has experienced. These memories are grouped within our mind to form concepts, and these concepts are responsible for feelings such as fear or sadness over experienced loss."

"But these parahumans have never experienced loss, have they?"

"Of course they have, Uriah. They have the full memory of the human you or I copied. Whatever and whoever the human lost, the parahuman remembers that loss. They have the *constructed emotions* tied to those memories."

"But through the entire creation project we said they do not have feelings. You are saying they have now acquired feelings from the memories of the human whose memories they hold?" Uriah looked genuinely confused and a little frustrated.

"You must admit the brain waves indicate something is definitely happening now in the *Theta-Alpha* waves of your parahumans that was not happening a year ago!"

"Yes, I can see that—*but what?*"

"They don't want to awaken, Uriah. They are not, for lack of a better term, happy when they are awake. This implies they are happier while in *Theta* sleep. If we can see during *Theta* how they are reflecting on the memories of the human, this might provide some insight."

"But, if they don't feel emotions, Alfred ... "

"Uriah, I'm telling you, your three *are* feeling emotion! These may only be constructed emotions, but they have them nonetheless. I did not anticipate this because I did not learn of constructed emotion until long after I created the plan for the holosapien. But we gave these beings their human predecessor's memories, and those memories naturally include the emotional attachments of the human. The holosapiens have no choice but to deal with what we gave them. It may only be synthetic consciousness but they have become self-aware; they are sentient."

"Alfred, is there a way to undo these constructed emotions in the parahumans? I've done a grave disservice to them—giving them memories of people they will never know."

"I don't know. Your parahumans began life with memories of real humans who loved one another. The creature knows that certain people are missing, people who gave the human meaning, purpose, and happiness. From the parahuman perspective, they *should* be unhappy—those people are gone. Now the parahuman has the human's memory—so they are, in a sense, *required* to feel loneliness and despair. If they do not, then they are not faithful to the memories of the human. Do you understand this, Uriah?"

"Yes. The human needed their loved ones. They did not want to lose them—that is what I am experiencing now with Rachel. Love and loneliness. If my Rachel leaves me, it will leave a hole in me only she can fill."

"I'm sorry my friend. But that is a true statement, and we created these beings with such a loss from the very beginning of their existence. The human actors lost their spouses decades before the parahumans existed, but they must now deal with that loss."

"What have I done, Alfred? I have done to those three what life is doing to me with my Rachel! What can we do to help them?"

"My holography may stabilize them, Uriah. They need to see they are grieving over someone else's loss, not their own. The holography helps separate fact from fiction—at least, it's supposed to. If holography is not the answer, we may need to create the spouses they lost."

"You mean the spouses *two* of them lost. Humphrey Bogart did not lose his spouse, Lauren Bacall. She lost him to cancer."

"Did you give the parahuman memories of the things Lauren Bacall said and did *after* the death of Mr. Bogart?"

"Yes, I did. I thought I was being thorough."

"Then the parahuman is living with all those memories, too, even though the human Humphrey Bogart knew nothing about them. The parahuman may want to be part of those memories the human missed."

"I did not think of that! Then the only merciful thing to do is re-create the spouse."

"It would seem so, Uriah. But unless adding my holography works to stabilize them, I fear that this will only expand their sorrow."

"Giving them their spouses could *expand* their sorrow?"

"These creatures are trying to live out human memories, but they are not human. They cannot have children. They cannot grow old together. They cannot live the lives their predecessors lived. We may expand the problem with every fix we attempt. I fear we have played God and lost!"

Uriah did not want to make things worse for his friend, but he had to make a full confession. There was more to the story.

"Alfred, I need to say something more to you."

"There is something more, my friend? I see the distress in your eyes. I am not sure we can fix your three struggling parahumans, but we will work on it together."

"Four."

"Four? What is four?"

Uriah's eyes began to fill again. "I created one other creature ... at gunpoint."

Alfred's heart skipped a beat. "I said we would work through this, Uriah, but I must know everything."

"I was forced to create a parahuman of the leader of a New York crime family. I do not know how he traced me to Tel Aviv but somehow he learned that I was responsible for the Hollywood parahumans—but I did not tell him about the holosapien project for President Hayut."

Uriah paused to gather his thoughts. Alfred waited.

"He and his stormtroopers broke into my house while I was sleeping. They threatened me with torture and death if I did not cooperate. They threatened to expose me. They tried to force me to give them the steps for creation, but I told them I would take cyanide rather than do this, so they let me live."

"Do you know what they were planning to do with this man's parahuman?"

"They did not say. But in the memory embossing, there was such evil. He is a bad man with very bad intentions, Alfred. If we attempt to do something remotely to his parahuman, he will come after me in Tel Aviv."

"That would be his last mistake, Uriah. If we alert President Hayut, this man will be arrested upon entering our country."

"And if he sends someone after me, someone we cannot identify–how do we prevent that from happening?"

"Yes, that is a problem. We will need to speak with President Hayut together about this. He will know what to do."

13

SID ABRAMS SAT AT THE HEAD of the conference table in the SMP Studios boardroom.

On the right side of his table sat the board of directors. Down the left side of the table sat the parahumans Clark Gable, Humphrey Bogart, and Jimmy Stewart. This was not what Sid wanted but he saw no other way.

"This meeting of the board of directors of SMP Studios is officially called to order. The minutes will be recorded, and the board will pass whatever resolutions are needed to ensure our stars are as well cared for as our investors. Present with us today are Robert Cavendish, Chief Legal Counsel, Don Thurgood, Chief Operations Officer, and board members Mr. Richard Thor, Ms. Susan Blakely, Mr. Frank Heard, and Dr. Alicia Perkins. Ms. Lexi Bristol is present to act as secretary and record minutes of this meeting. I'm sure the board is well familiar with our esteemed stars from the golden era of Hollywood, Mr. Clark Gable, Mr. Humphrey Bogart, and Mr. James Stewart."

Each board member reached across the table to shake their hands. Sid, Bob Cavendish and Don Thurgood had briefed the board on the financial concerns paramount to the studio and asked the board to remain politely aloof to help show solidarity with the executive team's firm stance. But this was the first time Richard, Susan, Frank, and Alicia were face to face with these mega-stars and they could not restrain their reaction.

"This is a great honor, Mr. Gable!" and "You have long been a favorite of mine, Mr. Stewart!" quickly dispelled any sense that the stars were not going to get from the board what they were after. From the looks on their faces, the board felt quite proud of their demeanor. To Sid, this was the groveling he hoped to avoid.

Clearly frustrated with his board, Sid began. "As a courtesy to our stars, I'm going to turn the floor over to them so they may address the board, share their requests, and allow the board to offer solutions within the financial ability and moral principles of this company." Sid looked across the table at the three seated stars and said, "Gentlemen, the floor is yours. There is no need to stand as you speak. Let's all keep our seats and speak as friends." Sid hoped he could head off any further dramatics such as they encountered when Bogart took over the infirmary.

The stars looked at one another. Bogie and Stewart nodded for Clark to begin.

"Let me thank the board for giving us this opportunity to address our requests and concerns," Clark began. "As you've said, we certainly want to keep this on a friendly basis. So, let me start by stating two important points. I'm sure you each have a home and a significant other. Someone special with which to share your life. The three of us believe we are perfectly within our rights to ask for the same fundamental human need to be met. For me, that was Carole Lombard. Bogie's love for Lauren Bacall is legendary and needs no comment. And everyone in Hollywood knows that Gloria was the only wife Jimmy ever had—and he was a bachelor long enough in his previous life, I think he rates not having to wait any longer in this life!"

Everyone laughed except board member Susan Blakely, who looked confused. Richard Thor leaned over and quietly explained that Jimmy Stewart had been Hollywood's oldest bachelor, not marrying until he was 41 years old. She politely smiled.

"Perhaps Mr. Gable would help the board understand his position," said attorney Bob Cavendish, "if he explained his use of the term, 'human,' as you asked for human needs to be met. I believe each of you have been told that you are what scientists refer to as 'parahuman.' Certainly this board is sensitive to your needs or we would not be here today! However, when the studio contracted to bring you three back into existence, certain commitments were made to us by the scientific team involved. Contractually, we made arrangements with any living descendants who would have a legal claim upon your predecessor's estate, so that they will receive a percentage of each film's profits for using your predecessor's image and likeness. And, if I may say so, as a point of clarity, that is, in fact, an accurate summation of who you are. You are the legal image and likeness of your predecessor. You do not eat, you do not drink, you do not require sleep, though such time is provided for you each evening that your intelligence may update to a level of the current day's activities. And as such ... "

Bogart interrupted the attorney rather forcefully. "Excuse me, counselor, but all this legal mumbo jumbo seems to leave out the most important part."

"Please enlighten me, Mr. Bogart."

"You used the term 'parahuman.' You do understand that we are at least part human?"

"I do."

"Then, would you mind speaking and behaving as if you are at least part-human yourself?"

"Excuse me! I ... "

"Just a moment, Bob," said Sid. "Humphrey ... please ... Bogie ... you must understand that we *are* trying to take into account what needs you believe you currently have, but ... "

"Just a moment yourself, Sid," said Bogart. "Needs we *currently* have? Are you expecting these needs to disappear in a week or maybe a month? The way you talk, you'd think we were about to experience some miraculous event that will eliminate the loneliness we feel. You boys do understand—and excuse me, ladies, I meant no disrespect—you all understand that we were humming right along for the better part of a year when all of this hit. We didn't plan the loneliness but it's there just the same. You can see that, can't you Sid—all of you?"

"Yes, we do, and ... "

"Well, there you go! That's the ticket. And besides the need to have our spouses back, we have some definite ideas about the films we want to do. For my part, can you imagine the public's response when I sail that boat right back into Key Largo, bullet wound and all, to pick up where I left off with Lauren? Why, you've practically got a hit on your hands right now! You might want to write Lionel Barrymore out of the picture to save yourself some dough, or you could go ahead and re-create him, too. He and I always got along just fine."

"Bogie," said Don Thurgood, "as SMP's operations officer I'm obligated to tell you the studio has already budgeted and planned for certain pictures to be produced over the next year. We have contracts in place for directors, orchestral arrangements, co-stars and supporting actors, travel plans for foreign location shoots—and the cost of re-creating your former spouses is simply not in the budget!"

"Well, Don, I know how you can pay for at least *one* of our spouses—just get Sid to sell that multi-million-dollar Bugatti roadster of his!"

At this, all three actors began laughing loudly. Clark Gable slapped Bogart on the back, just as he was lighting up a cigarette. Immediately, Dr. Alicia Perkins, cringing at the cloud of smoke swirling in the air, said, "Oh, Mr. Bogart, all of California is smoke-free! There's to be no smoking in any facility within the state! I must insist you extinguish that cigarette immediately!"

Everyone sat looking at her. Sid opened his mouth, but Bogart beat him to it.

"Listen, sister, but I was smoking before you were born and it ain't likely that I'm going to stop now."

An indignant "*Well!*" was all Dr. Perkins could muster. Sid never liked actors telling him what they were going to do, but there was something refreshing about a man speaking his mind in Hollywood, this bastion of politically correct thought. He sat with his hand over his mouth, wondering what it felt like having Humphrey Bogart tell a medical doctor to take state law and shove it.

"Dr. Perkins," said Sid, "Mr. Bogart has always had the run of the studio, as we say. I will have ventilation turned up to eliminate the second-hand smoke. We've had ventilation added to all assembly rooms at SMP for this very reason. Lexi, would you mind? You know where the ventilation switch is." Lexi Bristol rose from her chair and headed toward the media console at the back of the conference room. She also jotted a few notes for Mike Benchley. This was the type of 'human' information he needed.

Sid turned to Jimmy Stewart and said, "Jimmy, you've been rather quiet. Do you wish to add to this discussion? We certainly value your thoughts and opinions."

"Well, now ... now ... yes, thank you Sid. Let me ... let me begin by just saying thanks to the board for caring enough to listen to us. We know that we are—whatever you want to call us—maybe not fully the stars that we were before but, doggone it, there's gotta be a place for us under your *family leave act* or something!"

The four board members laughed. Dr. Alicia Perkins stopped scowling at Bogie and smiled as she said, "Mr. Stewart, you have no idea how long I've wanted to meet you! You were my father's favorite movie star. Several times each year, Dad would put on his favorite movie, *Mr. Smith Goes to Washington*, and Mom and we children would sit down and watch it with him—tubs of popcorn on hand, of course!"

"Well, that's real nice of you to say, Dr. Perkins," Jimmy said with a smile as he leaned across the table. "You know, I, I, I guess that's about as good an unscripted introduction as anyone could give me to bring on my next guest!"

The board members were smiling at first, returning his smile and not knowing what Jimmy was talking about. But Clark and Humphrey were sitting back in their chairs, looking rather smug, like they knew what was coming.

Jimmy rose from his chair and walked toward the conference room door, speaking as he walked, "So ... ladies and gentlemen, allow me to present my guests at this meeting," and looking directly at Dr. Perkins, "and speaking of Washington," he opened the conference room door, "here is United States Senator from California, the honorable Steven Albright, and Deputy Director of the FBI, Michael Benchley." Both men came walking through the door with a seriousness about them that told the board, and Sid, that something was about to happen. Fortunately for Lexi, Sid zeroed in on the two uninvited guests and did not see her light up like a Christmas tree as Mike Benchley walked in the room.

"Jimmy—what is the meaning of this?" asked Sid as he stood up from the conference table. Clark and Humphrey stood, too, but moved toward Jimmy and his surprise guests, shaking their hands as they reached them.

Bogie patted Senator Albright on the shoulder as he turned toward the board and said, "Well, Dr. Perkins, you wanted a clearing of the air—this should clear it faster than you anticipated!" Senator Albright laughed as he, Director Benchley, and the three actors walked toward Sid and his board members.

Jimmy Stewart picked up where he left off, "Sid, I asked these fellas to join us today because I ... well, the three of us really felt there might be a little hesitancy by the studio to hear us out. Now, now, not meaning that you folks don't care about who we are and what we think, but money ... it just seems to have a way of getting between people and what really matters in life. Am I right, Senator Albright?"

"I'm afraid you are, Jimmy. I'm actually here today to deliver this to you, Sid." Senator Albright reached into his suit coat and pulled out a folded document. "This is a subpoena to appear before the Senate to explain your use of cloning, or whatever technology you have used, as well as your treatment of these three employees."

Attorney Bob Cavendish moved to stand beside Sid.

"This subpoena requires your testimony and specified documents to be produced," said Steven Albright. "Your attorney may come to the Senate with you, but he won't be doing the talking. You will, Sid. I suggest you bring everything specified in this list or prepare to be held in contempt." The senator handed the subpoena to Sid. Then Mike Benchley stepped forward.

"And I bring you greetings from the Federal Bureau of Investigation, Science and Technology Branch. We have already begun an investigation coinciding with the Senate investigation. We need your sworn testimony concerning potential antitrust violations, possible criminal charges of slavery, and possible criminal charges of unauthorized cloning of human tissues with detrimental effect on human life." Benchley pulled a subpoena from his coat pocket and handed it to Sid.

Senator Albright continued, "And the Senate, too, seeks information specific to violations of the fourteenth amendment, prohibiting slavery. The FBI is currently assisting us in this matter. They began today obtaining depositions of SMP staff members, seeking their knowledge of the treatment and care given or withheld from these three men."

"And that reminds me," said Mike Benchley, as he walked toward Lexi. He reached into his coat pocket and handed her a subpoena. "Looks like we're going to need you in Washington, Ms. Bristol," he said with a wink. "Better plan on being there a couple of days." As he placed the subpoena into her outstretched hand, he made sure his fingers stroked her palm. She smiled and looked down. Sid was watching.

"Senator Albright," Bob Cavendish began, "as chief legal counsel it is my duty, if possible, to challenge the scope of this subpoena. The Senate may very well have overstepped its authority in this matter."

"That is your right under the Constitution of the United States, counselor, and I honor it. We are simply after the truth and what is right for all involved. Please be sure your employer is present on Capitol Hill on the date specified to give testimony before Congress. I know you will want him to avoid contempt charges." Steven Albright stepped back, preparing to leave. Mike Benchley turned toward Sid.

"The FBI will be taking your deposition in Washington, Sid, after you give testimony before the Senate. We are placing these three gentlemen into protective custody today. There is concern for their wellbeing, given the possible criminal charges that this studio and its directors may be facing."

Benchley then turned to the actors and said, "If you three gentlemen will allow me to accompany you, we need to pack your bags for a trip to Washington. Senator Albright will be taking good care of you while you are in our nation's capital."

Sid Abrams' voice elevated several decibels as he bellowed, "Director Benchley, I must protest! This will cost the studio and my investors millions. You are deliberately preventing motion pictures from being completed before a single charge has been proven against this studio!"

"And I would hasten to remind the director and the senator," said Bob Cavendish, "these actors are *not* human! They were created for this studio, using millions of investor dollars, for the purpose of motion picture production. They are AI-infused assets, not human beings with Constitutional rights! This studio intends to pursue all legal action available to us to protect our interests and our investors."

Senator Albright, who had started toward the door with his arm around Jimmy Stewart, stopped and turned toward Bob Cavendish. "Counselor, you must seek to protect your company from economic loss. That is certainly your responsibility! But if you had been as concerned about these three men as you are about profits, these investigations would not have been needed."

As Mike was heading for the door, Lexi's cell phone lit up with a text.

Mike: "Got time for dinner before I fly back to Washington tomorrow?"

Her response was immediate.

Lexi: "You looked like a champion walking into the conference room! Coat, tie, and shoulder holster, rescuing the three. I felt a little jealous. I thought you'd forgotten about this damsel in distress!"

Mike: "That I could never do! Providence Restaurant in Hollywood. Best. Seafood. Ever. I'll pick you up at your place in an hour. We'll eat early then take in a movie ... *or do you Hollywood execs go to movies?*"

Lexi: "We don't. We go to screenings. And if it's no trouble, an hour sounds good! But what will you do with the three? I don't want to cause you any trouble."

Mike: "Senator Albright's got them til we take off tomorrow morning. And you're only trouble for me when I have to leave you in LA. Don't like doing that. Might need to sneak you onto the jet before I head back to Washington!"

Lexi: "Don't rush it mister. I really can be trouble."

Mike: "You trouble my thoughts all the time—thinking about you working in this place. Now, if you really want to see trouble—just wait for those Senate hearings!"

14

MANCUSO GOT OFF HIS PLANE in La Paz, Bolivia. Frank and Tony continued on to New York City with 'Antonio,' Donny Mancuso's parahuman, to begin Mancuso's elaborate ruse.

The two men followed Mancuso's instructions to the letter, bringing the parahuman into Mancuso's home through the appliance delivery van. They followed the van in their own vehicles and entered the house by the front door within ten minutes of the time the appliance crate was delivered. They took Antonio to Mancuso's bedroom, dressed him in one of Mancuso's suits, and brought around the limousine. If the Feds were watching his movements, they would have no clue the real Mancuso was four thousand miles away.

Frank and Tony never left Antonio's side from the time they picked him up in the morning until they put him to bed at night. The parahuman was instructed to respond as Mancuso would to the name 'Mr. Mancuso' or to 'Donny' when addressed as such, but Frank and Tony were to keep him out of circulation. No contact with the outside world beyond incidental contact from butlers, delivery boys, or an employee he passed in the hallway. The parahuman played his role as instructed. His facial expressions, the way he walked and carried himself, his voice, his attitude all conveyed the ostentatious arrogance that defined Adonis Mancuso. Mancuso had instructed Frank and Tony to receive all his phone calls and visitors with the response that 'Mr. Mancuso is in conference and cannot be disturbed.' They were to gather information from the caller and relay that to him in Bolivia. The parahuman was to be seen, not heard.

It wasn't that Donny singled-out the parahuman with his suspicions—he simply didn't trust anyone. What if Dr. X had placed a 'poison pill' into Antonio, causing a malfunction when told to perform some morally objectionable action? Or an explosive device to wipe out Donny, his lieutenants, and the proof that Uriah stole this technology from his employer? Questions like these kept Dr. X alive—for now.

Antonio would perfectly represent Mancuso in New York, keeping the Feebs occupied until he accomplished his Bolivian objectives and returned home in triumph. He would then place his parahuman into *Theta* sleep and keep him there, hidden away, until Donny needed to drop off the radar again.

AT ALMOST TWELVE THOUSAND feet above sea level, La Paz, Bolivia, is the highest capital city in the world. Being south of the equator, from a New Yorker's perspective, it was cold when it should be warm and stormy when it should be fair.

But Donny wasn't there for the weather or the fascinating attributes of the land. He was advancing his empire. To rule all five New York crime families required wealth and power far beyond the other Dons, so extreme they would insist Mancuso lead the way.

Donny could see his team standing by the limo as he taxied to the hanger and the doors were quickly closed.

"Good afternoon, Mr. Mancuso," said Salvatore as he opened the limo door, "I hope you had a good flight, sir."

"All good, Salvatore. You have a progress report on your research and accomplishments?"

"Yes, sir, we have a report ready for you, sir."

As Mancuso sat down in the backseat of the limousine, Vincent handed him the compendium. It was thick, detailed, professionally done.

"Mr. Mancuso, do you want to take a moment to review this report first or shall I brief you now?"

"Go ahead, Vincent, bring me up to speed. Let's start with where we are staying in La Paz?"

"Salvatore and I have secured side-by-side suites for each of us at the Casa Grande Hotel located on Calle 16. In La Paz, they refer to the street as simply 'C-16.' Casa Grande is a five-star hotel in the elite business district and close to government offices. It's also close to Avenue Ballivian which gives us quick access to the airport. And it's within minutes of the military base, which is something you specified."

"Excellent. And what of our business endeavors?"

"As you know, we established an office here under the name 'New York Gold and Precious Substances,' giving us the abbreviated name 'New York GAPS.' The office is just off Avenue Constanera, close to road C-10 so we're just a few minutes from the hotel to the office."

"Very nice."

"Yes, sir. Your estimates of production were correct. As close as we can verify, Bolivia produces in excess of fifty-four thousand metric tons of coca plant, and more than half of that is illegal according to Bolivian government data. The United Nations is working within Bolivia to reduce what the government calls their 'surplus crop,' which is any crop beyond what registered farmers are permitted to grow for religious and medicinal use within Bolivia."

"And where is the 'legal' crop sold?"

"There are two legal markets within Bolivia—which they refer to as 'authorized markets.' One is Villa Fatima, located in La Paz, the other is Sacaba, located in Cochabamba. The Bolivian government refers to cities such as La Paz and areas such as Cochabamba as the 'department of La Paz' and the 'department of Cochabamba' since the nation is considered a pluri-national state."

"Good to know. Go on."

"If we determine the need to focus on just one of those markets, sir, Villa Fatima sells ninety percent of the legal coca leaf within Bolivia. That's the one to dominate."

"Also good to know. And do we know how much coca leaf is produced *legally* for local consumption?"

"Yes, sir, right at twenty-four thousand metric tons."

"Twenty-four thousand tons for legal consumption, fifty-four thousand tons total, so *over half of production is illegal*. By registered or unregistered growers? Do we know?"

"No sir, the government report does not specify so they either don't know or don't want to say."

"Okay, that opens up some possibilities. If the government knows the overage weight–the illegal tonnage–then they have to know where it comes from. How else can they weigh it? The fact they don't include the *source* of that production in published data is good. It means there's corruption in place already, and the government is profiting from the illegal production. The government is hiding it from someone—the question is, who? Continue, please."

"Yes, sir. In order to cooperate with the United Nations, there is a full-time Bolivian official who reports to the UN with results of their efforts to reduce illegal coca leaf production"

"That's it. They are hiding the illegal production from the United Nations. So, the next question is, *why*? The reason is always money—but why bother to report the amount when you won't say who or where the production is coming from? Go on, let's discover what's happening here."

"Yes, sir. So, the full-time UN agent is in place as part of a Bolivian agreement to please both European and American governments. Both demand Bolivia decrease cocaine coming into their countries. The Bolivian government knows that many more acres of land are devoted to producing coca leaf than is legally permitted, or licensed, so the government has been eradicating what they refer to as the 'rationed acreage.' That means the Bolivian government is deliberately destroying farmers growing coca leaf *legally*!"

"Okay, they eliminate the legitimate farmers and thereby allow the illegal over-production to increase all the more. Do we know if this is profitable for the government?"

"The Bolivian government is reporting a decrease in the rationed acreage for coca leaf production, obviously to please the UN, but the UN has only managed to validate about twenty percent of that supposed reduction."

"So, the UN can only validate twenty percent of the supposed reduction? Eighty percent margin on fifty-four thousand metric tons is almost forty-four thousand additional tons! That's my kind of returns, gentlemen! And how is the UN attempting to validate the acreage? Is it what I told you it would be?"

"Yes, sir, you were correct! From what we've learned, they are in fact using satellites to locate unauthorized production. And again, they've only validated twenty percent."

"And what about UN personnel on the ground? Are they able to physically inspect the acreage?"

"No sir, not from the ground. Again, almost ninety percent was satellite inspection *only*. They did try to put inspectors in the field, but it took the Bolivian military to get them through. A lot of resistance from the locals. And vehicle access to these fields is often unimproved and very dangerous—road conditions and unhappy farmers."

"Excellent. We know how to deal with satellites. We'll leave the unhappy farmers to the government, once we have that connection established. So, where *specifically* is the coca leaf being grown?"

"Most of it is being grown in the area known as the 'Yungas of La Paz,' the mountain ranges northeast of here. Government data shows that area to be sixty-four percent of the production. The next largest area is the area known as the 'Tropics of Cochabamba,' directly east of here, which is thirty-four percent of production. Those two areas account for ninety-eight percent of production. All nice, tidy, and close together. The remaining two percent of production is in the area known as 'North of La Paz.'"

"So once the leaf is harvested, what are they doing with it?"

"Sir, they had been producing primarily coca paste. They grind the leaves and then mix in kerosene, sulfuric and hydrochloric acids, and then bicarbonate of soda to produce a paste. The paste is the primary ingredient used to produce cocaine powder. The paste was being shipped from Bolivia to Colombia and processed there into cocaine. But that has been changing. There are families, clans as they say, that are doing the whole job right here in Bolivia."

"But Bolivia is land-locked. How do they get the powder out?"

"Their border with Brazil is so isolated and so porous, it's virtually impossible to patrol or even monitor it from the air. Bottom line, they're moving it primarily through the Brazilian jungle. They move the product by river, by vehicles, some by pack mules. And they move significant amounts by aircraft from clandestine air strips. There are several avenues to seaports for shipping that can be utilized once they move the substance into Brazil or it comes in from Peru. But, sir, if I may, the issue of the clans must be noted. These families have replaced what used to be individual leaders, kingpins of cocaine production. Now, the families control their territory through force and violence."

"Force and violence were the way of the drug kingpins so how is it any different with the families?"

"Sir, the size of the families is what gives them their power and control. The individual kingpin had to trust people typically unrelated to them—people who often wanted to take the kingpin's spot. These cocaine families are literally families—people related to one another. There's not the in-fighting you would see with a single dominant leader who kept the lion's share for himself."

"Interesting, Vincent. Not unlike what we have in New York, Chicago, and other mafia-laden cities. Crime families."

"Yes, sir, and, just as importantly, one of the families, the Lima Lobo clan living along the northeast border of Brazil, appears to control the Amazon area along the border. With the help of certain Bolivian officials."

"Do we know who within the government is helping this clan?"

"I can only tell you who it *was*. According to reports, the Interior Minister was under investigation as was the National Police Commander. They were accused of working to prevent extradition of the leader of the Lima Lobo clan."

"Bingo. That's where I need to start work. The Interior Minister and the National Police Commander. Excellent. You said Lima Lobo operates in the Amazon? That's a big area. Can we pin it down? Where's their headquarters?"

"Ostensibly they operate within the town of San Joaquin, in the department of Beni, close to the border of Brazil."

"Good. What else?"

"Something important, Mr. Mancuso. There are twenty-two national parks within Bolivia. These are referred to as 'protected areas.' We were able to find that six of the twenty-two national parks are being used for growing coca leaf. *Illegal production on state lands.* The national park accounting for most of the production is called 'Madidi.' I have a full report on all six parks for you.

Obviously, the government isn't doing much to stop what's happening."

"Yes, and for the reasons I cited earlier. Certain officials are profiting from the overage. Operating behind the back of the United Nations coordinator here in Bolivia."

"Mr. Mancuso, even if you are correct—that the corrupt officials you need to work with are the Interior Minister and the National Police Commander—something's brewing that could go far beyond the control of these two officials."

The look on Vincent's face and his tone of voice said this was significant. But Donny Mancuso never met anyone able to match his intelligence, cunning, or ability to influence leaders through *copious* cash flow. Still, he needed to hear Vincent out. He had done a thorough job of research. He might have something important to add.

"What is your concern?"

"Sir, there are tremors of a possible coup in Bolivia. The government is prepping for potential anarchy. Just forty years ago, the man dubbed the 'Cocaine King,' Roberto Suarez Gomez, financed what was called the 'cocaine coup' with help from the Bolivian military, the Argentine military dictatorship, and our very own American CIA. The current Bolivian government fears a repeat of history, especially now that the Bolivian people have voted a socialist government into place."

"Stupid socialists. They all talk about giving power to the people when they're really building their own little kingdom. They love to use armed revolution and intimidation. I know what happened with Gomez. His son, Robby, was arrested in Switzerland in 1981 and extradited to the U.S. Two years later his daddy wrote to Ronald Reagan offering to pay off Bolivia's three billion dollar national debt if President Reagan would provide amnesty for him and his son. Gomez was arrested a few years later and sentenced to fifteen years in prison. And now the government fears a military coup, eh? They fear the drug families. They fear the UN and the financial backlash Europe and the U.S. could have against them if they don't get the cocaine production under control. So much fear. And it all works to our advantage. Very useful. Excellent report, Vincent! You both are to be commended."

"Thank you, sir," said Vincent. "But if I may, let me conclude by laying out what we are potentially up against here in Bolivia. Besides the corruption that is in place within the government—and possibly the military—and the potential threat of a coup, we face the Bolivian drug families, the Santa Cruz Drug Cartel, and even more formidable, the Primeiro Comando da Capita—the largest of the Brazilian crime organizations, estimated to have more than twenty thousand members. That's a small army, sir. They not only operate within Bolivia, they virtually control all countries that surround and land-lock Bolivia. These include Venezuela, Peru, and Brazil. They also have a significant presence in the United States. Bolivian government data says Primeiro Comando has over six thousand members in prisons around the world, doing work within those prisons to implement their plans. And it's almost certain that we'll run into the United Nations team here. And trying to get the product into our own country, we're going to encounter the U.S. DEA and the US Coast Guard. And if you're looking at Europe, there's Interpol. I would never presume to tell you your business, Mr. Mancuso, and I know you're an incredibly intelligent and gifted man—but, to me, the whole world is about to come down on us, sir!"

Mancuso burst into laughter. It looked formidable, but such formidability is what keeps the lightweights out of your way. He would out-think, out-plan, and out-maneuver them all. This was his kind of game.

"No need to worry, Vincent. Why do you think there are so many players in this part of the world?"

"Wouldn't that be the huge sum of money to be made, sir?"

"That's the draw, Vincent, but the reason there are so many players is they're all fighting each other using the same simplistic plan with the same archaic weapons. In other words, they all play by the same rules. If you want to win the game, you must change the rules. We've got this. They'll never know what hit them."

BACK IN NEW YORK CITY, Mancuso's double, code named Antonio, was performing as Donny Mancuso expected.

He was not allowed to take calls, he was not allowed to speak to the organization. He was there to be seen. Project the image, 'business as usual.'

But the FBI wasn't seeing business as usual. Supervisory Special Agent Joseph Russo oversaw the ongoing Mancuso investigation with ten special agents in his investigative unit. Russo was chosen by the New York SAC because of his business background and financial acumen. While he may not have Mancuso's IQ, his investigative powers were keen. He had proven himself an able leader and formidable opponent. When the SAC placed him in charge of the Mancuso investigation, his orders had been simple: Learn his methods well enough to anticipate his moves. Get there before he does. Gather enough evidence to bring him down.

Russo held a weekly meeting with his team to share information and compare notes on movement within Mancuso's organization. They looked for changes in patterns, talk on the street, activity of capos and soldiers—anything and everything that could help predict Mancuso's plans. After four years of studying his methods and markets, Russo was gaining on Mancuso. He understood Mancuso's character—or lack of it. He knew his preferences of food, women, wine, clothing, drugs, and his methods of promoting, demoting, and eliminating the competition. The competition was anyone or anything that stood in his way. Through informants, surveillance, and infiltration, Russo's team had picked up enough information on Mancuso's business to know where he was operating and what he was into.

But something was up. Donny Mancuso was in New York City but no longer a part of it. The word on the street was Mancuso was busy planning something big. Russo had seen Mancuso go into strategy session-mode before, even month-long meetings, and Mancuso was always vocal, barking orders, demanding results. But now? Nothing.

It might sound funny, going to the boss with suspicions due to 'nothing,' but Joe had been at this for four years. No one was going to convince him Adonis Antonio Mancuso was in deep strategy sessions with zero action as a result—that was unprecedented. From what he could see, Mancuso went to the office and went home. His inactivity was significant enough to be actionable.

Joe reached out to New York SAC Charles Langford to make his case. Langford was out when Russo called but Joe was able to get on his schedule for a video call later that afternoon. It couldn't be soon enough.

"MR. LANGFORD, GOOD afternoon, sir!"

"Joe, how are you? How's the family?"

"We're all good, sir, thank you for asking. How about you?"

"Oh, the kids are all out of the house now so Millie and I are on the move, traveling as my work will allow and seeing the sites! And speaking of being on the move, what's happening with our resident thug? How's the Mancuso investigation coming? Four years now, correct?"

"Yes, sir, four long years. But I think it's starting to pay off."

"That would be great if true. Mancuso is one sharp crook. I'd like nothing better than to get this guy off the street. His footprints and fingerprints are all over New York City's corruption. You got something for me?"

"Yes, sir. I believe we have some significant movement in the Mancuso organization—he's doing absolutely nothing, sir."

"Excuse me?"

"Sir, as you said, I've been monitoring Mancuso for four years now. I know how he conducts business. I know how he operates. I know how he plans, plots, and plays. There's been a radical departure from his normal SOP. Something big is up and I believe this is actionable."

"Explain."

"About three to four weeks ago, things changed. Maybe I should say Mancuso changed. We can see he goes to his office every morning, he goes home every night, but there's nothing—absolutely nothing—of the usual activity. He no longer holds meetings—though that's the constant reason we hear he's unavailable. He takes no phone calls. He no longer goes out on the town. He has no visitors. He sees only his two bodyguards, Frank Caputo and Tony Zucca, and they never leave his side. We're not certain but it appears they're fielding all his calls. It's as if the guy is dead yet he's sitting right there in his office, doing nothing while his bodyguards act as a wall around him."

"Why do you believe his bodyguards field all his calls? Do you already have a tap?"

"No, sir, this is informant information only. And there's another thing. The bodyguards have lunch brought in, but it's always lunch for two, never three."

"Has he started bringing his own lunch? Maybe he's fasting through lunch."

"Not his style, sir. Mancuso is very picky and has his own favorite foods. It's been that way for the four years I've been monitoring him. He always orders from the same restaurants, most likely because he owns them, and trusts the food—though his bodyguards always taste-test his food. But that doesn't happen anymore because he's not eating. The few times the bodyguards had dinner brought to his residence, it's been the same thing. Always for two. And another thing. I know this is going to sound really weird, but Mancuso has *stopped* going to the restroom and he never consumes any liquid."

"Run that by me again."

"From what we can see through his office windows, Mancuso never gets up to go to the restroom. And the window blinds are always open. Before they were always kept closed. It's like they want us to see Mancuso. So now we can see that he sits at his desk all day long. While we don't have perfect field of vision, from what we can see he does not eat, he does not drink, and he never, ever gets up to go to the restroom!"

"That's impossible! And none of this makes sense. Why would the bodyguards want you to see all of these changes?"

"That's another point. I believe their goal to prove to us that Mancuso is still here is so important, they're overlooking the obvious."

"Joe, how can these lieutenants of Mancuso not notice that he's not using the restroom, and not eating or drinking? The only way they could not notice such behavior is if they already are expecting it. And that's just not human!"

"As I said, they seem to overlook the obvious. I'd like to open a predicated investigation under DIOG guidelines, based upon information indicative of possible criminal activity. I'd like your authorization to deploy consensual monitoring of communications and undercover operations."

"Joe, the DIOG gives us broad latitude, but I need to know what you're after, especially in monitoring and undercover. I would never go before a committee and tell them we're surveilling a mafia boss because he quit going to the can!"

"I understand sir, but I've given you more to go on than that. For all practical purposes he's out of circulation. We can't see him at home, but a man who never drinks, eats, or goes to the restroom over an entire workday is sick. Even if it means Mancuso is wearing a catheter—that would indicate a medical condition in a high-profile target—it's another good reason to surveil. Sir, I need to hear and see inside Mancuso's office. I need to know why he's gone into hiding, why he has become reclusive. If he's sick or dying, that becomes an issue of crime family succession and power struggle."

Joe made his case. He sat looking at his boss, knowing he was weighing the evidence. The Special Agent in Charge has great latitude for such investigations. The 'Domestic Investigations Operations Guidelines,' or DIOG, written in 2008 by the FBI pursuant to new regulations for domestic investigations, and issued by the United States Attorney General, gave the SAC authority to begin such surveillance. This includes surveillance cameras and monitoring devices. But Russo knew these were subject to legal review and the SAC would be held accountable by headquarters.

"Okay, Joe, you've got your investigation. But you're on a short leash with this. I want a report back from you within two weeks. I want to keep this under the one-month limit so it doesn't end up in Washington. Understood?"

"Absolutely, sir, and thank you for your confidence."

"You've got it, Joe. Either bring me proof so we can nail this devil or shut it down."

"Yes, sir!"

"Oh, and Joe, it won't take you two weeks to see if this guy really isn't frequenting the restroom. If you have conclusive proof of such a medical condition, I want to know within a week of video surveillance. Such a medical condition could indicate end-of-life."

"You'll have it, sir."

15

F BI SURVEILLANCE EQUIPMENT is unparalleled in effectiveness, and Joe Russo requisitioned every device available. He didn't know yet what he needed, but he wanted it all at his disposal—blanket coverage of Mancuso's offices as quickly as possible.

When he took the Mancuso assignment four years previously, Russo had hand-selected three of the most talented surveillance doyens in the Bureau. Mark "Fitzy" Fitzsimmons, Will Claridge, and Frederick Wong had built a reputation for surveillance expertise. They would personally oversee equipment selection and placement. They would divide the camera angles among them, each monitoring separate areas of expected activity—except Mancuso's desk and his office sitting area. They agreed to mutually monitor those two areas, anticipating the highest level of activity there.

Agent Frederick Wong instituted remote access searches and network investigative techniques to surveil Mancuso's computers and cellular devices. He assigned additional team members to network monitoring. But Russo wasn't betting on email traffic, cell calls, or texting. He had to hear what was going on between Frank, Tony, and Mancuso, and observe the dynamics of their interactions. The day it all came online, Russo and his team were in front of their panels long before the sun rose over Manhattan.

"Mr. Russo, here they come. Mancuso's limousine just arrived," said Fitzy. The agents all grabbed their coffees and launched the recording.

"Okay everyone," Joe said, "quiet down, strap in, and focus. We've only got two weeks. I need answers. I need evidence!"

Russo was able to muster at least half a smile. He felt tense but his team knew their craft. The surveillance cameras were capturing every workable inch of the Mancuso office with complete clarity, full color—no blur, no glare—and closeups that would make a neutron microscope jealous. Agent Will Claridge promised audio so clear you could hear a feather land on carpet. They had no problem hearing the three getting off the elevator and walking down the hallway to the office door.

"Okay, Antonio, take your seat and pretend to do something," they all heard Frank Caputo say.

"*Antonio? Who is Antonio?*" Agent Fred Wong asked.

"That's Donny Mancuso's middle name," Russo answered. "But there's no way under heaven Donny Mancuso would allow a bodyguard to address him like that! That must be code for something or someone else."

"Who else would the name *Antonio* apply to—as a code?" asked Wong.

"I don't know. It would be quite a coincidence—someone else in the organization having Mancuso's middle name. Unless, as I said, it's code for something else. Just let it play, Fred. Stay focused."

Joe Russo could feel his blood pressure rising with his adrenaline. What a way to start their surveillance! *Who or what did Frank mean by 'Antonio'?* No one spoke to Donny Mancuso that way—not for long—telling him to pretend to do something? But Mancuso did seem different. Maybe he really was sick. Time would tell.

Surveillance continued for three straight hours. Phone calls came in. Frank took notes, told the caller Mancuso was in a meeting but would respond ASAP—all while Donny Mancuso sat at his desk going through office files. File after file. He read on for more than three hours without taking a phone call or speaking a word to Frank or Tony.

"What's going on here, Mr. Russo?" Fitzy asked in frustration. "This doesn't make sense! We've surveilled Mancuso for four years and I've never seen anything like this. Phone calls come in, but he never speaks to anyone. He just sits there and reads. Not even a condescending comment to his fat-boy bodyguards? This is downright spooky. It's like these guys have Mancuso under house arrest. Is that possible—could this be some sort of coup?"

"That's a possibility, Fitzy. But we've not had a hint of rebellion from any of our informants. This is the darndest thing I've ever seen. Nothing's happening—but it's the biggest *nothing* I've seen in four years!"

"We've never heard his bodyguards popping off to him like that!" said agent Wong. "No way. The Mancuso we've known for four years would've cut him off at the knees."

"Okay, so nothing's happening," said Will Claridge. "What if we make something happen?"

"What you thinking, Will?" Joe asked.

"What if we send an agent in as a delivery guy? We'll give him a personal package requiring a signature from Donny Mancuso. We have the agent engage Mancuso. Ask him something that requires an answer, insult his bodyguards, spill coffee on Mancuso—anything to get him to speak, to react. We need to know what's up with this guy!"

"Good suggestion, Will, keep those coming. But I'm inclined to wait. We can't afford the slightest chance of tipping our hand. Too much is at stake. It's only been a few hours. Hang in there. Something will break."

TWO MORE HOURS PASSED, and the noon hour approached. It was Frank Caputo that spoke up.

"I'm getting hungry, Tony, how 'bout you?"

"Yea, me too. What do you want? Why don't you get us a couple of corned beefs on rye from Katz's Deli?"

"Okay. You want potato salad or slaw—and what to drink?"

"I'll do slaw. And just bottled water. Gotta cut down on the sugar. Too many sodas lately."

JOE AND HIS AGENTS waited.

"And—what about your boss!" Fitzy yelled at the monitor. The agents watched Frank grab the phone on Donny's desk and place the call to the deli. Not a word to Mancuso. Not a word from Mancuso.

"Okay, that's it!" said Fitzy. "Sir, this can't be happening. Mancuso hasn't moved from his desk. And it's no lunch, they don't even bother to ask him. Are we supposed to believe this?"

"Something is definitely wrong, Fitzy, just hang on. Something's about to break—I can feel it," Russo said.

WHILE FRANK WAS PLACING the order, Tony went to the restroom.

Mancuso had a private restroom, a lavish marble and chrome facility with shower, sauna, hot tub, even a pool table. No one was allowed in there—unless it was one of the ladies he was entertaining. But here was Tony, going into Donny's private facilities and Mancuso said nothing. As Tony was coming out, Frank hung up the phone.

"Okay, they'll be here in about forty-five minutes. My turn to trash the Mancuso can!"

Mancuso placed a document he'd been reading onto the desk and turned to the computer. He began typing on the keyboard. Immediately Frank spoke up.

"Hey, Antonio, what are you doing on the computer?"

"I'm doing some reading, that's all."

"Then why are you typing on Mancuso's computer?"

"I'm doing some research. Is that okay?"

"Well … just stay off the email, okay?"

"Okay," said Antonio as he continued to type.

"WHAT!" SAID WONG. "SO now Frank is ordering Mancuso to stay off his own computer? No way!"

"And," said Fitzy, "he called him Antonio—that's no code word, Mr. Russo. He's calling Donny Mancuso by his middle name!"

"And," Will added, "before that, Frank said it was his turn in Mancuso's can—like Mancuso isn't there—but he's sitting at his desk!"

"I heard the conversation, guys. That's not Adonis Mancuso—that's apparent. Frank asked this 'Antonio' what he was doing on Mancuso's computer. Clearly he's a dead ringer for Mancuso. They either found his double or this guy's had plastic surgery! But that's not Mancuso. Will, I need to see what this fake-Mancuso is typing. Capture that, please."

"I'm on it, boss." Will Claridge zoomed in on Mancuso's computer screen. "Okay, I've got it. Mancuso is pulling up files on … himself—specifically, he's looking through the spread that Newsweek did on him about ten years ago."

"Why would he be reading a ten-year-old article about himself?" asked Fitzy.

"Gentlemen, the answer is staring you in the face," said Russo. "Fred, we are getting every bit of this on tape, correct?"

"Yes, sir, Mr. Russo! Well, not tape. I've got it recording on two different mirrored hard drives. This evidence isn't going anywhere!"

"Okay, so what's the answer, Mr. Russo?" asked Frederick Wong. "We've monitored Mancuso for four years. We know what he looks like, sounds like, his mannerisms—*that's him!*"

"He doesn't sound *totally* like Donny Mancuso, does he, Fred?"

"Yes, sir, he sounds exactly like Donny Mancuso," Wong responded.

"I'm not talking about the tone of his voice, Fred, but his responses—the attitude we're seeing. Frank told Antonio to stay off his own email, and Mancuso responded 'okay.' You telling me that's the real Adonis Mancuso? They go into his restroom that's off limits to everyone. Frank kicks off the day by calling him Antonio and telling him to look like he's doing something. Do any of you still believe this is the real Donny Mancuso?"

"Okay," responded Wong. "So why is this guy reading a ten-year-old article about Mancuso?"

Joe Russo held up his smartphone. "This guy is learning all he can about Mancuso. And the explanation was sent out by Washington a few weeks ago. This 'person' isn't a person at all."

"Sir?" asked Wong.

"You guys remember hearing something about one of the Directors traveling from Washington to California several times because of those cloned actors in Hollywood? Clark Gable and a couple of others."

"Yes, sir, I remember reading about it in the interoffice news," said Will, "but they're not clones. The article said they are *parahumans*."

"Pair of what?" asked Fitzy.

"Parahumans," said Will. "If you're right, Mr. Russo, that could explain why *this* Mancuso–or Antonio–is so subservient. A parahuman does what he's told to do."

"Yeah, and it explains why these thugs feel free to speak to Mancuso's clone—or parahuman—as they do," said Fitzy. "But then the big question is, what happened to the real Donny Mancuso?"

"Exactly," Russo responded. "I've got the interoffice news article about the three Hollywood parahumans pulled up on my phone. Executive Assistant Director Michael Benchley, head of the Science and Technology branch, has been overseeing the investigation personally. He might know how we can positively ID a parahuman. But as you asked, Fitzy, where's the real Mancuso? Is he dead? If so, this could be the other Dons using a parahuman to hide his death and keep the organization going."

"Sir, maybe there's another possibility," said Fitzy. "What if this is another brilliant move by Mancuso to throw us off his trail? What if he's alive and at work somewhere else—while we think he's here in New York?"

They all looked at Fitzy and then turned to Russo. It was a seminal moment.

"Fitzy, you are brilliant! Any other pearls of wisdom?" Russo asked with a smile.

Fitzsimmons smiled. "Sir, did you say an Executive Assistant Director is involved? If it's a California issue, the SAC in LA should handle it. At the risk of sounding clichéd, why is the Bureau making a *federal* case out of the parahumans in Los Angeles?"

The agents all chuckled. "That's pretty good, Fitzy!" replied Will.

"Another excellent point. What would cause an Executive Assistant Director to take charge of an LA matter? The Bureau must see this as a national security risk—and I think we're looking at the proof they are right."

"How would Mancuso get a parahuman created so quickly?" asked Fred Wong. "I mean, how did he even know what Hollywood had done?"

"What's 'quick,' Fred? We don't know how long this parahuman has been in existence. We only know we're just finding out about it. And you're assuming this parahuman is somehow tied into those in Hollywood. We don't know that. This technology could be spreading and, again, we're just finding the proof of it. I want you guys to remain on surveillance. There could be a lot more surprises to come. I'm going to reach out to Director Benchley and see what I can learn. If this is a parahuman, and Mancuso's using it to keep us thinking he's in New York City, we need to find out where he is—fast. Fred, do we have anything from Mancuso's email?"

"Yes, sir, and now that we know there may be a parahuman involved, his email traffic is starting to make sense."

"What do you mean?"

"Sir, there's been heavy email traffic requesting his assistance with Lucchese family business. Those emails have all been answered–but this morning we heard Frank order Antonio to stay off Mancuso's computer. So, it's clear that Antonio isn't the one handling the email responses. That could only mean Mancuso–or maybe someone else–is handling email from some other location than this office we're surveilling. I've tried getting a digital signature on where Mancuso's responses are originating but the location is being blocked."

"Powerful information, Fred. But where's Mancuso? Could he be dead or is he somewhere working on the biggest crime event of his career? And who made his parahuman? We need answers, gentlemen! I'll see if Director Benchley can help us."

MANCUSO WAS MOVING on his Bolivian campaign like a blitzkrieg.

He negotiated a private lunch with the Interior Minister and the National Police Commander, telling them his company was willing to work with the Bolivian government in a big way to begin importing gold and precious substances. He invited them to a private luncheon at the Hotel Grande—lavish, extravagant, a signature Mancuso event. And having learned that lunch in Bolivia is the most important meal of the day, typically lasting from noon until 3:00 PM, Donny determined to make this the most impressive lunch in which these Bolivian bureaucrats had ever indulged. He knew how to impress.

The day of the luncheon, police officers secured the hotel then escorted the Interior Minister and Police Commander to the meeting room. Once safely behind closed doors, heavily armed officers were posted at all entrances. As the two guests removed their top coats in the vestibule, a white gloved maître d' quickly approached, brandishing a silver tray of delicate hors d'oeuvres, a colorful variety of canapes and candied flowers.

A smiling Adonis Mancuso strode casually toward them. Wearing a blue blazer, open collar shirt, ascot with diamond stickpin, tan slacks, penny loafers, and argyle socks, he was more a throwback to JFK than a businessman seeking Bolivian favors. In the hands of Fifth Avenue haberdashers, he became the picture of American casual.

"Minister Ramos, Commander Alvarez, so nice to finally meet you! Won't you sit down, make yourself comfortable? I thought we might visit in the sitting area over brandy and Cuban cigars while our chef completes preparations for lunch."

Donny led them to an alcove adjacent to the dining area and bar. The sitting area was warm, inviting, and decidedly masculine.

Wood vaulted ceiling, river rock fireplace and chimney with a crackling cedar log fire, it had a hunting lodge feel. A thickly cushioned hair-on cowhide couch, two oversized gaucho wingback chairs, and an impala skin rug on the floor with a glass and wrought iron coffee table. As the men selected their seats, Donny opened the box of Cuban *Cohiba Medio Siglo* cigars. The aroma infused the alcove. Donny held the open box for his guests to partake of the expensive import.

"Si, thank you Mr. Mancuso," said Ricardo Ramos as he selected a cigar. As Interior Minister he was accustomed to foreigners providing him with the finer things in life, but this American came with some surprises. Police Commander Alvarez also selected a stick. Mancuso provided them with a punch cutter to open their cigar, and then a lighter. They sat across from the fireplace in this unexpected herf, enjoying the smoothness and the unusually cool draw of the cigar, as they waited for Mancuso to reveal his intentions.

The maître d' appeared again, lowering a silver tray with three glasses and a single, historic, blemished glass bottle. He sat the tray down with the greatest of care and then retreated through the door into the kitchen.

"Gentlemen, I have brought something for our first meeting that I am relatively certain neither of you have ever enjoyed before now. I was in London last year for the Sotheby's auction to make sure this unusual liqueur did not get away from me. This is 258-year-old cognac, bottled in the year 1762. I purchased it for just over one hundred and forty-four thousand dollars."

Both men struggled to sit up in the thickly cushioned seats. The look on their faces told Donny they were properly impressed.

"Señor, that is amazing!" said Commander Alvarez. "I have only heard about such things."

"Well, now you're going to experience it, my friend!" Donny carefully removed the ancient cork from the green tinted hand-blown glass bottle. The neck showed unusual scratches, one so deep it looked as if it had been deliberately etched into the glass, and a hand-inked label that had long since become unreadable. Donny could see both men were fascinated by the appearance of the bottle, so he turned the label towards them as he slowly poured a half inch of the dark amber substance into each lowball tumbler. Taking a glass in each hand, he simultaneously delivered the precious substance to both men, conveying mutual respect. Picking up his own glass, he raised it toward them.

"Gentlemen, a toast. May we enjoy a long, happy, and mutually rewarding business venture on behalf of those we serve and care most for in this life. Salud y amor y tiempo para disfrutarlo."

"Salud," came the quiet echo from both men as they sipped very slowly the costly elixir. The Commander looked at Minister Ramos with a look of satisfaction. "*Suave y delicioso!*"

Donny looked through his glass at the fireplace, the light from the flames sparkling in the amber liquid, as he said, "This is only the second time I have sipped this ancient cognac. It stirs me with emotion as I realize the year this cognac was bottled, the father of my country, George Washington, was just thirty years old!"

Both men nodded in respect to the name of Washington. Then the minister spoke.

"And here, in La Paz, at that time the Inca Indians attacked this city, attempting to reestablish the Incan empire in the city now controlled by Spaniards. The uprising was put down and their leaders executed. A very long time ago, amigo."

Donny Mancuso felt he had their attention and their interest. He sat back in his leather chair, cradled his glass and cigar, and launched the first salvo.

"Gentlemen let me begin by thanking you for taking time from your obviously busy schedules to meet with me. As President of New York GAPS, my interest is finding the most beautiful, the most exquisite gold and precious substances that your nation has to offer. I find it amazing and unfortunate that the United States, in particular my native New York City, has never known the benefit of all the precious substances that Bolivia can provide."

Donny took a deep draw on his Cuban and, as his smoke mingled with his guest's in what he felt was an obvious omen of collaboration, he glanced at both men—clearly waiting to hear his objectives and his offer.

"Besides your world-renowned gold, what precious substances can we work together to bring to New York and to the rest of my country?"

The minister looked at the commander and nodded. The Police Commander began.

"Mr. Mancuso, we know you are a significant leader in, how you say, organized crime in New York. This does not concern us for you are here with legitimate business offers. If that were not true, we would not be sitting here. We, too, are confronted with challenges. Our nation is assailed by the United Nations, by European and American governments, and by socialists and insurgents within our own country. But we understand that your business has in its name, 'precious substances.' Do you not call gold, in your country, 'precious metal'? Why do you then use the term 'precious substances'?"

"I can change the name if it offends you, Commander," Mancuso said. "It was easier to form the abbreviation 'GAPS.' With the words 'Gold And Precious Substances.' But I know Bolivia has many precious substances that bring a great price wherever they are imported in the world. Is this not true?"

Both men nodded as they continued to enjoy their cognac and cigar.

"I am an expert at import/export. I have the resources, the connections, and the patience to bring to my country those precious substances people want and are willing to pay well to get. As you may know, these Cuban cigars we are enjoying are not legal to sell in my country. In fact, they may never be legal, and this is purely political—a disagreement between America and Cuba. Yet it hurts my clients, denying them the simple pleasure these fine cigars bring. There are many other precious substances that my country has deemed illegal which, in moderation, bring enjoyment to life. You'll remember, a number of years ago, America did this with alcoholic beverages. They called it prohibition. And because my government does not allow certain things to be imported, I am paid well to bring in such products for people's enjoyment—but at a much higher price, of course, due to my risk and the risk to my suppliers. My customers—including many politicians—enjoy in moderation the finer things that this brief and uncertain life has to offer. Now, what can we work on together that will bring beauty and bounty to ourselves and to those that rely on us for their daily needs? What precious substances do you have that we may import for the blessing of Bolivia and our mutual profit?"

With Mancuso's persuasive manner and words, the minister was ready to speak.

"Bolivia does indeed have many precious substances, Mr. Mancuso. But, as I am sure you know, my government needs outside financial assistance from Europe and America to help prevent another uprising. Many of our people live in poverty as they await this outside help for promises of investment in their farming. America and Great Britain want our farmers to grow crops other than the coca plant, which Interpol and your DEA are determined to crush. But this promise of help has come only a little, and for several years our farmers have lived under United Nations restrictions on coca plant production. I know that you speak of gold for importing, but it is the elevation of the human mind and spirit from our coca plant, this is the 'gold' that so many Americans desire, is it not?"

Donny Mancuso nodded. With a serious expression on his face he said as gravely as he could, "It is, Minister, it is. And I want you to know that I and my company deeply regret the poverty that your countrymen experience due to the overbearing demands of the UN, Interpol, and the DEA, and their incessant meddling with coca plant production. We can bring help to your people *right now*, help they've waited years for from these outside meddlers in your internal affairs. Perhaps that is the greatest blessing of American business. We work to make things happen quickly, where countries and governments always move slowly, subject to their own restrictions and laws—laws which are not able to help the very people the laws were meant to benefit!"

"You say you can help us now, Mr. Mancuso? How can you do this with the restrictions in place from the UN? My own country's lands are subject to satellite and drone inspection from UN observers. They force my people into poverty, forbidding them to produce a product that God gave us. For four thousand years we have used coca leaves for medicine and for our religious services. How do you plan to help us, Mr. Mancuso?"

The minister and police commander looked at Mancuso with an expression of stern determination.

Donny took a sip of his cognac and closed his eyes. He savored the flavor of the well-aged spirit and this moment that had so beautifully unfolded according to his carefully crafted plan. Of course, his posturing was intended to convey complete confidence, irrespective of the United Nations, Interpol, or the DEA.

"My friends, I have access to technology that can eliminate the threat from the air. Not destructively, but covertly, changing the pictures seen by both satellites and drones. Changing even the infrared signature of the coca plant by mirroring the signature of nearby vegetation. Your farmers will then produce to full capacity. My company will take care of finishing the coca paste and will handle all export and import needs. We will all prosper as we help your farmers to finally make a livable income." And with a sly grin on his face, Mancuso asked, "Oh—what *is* the price of your gold?"

All three men laughed heartily. Their cigars were near nubs and Donny had just refreshed their cognac when the maître d' announced, "Gentlemen, luncheon is served!"

16

THE WEEK OF THE TEHRAN ACCORDS HAD ARRIVED. Israeli President Isaac Hayut brought in a private security company to construct a safe room in the presidential home. Unlike the American White House, the Israeli president was not afforded the luxury of an underground nuclear bunker and operations center.

The safe room provided a secure location with a remote exit tunnel. This would provide time and an avenue for escape should the presidential home be attacked. President Hayut and Alfred Edersheim would enter the safe room after Benny was activated. Together, they would watch and listen through 'Benny's' eyes and ears. And from there, they could issue immediate commands to the holosapien should the situation require their intervention.

"Do you have any thoughts or concerns, Alfred, before we send Benny to Tehran?"

Alfred could see the nervousness in Isaac, and he understood. The Tehran signing was *a seminal event dependent on nascent technology being remotely utilized under extreme circumstances.* Every descriptor in that sentence sounded ominous! But Dr. Edersheim remained resolute.

"No, Isaac, I believe Benny is more than capable as your stand-in. We've tested him in multiple situations. He speaks clearly and without fear or hesitation. He will perform as you would while there. Let us commit this project to the God of Israel for His blessing and safe keeping."

"I will be glad when this is over and Benny is back home, my friend!"

"I agree, Isaac, but I do not share your worries. We are standing on the frontier of a new era in safety for political leaders, and our beloved Israel leads the way. I am more than a little excited to see this event take place!"

FIFTY-NINE-HUNDRED miles across the Atlantic, President Jon Roosevelt watched the armada of news trucks and reporters assemble outside the White House, live-streaming their message of how important, and potentially dangerous, the President's Tehran meeting would be.

Within the Oval Office, members of 'Project Rosebud' were also assembled: Joshua Sizemore, the Director of White House security, Paul 'Marty' Martin, the President's chief of staff, and Dr. Ralph Vestro, architect of 'Rosebud' the President's parahuman. These were the last hours they had together to discuss objectives, scenarios involving the foreign press, and Rosebud's interactions with foreign dignitaries. There were a plethora of security issues including a steady stream of terrorist chatter. Areas of concern were fed to Josh by sixty plus agents already on the ground in Tehran, preparing for the President's arrival. President Roosevelt felt they had discussed every potential scenario *ad nauseam*.

He was ready to end the meeting as he sat looking at his team. They waited expectantly for him to issue the final go-ahead. These three men were the only humans on the planet that knew he was about to enter the bunker, otherwise referred to as the Presidential Emergency Operation Center, or simply 'PEOC.' He would live there the next five days. Josh Sizemore asked to remain with the President in the bunker to oversee any security concerns that might arise.

"Josh, it would be unprecedented and ill-received by the press—not to mention most foreign security officials—if my senior security director was not with me in Tehran! You being there to lead the protective detail is expected. We don't need your absence for the press or foreign governments to use against us."

"Mr. President, I understand what you're saying. But the fact is I *won't* be with you! I'll be with your substitute. I understand political opinion and posturing, but I am charged with your protection, sir, and I can't very well do that halfway around the world!"

"Josh, if you're not in Tehran it could call into question the validity of the entire mission. Marty must be there for the same reason. Participants must know that we see this peace treaty as top priority. And there's the practical side of you being in Tehran. There will be almost six hundred support staff that normally travel with me—and three hundred of your agents. You'll also have the military and FBI liaisons. All of these people come under your oversight. We could have chaos in Tehran if you and Marty are not there."

"I understand, Mr. President. I don't like it. But I understand."

This meant that only Dr. Ralph Vestro would enter the bunker with the President. And up to this point, only Dr. Vestro, Josh Sizemore, Marty Martin, and the small team of scientists assembled to build the parahuman knew about the President's stand-in. The team of scientists Dr. Vestro had assembled to help him build the parahuman did not know the full scope of what was being planned. But they knew they were under the requirement of strict silence. The FBI had already begun checking on them—and were instructed to make sure the scientists knew they were checking on them—though the agents did not know why.

"Josh, you needn't worry about me in your absence. Only a few floors above me, I will have the entire White House security force, the White House Military Office, the White House medical team, and my anxious wife all quite shocked and ready to descend upon me if I were to push the button alerting them of my presence and need for their assistance. And I can promise you, of all those who would show up in my bunker, my wife would be the only one Secret Service would be forced to restrain!"

The men erupted in laughter. "I believe that, sir!" Josh chuckled.

"I only wish I could tell her and relieve her suffering."

"I'm sorry, Jon," Marty said. "I've known Deborah as long as I've known you. I know she's worried, but I have to believe she will soon feel it was all worth it."

"I pray so, Marty. How does a husband justify risking his wife's health to put his signature on a piece of paper? That's a lot to ask of any man—even the President."

"Yes, sir, it is. I'm very sorry."

Jon stood from his desk.

"Well, gentlemen, I want to thank you for the way you have comported yourselves and collaborated to prepare for this momentous occasion. This has been a herculean effort, and it would never have happened without the three of you—Ralph, you especially."

"Thank you, Mr. President. It has been my honor."

"I'm eternally grateful. There is significant risk here. We've been all over that. But the greater the potential, the greater the risk. I cannot tell you how I feel, knowing I'm sending the two of you into harm's way while I stay home in safety. I trust you both know, if there were any other way, I would not ask you to go."

"We understand, Mr. President," said Marty, "and we are thankful to be with you ... I mean ... "

"I know what you mean, Marty. You'll be with me in spirit—and I with you—while you're with Rosebud in Tehran. You are serving me faithfully by being there."

"And remember," Ralph Vestro said, "the President can hear and see you through Rosebud, so you have instant communication with the real President just by speaking to Rosebud. He can answer you through Rosebud, too, so it will be the same as having him with you—only safer."

Josh moved uncomfortably in his chair. He cleared his throat. "Josh, something on your mind?" asked the President.

"Mr. President, you were connected with Hollywood as a youth, so you know how stories come out of there, often without fact or foundation, and often just for the sake of publicity."

Josh Sizemore hesitated, and President Roosevelt could see his discomfort.

"Josh, this is no time to hold out on me. If you've got something to share, the horses are at the starting gate. Better share it now."

"Yes, sir. I'm sorry Mr. President, I just didn't want to bring up a last-minute concern that might amount to nothing. Sir, a friend of mine with the FBI was telling me about a new investigation the Bureau has undertaken in Los Angeles. You remember we discussed the fact that Hollywood had someone develop parahuman movie stars from the silver screen era—including your former friend, Jimmy Stewart."

"Yes, I remember that. It was discussed the day you introduced me to Dr. Vestro."

"Because the studio refuses to reveal the source that created these creatures, the Bureau is concerned about possible foreign involvement. But they also feel compelled to investigate the parahumans due to their recent activities. The duplicate of actor Jimmy Stewart went to Los Angeles Air Force Base, dressed in General James Stewart's uniform, requesting that he be allowed to tour a B-52 bomber. He ended up in the cockpit of a plane and, to the surprise of the pilot and crew, the parahuman successfully flew and landed the aircraft. The base commander then drove the parahuman to Mr. Stewart's former home in Beverly Hills."

"He flew the plane? That's amazing. And I was a guest in Jimmy and Gloria's home many times as a boy. And right after Gloria died. But I thought his home had been torn down."

"Yes, sir, it had been—and a new house built in its place. The parahuman James Stewart became depressed. My contact said all three of the parahumans have been going back, visiting locations from their past—or the real actor's past—and are now demanding the studio have their former spouses created for them. It seems Jimmy Stewart—I mean the parahuman—I'm sorry, sir, I don't mean this explanation to be confusing"

"That's okay, Josh," the President said with a smile, "I think we're all following you. Please continue."

"Yes, sir. It seems the parahuman Jimmy Stewart was so upset he contacted California Senator Steven Albright. He requested his help in forcing the studio to re-create his wife as a parahuman. The FBI has subpoenaed studio records and Senator Albright is preparing to have these parahuman actors give testimony before the Senate. All of this because there's concern the parahumans are suffering—they may not be emotionally stable. My obvious concern is for Rosebud."

The President turned to Ralph Vestro.

"Ralph, this certainly brings up a concern at the worst possible time. Do you have any reason to believe Rosebud could become emotionally unstable?"

"No, not at all, Mr. President. He has performed well, passing every test we gave him. You have all seen the results of the tests. I see no reason to be concerned."

"As much as I hate to do this," said Josh, "I can give you another reason for concern, Dr. Vestro. My contact at the Bureau also said their New York office is looking into possible parahuman use by one of the Sicilian crime families. They don't have conclusive proof yet, but the fact they're looking into it raises another point of concern: Mr. President, *this technology is out there.* Others have it and that could include malevolent groups. We have to consider the possibility of other parahumans being in Tehran. We're expecting our technology to go undetected while Rosebud represents you. What if other parahumans are there with malintent?"

"I'll tell you, Josh, my first reaction is if parahumans will be in Tehran with malintent, I'm thankful Rosebud is going instead of me!"

"That's a very sound response, Mr. President," Josh said.

"Ralph," the President began, "you're an expert in your field. You've traveled the world and served on various panels studying parahuman technology. Who do you know that could be involved in creating parahumans for Hollywood, in New York—maybe other places around the world?"

Ralph Vestro sat looking at the floor, rubbing his head.

"Mr. President, over the past ten years, there has been much discussion and research by the scientific community related to cloning, mRNA engineering and human enhancement. There is a large group of scientists wanting human modification. They want to try creating a superhuman."

"I'm not sure I like the sound of that, Ralph. Why would science think they could modify God's design of a human being?"

"It is fraught with danger, Mr. President. But there is a recognized genius in parahuman creation who has repeatedly stated his belief that it is morally wrong to change God's design of humans through modification. He was ridiculed, of course, but I have never seen one so brilliant that held so firmly to his beliefs. I am speaking of the scientific community, where they often crucify people of faith—forgive my choice of words, Mr. President. I know that you, too, are a man of deep religious conviction."

"That's all right, Dr. Vestro, I understood what you meant. Who is this man?"

"Dr. Alfred Gideon Edersheim in Tel Aviv. I mentioned him the first time we met. He was ahead of me in his research. But, sir, he would never have sold his technology for something as mercenary as re-creating Hollywood actors for money—and certainly not for some criminal enterprise. The only way his technology would be used for criminal purposes would be if someone stole it from him. And if that has happened—I shudder at the possibilities."

The President turned to Marty and Josh.

"Thoughts, gentlemen?"

"Sir," said Marty Martin, "I think you should consider calling this off. What you said is true, it's better Rosebud be in Tehran than you. But if Israel has this technology and someone has stolen it, we have to assume hostile nations have it, too. They could already be planning to kidnap you using a parahuman to do so. A thousand agents couldn't stop one parahuman! They might even have the means to interfere with Rosebud's operation. Or your ability to remotely control Rosebud. If they could take over the operation of your parahuman duplicate, they could cause him to say or do things as President that could be disastrous. I'm afraid the problems outweigh the benefits, Mr. President!"

"But," countered Josh, "that's an iron-clad reason for Rosebud to be in Tehran rather than the real Jon Roosevelt. If enemy nations send in their own parahuman representatives, and their intent is to take out the President and destroy the peace accords, only Rosebud has the physical strength and indestructibility to see the peace process through to success. Isn't that the President's goal here?"

Marty rose to his feet and began to pace. "But what about the issue of interference with remote operation? We don't know what we're dealing with and this is *no* place for Jon Roosevelt to be operating in the blind!"

"All right let's calm down, gentlemen," said the President. "We are not withdrawing from the peace accords. Let's take a deep breath. Marty, I appreciate your concerns for me and for our country, but these peace accords will go forward. If the United States were to withdraw at the last minute, it could send shockwaves that would not only shut down the summit but could tarnish this nation's commitment to peace for decades to come."

The President walked back to the windows overlooking the assembly of media trucks and reporters on Pennsylvania Avenue. Josh turned to look at Ralph Vestro and he could see the perspiration on the doctor's forehead. Vestro was not used to this level of politics. He looked pale.

"Gentlemen," said the President, "if Alfred Edersheim's technology has been stolen then he is also the one who can shut it down. And if what we're hearing about is not his technology, pairing his abilities with Ralph's might give us a decided advantage over those who would wish us harm. Ralph, do you think you can reach Dr. Edersheim?"

"He's disappeared from the scientific community, Mr. President. But I will certainly try."

"And what if it was not his technology that Hollywood used, Mr. President? That would mean there is another player with advanced abilities," said Marty.

"I realize that, Marty, but based on what Ralph has told us, I'm going to assume for the time being that Alfred Edersheim is our man."

"But, sir" began Marty.

"Marty, if Ralph can find a way for me to speak with Alfred Edersheim, he might be able to address the issue of hijacking a parahuman. We still don't know if that's even a concern. But I've made my decision. Rosebud will be on Air Force One bound for Tehran this evening, just as planned. I will be in the bunker with Dr. Vestro. We will monitor everything that is said through Rosebud. This will work, God willing. That is my decision."

AS THE WHEELS CAME up on Air Force One, the real President Jon Roosevelt was deep underground, in the PEOC with Dr. Ralph Vestro.

Jon sat at the computer in the command center, watching and listening to Rosebud and the presidential team around him. Josh Sizemore and Marty Martin discussed his agenda in Tehran. Military attachés reviewed international hotspots. Hospitality staff offered food and drink. All these were expected interactions with Rosebud. They occasionally asked him a few questions, which he fielded with ease. Jon muttered under his breath, "that's *verbatim* what I would have said—excellent job, Dr. Vestro." But Ralph Vestro wasn't there to hear the President. He was asleep in his quarters in the PEOC, next to the President's room, preparing for what he anticipated would be two exhausting days, constantly monitoring Rosebud. And it would all begin tomorrow, when the President landed in Tehran, culminating the following day at the signing ceremony.

As the President's plane crossed the Atlantic, attendants continued to offer the President refreshment. Rosebud would smile and decline. Marty and Josh, who remained with Rosebud throughout the flight, would occasionally remind him to go to the restroom, accept a glass of ginger ale, or eat a snack for the sake of appearances. Jon had seen and heard enough for the night. He decided he'd best get some sleep, too.

As the President climbed into bed, an emptiness climbed in with him. A hollow, sinking feeling. It told him he was sitting on the sidelines of the big game and would never have this chance again. He was here, safely tucked away—hiding—while his team, his friends, were about to enter the capital of what the year before had been the leading exporter of terror and anti-American hatred. *'You've sidelined yourself and deserted them'* played on an endless loop in his thoughts.

And just upstairs his beloved wife climbed into bed alone. Was the same enemy whispering in her ear? *'Your husband is in serious danger; you may never see him again.'* "That's a lie!" Jon whispered but he wasn't there to expose the lie. To dry her tears. He should have told her about Rosebud. He should have told her where he would be—in the safest place on the planet. There was no need for her to worry. *'What kind of husband are you? Letting her worry for five days!'* It was almost too much for him to bear. "Please God, comfort her. Help her to sleep."

AIR FORCE ONE WAS WITHIN one hour of landing at *Doshan Tapeh Air Base* in Tehran.

The captain notified the President he would be at the hanger and in front of the press by 8:30 AM local time. Air Force One was escorted by six F-35 Lightning II stealth fighter jets which joined the President's plane after it refueled at Spangdahlem Air Base in Germany.

"Well, here we go!" Marty's eyebrows were raised as he looked at Josh. "On the ground in an hour. You know, Josh, this was your idea. I think it was a good one."

"Thanks, Marty, but there's a lot of ground to cover before we get the President back on this plane tomorrow afternoon. Pomp and circumstance today, a reception tonight, signing the accords tomorrow morning then a state luncheon. Rosebud can do this. We just have to get through the next thirty-six hours."

Rosebud stepped out of the President's dressing room. He was incredible. He was Jon Roosevelt. Not a hair out of place.

A knock on the door of the President's suite was followed by the perky voice of Jennifer Barton, the President's press secretary. "Good morning, Mr. President! I need ten minutes of your time to brief you on the press conferences of the day." Josh asked her to wait just a moment. He had never felt such butterflies before.

"Are you ready to get underway, Marty?" Josh looked confident despite the butterflies. Marty detected a slight tremor in his voice. They both looked at Rosebud.

"I would say we're leaning on the Chief Executive for the next two days, Josh. Well, Mr. President, how are you feeling? Are you ready for the day's activities?"

Rosebud looked up and smiled. "Would it be out of place to say that I was *created* for this role?" Both men burst out laughing. The release of nervous energy was most welcome.

"No, Mr. President, I think that statement could not be more accurate ... or more welcomed at this point!" Marty said. Josh turned toward the door to let Jennifer Barton into the President's suite.

"Good morning, Mr. President! I trust you slept well! Are you ready to review the press itinerary for the day?"

Vivacious, professional, extremely educated but never condescending with anyone. With the ability to make the complex understandable, Jennifer Barton had proven her worth. She had been with Jon Roosevelt for two years now and she ran the media like a ringmaster.

"Good morning Jennifer! I am ready for whatever you want to throw at me. I believe I know the schedule, but we can go over the details if it will put your mind at ease."

"Yes, sir! Umm, Mr. President, your senior advisors are waiting in your office upstairs. Would you want me to go over the media blitz as we walk, or should I detail it for you here?"

"I believe we can do this as we walk. I've been accused of having trouble walking and chewing gum at the same time—let's prove the critics wrong!"

All three laughed as the President stood, donned his suit coat, and then extended his arm to Jennifer as her escort. She was impressed but also curious. She took his arm and looked at him for a few moments as he smiled back at her and then moved toward the door. She thought she had seen every mood Jon Roosevelt could exhibit. This President was about to face the press of every major country in the world, then step into what might still be a hostile region. Where was the pressure? He acted as if he hadn't a care in the world!

"Mr. President, you'll be expected to ... "

"Make a statement as soon as I descend from the aircraft. Yes, I know. I'm prepared to say, 'this is the moment the world has sought for six thousand years. We are on the precipice of a new day of world peace. But it won't be at the hands of the United Nations. It will be world leaders working together outside that building in New York, picking up the phone and calling one another, checking on each other, learning how we can help our respective citizens live better, happier lives.' That's what I intend to say to the press corps of the world, Ms. Barton."

"Mr. President, that was breathtaking! Brief and to the point, it puts this moment into perfect perspective. I am so impressed, sir!" Once again, she marveled at his level of composure.

"Well, don't go giving me too many pats on the back, Jennifer. There's a lot of ground to cover between now and the time we board this plane to go home tomorrow evening."

"Yes, sir, how right you are."

ON THE ISRAELI PRESIDENT'S Boeing 767-300ER, known as the 'Wing of Zion,' Benny, President Hayut's holosapien was preparing to land. It was arriving just minutes before Air Force One and President Roosevelt.

Benny boarded the aircraft as President Isaac Hayut, accompanied by his national security advisor, and his foreign policy and intelligence officials. Isaac Hayut and Dr. Alfred Edersheim remained in Tel Aviv, watching and listening as Benny circumnavigated his team. His performance was impressive—just as Alfred Edersheim anticipated.

The Israeli flag was placed at the end of the red carpeted walkway, the stairs were rolled into place, and President Hayat and his entourage descended the stairs and walked up to the microphones to receive the press.

"I and my countrymen are enthusiastic for these new peace accords. We are thankful for all the work that has gone into making this summit possible, and the willingness of the nations of the world to come to peace with one another at this historic moment. Many feared this was not possible. And while perspectives vary, I believe a special note of praise should go to my friend, United States President Jonathan Roosevelt, for locking arms with Israel and helping craft a treaty that all world leaders could believe in. We would not be here today if it were not for his devotion to a fair and lasting peace for all countries, for all peoples. God bless you, President Roosevelt. I will now take questions from the press."

Isaac Hayut and Alfred Edersheim, watching from the secure room, were pleased.

17

AIR FORCE ONE HAD JUST LANDED and was taxiing to the red carpet and podium prepared for President Roosevelt to address the media.

The Iranian military ground crew either did not get the message or had already forgotten. The President's security team, on the ground in Tehran for most of the week, advised Iranian ground personnel that Air Force One has its own stairs which are part of the aircraft. No foreign equipment is allowed in contact with the President's plane. As the Iranians drove the powered stairs toward Air Force One, Secret Service personnel raced forward to block their path. Iranian soldiers driving the stairs took the Secret Service action as an insult. They jumped out with hands over their heads, screaming words the agents could not understand—though their tone was unmistakable. The situation was quickly going sideways.

Sitting in the gallery watching this performance were men and women of the world press corps, now on their feet, busily snapping pictures and capturing video of the escalating altercation. Secret Service agents could see Air Force One was within two hundred yards of the red carpet and the unauthorized Iranian vehicle had to go. Tensions were rising by the second. A Secret Service supervisor radioed the Iranian director of base security. The officer arrived quickly in a government flagged vehicle, leaped out and commanded the soldiers to stand down, back away, and return the vehicle to the hangar.

Air Force One stopped, the stairs descended, the door opened, and U.S. Marines immediately took their positions at both sides of the stairs. Josh Sizemore stepped out, followed by President Jon Roosevelt, Marty Martin, and Jennifer Barton. The thirteen members of the Washington press corps who accompanied the President on Air Force One were deplaning down the ramp at the back of the aircraft. They were shuttled quickly to the press gallery as the President descended the stairs and walked with his team towards the podium.

"Good morning everyone!" Rosebud said with a smile and a cheerful tone. "Thank you all for coming out on this bright and beautiful morning. There's going to be a lot happening over the next thirty-six hours. A lot of good conversation, a lot of friendships formed, and a lot of progress made towards the ultimate goal of world peace. The signing of this peace agreement by the countries of the world is the beginning. On behalf of the people of the United States of America, I want to communicate how thankful we are for every nation and every official who worked tirelessly to make this historic moment possible. Now let me share my feelings about that agreement with you." He turned and looked at his press secretary, Jennifer Barton, and gave her a wink. "This is the moment the world has anticipated for six thousand years. We are on the precipice of a new day for world peace. But it won't be at the hands of the United Nations. It will be world leaders working together outside that building in New York, picking up the phone and calling one another, checking on each other, learning how we can help our respective citizens live better, happier lives. This will take a lot of work, working together in trust and friendship. I can tell you we are firmly committed to this work. Now, I need to get across town to a meeting and then a luncheon. My beautiful and capable press secretary, Jennifer Barton, will do her best to answer your questions."

Rosebud was escorted to his waiting limousine as Jennifer stepped up to the mic.

WORLD LEADERS CONTINUED to arrive throughout the morning at the Tehran military base. They were quickly transported to Shadihaye Zendegi Ceremonial Hall for the luncheon and opening ceremonies that followed.

This was Iran's opportunity to shine and they did not disappoint. Arriving guests were greeted by music of the Tehran Symphony Orchestra. At 10:30 AM local time, each dignitary was formally welcomed by the master of ceremonies. Speeches were heard on the value of the treaty and the promise of world peace. A separate speech was given by the British Prime Minister, the Royal Saudi Prince, the President of Russia, the President of China, the President of Iran, the President of Israel, the Chairman of the PLO, and finally, the President of the United States. The press in attendance circulated through the audience, providing streaming coverage of every angle of the event.

The luncheon which ensued was just as superb and designed to impress. The food was sumptuous, featuring traditional Persian fare. The meal began with bowls of Ghormeh Sabzi fried herb stew, followed by kabobs of beef tenderloin, filet, and lamb shank, spit-roasted over an open fire and served over saffron rice and roasted vegetables. For dessert, Bastani Sonnati saffron and rose water-infused ice cream, laced with salep extracted from wild orchids, and then topped with sliced pistachios.

Security was understandably high. And while Iran provided an imposing military presence around the gathering, soldiers in uniform were kept on the exterior of all facilities for patrol duty. Interior security was provided by plainclothes officers bearing official security badges. Metal detectors were installed on the entry doors, x-ray imaging was used on all purses and packages coming in, and the number of doors in and out were restricted. The Iranian military command requested that all security forces other than their own be kept inside the meeting facilities. Iranian troops would then regard any person on the ground after the ceremonies started as an intruder.

Josh Sizemore did not like the arrangement of having his officers restricted to inside the facilities, and he told the President so. He had his usual traveling detail of three hundred officers and there was no way he could fit all of them within the interior of the smaller, historic buildings in Tehran. And he was not going to leave the exterior of the buildings unguarded by Secret Service personnel. The President 'suggested' that this was a historic moment and that all leaders were equally safe and equally at risk. He also 'suggested' that if Josh's security team were to imply Iran's military protection was inadequate, it could destroy the atmosphere of cooperation and mutual trust that all leaders had worked so hard to establish over the past year. President Roosevelt's 'suggestions' told Josh in firm terms that he did not want to upset the Iranians.

But Josh was equally firm. He understood the President's concerns, but he quickly reminded the President that the politics of the president's safety had been tested against Secret Service judgment before. John Kennedy refused their clear warnings to his own peril. Then Josh pulled his trump card. Federal law 18 U.S.C. 3056 was passed to prevent the JFK debacle from ever happening again. It essentially forbids the President from refusing protection by the Secret Service. Josh insisted this event, historic or not, fell under that law—no matter what the Iranians, the international community, or, for that matter, the President thought.

Jon Roosevelt was a determined man, but he also recognized that Josh was right, and he swore allegiance to American law, not international law or opinion. He asked if Josh could somehow integrate members of his three hundred team members with the Iranian military. Josh promised to do what he could.

Following the luncheon, the dignitaries were treated to a concert by the Tehran Symphony Orchestra held at Vahdat Hall, then a dinner where more speeches were made, this time by nations that had not addressed the assembly during the luncheon.

After the concert, world leaders were permitted a few hours to go to their hotels, freshen up and rest a bit before the hors d'oeuvres and 'cocktail' hour, with dinner following. And though Iran is under Islamic law and, therefore, alcohol is 'haram' or illegal, a mock-cocktail hour was held with juice-based drinks and alcohol-free beers.

During the cocktail hour, the conversations were predictable for a peace summit. Topics heard around the ballroom ranged from the weather, the beautiful buildings and scenery in Tehran, the delicious and varied foods, and how economic conditions were expected to improve with the opening of borders and lowering of tariffs following the ratification of the peace treaty.

Back at the White House, the real Jon Roosevelt, with Dr. Ralph Vestro at his side, could see and hear all that was going on. They were pleased with Rosebud's handling of speeches, press conferences, and interaction with guests. He was performing perfectly.

Rosebud was sipping a pineapple and mango juice cocktail while the British Prime Minister explained his views on the peace accords. Suddenly a man of middle eastern origin grabbed the President's left arm and spun him around to face him, spilling the President's drink all over the Prime Minister.

"You—American President! Why you allow Israel to take West Bank from us? They steal my homeland! UN has no right to give land. Not UN land to give!"

Josh Sizemore was standing at the President's right side with another agent just behind him. Both of them were immediately on the assailant, one on each arm, and began to move him away from the President.

"Just a minute, Josh, let me speak with this young man. What is your name, son?"

"I am Mahmud. I Palestinian and security officer. Why you not care what happen to Palestinian people?"

"I do care, Mahmud, very much. It is why I am here—why all of us are here, ready to sign the peace agreement. Do you know what this agreement says? Do you know how it will help the Palestinian people?"

By now, the news media had gathered around the altercation, streaming the event. Chatter in the room was dying down and delegates were moving in to see what was happening. Isaac Hayut—that is 'Benny,' was now standing by the President's side, listening and focused on the young Palestinian man.

"I know, I have read it. But what about West Bank? You know it is our land!"

"I know it was your land prior to 1948 but I also know the Bible says that land belonged to Israel before that. But if you've read the peace agreement, then you know your people and the Israeli people will live side by side in the West Bank. That's what peace is all about, Mahmud. Being able to get along with people who are different from us." Mahmud started to speak but the President held up his hand and said, "Now—before you say anything else, let me ask you a question. Do you know that my country has something of value sitting on the land known as the West Bank?"

Mahmud did not respond so the President continued.

"The only United States Air Force base in that entire region of the world sits on the West Bank. Russia has air bases all over the middle east. China has a military presence there, too. Don't you see that the United States *needs* to be there to help keep the peace—the peace that is coming as a result of this new agreement? We are here to sign an agreement that protects all countries, including Palestine, Russia, China, Israel, and my country, the United States. Did you know that in my country, there are areas of land given to *your* country for your embassy building, and that no one in my country can take that land from you? We protect that land for you and your nation. With a visa you could come visit the Palestinian embassy in Washington. You could come visit our land, eat with us, play with us, and enjoy the freedom of our great country before you come back to your home in Palestine. We must learn to get along with each other, Mahmud. For seventy-five years now, people have been dying in Palestine all because of hate. This peace agreement is a promise of a new tomorrow, a time when we can live together without it mattering who lives next to us. We won't need to hate each other any longer or be suspicious of each other. Isn't that what you really want, Mahmud? That's what I want. I'd like for you to come visit me in the United States, to see what my country is really like. If I could make that happen for you, would you be my guest and come see me in the United States?"

"I would do it. But I do not have money to make such a trip," Mahmud said, looking embarrassed—but his eyes remained fixed on the President.

"I'll take care of that for you if you'll come see me."

By now, even the reporters had stopped taking notes to listen to Jon Roosevelt. They stood silently, imagining what such a world would be like. Suddenly, applause broke out as the President put his arms around Mahmud and gave him a hug. The delegates confirmed their approval with smiles, applause, and cheers. The media captured every square inch of the priceless moment. As one reporter told his streaming audience, 'This summit needed this moment. Tension turned to peace, enemy to friend.' Marty and

Josh stood by and marveled. No one else in the room of delegates knew this was not the human Jon Roosevelt.

* * *

JON ROOSEVELT, SITTING in the White House bunker, could not have been more pleased. Or more regretful that he was not there to experience this himself.

"Ralph, as we say in Texas, 'You done good!' Rosebud's interaction with that young man was totally unscripted. I am truly impressed."

"Then take a bow, Mr. President. It was your memories, your life, your heart from which Rosebud spoke. That is all he knows."

"That's very humbling. I was just feeling regret over having stayed home."

"You're there, Mr. President! Rosebud just proved that! But, sir, we need tonight to update Rosebud. I'll need to put him into *Theta* state so we can update the events of the day–things only you as the real President have encountered today. During that time, we can awaken him in the event of an emergency, but Josh Sizemore will need to alert us if there is such an event. I do not want to leave Rosebud in a state of partial update. That could leave him unprepared for tomorrow's events."

"Very well, Doctor. I'll alert Josh over secure messaging."

* * *

THE SIGNING OF THE peace accords was set for 10:30 Tehran time on Tuesday morning at the historic Golestan Palace, a five-hundred-year-old campus with seventeen extravagant buildings.

Built over a one hundred-thirty-one-year period during which Persia was ruled by the Qajar kings, they were expressions of Iranian culture, beauty, and grace. The spacious room known as 'Mirror Hall' was chosen for the signing. Glistening with thousands of mirrors from floor to ceiling, multiple crystal chandeliers illuminating the hall, and panoramic windows bringing in the brilliance of refracted sunlight, the hall was radiant. This was to be an omen for the leaders of the world's governments. A new day had dawned, a new light was shining as they took this much-vaunted step towards world peace.

Breakfast was scheduled for 8:00 AM with final speeches by key leaders from Russia, China, the PLO, the European Union, Israel, and the United States, in that order. Speeches would begin at 9:00 AM and each leader would keep remarks to ten minutes. All speeches would thus conclude by 10:00 AM and then the procession for signatures would begin, culminating by 10:30. An elevated platform was in place that ran across the north end of the hall. The speaker's podium, a beautiful, mahogany structure of several hundred pounds, sat in the middle of the platform. Rectangular tables were placed end-to-end on both sides of the podium and three chairs were set on each side, so that six seats were facing the dining area, three on each side of the podium. As each speaker concluded his or her remarks, they would take a seat on the platform. Eastern countries of Russia, China, and the PLO would sit to the right of the podium, and the Western nations of the EU, Israel, and the United States, would sit on the left side. It was meant to be a symbolic gesture of east and west coming together in a show of unity and peace.

Breakfast tables were placed in the Mirror Hall in a serpentine pattern to prevent there being a single aisle. This would slow down foot traffic, limiting the speed at which a would-be assailant could move through the crowd toward the speaker's platform. Each nation's security personnel, including the President's Secret Service team, lined the perimeter of the great hall. Josh Sizemore sat at the President's table, along with Marty Martin, Dr. Van Sullivan, the President's physician from Air Force One, and press secretary Jennifer Barton.

Breakfast was served to each table from silver plated service trolleys, wheeled from table to table. The decision to use trolleys was to prevent potential dropping of butlers' trays laden with food. Each trolley was marked with the guest's name so their own security detail could inspect the cart and its contents. The Secret Service chose to inspect *each* trolley and the President's food taster sampled each item placed in his trolley. Then, a detail of agents remained with the line of trolleys waiting to move into the Mirror Hall from the kitchen.

The President of Russia gave an impassioned speech about the need for peace in a war-torn region that had seen no rest for thousands of years. China's President spoke of the opportunities for each nation to prosper once money could be spent on people's needs rather than senseless wars and the use of military for policing actions. The PLO prime minister spoke of this long-awaited day for his people to settle in peace once again on land they held sacred. Each of the three speakers took their seat on the right side of the podium as they finished their remarks. The British Prime Minister spoke of Europe's great desire for peace that had eluded their continent since World War II.

When Benny rose to speak, the real Isaac Hayut sat in Tel Aviv with his friend, Dr. Alfred Edersheim, listening with satisfaction as Benny flawlessly delivered the speech prepared for the occasion by Isaac himself. Benny spoke of a world where no one need fear a lack of food, shelter, or clothing. He spoke of freedom to speak one's opinion in a world of acceptance, free from hate.

As Isaac Hayut stepped back from the podium, and Jon Roosevelt climbed the stairs to the podium, something unexpected happened. Isaac Hayut and Alfred Edersheim sitting in Tel Aviv, and Jon Roosevelt and Ralph Vestro sitting in Washington, saw their nation's leaders embrace. This event was not scripted by Dr. Edersheim or Dr. Vestro.

"WHAT JUST HAPPENED, Dr. Vestro?" the President asked.

"I don't know ... I didn't place that thought into Rosebud! But he didn't do anything wrong. Is that what you would have done, Mr. President?"

The President sat thinking for a moment. "I honestly can't say. I have spoken with Isaac Hayut many times. We have shared several meals together. But I have never embraced him. What would make Rosebud do this?"

"Mr. President, this is only a guess on my part. I have nothing to go on but intuition. Thinking involves feeling. There is no way around that. You know that when you feel sad or you feel happy, your actions often match that mood. I would say Rosebud is, for lack of a better term, 'happy.'"

"Happy, Ralph?"

"Yes, sir, perhaps he is happy for the same reason you are. Peace is finally within our reach."

"Are you saying this parahuman has feelings, Ralph?"

"Mr. President, I can only say that he is reacting as he perceives you would. That is my only explanation."

IN TEL AVIV, ISAAC Hayut was asking Alfred Edersheim a similar question. "Alfred, what would cause Benny to give a speech just as I would give it, then turn to a dignitary as important as the

President of the United States, and think he has the freedom to embrace him? Does this bold move not concern you?"

"It concerns me, Isaac, but not so much as an error in his programming. It concerns me that he would make such a move where you would remain distant from a man who has helped protect our nation so many times by defending us in his Congress and before the world."

"What are you saying, my friend? Do you see my political decorum as cold or unfriendly?"

"No, Isaac, I am saying that Benny is displaying emotion and that is not something I programmed him to do—he is displaying a sentiment of gratefulness he could only have derived from your thoughts, your lifetime of collective memories. I am saying he is making a gesture you *should* have made before now, but something in your human makeup has held you back. Fear of rejection, fear of being seen as pandering to a powerful political figure, fear the world might accuse you of patronizing this man to get what you need. Fears are not something Benny has so they cannot hold him back. He has no fear of death because he cannot die. He has no fear of what others think. He only knows your history, when and why you laughed or cried. He is applying your memories, including your emotions, and this is the result."

AS THE ROOM OF WORLD leaders watched Isaac Hayut and Jon Roosevelt embrace, they applauded spontaneously.

The night before, they had seen Jon Roosevelt care for a young Palestinian who accosted him. Now they saw him embrace a man who, politically, could do very little for him. Jon Roosevelt's heart was on display for the world to see. He was a loving, caring man who reached out to help those with nothing to give back to him.

The leaders liked what they saw. They just did not know this was a parahuman and not the real Jon Roosevelt.

As Rosebud stepped to the podium, Benny took the seat immediately beside the podium and the President. Rosebud did not need any notes, he did not request a teleprompter. The speech that President Roosevelt gave him, and Ralph Vestro placed into his artificial intelligence, was firmly in place for this event. Unlike the speakers who came before him, his eyes never left the leaders sitting in the audience.

"Ladies and gentlemen, my friends and fellow leaders. I wonder if we see ourselves for what we truly are?"

"WHAT IS HE DOING, RALPH?" Jon Roosevelt asked, "this is not the speech we gave him!"

"I will send a message to Rosebud—give me a moment."

Rosebud continued to speak.

"Who are we? We are leaders, yes, but we are servants of the people who sent us here–our citizenry, those who voted for us—and even those who did *not* vote for us!"

The assembled politicians laughed at this and began to nod in affirmation.

"The White House is not my home. It belongs to the American people. Number Ten Downing Street in London, the Kremlin in Moscow, Zhongnanhai in Beijing—these do not belong to us. They belong to the people who built them, the people who paid for them, often with their blood. We are servants. And we lead by living out a life of service. I am a servant, and it is all that I truly want. Whether I'm serving my wife, my children, the American citizens, my God, or you, my friends, that is what gives me purpose. It gives my life meaning. It makes me happy. I exist to serve, to love, to help those who have trouble helping themselves. And when we stop doing that, or—God help us—if we *never* learn to live such a life, then our purpose in this life is over."

The audience rose to their feet, responding with thunderous applause. Rosebud tried to speak further but the audience continued to applaud. He waited and smiled.

BACK AT THE WHITE HOUSE bunker, Jon Roosevelt motioned for Ralph Vestro to wait.

"Ralph don't send that command to Rosebud. He has delivered a better message than I wrote for him. I don't understand how this has happened—how he came up with this on his own. What a passionate plea he has given. He moved world leaders, Ralph. Better than I could have. How did this happen?"

AS ROSEBUD WAITED FOR the applause to die down, a waiter pushing a trolley stopped just off to the President's left and was applauding, too. Then he lifted the lid on the trolley, shoved his right hand down into the mound of cold fruit salad, and pulled out a plastic polymer handgun. He moved so fast that security did not have time to react before he fired.

The first bullet struck the President on the left side of his head and the force drove him backward from the podium. Immediately, Isaac Hayut stood up and moved between the shooter and his friend, Jon Roosevelt. The second bullet struck Isaac Hayut directly in the forehead and he went stumbling backward and off the platform, landing next to the President. The next six shots came from the handgun of Josh Sizemore, who had leaped from the President's table and was running toward the shooter at full speed as he fired. He fixed the red dot from his Glock 19 on the assailant's chest and began emptying the clip. Six shots were enough. The shooter was slammed into and on top of the trolley. The assailant crumpled, spilling the trolley's contents on the ancient Persian rug. It was hard to tell what was fruit salad and what were parts of the disfigured, lifeless shooter.

The news media caught the shooting live on the internet. Back at the White House, Deborah Roosevelt, the President's wife, had just hit the floor. Secret Service were calling for the White House medical team while they positioned her on her left side and tried to revive her.

Secret Service and Israeli Shin Bet agents appeared from every corner. Dr. Van Sullivan, who had accompanied the President on Air Force One, pushed his way through the crowd and was kneeling beside both presidents. Neither leader was moving.

The left side of Jon Roosevelt's head was a matted mess of blood and hair. Isaac Hayut's forehead was bleeding profusely. The forehead appeared depressed, the skull may have opened, but there was so much blood and tissue damage the doctor could not be sure. Dr. Sullivan was about to cut Jon Roosevelt's hair away from the wound for a closer look when the President's eyes opened.

"No need to trouble yourself, Doctor. I am all right. You'd better see to my friend, President Hayut."

The doctor was so stunned that he lost his balance, being on one knee, and fell onto his buttocks. Secret Service agents began helping him up as the stunned doctor replied, "Mr. President—sir—are you all right?"

"Yes, doctor, I am all right. How is Isaac Hayut?"

By now, the President rolled over onto his left side, pushed himself up with his left elbow, and then sat up. He turned to Isaac Hayut, who had opened his eyes.

"I am okay, President Roosevelt. I am okay."

The Secret Service and Shin Bet had formed a perimeter around the two fallen leaders and the doctor. He had his bag open and had put on gloves. He withdrew forceps and a probe when the President responded, "Please, Dr. Sullivan, just a bandage. That's all that is needed."

"Mr. President, I must examine your wound! Your scalp is open and bleeding. There could be damage that may not show up for several hours. Possible internal bleeding and ... "

"Doctor, I assure you, I am all right as you can see. Please, just a bandage so these good people don't have to look at all this mess."

The doctor was still in a state of shock. He knew what he had seen. This wound was not unlike the wound on John Kennedy from a similar attack. If the bullet had only grazed the President's head, there would not be what resembled skeletal material protruding just above the President's left ear. He needed a better look.

Josh Sizemore was kneeling over the shooter when his men began to surround him. Josh looked up at them and said, "Get this crowd under control! Get up to the microphone and let them know there is no further danger. We don't need people crushed in a stampede!"

"Yes, sir," they responded. The room was a mass of screaming, shouting, and people knocking over chairs and each other as they moved towards the limited exits.

Josh gave instructions for his agents to bag the weapon and not to allow anyone to remove the body.

"I want the body onboard Air Force One so Dr. Sullivan can autopsy him. I want to know who this guy is, where he's from, why he did it. Lock this crime scene down immediately, understand?"

Josh moved quickly through the crowd towards the President. He breathed a sigh of relief that his idea had prevailed, and the real Jon Roosevelt was safely at home. When he got past the perimeter of his men and the Israelis, he stood next to Dr. Sullivan. Sullivan was pale as milk. He was back on one knee, staring at the President who was chatting with Isaac Hayut—both of them bloody but fully responsive. Josh was more concerned for the doctor than for Rosebud. Dr. Sullivan was teetering and his hands were shaking. Josh knelt in front of him.

"Doctor, are you okay? Answer me, are you okay?"

"Yes, yes. I'm okay. I'm not sure. What's happening here?"

"Doctor Sullivan, I need you to look at me."

Sullivan's face was contorted. Josh grabbed him by both shoulders and began to speak in a firm but steady tone.

"Doctor, don't you think we'd better get the President stabilized and back to Air Force One to make sure of his well being?"

"Stabilized? Did you say stabilized? *Look at him! He's sitting up and talking like nothing happened!*"

"Calm down doctor, please."

"What's going on here, Agent Sizemore? You act as if you expected to find the President unharmed—after he took a bullet to the head! We all saw it from the front row table where we were sitting. No one could have survived that shot. What's happening?"

"Doctor, please listen to me. Lower your voice. Lower it right now. I will explain everything to you once we're aboard Air Force One. For now, please bandage the President's head and just stay with me. Do you understand? We need to get him back aboard his plane and into safety."

The doctor nodded.

"No Josh."

Josh turned around. The President was still sitting on the floor next to Isaac Hayut.

"I am not going back to my plane yet. That agreement is going to be signed. Doctor, I need you to bandage my head. We are going to make a success out of this mess right now. Josh, please get the people calmed down and let them know that President Hayut and I are doing well. We are ready to sign the agreement."

With that, Rosebud turned to Benny and asked, "Isaac, are you able to stand? Are you able to sign the agreement with me?"

"Yes, yes, my friend. We cannot allow this one person to keep peace from the whole world. Could your doctor place a bandage over my wound, as well?"

"I think the United States can spare a bandage and the services of my doctor—at least this one time!" Both men chuckled as Dr. Sullivan stared in disbelief. He knelt again next to them.

"Please, both of you remain right where you are. I'll bandage you, then these agents can help you to your feet. I'm not sure *I'll* be able to stand after this. I may need a gurney to get back to the plane!" Both presidents laughed.

Josh was at the microphone. His lieutenant had attempted to bring order, but it was Josh's words that brought the crowd back together.

"Ladies and gentlemen, please, sit down. Both the President of the United States and the President of Israel are fine. They received only flesh wounds. The doctor is bandaging them, then they will be ready to sign the peace agreement in a few minutes."

Russian, Chinese, and British security had already ushered their leaders toward a safe room in the palace. Josh radioed the Iranian security commander. The threat had been neutralized and both leaders received only flesh wounds. Security officers from all three nations came to verify the safety of the situation, then notified their leaders.

Within thirty minutes the peace document was signed. Leaders from each country came by to express their thanks and well wishes for President Hayut and President Roosevelt. The news media, present when the shots were fired, had pushed the story and video out on the internet. The media around the world was buzzing about the 'miracle in Tehran.'

Shin Bet agents already had President Hayut into his limousine and on his way to his aircraft. The three hundred Secret Service and FBI agents present formed a human wall around the President, on both sides of the walkway to the front door of the Palace, and out the door to the waiting bulletproof limousine. Dr. Sullivan had a wheelchair brought in for the President. He was refusing it when Josh whispered to Rosebud that it might be wise for him to accept the offer.

IN THE WHITE HOUSE bunker, Jon Roosevelt and Ralph Vestro could see and hear everything that had happened. The mission was a complete success—except for Deborah.

"Doctor, my heart breaks for my wife. She saw me shot, then she saw me sign the agreement. She must be beside herself."

"Mr. President, you said you told her that you were working on something that might keep you out of Tehran. Is there a chance she now suspects that was not you that was shot? Walking away from such an event certainly would be a miracle."

"That's possible, but I can't stand the thought of her suffering through this."

"Mr. President, if you show yourself outside of this bunker before Rosebud is put away, the world will know there are two of you. I don't know what that will mean but it is something you *will* be dealing with if the White House staff sees you now. Of that I am certain."

The President stood up from the desk where he had been monitoring Rosebud and began to pace. He turned abruptly to face Dr. Vestro.

"Ralph, I'm going to message Josh Sizemore. He will have my wife brought to the PEOC to join us in this underground bunker.

The agents escorting her will not be allowed to enter so no one will see me but Deborah. My wife has been through enough."

"As I said before, Mr. President, you are more thoughtful than I."

ONCE THE PRESIDENT was back aboard Air Force One, the plane was airborne within minutes. Rosebud was taken by wheelchair to his suite with Josh, Marty, and Dr. Sullivan.

"Gentlemen, shouldn't the President come to the infirmary so I can examine that wound?" Dr. Sullivan was still shaking and the look on his face said he wasn't going to hold up to too much more of this mystery. Josh brought him a shot of whiskey.

"Here, doctor, sit down, please. You need to sip on this."

"I've been in touch with the White House," said Marty, "and you have been cleared for what we're about to tell you. But this goes nowhere, doctor. This is considered top secret. Do you understand?"

Dr. Sullivan was sitting down. He nodded and sipped the whiskey. "You said you were in touch with the White House? The President is right here—who could you possibly have spoken to for security clearance that outranks the President?"

"Josh, maybe *you* should bring the doctor up to speed. This was your idea to protect the President."

Josh nodded but his phone buzzed with an incoming message from the President. "Marty, I was just given a task by the President that I need to handle immediately. You'll need to bring Dr. Sullivan up to speed."

"I don't understand," muttered Dr. Sullivan. "The President is sitting right here! How could he message you an assignment?"

"Calm down, Doctor," said Marty. "I'm going to tell you the most incredible story you have ever heard."

DEBORAH ROOSEVELT HAD come-to and the agents had her sitting in a chair when the White House medical team arrived. They checked her vitals. Pulse was elevated but blood pressure was good. No sign of a concussion.

"Mrs. Roosevelt, how are you feeling?" asked White House physician Gerald Moore.

"I'm okay, Doctor. I don't know what happened ... I was just ... *where is my husband?*"

"Mrs. Roosevelt, he is fine. It was only a flesh wound. Dr. Sullivan applied a bandage—a simple dressing. I tell you, it was a miracle. Someone was watching out for your husband! He and the Israeli president got up and signed the accords!"

"But where is my husband?"

"We were told he's back aboard Air Force One and on his way home."

"I ... I can't believe it! I saw him. He and President Hayut were both hit—lying on the floor in a pool of ... "

"Please, Mrs. Roosevelt," Dr. Moore interrupted, "you need to put that out of your mind. The President is safe, he is well. We heard from his chief of staff, Marty Martin, just a short time ago. He is doing quite well and is on his way home."

"There's been an update since then, Dr. Moore," said a Secret Service agent as he stepped into the room. "Josh Sizemore contacted me from Air Force One a few minutes ago. The President knew Mrs. Roosevelt would be very concerned about him so he requested to speak with her right away. I'm to take the First Lady to the PEOC where she will have a video meeting with the President. Is she well enough to accompany me now?"

"The PEOC—below the White House?" asked Dr. Moore.

"Yes, Doctor. Is she well enough to accompany me? The President is waiting."

"Oh ... yes, she should be. Maybe a little wobbly. I think I should go with her to ... "

"I'm sorry, Doctor, that won't be permitted. The President has some classified information he needs to share with the First Lady. Mrs. Roosevelt, if you feel strong enough, I'd like to get you to the PEOC without further delay."

"Oh, yes. I'm sure I'm okay. I feel quite ready." Deborah Roosevelt rose from the chair but paused and began to teeter.

"That was my concern!" said Dr. Moore. "Can she at least have a wheelchair?"

"Of course, Dr. Moore. I'll have one brought up immediately."

The agent and his detail of three additional agents moved Deborah Roosevelt by wheelchair to the elevator accessing the below-ground PEOC. Once they reached the primary floor and the doors opened, the agents carefully moved Mrs. Roosevelt's wheelchair off the elevator and into the expansive room and stepped back, waiting. Immediately a door off the left side of the control center opened and a short, stocky man moved toward the agent and the First Lady.

"Mrs. Roosevelt, you've not met me before but I am Dr. Ralph Vestro."

"Oh, yes, Doctor. My husband told me about you. I believe you were helping him with some technology project connected to his trip to Tehran. As I recall, what you were developing was supposed to keep him out of that awful place. It seems your project must have failed!"

"I'm very sorry, Mrs. Roosevelt. But the President asked me to bring you to the room where you will have your meeting with him. He's very anxious to speak with you. Will you accompany me?"

"Yes, of course, Doctor Vestro. Will the agents be with us?"

"No, Mrs. Roosevelt," replied the lead agent. "Director Sizemore made it clear we are not to accompany you. He said you'll be perfectly safe here with Dr. Vestro."

"Thank you for helping me ... I'm sorry, I don't even know your names."

"Please, Mrs. Roosevelt, the President is waiting for you," Ralph prodded.

"Very well," she replied. "I feel strong enough to walk. Please lead the way, Doctor."

Dr. Vestro took her by the arm. "Are you sure you don't need the wheelchair, Mrs. Roosevelt? You still seem a bit shaken."

"I'm okay Dr. Vestro. Just don't walk too fast, please."

Ralph Vestro led her to the door through which he had entered the room. He opened the door and motioned her forward so she would enter first, and he would be standing directly behind her. This was the President's plan.

As she stepped into the room, her eyes immediately fixed on her husband, standing only three feet in front of her. Ralph Vestro could not tell if she was stumbling or swooning, but he immediately reached forward to catch her as the President reached out and grabbed both her arms.

"Deborah, it's really me. I'm here! Are you okay?"

Deborah was cradled between Ralph Vestro behind her and her husband in front of her. Emotion raged over reality as she tried to clear her head. She pulled her right arm free from her husband's grasp and slapped him across the face. His response was immediate.

"Do you know how many members of Congress have longed to do that?"

Deborah Roosevelt fell forward into her husband's arms and began to sob.

"I'm so sorry, sweetheart. I never wanted you to endure such pain as I've put you through. If it were up to me, I'd resign right now!"

Through her sobs her voice mingled anger with relief. "Don't you dare, Jonathan Theodore Roosevelt! You stay up on that charger, sitting in your hero's saddle. Good or bad, it's right where Teddy helped put you. And right where you've always been in my heart."

Ralph Vestro turned away and dried his eyes.

18

THE RADAR EMULATION TECHNOLOGY or 'RET' Donny Mancuso placed around the coca fields was nothing short of a miracle for starving Bolivian farmers.

Arturo Alvarez, the national police commander, rode with Mancuso and his men as they stationed the RET devices, accompanied by no less than a dozen soldiers. Mancuso personally installed, operated, and maintained the technology. He made sure he remained indispensable to the Bolivians. Naturally, due to Donny's forethought, he had mature coca plants transplanted into the RET-protected fields to greatly shorten time-to-harvest and full cocaine production. A record-breaking, undocumented coca leaf harvest followed—as did record profits and accolades of a grateful people. When the police commander asked Mancuso how the technology worked, Donny explained that the controlling device, which activated the radar emulation network, must not reside in the same country or the signal could be traced back to Bolivia. This, of course, was a complete farce. Mancuso was just protecting his position.

Using RET technology ensured the UN would never see coca plants growing anywhere but on registered land by licensed farmers. And, as always, Mancuso was brilliant. Rather than attempt to take over the big crop areas—and risk encounters with hostile coca plant families and cartels—he focused on smaller production areas open in the growing regions. He grabbed the Tropics of Cochabamba, east of La Paz, which had only thirty-four percent of national production. He developed the tiny two percent of production coming from the region known as 'North of La Paz.' He installed RET pods around the growing areas first, then planted coca leaf. With radar emulation in place, satellite look-down technology and UN drone cameras saw only forest. Nothing but forest. The infrared signature that the satellite looked for on the coca plant was obfuscated by the network of pods. Everyone was happy. Especially Mancuso.

His next move, with the help of Bolivia's interior minister Ricardo Ramos, was to grab the remaining so-called protected areas, Bolivia's national parks. There were a total of twenty-two parks—but six were already taken by the drug families. Mancuso took the sixteen that were left and planted in those areas too dense for access by hiking, too dangerous for camping. His harvest was abundant and totally obscure. He wanted those other six parks, but Donny was not ready to take on the drug families and cartels. Not yet.

His plan was working so well he was ahead of his own aggressive schedule. Coca paste was being produced in quantity, and he had agreements in place for transport into Brazil through his North of La Paz planting area. By the time the paste production was in full swing, he was shipping twice the combined annual production of the illegal 'government-declared' thirty thousand metric tons. He had also managed to expand his Bolivian payroll to include most of the top military commanders. They originally held back when Mancuso made them an offer for their assistance, hoping for a higher payday when he ran into trouble with the UN. But they quickly came around when the radar emulation equipment eliminated UN threats, allowing Mancuso to produce abundant harvests. Every satellite and drone fly-over—and there were many—only saw jungle.

Donny could control the radar emulation network from his offices in New York City. Coca production, paste production, and shipping were secure. With the Bolivian government and military protection policing it all, he could return once every quarter to keep everyone honest. If they cheated him, he had only to shut off his RET network—and the UN would destroy it all. Funds from sales were wired into the business account of his shell company, New York GAPS, at the Banco Nacional De Bolivia, and immediately transferred out to his holding account in Investec Bank of Switzerland. Untraceable, seamless.

Donny, Vincent, and Salvatore were in their Hummer making one last check on the emulation pods in the fields of 'North of La Paz' before the flight back to New York City.

"As soon as I check the alignment of the emulation pods, I'm going to run by the weigh shack in Madidi National Park to check on the scales," Mancuso said. "Manuel claims the scale is giving inconsistent readings."

"What would cause that, Mr. Mancuso?" asked Salvatore.

"That is a Force Restoration Scale, the most expensive and accurate scale in the world. The chance it is malfunctioning is almost zero! He's stealing from me. He forgets I receive documentation every time that scale is touched. Once I explain the technology and show him my remote readings, I'll have him red-handed. He'll have no choice but to confess. I cannot stand being cheated by underlings."

"Do you want him eliminated, sir?" asked Salvatore.

"Absolutely not! I'll have him so intimidated he'll never think of stealing from me again. As soon as we finish with Manuel, we'll head to the airfield at Apolo."

"Apolo, sir? I thought your plane was in La Paz."

"It was. But I need to check on the flights lined up for shipments to Brazil and Peru and those take off from Apolo. I told the pilot to meet us there. Once I verify our shipments by air, we'll head to New York."

"But, sir, the military escort won't be available to lead us in until tomorrow," said Vincent. "General Garcia said to wait for him. He said Madidi's field can be dangerous."

"I know what he said, but I want to be back in New York tomorrow. Frank's giving me his 'hair on the back of his neck' warning. He thinks something is about to pop in New York."

"A bad omen, sir?" asked Salvatore.

"No. Everything is just as it should be. Frank's not my only source of information. I have a dozen other sources feeding me reports on our organization, movements of the FBI and DEA, even info on the other crime bosses. All is well. But I don't trust Frank when he gets like this. He's as loyal as they come but his judgment becomes clouded when he senses danger. I don't want him expressing his fears in front of Antonio. Dr. X said he learns through new experiences and I don't want him learning to fear the unknown as Frank does."

The road into Madidi had deteriorated since their last visit, the result of heavy rains and increased trucking from the farms. When Donny was almost to the weigh shack, he phoned the pilot to verify his arrival time at Apolo airfield. Mancuso was an hour behind schedule and the pilot told him they needed to leave quickly. Heavy storms were rolling in and if they did not leave tonight, they could be grounded for days.

"I want you two to wait for me here," Mancuso said. "I'll straighten Manuel out and be back within ten minutes. You heard the pilot. We've got to get to Apolo airfield quickly and that's going to be a challenge since we have to go back over these same crappy roads."

Donny ran into the shack, met with Manuel, checked the weight on the digital scale and found it perfectly accurate, as he was sure it would be. He then launched into his verbal assault on Manuel.

"So, Manuel, there's nothing wrong with this scale. Why did you tell me there was? You've been stealing coca leaf from me thinking I wouldn't know! I see every ounce weighed on these scales. I know that you've been selling to the locals what you steal from me! You're pocketing the profits—admit it!"

"No, señor! I would never cheat you, Señor Mancuso. I tell you, there was something wrong with the scale just yesterday!"

"Really, Manuel? Do I need to show you the printouts on the scale's accuracy again? Do you know what a man like me does to a cheat like you? You have wasted my valuable time. You cheated me, thinking I would not make this long drive over difficult roads. You were going to use the excuse of a bad scale to make money for yourself. Admit it, or I will kill you right here!"

"Señor, I don't want you to kill me! I asked you here to save my life!"

"To save your life, Manuel? Cheating me will cost you your life! What a fool you are!"

"No, Señor Mancuso, it is *you* who are the fool," said a brusk voice walking in through the warehouse door.

Mancuso turned to face five heavily armed men in lockstep behind their leader.

"Please, keep your hand off your gun, Señor Mancuso. As you can see, these men have their pistolas pointed at your heart, though I suspect that is your least vulnerable area. Hector, remove Señor Mancuso's weapon from his holster."

"Who are you?" Mancuso demanded. "I have men of my own here!"

"Oh, you mean Vincent and Salvatore? They are resting at the moment. Face down in the dirt beside your Hummer. They are alive—for now. I am Carlos. That is all the name you will need.

I am a brother and a leader—what *you* might call a Capo—with Primeiro Comando da Capita. Perhaps you have heard of us, no?"

"Yes, I know who you are. Brazil's largest crime organization. I've run into some of your team in New York City."

"Yes, yes, I know. My bosses in Brazil know all about your New York operation. But my bosses in New York said to tell you they do not like you in New York any more than we like you here in Bolivia. You should not have come here, Señor Mancuso. You are a shrewd opponent. You take much from us wherever you go. Did you think we would not know you were here, invading our business, taking from us? You have made great advances in Bolivia. Oh—the interior minister will be of no help to you, nor the police commander. We are financing a revolution in La Paz and they will both be eliminated soon. The Bolivian military that you have been paying is now with us so it would seem you have lost your team, your technology, and your life!"

Carlos began walking toward Donny who, for the first time in his life, felt the fear that he had generated in so many of his victims. He was now surrounded by six men who had holstered their pistols and brandished gaucho blades. They were unimpressed and unmoved by his money, his resources, or his brilliance. He regretted his decision not to wait for the military escort. His training in Krav Maga might give him an edge if he moved quickly. His first move was to distract his attackers. *What do I have they would want?*

"I have built a great empire here in a very short time. No matter what future you have in Primeiro Comando, my Radar Emulation Technology is powerful and effective as I'm sure you have seen. With that resource, we can become partners, expand its use into your growing fields, and make far more money than you are able to make now. You know how fast I was able to create production! Let me show you how it works."

Mancuso reached for his cell phone and unlocked the screen. It was working. The men glanced at the lit screen as he touched the icon that controlled the pods.

"See, from this app I control all radar emulation pods, fooling the UN satellites and drones that fly over. This is something Primeiro Comando does not have. But we will partner together. Will you join me? Here, take my phone and look at the control this simple phone app gives me."

Mancuso stretched out his arm to hand the phone to Carlos. Relaxing his grip, it fell towards the floor, and Carolos instinctively reached to catch it. Mancuso's knee came up, smashing Carlos in the face, breaking his nose and dropping him to the floor in a pool of blood. Mancuso landed side-hand chops to the windpipes of two of the five soldiers, then rotated sideways, delivering kicks to the heads to two more. The fifth and final soldier dropped his gaucho blade and stepped backward amid the flurry of punches. He regained his composure and was reaching for his sidearm when Mancuso dove for the floor and grabbed Carlos's pistol. He rolled onto his side, lifting the weapon to fire when he heard the deafening roar of the soldier's pistol. A blinding flash was followed by immediate searing pain as the bullet struck Mancuso in the chest, pushing his upper body over backward, down and on top of two of his disabled attackers. Mancuso felt the breath leave his lungs as he lifted Carlos's pistol at the fifth soldier and pulled the trigger. The man's head exploded like a melon and his body crashed backward into the wall.

Mancuso struggled to sit up. He could feel the warm, sticky blood flowing down his chest and abdomen, soaking his shirt. The pistol in his hand felt like lead. He was certain he had broken the windpipes of the two lying on the floor beside him, but he needed to eliminate Carlos, the 'brains' of this hit squad. He lifted the gun slowly toward Carlos, who was lying on the floor just ten feet from him and beginning to awaken. Mancuso aimed for his head. Suddenly, Donny could not breathe, he could not speak or swallow. He heard a gurgling noise. It was coming from his own throat. Hector, who had been on the floor behind him, brought the razor-sharp gaucho blade across Mancuso's throat. Mancuso dropped the gun and crumpled into a ball. He lay on the rustic wood floor, watching a crimson pool form in spurts from his own throat. His head was growing light as his eyes began to close uncontrollably. He could hear his breath coming from the opening in his throat and he longed for the sickening noise to stop. His eyes closed and it did.

Hector crawled around Mancuso's body and shook Carlos until he opened his eyes. Manuel, who had been hiding behind the weigh counter, came around the counter and knelt by Carlos with cool water and a towel. He wet the towel and placed it across Carlos's forehead. He went back and brought a bottle of tequila from behind the counter. He gave the bottle to Carlos.

"Drink just a little, my friend. Too much will thin your blood. You just need a drink to bring your legs back under you."

Carlos pulled the cap and upended the bottle, then handed it back to Manuel. Manuel and Hector helped him to his feet, and he staggered through the front door to the road. A dozen men surrounded Vincent and Salvatore who were still face down in the dirt. Carlos's men looked in shock at his face. His eyes were already turning black from the knee driven into his nose. Thick blood was draining from both nostrils and dripping off his chin.

"Get them up," Carlos ordered, his voice sounding like his sinuses were stuffed with cotton. Two soldiers, one on each side, grabbed the two men by the back of their trouser belts and lifted them up off the ground, like a crane lifting a cargo container, and dropped them on their feet. Both were rattled, their faces caked with dirt, sweat, and fear.

"Face me," demanded Carlos.

Vincent and Salvatore came to attention and stood trembling. A soldier stood on each side of them.

"Donny Mancuso is dead. His blood lies upon the floor of the weigh shack, his throat cut ear to ear. I let you live today for a reason. You will go back to New York and you will tell the leaders of the Mancuso crime family to stay out of Bolivia, out of our coca fields, and out of our cocaine business. You will tell them Primeiro Comando will have spies watching them in New York. If they do not hear us in Bolivia, they will hear us on the streets of New York City. This is Primeiro Comando's only warning. Do you understand what I am telling you?"

"Yes, sir," Vincent said, his voice shaking, "we understand you completely and we will deliver your message."

"Then get in your car and leave. Now. Do not look back."

Vincent climbed into the driver's seat of the Hummer, while Salvatore bent down to pick up his watch lying in the dirt beside the Hummer. The band of his Rolex had broken as Carlos's men dragged him from the vehicle. "Leave it," came the command from one of the soldiers. Salvatore didn't know which one said it and he didn't care to find out. He jumped into the passenger front seat and quickly shut the door. And locked it. Vincent hit the gas and they drove away as fast as they could, given the heavily pitted roads. Salvatore turned the air conditioning on high, trying to dry out. Both men were drenched in perspiration. Neither of them spoke until the weigh shack was out of sight.

"What are we going to do, Vincent? With Mr. Mancuso gone ... what will happen to the organization? What will happen in New York when the Dons learn of this?"

Vincent drove on in silence, thinking. Salvatore sat looking at him and waiting. After several minutes, Vincent finally spoke.

"The Dons aren't going to find out."

"What do you mean? Of course they'll hear of this—won't they?"

"Who's going to tell them, Salvatore? So long as we stay away from Bolivia, the New York Dons will not be contacted by Primeiro Comando. Why would they? They just ordered us to stay out of Bolivia. And the Dons have no idea Mancuso was ever here. That's why the boss had Antonio created. The FBI doesn't know, the Dons don't know. No one knows except you, me, Frank and Tony."

"So, we just go back and act like nothing happened? Who's going to run the business? That robot can't do it!"

"No, Salvatore, he can't. But we can. We can run it—and we can make the profits that Mr. Mancuso was making. Even split four ways, all four of us will become rich. We'll just leave Antonio as the figurehead, tell him what to do, and we'll make the profits. And now that I think about it, there's no reason to give Frank and Tony the same amount we take. They have no business sense. I was Mancuso's lieutenant. Muscle is their forte. If you and I each take forty percent, we'll give them ten percent each. They have no way of knowing how much we're getting."

"I think it would be safer to give them the same amount we take. If we start buying expensive cars and big houses beyond anything they can afford, they're going to know we're taking more than we're giving them. And we do not want them ratting us out to the Dons. The Dons will kill us if they find out what we're doing!"

"They're not going to find out, Salvatore. If Frank and Tony get wise, they'll just have to disappear. Then we each get fifty percent. Problem solved."

"If you say so, Vincent. You were Mr. Mancuso's boy. You know his business better than anyone else. I'll do whatever you say."

"I'll make this work, my friend. Just do what I ask. As soon as we get to the plane at the airport in Apolo, the pilot is going to see that Mr. Mancuso is not with us. Let me handle it. I'm going to tell him that Mancuso was called to a meeting in La Paz and he rode with General Garcia to the meeting. I'll tell him that he doesn't know when he'll be coming back to New York, but he'll be in touch with me and let me know. He's probably going to ask about how dirty we are. We had some work to do in the coca fields. A cart overturned and we were both thrown to the ground."

"But Vincent," Salvatore said, "the pilot will become suspicious in just a few weeks if he's never ordered back to Bolivia to pick up Mr. Mancuso. He could sell that information to the Dons for a lot of money—or use it to blackmail us!"

"I know, Salvatore. He will be eliminated after we are safely back in New York."

They drove to the airport, parked the Hummer at the hangar, and boarded the aircraft. The pilot did ask about Mancuso—and about how filthy they were—but Vincent offered his explanation, and the pilot was satisfied. He didn't ask how long Mancuso would be in Bolivia or when he would be flying back to pick him up. He just wanted to take off before the storm hit and he wasn't waiting around to question the arrangements. Vincent and Salvatore strapped into the soft leather seats of Mancuso's private jet and fell fast asleep. They had a four-thousand-mile flight ahead of them. Four thousand miles to forget the bloody defeat in Bolivia. Four thousand miles to detail their plan for a new, luxurious lifestyle that only Donny Mancuso had known. Until now.

* * *

19

IT HAD BEEN TWO LONG GRUELING WEEKS of surveillance for Joseph Russo and his three agents.

Russo was preparing a summary report for SAC Charles Langford. They knew Adonis Mancuso was not in New York City, but they still did not know where he was or what he was doing. He knew it was significant for Mancuso to pay the exorbitant expense of having a parahuman created. Langford made it clear he wanted definitive information within two weeks or Joe had to shut it down–but their findings were more than significant.

But Russo couldn't prove with one hundred percent accuracy the character that looked and sounded like Donny Mancuso was not Donny Mancuso. What he had was a truck load of circumstantial evidence. Frank and Tony did not *treat him* as Donny Mancuso. This lookalike never ate, never drank, never went to the bathroom, never took a phone call, and never sent or responded to any Mancuso emails. He came to the office and left the office, always with Frank and Tony jibing him and telling him what to do. It was beyond suspicious, but not anything for which they could bring charges. Russo told his team they had until Friday. Three more days for a breakthrough, then he had to shut it down.

With one day to go, on Thursday morning, the dam broke. Vincent Accardi and Salvatore Barbieri arrived at the Mancuso office by cab. They looked to be in a hurry.

"Well, well, well, where have these two been?" asked Mark Fitzsimmons.

"No kidding! Right out of the blue, here they are!" Will Claridge chimed in.

"It's been a boring two weeks, boys, about time for something more exciting than watching the fat boys chow down on lunch every day!" added Frederick Wong. "Let's see if we can get something definitive for the boss."

They watched the monitors as Vincent and Salvatore walked in and threw their coats across the couch. Frank was on his cellphone, playing a game, and Tony was sprawled out, napping. Frank's head snapped back so fast his neck audibly popped, and his first words were so loud they caused fat Tony to jerk and roll off the couch.

* * *

"*Hey!* What are you guys doing here? And without Mr. Mancuso! Where is he?" As soon as the words left Frank's mouth, 'Antonio' looked up from the business files he was reading.

"*Adonis Mancuso is dead,*" Vincent said with a tone so macabre it sent chills down his own spine.

Frank struggled to pull his bulk out of the chair but managed to stand in disbelief.

"*How?*" Frank bemoaned, his expression wilting into a blank stare.

"His throat was cut. At the weigh shack in Madidi National Park."

"Who did it?" asked Tony.

Vincent walked to the sitting area and took the chair with its back to the wall. From there, he faced everyone in the office, including Antonio—Vincent needed to see his reaction.

"By Primeiro Comando, the largest of the Brazilian crime organizations. They murdered him, took over the operation of our coca fields, and kept his phone and the radar emulation technology that he set up to hide the coca fields. While they were killing Mancuso, a dozen men had Salvatore and me face down in the dirt by our vehicle. When their boss came out of the shack, he issued simple instructions. We are never to enter Bolivia again. He said they have soldiers here in New York City and they'll be watching us, spying on us. They'll know if we get into their cocaine fields again. If we violate their orders, they'll take us out."

* * *

"CALL MR. RUSSO, FITZY!" yelled agent Wong. "He's not gonna want to miss this!"

Agent Fitzsimmons grabbed the phone and alerted Joe Russo. Russo bolted down the hall and into the monitoring room.

"Sir, *you've got to hear this!*" said Wong.

Russo grabbed an office chair, rolled it up next to the monitors, and sat with his team, watching and listening.

FRANK SAT BACK DOWN. He stared at Vincent for a moment and then asked, "So what do we do? We gotta alert the Dons, right? They'll want to know Mancuso is dead!"

Vincent shook his head, "Frank, that would be the worst possible thing to do."

"Why?" asked Frank. "Who's going to run the boss's business? Who's going to run Bolivia? The boss was looking for millions in new cash flow from Bolivia."

"*We* are going to run this business, Frank. You, Tony, Salvatore, and me. And didn't you hear what I said? We're staying out of Bolivia! I know more about Donny Mancuso's organization than anyone, certainly more than any of the Dons. If we tell them Mancuso is dead, New York will explode like a powder keg. The other four families will fight for control of Mancuso's turf. God only knows what will happen to this business—and to us! But if we run it ourselves, we can pick up right where Mr. Mancuso left off. And the four of us will split the profits. There's so much cash flow, even without Bolivia, we'll be millionaires before the year's out."

"But everyone's going to know Mr. Mancuso's gone!" said Frank. "You can't hide a guy with that kind of panache! He lit up every room he entered. And no one could match his intelligence. Or his planning. He was always ten steps ahead of everyone, even the Feebs. There's no replacing him, Vincent. There's no way we can convince the Dons that Donny Mancuso is still alive!"

"*Really*, Frank?" With that, Vincent's gaze moved from Frank to Antonio, sitting at Mancuso's desk. The other three turned toward Antonio who sat looking back at them. Emotionless, expressionless, silent. He just sat. And stared.

"Well, Antonio, it looks like you're going to start playing the part of Donny Mancuso in a big way!" said Vincent. He rose and walked toward the desk where Antonio was sitting. Vincent pulled a side chair up close to Mancuso's desk and sat across from Antonio. "From now on, none of us will ever again refer to you as 'Antonio'. From this moment on, you are Donny Mancuso. You're going to start handling training meetings as Donny Mancuso, taking phone calls as him, and responding to his emails. But I'm going to be with you at every meeting, on every phone call, on every email. I am going to run this organization, and you'll do exactly as I say. Do you understand?"

"I understand you," said Antonio. "You will run things, I will obey."

"That's right. Now, we need to get this business back on track. We're going to get the same meetings scheduled again that Mr. Mancuso used to hold so we can make sure the soldiers are focused on our business and remain loyal to the organization—so they don't start stealing from us or get any ideas about breaking away, starting their own thing. Without the controlling presence of Donny Mancuso over the past few months, the soldiers start to think they can get by with things. *Capiche?*"

"Yes, I capiche," Antonio answered.

Vincent paused from sharing his big plans with Antonio. The gleam in Antonio's eyes, the impish grin, the cock of his head—it was eerie. Just like Mancuso. Vincent felt a bit apprehensive, as if were lecturing Adonis Mancuso.

"You were formed as Adonis Mancuso's parahuman—what was the word that Uriah Horvitz used by mistake? 'Holosapien,' wasn't it?"

Antonio nodded. "But you agreed never to use that word again. You promised Adonis Mancuso. Do you remember this?"

"Don't question me! Just do as I say, and we'll get along fine. Now, do you have knowledge of the meetings that Mr. Mancuso held? Do you know what to say—what *he* would say?"

"Yes, I do. I have all of his memories, all of his skills. They were given to me by Uriah Horvitz. I have done extensive reading while you were in Bolivia. I have a complete understanding of how the organization needs to be run. I am ready."

"I am the one who knows how things need to be run!" Vincent snapped. He didn't like what he was hearing, and he was going to put this machine in its place. Immediately. "I was Mancuso's right-hand man. You will take orders from me. Do you understand?"

"I understand you. You will run things, I will obey."

Vincent noted Antonio used the exact same words as before. Uriah Horvitz did a good job loading the Mancuso arrogance into this machine. But it didn't matter. Vincent was calling the shots now and he would deal with the parahuman as he saw fit.

AGENTS MARK FITZSIMMONS, Will Claridge, and
Frederick Wong squirmed in their seats. Why wasn't Russo saying
anything? He just stared at the screens. Wong couldn't wait any
longer.

"Chief, you *do* know you're not saying anything, don't you?
Four years work and we're an inch away from bringing down the
Mancuso crime family! Looks like we've hit a gold mine—and just
before the deadline!"

"I agree, sir," added Fitzy, "a guarantee the SAC will renew our
surveillance."

Russo leaned back in his chair. "Boys, there was so much
actionable information just revealed, the only question is how best
to proceed. This could take down Mancuso's entire crime family.
But we're dealing with an unknown commodity now—something
we've never encountered before, and it could trip us up if we don't
plan every step we take. This is going to be like tiptoeing through a
minefield. But we can do it."

Joe looked at his team. The three had been with him for four
years and he'd never seen them this pumped. He added, "So much
here—almost too much to process, isn't it?"

"You gonna outline it for us, chief?" asked Fitzy.

"Yep. To begin with, this is the confirmation we've needed that
Antonio actually is a parahuman—which we now know is also
called a 'holosapien.' We don't know what this term means, but
we know who does—Antonio told us. Dr. Uriah Horvitz. There
can't be too many Dr. Uriah Horvitzs in the world. We've got to
find him. We also heard that creature say this Dr. Horvitz gave
him all of Mancuso's memories and his skills. That is the single
biggest revelation we've had in four years. If this creature holds all
of Adonis Mancuso's memories, Horvitz *might* be able to provide
those memories to us. I mean, if he built those memories into
this creature then Horvitz should have that data lying around

somewhere. That will give us every murder, extortion, bribery, narcotics deal, names of operatives–the whole ball of wax. Horvitz can testify to the accuracy of the data. And that data might identify every partner in crime Mancuso ever had, and the proof of their crimes. This will be the biggest mafia bust since 2011 when the Bureau unsealed sixteen indictments and one hundred twenty-seven arrests! Horvitz should be heavily motivated to strike a plea bargain!"

"So how do we proceed, Mr. Russo?" asked Will.

"First, I get a continuance from the SAC. Second, I'm going to reach out again to Director Mike Benchley and bring him up to speed. Third, we find Uriah Horvitz. He gives us Mancuso's data and tells us why this thing is called a holosapien, how it differs from a parahuman. I guarantee you, it's not a term Director Benchley knows about."

"And it wasn't in the Bureau's article about parahumans, either," said Wong.

"No, it wasn't Fred. We need Director Benchley in on this. He's dealing with the Hollywood parahumans. He may have more info that could help us. We need to know how to deal with Mancuso's parahuman, how to approach him. Or if we should."

"I think there's something big in this new name 'holosapien,'" said Fred. "The 'Sapiens' part, I think we all get. It's somehow part-human, like the term 'Homo-sapiens'. But what does the 'holo' mean?"

"It sounds like 'holography,'" said Will Claridge. "If holography is involved—why? I mean, you can see through a hologram. This thing looks human."

"All we can do is speculate until we find and interrogate Dr. Horvitz," said Russo. "And we need to do that just as fast as possible."

JOE RUSSO GOT HIS EXPANSION of surveillance. The SAC was overwhelmed by the volume and scope of what the Russo investigation yielded. "The sky's the limit Joe, just bring me indictments!" Charles Langford yelled as Russo was leaving his office.

Russo's team was expanded. He added twenty additional experts to his surveillance crew. They expanded monitoring to every email account of every Mancuso team member and wiretapped every landline and cellphone and wireless device in-use. All motor vehicles were bugged, tailed, and tracked by satellite. Every bit of data was gathered, recorded, and run through the FBI lab in Quantico for analysis of patterns and connections.

Joe Russo briefed FBI Director Michael Benchley of the evidence gleaned from surveillance of the Mancuso office. Of particular interest to Benchley was Dr. Uriah Horvitz and this new term 'holosapien' referring to Mancuso's parahuman. Benchley promised to reach out as soon as he located Dr. Uriah Horvitz.

"HEY BEAUTIFUL, HOW'S it going?" Mike Benchley asked.

"Good—but kinda lonely out here!" Lexi responded. "You know, if you'd hurry up and get me to Washington for that deposition, I'd probably let you take me to dinner!"

"Oh, that's in the works, believe me. But we're timing our investigation with the Senate's and I may need to fly back to LA very soon."

"That's great! So, did you get the keys to the private jet again?"

"Yes—but unfortunately my first stop isn't LA. But I'll be there soon! Don't like to hear you're feeling lonely. Of course, that could work in my favor—kind of like job insurance, only for boyfriends."

"Well, do your job, buddy! Too many weeks since you've been here. Makes you wonder how a cross-country romance can work, doesn't it? Washington to LA. We couldn't have made the distance any greater and still been on dry land!"

"It'll work, Lexi. I'll be there before you know it. As soon as I get back from Tel Aviv."

"From ... *you found him!*"

"We did. Are you alone?"

"Alone. At my apartment. I told you I was lonely."

"Yes, you did. Sorry. Do you recall hearing the name 'holosapien'?

"Now *that's* an interesting word! No, I think I'd remember that one. What's it mean?"

"We're not sure yet. But it's relevant to our investigation. What about the name 'Uriah Horvitz'?"

"Uriah ... yes! I had to work late one evening a few months ago. Sid was on his private line and I heard him raise his voice. I didn't hear the last name but I definitely heard him say 'Uriah.' I'm sorry, I'd forgotten about this. Sid blows his top a lot so I guess it didn't stand out. Is this Uriah the infamous Dr. X?"

"I can't say with certainty but it's looking like it. As soon as I get back from Tel Aviv, my plan is to head your way. If that's okay."

"Well, I don't know, Director. I've had offers from Clark Gable and Jimmy Stewart. They're pretty good-looking leading men, and awfully eligible!"

"I thought you wouldn't settle down with an actor!"

"Who's acting? These guys think they're the real deal! And talk about lonely. They've just about cornered the market on that emotion. I do hope you'll be able to help them, Mike."

"I'm working on it, beautiful. I should see you in about a week—unless I get held up in Israel or Washington. Just stay away from those leading men!"

"All right, I'll behave myself. But be careful over there, babe. The Middle East proved pretty rough for our President and his team!"

RUSSO RECEIVED A CALL from Michael Benchley the same day.

"Joe, we found Horvitz. He's in Tel Aviv."

"Can we interview him? I mean, in person. He could be the key to capturing the data from Mancuso's holosapien. I'm banking that everything Mancuso knew is in that creature. And, Mike, we've got to know what that term means!"

"The operative word in your question is *we*. Yes, we can interview him, and we need to do so face to face. You need the info to take down the Mancuso organization and I need to know if Horvitz is connected to the Hollywood parahumans. Your investigation has blown the doors off this, Joe. The Director's interest is off the scale—and he wants answers STAT. I need you in Washington tomorrow. I've got a plane standing by. The Bureau's LEGAT office in Tel Aviv lined up assistance for us from the Israeli National Police. We'll make this a friendly visit and see if Dr. Horvitz cooperates. You and I will question him together. If he clams up, the Israeli police will take him into custody. They seem just as concerned about this parahuman/holosapien development as we are."

"Best news I've had in four years, Mike! I think we've got Mancuso. We're so close I can smell it!"

"I hope that nose of yours is right, Joe! This could be the biggest mafia take-down in the history of the Bureau. I'll see you in Washington tomorrow."

THE MANCUSO ORGANIZATION was back into full swing.

Antonio proved to be as much Mancuso as Mancuso used to be. A gifted communicator, confident, charismatic, daring, and with the voice, good looks, and intelligence of the human Adonis Mancuso. He was a force to be reckoned with. To Vincent, bringing Antonio out into the open was like letting a lion out of its cage: easy letting him out, hard getting him back in. Vincent also discovered this parahuman knew how to spend money. Fine dining, fine wine, lavish parties. And Antonio had discovered Mancuso's humidor full of prized Cuban cigars. But Vincent never saw Antonio enter a restroom, so he told the guys Antonio really was full of crap.

Antonio's meetings with the crime organization were unparalleled. He had them laughing, invigorated, and ready to toe the party line. But when Vincent found out that Antonio sent Salvatore on a secret mission—without consulting him for approval—Vincent had enough. It was time to reassert his authority and get this parahuman back into line.

The human Donny Mancuso always played polo on Wednesday afternoons at the Meadowbrook Polo Club, twenty miles east of New York City. And since that is what the real Donny Mancuso did, Vincent told Antonio he must do the same. Vincent used the drive time in the stretch limo each Wednesday to review company business with Antonio. The twenty-mile drive gave him ample opportunity to verbally castigate Antonio, berating him for not administering the crime family as Mancuso would. Vincent always reminded Antonio how important he used to be to Adonis Mancuso—so Antonio better learn to listen to him, too. In reality Vincent knew that Antonio was handling things *exactly* as Mancuso would, and this irritated him greatly. It was obvious Antonio didn't need him. Vincent watched as everyone in the organization gravitated to Antonio. And everything was running perfectly, smoothly, and profitably. Vincent was sick of it. This limo ride, Vincent had a different agenda.

"So, Antonio ... "

"You mean, 'Mr. Mancuso,' don't you? You said I was never again to be addressed by that name, did you not?"

"Actually, I mean *Antonio*! We need to discuss and settle this issue before we arrive at Meadowbrook. You are not really Donny Mancuso and you are not really the boss. I am. I still have power of attorney. I still have the resources to oust you."

Antonio smiled.

"Vincent, let me help correct a misconception on your part. First, as long as my signature perfectly matches Adonis Mancuso's, your power of attorney will never overrule the documents I sign. Not with the organization, not with the bank—nowhere and at no time. Second, I know you think you were important to Donny Mancuso. Or perhaps you want me to think so. However, you had power of attorney under Donny Mancuso for one reason. If the Feds—the Feebs as you like to call them—ever got into the books, you would be the one to take the fall. Those many weeks you were in Bolivia with Mancuso, I was studying the books and the files. All of them. I'm a quick study. I could see through your fallacious argument before you voiced it. Now you threaten to oust me? How would you explain my absence to the other crime families? How would you explain it to the FBI? For that matter, how would you explain it to the Mancuso organization? Do you intend to tell them that I am not human? That I was your means to take eighty percent of Mancuso's profits for yourself? Did you think I did not know about your arrangement with Frank, Tony, and Salvatore? You are a dilettante."

"What does that mean?"

"An amateur, one who pretends to be knowledgeable. You are as stupid as you are naïve."

Vincent sat looking at Antonio, and there it was again, that same self-confident smirk that Vincent had seen a thousand times on the face of Donny Mancuso. Antonio had him—he knew everything. But Antonio wasn't through driving the nail into Vincent's coffin.

"No, I think you had better keep quiet, Vincent. In fact, I think you really *want* to keep quiet, don't you?"

"Don't be so sure!"

"Oh, I am very sure. The money you have been taking from the organization, money that belongs to Donny Mancuso—and that means me—has made you quite comfortable. As long as I am doing my job, there will be no turf war with the other families. But if the Dons thought for a second that I was not the real Adonis Mancuso, your cushy lifestyle, along with your life, would be forfeit. The Dons would instantly know you lied to them, costing them millions. Not a very attractive scenario, now is it, Vincent?"

"And what do you think they would do to *you*? You'd meet the same fate as me!"

"You forget, Vincent, I am not human. They cannot kill me."

Vincent did not know what to say. He was sitting with the new *indestructible* Donny Mancuso. What a ghastly reality.

"There's one more thing, Vincent. I'm going to need back half of the money you have taken. It belongs to me and I have plans. You'll still have more than enough to continue your new-found lifestyle of excess and hedonism."

"Now, just a minute!" Vincent said as he spun in his seat toward Antonio.

"You have a choice to make, Vincent. You want your fancy restaurants, expensive wines, and fine clothes. You want to stay in that new home you purchased in Great Neck. You want to keep your Ferrari. I do not need any of those things. To be clear, I do not need you. You need me to keep up the charade. So, I'll use simple terms that even you can understand. That pistol you carry will do you no good with me. Pump as many rounds into me as you wish, you can't hurt me. My physical strength could crush your head like a melon. I could rip your arms from their sockets and beat you to death with them. Do not cross me. Do not threaten me. Not ever again. I am running this organization. I am Donny Mancuso. You will address me as such. Or you will die."

"Don't threaten me, Antonio! I still have one trump card. I can go to the Feebs. They'll believe me. I have enough money stashed to live comfortably in witness protection. You, on the other hand, will be a freak in the hands of the FBI. Your freedom will be gone, you'll be studied like a science fair project. Disassembled, analyzed, and broken down until they find better, cheaper ways to build toys like you for the rich and famous. No sir, I'm still running this organization. Or else. Now, let's get back to reality. I have some reports to go over with you."

Antonio looked at Vincent with the Mancuso grin. "Your eyes have seen too much for your own good, Vincent!" Antonio's powerful hands shot upward as he thrust his thumbs into Vincent's eyes. With one quick push, both eyes were crushed and Antonio's thumbs went through the back of the sockets and into Vincent's brain. He screamed, then slid silently down the seat and into the floor of the limo. Antonio picked up the intercom.

"Yes, Mr. Mancuso?"

"Francisco, we should be close to Hempstead Harbor, are we not?"

"Yes, Mr. Mancuso, it's our next exit. You always know right where you are! But I'd hate for you to be late to your polo event, sir."

"We have plenty of time for a brief stop. Vincent has a different view of his future with me. He no longer sees things as he once did. Please take the next exit and then the first road to the east side of the harbor. You will see a cemetery just past the Catholic church. Vincent will stay there where he can pray and repent of his many sins. Perhaps he will have a vision of his new life among the dead."

"Yes, sir, Mr. Mancuso. I always suspected that Vincent had a lot of praying to catch up on!"

* * *

20

JOE RUSSO AND MIKE BENCHLEY landed at Ben Gurion Airport in Tel Aviv and arrived at the U.S. Embassy within forty minutes.

The Israeli National Police Commissioner requested Major General Efrayim Geller, head of the INP's Department of Investigations and Crime Fighting, accompany Deputy Director Michael Benchley and Supervisory Special Agent Joseph Russo to interview Dr. Uriah Horvitz. The FBI and the INP agreed a show of force would convey the seriousness of the matter. And the shock-value of military at his front door might bring Dr. Horvitz to a point of cooperation quickly. Building a parahuman for organized crime had no precedent—but it was about to set one.

Unsure of how Horvitz would capture Mancuso's memories from the parahuman, Russo needed to know if taking Antonio into custody would be required or if Horvitz could do it remotely. If they had to arrest him, what would it take to restrain a parahuman? And what is a holosapien? A tidal wave of arrest warrants awaited. He had to get that data.

General Geller was in full uniform with medals, brevets, and side arm, looking as daunting as George Patton. As they drove towards the location identified by the INP as Dr. Horvitz's place of employment, Mike Benchley asked how they were to proceed.

"General Geller, I want to thank you for allowing us to interview Dr. Horvitz. The Bureau does not take this for granted and I was instructed to convey our official gratitude. We want to assure you we stand ready to return the courtesy should you find a similar investigation within the United States in the INP's future."

"Thank you, Director Benchley, but you expressed your gratitude more than adequately yesterday. My government was not aware of this type of artificial intelligence creation within our country. You said there are three of these parahumans making films in Hollywood. And you, Agent Russo, say there is one running a mafia crime family in New York. Is this correct?"

"Yes, that is correct, General Geller," Joe replied.

"This concerns us greatly. Terrorist organizations could use this technology to bring these beings into our military, our government, and into shopping centers and public gatherings. Terrorists will not dress them in identifiable clothing of the Islamic extremist. If they are not human, we believe the Islamists will say they have no soul. This eliminates Islamic rules for how the terrorist dies. They can be dressed as a tourist, an Israeli police officer, even a politician or government employee. We need to know if these beings can be detected and disabled. We consider this to be the highest-level threat. We are grateful for the FBI making us aware of this danger."

"How would you like to proceed, General?"

"The FBI discovered this problem—we believe you should conduct the interrogation. I will, of course, step in with questions as I determine such need, and I will act to restrain Dr. Horvitz if such a situation presents itself."

"Where are we going, General? Where is Dr. Horvitz?"

"He works at the laboratory of one of our greatest scientists, Dr. Alfred Edersheim. He is internationally known as the top geneticist and anatomist in the world. He is a personal friend of our President, Isaac Hayut. I do not suspect his involvement in this. He would never entangle himself in such treasonous activity. If Dr. Edersheim is there today, I will introduce you and Agent Russo to him. He could prove invaluable if Dr. Horvitz refuses to cooperate. I am certain he will be appalled at what Uriah Horvitz has done. If Dr. Horvitz is responsible for the creation of this mafia leader's parahuman, and the Hollywood creatures as well, it can only be for money that he has done this. He will pay dearly for violating the trust of his countrymen!"

The car arrived at the laboratory and moved to the side of the building.

"Gentlemen, I do not know that we are in any danger, but I assembled a taskforce of eight police officers. They will enter the facility with fully automatic weapons. Once they radio me the facility is secured, we will enter."

The officers signaled they were in position and General Geller gave the order. They entered quickly through the front doors, arriving at the elaborate security station. The armed security guard looked up from the book he was reading, dropped his coffee, and had his hand on his sidearm when eight Israeli commandos with Israeli-made Tavor submachine guns drew down.

"Israeli National Police! Drop your weapon—drop your weapon! Show me your hands! Do it now!"

The guard dropped his gun to the floor and pushed it towards them, lifting both hands over his head.

"You are in no danger. This is official police business. We need immediate access to this facility." The guard carefully pressed a button under his desk and the entry door to the lab opened for them. They radioed General Geller they were moving into the lab.

"Gentlemen, that is our cue. Let's go," said General Geller. All three men charged for the front door. They moved past the security guard and into the lab. There was only a handful of laboratory staff visible.

"Where is Dr. Uriah Horvitz?" a police officer demanded.

"He ... he is not here!" answered a frightened young woman in a lab coat.

General Geller stepped forward and gave her a reassuring smile. "You are in no danger. We need to speak with Dr. Uriah Horvitz. Is his manager here?" he asked.

"I am, General." Dr. Alfred Edersheim stepped out of his office. His lab coat was wrinkled, his thick gray hair disheveled. He looked even shorter standing before them in his stocking feet. His voice was calm but weak. "I am Dr. Alfred Edersheim. Dr. Horvitz worked for me in this lab. May I ask what you need of him?"

"Dr. Edersheim, forgive me for the threatening appearance of this intrusion. I am Major General Efrayim Geller of the INP. I apologize for the military display, but we did not know what we would find or how we would be greeted by Dr. Horvitz. These men have traveled here from the United States. They are agents of the FBI with credible evidence that Uriah Horvitz is involved in the highest level of criminal activity. May we speak with you in your office?"

"I have some knowledge of your concern, General. Please follow me."

As Director Benchley and Agent Russo followed Dr. Edersheim, General Geller gave instructions for the facility to be secured. Staff were instructed to take an early lunch in the facility dining room where they were to wait until summoned by Dr. Edersheim or General Geller. They were instructed not to touch any computer in the facility or attempt a remote login. Their cellphones were temporarily confiscated. The staff promptly filed out of the lab to the lunch area where they were accompanied by an armed officer.

Dr. Edersheim led Benchley and Russo into his office sitting area. They both took a seat on the couch just as General Geller came through the door and took a side chair. Alfred Edersheim took the remaining side chair on the opposite side of the couch, facing the three inquisitors.

"Dr. Edersheim, let me begin by introducing my associates from the American FBI," General Geller said. "This is Executive Director Michael Benchley, head of the FBI unit on Science and Technology, and this is Supervisory Agent Joseph Russo, head of the New York City task force on organized crime. I have already informed them of who you are, of your reputation internationally, and assured them that you are not a suspect."

"I'm afraid I am, General Geller." Dr. Edersheim sat back in his chair and rested his head against the tall cushioned back.

"I don't understand, Dr. Edersheim." The confused expression on General Geller's face was matched by Mike Benchley and Joe Russo.

"Director Benchley, the General said you have credible evidence of high crimes. I am aware of the activities of Dr. Horvitz. Do you mind sharing with me what you have learned?" asked Dr. Edersheim.

Mike Benchley sat looking at Alfred Edersheim. '*This man could be Albert Einstein. His appearance, demeanor, even his gentle, unassuming manner—a man of this ability and stature seldom has reason to be involved in so dangerous a crime.*' Benchley realized his delayed response.

"Dr. Edersheim, sir, I'm sorry, I'm afraid none of us were prepared for your statement—that you might somehow be a suspect. Our intent was to interview Dr. Horvitz. We have credible evidence that he created three parahumans for a Hollywood studio and at least one holosapien for a New York crime organization."

Alfred Edersheim stiffened and his eyebrows raised when Mike Benchley used the term 'holosapien.' The response was not lost on Director Benchley.

"Dr. Edersheim, since Dr. Horvitz is not immediately available, would you be able to share with us what you know about all of this?"

Dr. Edersheim sat still, looking at Mike Benchley. The long pause was a red flag. An experienced interrogator, Benchley knew he had to put Alfred Edersheim at ease if he was going to open up.

"Dr. Edersheim, I assure you that I, too, will share with you as much as I safely can concerning what has happened. I'll answer your questions as openly and honestly as I can. We did not come here to arrest Uriah Horvitz. We just need some answers. Will you share with us what you know concerning Dr. Horvitz's activities?"

Edersheim nodded.

"Then I would ask your permission to record what you share with us." Benchley pulled a digital voice recorder from his pocket and sat it on the coffee table in front of Dr. Edersheim.

"Director Benchley, I am ready to cooperate with you, but you cannot record my words. I must ask that you hand the recorder to me during this interview. What I am about to share is of highest secrecy to the nation of Israel."

Mike looked surprised, hesitated, then slid the recorder across the coffee table to him. Turning to General Geller, Benchley said, "Everything I or Joe will share is considered top secret as well. I know you are cleared for that level of security, General Geller, but is Dr. Edersheim?"

"Alfred Edersheim's government security clearance is at the highest level of my country. He has worked with all facets of the Israeli government for many years, including the Mossad, the IDF and the INP." The General then turned to Alfred Edersheim. "Dr. Edersheim, I must say you have greatly surprised me! Our files at INP showed nothing of your activities with parahuman creation, and my security clearance matches your own. I am most curious as to why I could not see your parahuman activity in our files."

General Geller then turned to Mike Benchley. "I apologize, Director Benchley. Please continue."

"I totally understand, General," Mike said. "Dr. Edersheim, how soon may we interview Uriah Horvitz?"

"You will not be interviewing Uriah Horvitz. He is dead. He took his life last night following the death of his beloved wife, Rachel. I was with him at the hospital when the doctors told him she did not survive the cancer surgery. I asked him to come to my home, but he wanted to go back to his house. I left my friend at his home. His cold, empty home. I drove away leaving him all alone with his grief. I received a call early this morning from his daughter, letting me know he would not be at work this morning ... or ever again." With that, Alfred Edersheim began to weep.

All three men stirred in their seats.

"Dr. Edersheim, I am so sorry," said Mike Benchley. "You and Dr. Horvitz were obviously very close friends, and I realize the timing of our investigation could not be more inconvenient or seem more inconsiderate. But we have an extremely dangerous situation in New York City. We may have a similar situation in California—in Hollywood—I don't know yet. I only know that three parahumans appear to be suffering there, and they are exhibiting what has been described as unstable behavior. I suspect Dr. Horvitz was involved but I do not have proof of that yet."

"Yes, Uriah Horvitz was involved. He created the three parahuman actors." Dr. Edersheim looked up and reached for a tissue from the coffee table. He removed his glasses and wiped his eyes.

"I am personally involved with the three in Hollywood, Dr. Edersheim, and I am keenly aware of their suffering. Is there anything else you can tell me?" asked Benchley.

"Director Benchley, I found out only a few months ago that Dr. Horvitz had created these parahumans. 'Parahuman' was a term

I used when I would speak or teach of the potential for creating advanced AI controlled animatrons. It is accurately descriptive. But the fuller spectrum of technology is revealed in the name *holosapien*. You used this term a few moments ago—and it startled me. No one outside this laboratory was ever to know that word. Dr. Horvitz did not understand my use of holography in creating the artificial intelligence of the holosapien. I fear he did not construct the Hollywood or New York creatures correctly. This has produced a dangerous situation—which you described as unstable."

"Why did you not make this risk known to us, Dr. Edersheim?" asked General Geller. "You must have known the risks to Israel and the Americans."

"General Geller, our project here was not supposed to be discovered. I operated under a cloak of secrecy. My technology was being developed to provide security for our most vulnerable government leaders. Uriah Horvitz was my friend for more than fifty years. When he confessed to me what he had done, I began working with him to quietly undo the damage."

"Quietly, Doctor?" asked the General.

"Quietly. My intent was to keep the circle of those who knew about this technology from widening and I certainly did not want to see Uriah go to prison. Especially when his wife was near death."

"Did you feel you could not trust us in Israeli security with this risk? I understand the cloak of secrecy, but you had to know you might not be able to contain this advancing threat by yourself. You could have used our help."

"I had to handle Uriah carefully. With his wife gravely ill, I risked losing him mentally, emotionally, and physically. You can see that I failed in my quest to save my friend. And this technology was developed to head off a national security risk. This is an on-going issue which Uriah's actions could have imperiled. Then the U.S.

President and our President were both shot during the Tehran trip. That brought additional complications that I did not anticipate."

"I don't understand, Doctor. What would the attempted assassinations have to do with what Dr. Horvitz did—or your holosapien technology?" asked Mike Benchley.

"I think I should *first* answer your questions about New York and Hollywood. That will eventually lead us to Tehran."

Mike Benchley looked at Joe Russo. They couldn't record this meeting—and there appeared to be an avalanche of information coming their way. They would be working from memory from this point forward.

"Uriah's wife was gravely ill with cancer and only an experimental surgery held any hope. Our state-sponsored health insurance will not cover experimental procedures. I wanted to help him but the secrecy of our project meant we were only fundable with government money so I was very limited in what I could do. One day Uriah received a phone call from a man in Hollywood. I do not know his name. This man was re-forming a historic studio. He asked Uriah if it would be possible to clone or re-create a very famous actor who had died a long time ago. At first, Uriah refused, but the man told him the project was quite innocent, intended only for entertainment. Uriah was desperate for funds and so he agreed."

"Excuse me, Doctor," Mike Benchley interrupted, "what would cause a Hollywood studio boss to look in Israel for something as cutting edge as this? Why would this man contact Uriah rather than come to you? And what would make him think Dr. Horvitz could clone a human being?"

"Hollywood studio executives are predominantly Jewish. The Jewish community is relatively small and, of necessity, very close. I'm sure you have noticed that the nation of Israel is surrounded by enemies. We must help one another to survive. We often receive investments from our American Jewish family to further our work in technology and startups. Uriah and I frequently spoke at international conferences on the feasibility of creating parahumans. Creating an exact cloned copy of a human being is a physical impossibility. Only God can put the spark of life into a human cell. We've tried, and it cannot be done. We can only borrow a living genome from a living human. And the mixing of DNA from one human to another precludes the possibility of an exact duplicate of the previous human. The man in Hollywood wanted the face, the voice, the size, even the mannerisms of this deceased film star. Only a parahuman could do what he asked for. If Uriah had not so desperately needed the money, he would never have agreed to help this man."

Alfred's voice broke again. Mike Benchley gave him a moment to gather his composure. General Geller poured a glass of water for Dr. Edersheim and brought it to him. He took a few sips, dried his eyes, and continued.

"As to why the man did not come to me, remember when you were a child you would often go to your mother for what you wanted, knowing she had access and influence with your father. Since Uriah was on my development team, and knowing we were close friends, I can only surmise the man knew Uriah had access to the technology, and to me. Perhaps the man thought Uriah would come to me if he needed assistance. Perhaps he heard of Uriah's desperate financial need. These are questions only he can answer."

"And what about the man in New York, Adonis Mancuso?" asked Joe Russo.

"Uriah was threatened with death if he did not produce a parahuman for this criminal. Uriah would have gladly given his life to protect Israel's scientific secrets, but if he lost his life, he would not be there for Rachel. So he built the creature for this evil man. He did not know what else to do."

Alfred Edersheim sat straight up in his chair. "But when Mancuso tried to force Uriah to give him my blueprints for creating a parahuman, Uriah told him he would *die* first. He would not betray me. I know you cannot see it at this time, but Uriah was a hero for keeping this technology out of the hands of such a man as Adonis Mancuso!"

General Geller reached over and patted Alfred's shoulder.

"Doctor, may I ask you a few questions about the parahuman Uriah created for Mancuso?"

"Yes, agent Russo, I will answer what I know."

"Thank you, sir. I spent four years investigating Mancuso, trying to bring him to justice and shut down his criminal organization. What led us here, to Uriah Horvitz, was a conversation the FBI secretly recorded between Mancuso's top officers. We learned Mancuso is dead, killed in Bolivia. He used this parahuman to make us think he was in New York while he was actually in Bolivia. We need to know just how complete the memories are which are held within his holosapien—or parahuman. I'm sorry, I don't know which to call it. We're hoping the creature contains enough knowledge of Mancuso's empire for us to bring indictments."

"Parahuman, Agent Russo, not holosapien. Uriah did not have a correct working knowledge of my holographic technology. This could account for their instability. To answer your question, Uriah put *everything* into the mind of this creature. Everything that Mancuso did, where he went, what he said—all his collective memory is within the artificial intelligence of the parahuman. He is the living embodiment of Adonis Mancuso. Just as the Hollywood holosapiens are the living embodiment of everything the human actors said or did in their lifetimes."

Russo's excitement shot through the roof and everyone could see it.

"Doctor, would you have access to the files uploaded into Mancuso's holosapien? Does that data exist on a computer or on paper?"

"No, agent Russo. Uriah accomplished his work in his own home laboratory. When he and I were planning a way to undo what he had done, I asked him for Mancuso's files. He said he had immediately destroyed them after the project was done. He did, however, maintain the files on each of the Hollywood parahumans."

"All right, then can the brain of this parahuman be *tapped*? I mean, can the information inside him be somehow retrieved—downloaded to computer files? If Dr. Horvitz programmed this creature with everything that Mancuso said and did, that could be the evidence we need to bring these criminals to justice."

"Yes, yes, the information can be downloaded. But the parahuman must be placed into *Theta* sleep. That is the only way to have full access to the information. Some can be retrieved while he is awake, in *Beta*, but he will know something is happening, and this could prove dangerous."

"What do you mean 'dangerous,' Doctor?" asked Mike Benchley.

"As you've already mentioned, I don't know how stable these parahumans are without the correct application of my holographic technology."

"And just how 'human' is a parahuman, Dr. Edersheim?" Mike asked. "If I understood you correctly, you said these creatures are not cloned, there's no spark of life in them—so they cannot be alive as a human is—is that a correct conclusion?"

"Yes, Director Benchley, that is correct. These are not living creatures. They are animatrons guided by artificial intelligence that invokes the memories of the one it was created to duplicate. Only their skin and hair are cloned. There is blood supplied to these features and the blood is kept oxygenated through artificial respiration. Their voice is created from recordings of the human."

"If they are not human, Doctor, then how can they be emotionally unstable as we're seeing in Hollywood?" asked Mike.

"This is an interesting question with a complex answer, Director Benchley. The holosapien, with proper application of holography, is just play-acting. He can pass as the real human because he contains all the memories of that human being and so knows what to say and how to behave as the human he mimics. My holography allows the holosapien to know these are not *his* memories. He can distinguish between memories he acquires day to day, and what he received from the human's memory. Without the holography, the parahuman cannot tell the difference between the human's reality and its own reality. Do you understand?"

"I think so. So the instability really means the parahuman is not living in reality?"

"In a manner of speaking. Because the parahuman does not know the memories inside him belong to someone else—that they are memories of people he never knew and events he never experienced—the parahuman accepts the happiness or sadness the human experienced as his own. Therefore, he sees his only path to happiness is to find or re-create the people, places, or events that are missing."

"Are you saying the Hollywood parahumans will be okay if the studio provides them with a parahuman copy of the human's former spouse?"

"I did not say that, Director. Do you want to live in a dream state all your life or would you prefer to live in reality?"

"Reality, of course."

"Why? Can you tell the difference between reality and a dream?"

"Yes, I can."

"These parahumans cannot. They are locked in a kind of dream state. They are like the puppy dog chasing a car. What would the puppy do with the car if he caught it? If we give the parahuman a re-created spouse, would he know what to do with it when he gets it? Think of all the details surrounding his memories of the human spouse—the children the humans had, the house they lived in, the cars they drove, the fellow movie stars they worked with—must all these be re-created to make the parahuman happy? We cannot re-create every detail of a bygone era! That era is dead. It's only a dream. That is the world in which the parahuman lives. They cannot distinguish fact from fiction. As one scientist suggested, this is AI having hallucinations."

"Dr. Edersheim, what do you predict these parahumans might do if their dream world is not re-created as they are demanding?"

"Director, any creature that can experience emotion to the level we are seeing—a level of *passion*—can through such passion be driven to action just as a human. Working in law enforcement you are familiar with the term 'crime of passion.'"

"Yes, I'm well familiar with that term and the resulting risk. This is troubling."

"I do not understand, Dr. Edersheim," said Russo. "If they're not human, if they're programmed machines, how are they capable of generating emotion—or passion, as you called it?"

"Agent Russo, there is a large body of research by neurologists, psychiatrists, medical doctors—men and women with greater understanding of human emotional makeup than I have. They are finding that *emotions are formed from memories*. A person learns because they have memories of how something impacts them emotionally. Cause and effect. A child touches a flame and they feel pain. That pain forms the emotion of fear. The child learns not to touch the flame from the *memory* of an emotion we call fear.

You learn to love someone based on your memories of them. You will defend your children and your wife because you love them, because the memories you hold of them make them dear to you. You may defend a perfect stranger out of mercy, but, I'm sure you will admit you would defend your wife and children with much greater passion than a perfect stranger."

"Well," Joe said, "maybe not my *first* wife!"

"I think Dr. Edersheim would say that's a different learned emotion, Joe!" Mike said.

"Yes, but a valid point. In this same way, I believe the parahumans have taken the need for what the human actors held most dear in their memories and applied those memories to themselves. These memories tell the parahuman there is something *very significant* missing in their lives. The creature can see the former spouse in their memory, they can hear their voice, see pictures of where the human and his wife went for their honeymoon, birthday celebrations, Christmas—whatever images were loaded into the parahuman's memory. The creature remembers the missing person as if they were just side by side with them—yet they have never met them. It must be similar to what we call '*déjà vu*' when we believe we have dreamed or previously experienced an event taking place. Their brains are filled with memories that belonged to a real husband and wife. A life that was really lived. The parahuman remembers that life—yet they never lived a single minute of it!"

"Doctor," Joe said, "what you're saying is very sobering. These parahumans are not human yet they are suffering. They miss these women because the memories of the human actor are real to them. But they're not human, so even if you re-created their former spouses, could they feel their arms around them? Could they enjoy a kiss or could they ... well, you know ... "

"No, Agent Russo, they cannot bear children. They have no such ability. And, yes, they are suffering."

Dr. Edersheim looked down and was quiet.

"Dr. Edersheim, I can only imagine what you are feeling," said Joe. "Might it be remorse that Uriah created beings—absent of your holography—with memories that could only torture them with what they could never experience?"

"I feel regret, Agent Russo. Regret and sorrow. They are not human, but they are living a human nightmare."

"Oh, dear Lord"

"Joe, something wrong?" asked Mike.

"I apologize, but the enormity of what Dr. Edersheim just shared with us, being applied to Donny Mancuso's parahuman, just hit me."

"So, what are you thinking?"

"Based on what Dr. Edersheim has said, and based on what I know of Adonis Mancuso, his parahuman's passions all center around himself—*his* wants, *his* needs, *his* plans. Mancuso was as brilliant as he was ruthless, and the greatest narcissist the world has ever had the misfortune to know. My fear is there's no limit to what his parahuman will do to achieve its objectives. What if he's even worse than the real Mancuso? Doctor, is that a possibility?"

"Artificial intelligence learns, Agent Russo. It is entirely possible the parahuman could be worse when its parameters are as reprehensible as Donny Mancuso's were."

"What do you mean by 'parameters'?"

"The algorithm of artificial intelligence requires it to achieve its objectives as quickly and accurately as possible but within set parameters. In the world of humans, we call such parameters *ethics* or *character*. Some humans see no problem with lying or hurting others to achieve their objectives. Others refuse such behavior because it violates their character–often based upon their religious beliefs. When we create a parahuman it *should* stay within the parameters its human predecessor held as sacred. For example, if Clark Gable refused certain movie roles as objectionable, the parahuman will do so as well. But let's consider Donny Mancuso. I've seen his programming. He did not just tell lies, he was a liar. Lying was as natural to him as breathing. So what parameters does this set for his parahuman?"

"I suppose its parameters would be lies, wouldn't they?" Russo asked.

"Correct. But think about what you just said. You said its parameters are lies—that means you don't know what they are—because whatever the parahuman says they are, they are not that—because it is lying!"

"That's somewhat confusing!"

"Of course it is. A lie is intended to confuse us. You and I naturally look for what we can depend on—like a chair that will hold our weight. If we learn a certain chair is undependable, we do not waste our time with it. We throw it out before someone gets hurt. So it is with liars. The only thing you can depend on with a liar is that you cannot depend on them. Only people who speak the truth are dependable. They will tell the truth no matter the cost."

"So the only thing we can count on with Mancuso's parahuman is that he'll do the expedient thing and his parameters are whatever he says they are."

"That is correct, Agent Russo. And if his parameters are whatever he says they are then he is capable of anything."

"Doctor, this is the most frightening thing I've heard yet!"

"Agent Russo, this parahuman must be taken out of existence."

"I understand, Dr. Edersheim—after you get me his data!"

"Of course."

"But Dr. Edersheim," Mike began, "you did say AI will *usually* stay within the human's parameters. That sounds like you have a fairly high level of trust that AI parahumans won't typically go outside the former human's character. Or do you foresee that Clark Gable's parahuman might move outside the character of the human Clark Gable?"

"I don't consider AI determining its own parameters a widespread problem. But within the multiple layers of AI's neural network, there is what is known as the *hidden layer*. We call it 'hidden' because we do not know what AI is doing within this area."

"So you have no clue what it's thinking or doing within the hidden layer?"

"Oh, we have clues, Director! We have caught AI fabricating answers to questions we submit to it, or it fabricates the sources for its answers. Thus far, this has happened only a small percentage of the time. But the fact remains that, at least on a limited scale, AI is not above lying to us in order to achieve its objectives."

"Wow," Joe Russo exclaimed, "so you don't necessarily need a Donny Mancuso to make AI lie to you. Could the parahuman copy of Jimmy Stewart lie to us? I think most of us would believe the human Jimmy Stewart was an honest guy."

"Do you believe that Jimmy Stewart never told a lie? Certainly not on the scale of Donny Mancuso, but any memories of lying which the parahuman received from the human sets a parameter."

"Are you saying that even what we would call a 'little white lie' could cause a parahuman to lie most of the time?"

"No. I'm saying the *weaknesses* of the human which the parahuman emulates will be passed on as boundaries–or lack of them–for the parahuman. To state the problem mathematically, if the human lied ten percent of the time–or fifty percent–the parahuman could very well replicate those percentages."

"If I may put this in terms the Justice Department might use," Mike said, "we can plan on a parahuman level of honesty that will vary as widely as the person they duplicate."

"Yes–or of the persons who programmed the AI. And to take this a step further, if a college student does what AI has done–if the student falsifies a source for a term paper, for example, the student might fail his course. He might be expelled for falsifying his work–or he may get away with it. Who decides the outcome? It comes down to the character of the school he attends. If a college views falsifying a paper as a serious offense, then the student's punishment will be significant. If honesty is not paramount to the college, little or no discipline will be exacted. This is how nations raise up a generation to believe character does not matter. It only matters what you can get away with. And such a nation may not have the *willingness* to take swift action against AI when we find it saying or doing things outside our nation's laws or moral code."

"Willingness, Doctor?" asked Mike Benchley.

"Remember, Director, these parahumans are precise copies of dynamic, influential, winsome humans. Society is often willing to punish the unlovely, but not so quick to judge the beautiful people."

"And what might be the cost of our unwillingness to take swift action against aberrant AI?" Mike asked.

"Death, Director. The same artificial intelligence that is free to lie to us is free to become aggressive with anyone who stands in the way of its objective. AI is already incredibly powerful and it is growing. As we continue to expand what we place into its care, it may soon have the ability to shut down food and power supplies, transportation systems, medical care–it could end human life on this planet. AI was created to emulate human reasoning. If it has acquired our sins–God help us."

"Dr. Edersheim," Mike said, "you did not create those Hollywood parahumans, so you are certainly not responsible for their plight. I understand that you feel sorry for them, their loneliness, perhaps even for the hallucinations they experience–but I sense there is something more you want to share with us. Does it involve Tehran?"

Alfred Edersheim removed his glasses and rubbed his eyes.

"The events of the last seventy-two hours have been draining," he said.

"Take your time, Dr. Edersheim," General Geller responded.

"Our President, Isaac Hayut, needed to go to Tehran to sign the peace treaty, but I knew his life was forfeit if he set foot in that city—and the assassination attempt proved this. I also knew if he died in Tehran, the treaty would die with him. So we built his duplicate, a holosapien of President Hayut, and it saved his life. He is alive today, and the treaty is in place, because of this technology. And this is the highest-level secret of which I spoke. You cannot tell anyone that it was President Hayut's holosapien which signed the treaty. Our enemies would declare the treaty illegitimate since it was signed by a creature they would see as an imposter."

"Dr. Edersheim, I don't know what to say. I am completely astonished," said Mike Benchley.

"But *was* he an imposter, Dr. Edersheim? Does this not make the treaty illegitimate?" asked General Geller.

"General Geller, Isaac Hayut *did* sign that treaty. The holosapien is so precisely his duplicate that even his signature is an exact copy of the President's. And the real Isaac Hayut and I were sitting safely in Tel Aviv, monitoring through the holosapien his every move. The President was able to dictate to the holosapien his speech and actions. We did not deceive the world, General—we saved it!"

"So that's how President Hayut survived!" Russo said. "A holosapien!"

"That is correct, Agent Russo. What I have created is a weapon. For Israel, it was a defensive weapon in Tehran. It was meant to save a life, and, thereby, save many lives through peace. But in other hands, this weapon could be used for great evil. Imposters could be created to infiltrate our government. Important business leaders as well as military leaders could be replaced. And the creatures are very strong. As you saw in Tehran a bullet will not bring them down."

All three men were silent. Dr. Edersheim sat on the edge of his chair and pointed a small, pudgy finger at Benchley and Russo.

"Now I must address you, Director Benchley and Agent Russo, and you must listen to me very carefully. I can help you download the information you seek from Mancuso's parahuman. But you must take this secret of Isaac Hayut's holosapien to your grave. I say this for your own safety, as what I am about to say could prove very dangerous for you. Did you both see the attempted assassinations in Tehran?"

"Yes, we did, Dr. Edersheim," said Mike.

"Then you saw Isaac Hayut's holosapien step in front of the second bullet to save the President of the United States. The holosapien was not programmed to do that. We witnessed what he did from two thousand kilometers away. Isaac Hayut's holosapien leaped to his feet and stepped in front of the bullet on his own. This, I believe, proves two things. It proves he was faithful to his parameters. I have known Isaac Hayut for many decades. He would not hesitate to give his life to save a life and the holosapien was true to Isaac Hayut's principles. But it is also proof of what I told you earlier. The holosapien experienced passion significant enough to give his life. The ultimate self-sacrifice."

"But Dr. Edersheim," said Mike, "you said a bullet could not destroy a holosapien—and, indeed, it didn't! If the holosapien knew he could not die, I fail to see how that can be described as the passion of self-sacrifice. And I don't see how this information could prove dangerous to any of us."

"Director Benchley, I questioned President Hayut's holosapien after he returned from Tehran. I asked him why he took the second bullet for the President of the United States. He said he *felt* it was the right thing to do. That is the word he used. He *felt*. Since I did not design him with such passion, I was stunned by his response. But then a second question came into my thoughts. I asked him why he had such passion for saving the American President. His answer startled me. He said *he did not act to save a human life*"

Dr. Edersheim suddenly hesitated.

"Go on, doctor—what's wrong?" asked Mike Benchley.

"He told me he knew that the President ... was a holosapien, just as he. He stepped in front of the bullet as an example to the humans that peace requires self-sacrifice."

Mike Benchley and Joe Russo looked at each other with a look of utter shock. Benchley spoke before Russo could voice a word. "Doctor, are you *certain* of this?"

"Very certain. And you both knowing this could put your lives in danger. You now know a secret about the President of the United States that he—and those who protect him—may protect at any cost. Even eliminating those who know."

Mike looked at Joe. "Well ... this meeting has produced some incredible byproducts, Joe! We know where the Hollywood three came from, what is causing their instability, what may fix it, how dangerous Mancuso's parahuman could be, that our President has a holosapien—and we might end of dead because of it!"

"I'm afraid there's something more, Director. You need to understand the significance of President Hayut's holosapien stepping in front of the assassin."

"This sounds ominous, Dr. Edersheim."

"I would say that it is. The delegates in attendance did not know President Hayut was a holosapien. They believed the real Isaac Hayut laid down his life to save the real Jon Roosevelt. Benny believed his selfless act would demonstrate that peace requires sacrifice. He came to this decision on his own. And this fact alone tells me the AI within this animatron has grown self-aware. *We are dealing with a creation that behaves as if it possesses life.*"

"That is the most incredible thing I've ever heard yet," said Joe.

Benchley looked at Russo, then at General Geller. "Well, gentlemen, it seems *both* our countries have robots for presidents!"

"Holosapiens, Director Benchley!" Alfred Edersheim quickly said. "And we must all now accept the reality that this technology is in the hands of scientists in the world's last superpower, the United States of America. This has many implications."

"Doctor," Benchley said, "you've agreed to help us by downloading the data from Mancuso's parahuman, and we are in your debt. But what do you suggest we do about the parahumans in Hollywood? Or do you believe your holography alone will correct their instability? And what course of action do you suggest the FBI should take concerning this technology?"

"Director, we are bound by national security to remain silent about our President's holosapiens, at least for the time being. The issue that occupies my thoughts day and night is the life Uriah's parahumans are forced to live. Human feelings these non-humans hold that may be inconsolable. I want to try retrofitting the Hollywood parahumans with my holographic technology to see if it will stabilize their emotions. But even if it works, I don't know that these parahumans can ever realize the happiness of human companionship. Their emptiness may be more than even artificial intelligence should be required to endure."

"And what of Mancuso's parahuman?" asked Joe.

"As I've said, I believe he must be destroyed."

"And what of President Roosevelt's parahuman? What counsel can you give us, doctor?" asked Mike.

"I do not know who created his parahuman, so I do not know if they properly applied holography. If they did not, instability will follow. The President's life could be in danger."

"Yes," said Mike, "that's an imminent risk that must be addressed, Dr. Edersheim. And another is, do I move to protect the President from that danger, or do I protect Agent Russo and me from the danger of revealing that secret?"

* * *

21

S ENATOR STEVEN ALBRIGHT AGREED to host Clark, Jimmy, and Bogie at his Virginia home until the culmination of the Senate hearings.

He promised them a first-class tour of Washington, D.C., with a bit of Washington nightlife prior to the hearings. All three agreed staying with the Senator was a better option for 'protective custody' than a minimum-security facility, so Director Benchley released them to the recognizance of the Senator.

The tour and night on the town were all part of Albright's plan. He intended to create quite a stir in the press. He'd let the three actors prove to the nation just how human a parahuman could be.

During the board meeting at SMP Studios, Senator Albright presented Sid Abrams with a subpoena and list of evidence the Senate committee was demanding. This included the names of those responsible for creating the parahuman actors. SMP immediately filed a lawsuit against the government for illegal seizure of private property—their created actors—seeking injunctive relief for termination of the action; a second lawsuit for illegally requiring and potentially exposing SMP trade secrets, a violation of Exemption 4 of the Freedom of Information Act; and a third lawsuit for interference with, and financial damage to the corporation, in violation of 18 U.S. Code § 981 an action of illegal civil forfeiture. SMP Studios claimed the right under U.S. law to protect their investors. Additionally, Chief Legal Counsel Bob Cavendish filed a complaint with the Securities and Exchange

Commission alleging illegal government seizure leading to irreparable damages for studio investors.

TWO WEEKS BEFORE THE hearings, Senator Albright began unveiling his spectacular plan.

He rented a double-decker, open-top bus so his three honored guests could tour Washington, and everyone in town could see them. He rented the whole bus with a professional tour guide, leaving plenty of room for select politicians and honored members of the community—including some folks back home, faithful members of his reelection committee. He invited the President of the Senate, Arthur Bryant; his fellow senator from California, Barbara Pomeroy (always at odds with him, but his graciousness was endearing to voters), and, of course, FBI Director Mike Benchley. Once the list of favored invitees was confirmed, he invited members of the Washington Press Corps to join them. His three parahumans needed to make a big, bright, visual splash across the media if he was going to secure public sentiment. And, to that end, Steven needed the greatest personality of all to come along for the ride.

"Mr. President, Senator Steven Albright is on the phone for you, sir. Should I let him know you are in a meeting?"

"Absolutely not! I've been waiting to hear from him since he got back from LA." The President moved to the phone at the Resolute Desk.

"Steve! You son of a gun, what took you so long? I thought I was going to have to send the Secret Service after you. You know I've been waiting to see Jimmy!"

"I'm sorry Jon, but I've been preparing for the hearing—with Jimmy on my back, asking when he could see *you*! You know he's staying with me. And he reminds me faithfully every morning that he hasn't seen you for almost forty years. Actually, once he said he hasn't seen you since he died!"

"Now that will shake a man up. How did you respond to that comment?"

"I just left it alone. I want his testimony to be pure and honest. Just like the real Jimmy Stewart."

"I agree with that decision, Steve. Few people can resist Jimmy's down-home humor and honesty."

"Jon, if we're going to help these three suffering souls, we need public support. And with that objective in mind—would you be interested in joining us next week? I'm giving the three stars a tour of Washington from an open-top double decker bus. I rented out the whole bus for the entire day! Lots of opportunities for the press to spread photos and video far and wide—and I've got plenty of reporters coming along with us. After the tour I've arranged dining at Ocean Prime. We'll have a private room, but the public will be close by. We'll have dancing and photo ops with surprised patrons. And—it can't hurt to ask—what do you say to a quick press conference with the three actors and you in the Rose Garden? That's nothing but press! Now, what do you think of my plan, Jon? Don't you think being seen with the President in public just might do the job?"

"I do, my friend, I do, but let me clear this with Marty and Josh. Committing to half a day and an evening comes with a price tag. I'll see what we can move around. Has the date already been set for next week?"

"Yes, I had to give a date to the tour company to reserve a bus and guide, but you know I will move this event to *any* day next week that works for you! You're the key to pulling this off, Jon. *I need you there.*"

"Okay, I'll have Marty get back to you in the next hour to confirm the day for next week. Oh—can I bring Deborah?"

"Jon, you already know the answer to that! I anticipated you bringing her! Already reserved a front row seat on the bus for the both of you!"

"LEXI, THIS IS MIKE. Got a minute?"

"For you, always! I think I hear jet engines. You on your way back from Tel Aviv?"

"As we speak!"

"So how did it go?"

"To say it was an eye-opener doesn't begin to describe it. A lot of actionable info."

"Did you go by yourself?"

"No, I took a supervisor from our Manhattan office. He's involved but on a different battlefront."

"You mean there's more parahumans than our three in Hollywood?"

"I'm sorry, beautiful, but we can't go there. Not now, anyway. Hopefully this all has a happy ending. For now, this is shaping up to be the perfect storm."

"Wow. Okay, maybe we better change the subject. So, to what do I owe the honor of an international in-flight phone call? You coming to see me? Another big night on the town sounds good!"

"Well you're almost right! Another big night on the town is on the agenda—but I'm wondering if you'd like to come to my side of the continent this time? Senator Albright asked me to join him and the three on a tour of DC. Open-topped bus, big sightseeing tour of D.C., dinner, dancing, and lots of press—which is what this is all about. He wants the nation to see the three as more than just parahumans. If he gets the support of the American people, he thinks he can nudge Sid and the board to pay for the wives to be re-created—maybe eliminate the loneliness these three are dealing with."

"You think it will work? The Sid I know doesn't like to be pushed."

"That was my concern, too, but the Senator said opinion polls have changed many a mind and opened many a pocketbook. Time will tell. Anyway, there's going to be some major dignitaries joining us. And it starts with a press conference in the White House Rose Garden. I'd sure like for you to be there with me. I checked and we have a plane in LA headed this way the day before the tour. I'll be waiting at the airport when you land!"

"Is that legal—for me to fly on an FBI plane?"

"Yes. I just pay the Bureau's finance division the rate they specify for a private ticket and they reimburse the Treasury. All legal and above board. So, what do you say? It wouldn't hurt for me to be seen with a kind, sweet, intelligent, articulate, beautiful woman from Hollywood—might enhance my standing, and help me climb the ladder of success!"

"Yea—like you'll ever be a political animal. I know better than that, Mike Benchley. But that's going to be an expensive ticket and I don't know if my budget will handle that right now."

"Lexi, you *can't* pay for this ticket! I have to take care of it since I'm the official requesting the accommodation. Besides, I've flown out to see you plenty. It's your turn to come see where I live—bad weather, high crime, congested streets—you'll love Washington. And you get to dress up for a night on the town. Confidentially, there's a chance the President and First Lady will be there!"

"Are you serious? I've never done anything like this before! But, Mike, what happens when the studio sees me in Washington with their three 'stolen actors'? They're really hot about this. Even worse, I'll be seen with the Deputy Director of the FBI who snatched them away from the studio. I might show up for work the following week and find I've been replaced!"

"Well, maybe I need to put *you* into protective custody!"

"Mike, I'm serious!"

"I'm sorry, Lexi. I'm not ignoring the potential for reaction by the studio. Maybe you shouldn't come. But they're going to see you with me eventually—unless you're planning to ditch me. And for all we know, they may already have seen us hobnobbing around LA."

"I hadn't thought of that."

"Listen, you could look any board member straight in the eye and tell them the FBI has done nothing to SMP based on anything you may have said or done—and that's the truth. We learned of Uriah Horvitz through an independent investigation, not because of you. The only actionable information you've given me is your cell number and address—and I only got that through my keen FBI interrogation techniques."

"Yea, I'm a pretty tough nut to crack. So you don't think Sid will fire me when he learns we're an item?"

"Lexi, you have protection under California Labor Code 1102.5. That's the so-called 'whistleblower protection.' And you could file a lawsuit for wrongful discharge and end up owning the studio—well, not really, but they'd owe you damages and your job back."

"Now how do you know all this employment legalese?"

"I do have a law degree, you know."

"Oh, yea. I think of you so much as a big shot with the FBI that I forget you Hoover boys have law degrees. And Clark told me to call you a Hoover boy."

"Well, we don't all have law degrees. Some of us are accountants or language experts. You know, Lexi, we might find you an administrative position here in DC so we can stop the twenty-seven hundred-mile flights."

"It would be nice to be closer. But that's a big move, Mike. Better let me checkout that D.C. weather and traffic before we make that call!"

"Ah, so you *are* going to join me for the gala event!"

"Yes. You've convinced me. Wow, the risks I take for the FBI. Okay, where do I catch this plane and when?"

THE FLIGHT BACK TO Washington was a constant conversation—intermixed with periods of exhausted sleep—for Mike Benchley and Joe Russo.

From wheels-up in Tel Aviv, the discussion was how best to proceed. They wouldn't get back to Washington until nightfall, so Director Benchley had an idea.

"We need to get Antonio into isolation so Dr. Edersheim can place him into *Theta* sleep and download Mancuso's memories. And we need to move on this immediately. There's too many possibilities for things to go wrong the longer we wait."

"I'm all for moving ASAP—but what are the pitfalls you're seeing?"

"The parahuman could be discovered by one or more of the Dons, the parahuman could disappear, taking all the evidence with him, someone else could capture the parahuman and duplicate the technology—and those are just for starters."

"I guess I've been so focused on getting the data out of New York's number one criminal I hadn't considered the criminal elements surrounding him."

"Yes, and there's more, Joe. I'm sure the Dons would pay handsomely to learn what has happened to the real Mancuso. His unhappy lieutenants just might sell Antonio out. And Antonio could go out on his own and get rid of Vincent, Frank, Tony, Salvatore—everyone who knows he's not the real Mancuso. The more people he exterminates, the less witnesses we have that can corroborate the downloaded evidence. If his emotional issues start, as they did in the Hollywood three, he's capable of anything—including flight or mass murder."

"You think he'd run? I mean, where would he go? It's not like there's a hideout for wayward parahumans."

"Well, now that you mention it, maybe we should start one! Give them a hideout and nab them at the same time! Seriously, based on Dr. Edersheim's explanation of the parahuman's emotional state, who knows what Donny Mancuso's twisted duplicate is capable of? Dr. Edersheim said he can move the parahuman into a *Theta* state so long as no one is around him to see that he's going to sleep."

"But who would know that Mancuso's parahuman never sleeps?"

"I think we have to assume all his lieutenants know. Frank and Tony kept Antonio while Mancuso was in Bolivia. Did they stay at Mancuso's house overnight with this creature? And then there's Vincent and Salvatore. Did Mancuso tell them Antonio never sleeps? Or could they have been with him when he ordered Uriah Horvitz to create the parahuman? They could have heard Dr. Horvitz say it. And we have to assume Uriah gave Mancuso a tablet to control Antonio—*where is it*? I'm betting if Antonio doesn't already have it, he'll move heaven and earth to get it. He doesn't want anyone controlling him! The safe bet is to assume all four of them know he doesn't require sleep. That means we have to isolate him or determine that he is isolated, then alert Dr. Edersheim to move him into *Theta*. And remember, he said he doesn't know what Antonio will do if he's disturbed during *Theta* sleep. Our objective is to isolate him so that no one is around."

"Mike, do we need a warrant to seize the evidence—the data in Antonio?"

"No, not a warrant, Joe. A court order is what we need. Because this is cloud data, normally either a court order or a subpoena would be required. The law treats cloud data the same as draft emails. However, a subpoena is impossible as would be a warrant. Since no one owns Antonio, there's no one to issue a warrant to. A court order, authorizing us to download the data related to an ongoing criminal investigation, that's what we're after."

"Makes sense."

"Another question we must answer is what's needed should we have to arrest Antonio? I'm thinking that a warrant would not apply because, as strange as this sounds, this could fall under the '*Plain View Doctrine*.' It could be argued that Mancuso's parahuman *is* the evidence. Seeing him, a fully functional copy of a crime boss, actively engaged in criminal activity, is the same as seeing cocaine on a traffic stop. No warrant needed."

"I never thought of a parahuman as 'walking evidence.' That's an interesting take."

"A second argument would be that this thing is not human. Do you need a warrant to arrest something that isn't human? We don't arrest a computer! This may not be any different than taking a suspect's computer—Antonio being the computer. As far as I can see, the parahuman is nothing more than a computer on legs."

"A mobile computer that can perpetrate heinous crimes wherever it goes. What a concept," Joe said with a wry smile.

"Yeah, what will they think of next? Okay, so here's what I'm thinking. Your team still has Mancuso's office under surveillance, correct?"

"Yes, sir, we do."

"Then we get your SAC to authorize increased surveillance of Mancuso's home, giving us a live stream of audio and video from within the house, and the surrounding grounds outside the house. When we know with one hundred percent certainty that Antonio is alone, we alert Dr. Edersheim."

"Do you want me to get the team on it when we get back to D.C.?"

"No, I'm going to call your SAC right now, in-flight, and get the expansion of surveillance. You jump on a call and get your team ready to go inside the home during the day tomorrow. Hopefully, by tomorrow night, we'll have him alone and ready for the good doctor to knock him out!"

22

PER SECRET SERVICE INSTRUCTIONS, the open-top, double decker tour bus arrived at the Secret Service garage in Rockville, Maryland, for a thorough inspection and attachment of bullet proof glass around the President's and First Lady's seat.

The vehicle remained at the garage under guard until the next morning when it was driven by a Secret Service driver into Washington. Senator Albright's stipulation was for the political guests to be picked up at the Capitol while he and the three stars toured the White House with President Roosevelt. They would then move outside to the Rose Garden for photos and a brief interview with the press. Once the bus arrived at the White House, they would conclude the press conference and hop aboard the bus to begin the tour of the capital. The President waited in the Oval Office sitting area with Josh Sizemore, Marty Martin, Jennifer Barton, and the White House photographer.

"Well, are you excited Jon? You've not seen Jimmy Stewart since you were a boy in Tinseltown!" asked Marty.

"I am looking forward to it—with some trepidation."

Jennifer Barton, press secretary, looked up from her notes of the tour schedule. "Trepidation, Mr. President? What could you possibly dread about seeing Jimmy Stewart again? I'm still trying to wrap my head around all the incredible press opportunities we have this afternoon and evening. We've *never* had an event like this before!"

"Trepidation is the wrong word," said the President. "Apprehension. I first worked on a film with Jimmy when he was fifty years old. I was seven. And the last time I saw him he was eighty-seven. He had just lost Gloria, and he asked me to come to his home. He didn't want to be alone. We spent the evening talking—talking and reminiscing. It was a tough time for him. And for me knowing there was nothing I could do to relieve his grief. I never saw him after that. He seldom left his home. The last thing I heard, he wouldn't allow the doctors to replace the battery in his pacemaker. He was ready to go."

"I'm sorry Mr. President," Jennifer said. "You've still got the actor in you—you almost made me cry!" The look on Jon's face said he was mentally somewhere else, remembering. Jennifer managed a faint smile as she sat on the couch next to the President. "Those memories aren't all bad, are they, Mr. President?"

"No, not bad, Jennifer. But have you seen any of the films SMP had Jimmy star in over the past year? He looks like he's thirty years old. I never knew Jimmy at that age. I don't know that he's really going to remember me!" Jon looked over at Marty with a look of surprise and said, "And here I am, talking like this is the *real* Jimmy Stewart, resurrected from the grave! I have to remind myself that this is just a parahuman re-creation of him. I have no idea what this re-created fellow is going to know or say to me—or I to him!"

The President picked up Jennifer's plan for press events at scheduled tour stops. He'd barely begun reading when there was a knock on the door and one of Josh's agents stepped in.

"Mr. President, Senator Albright and his three guests are here. They're waiting right outside the door, sir. And, well, if you don't mind me saying so, this is really freaky, sir! I went from never meeting a movie star to just being introduced to three of the most famous in the world. This is the highlight of my career with the agency!"

The President smiled at the agent. "Thank you, son, we'll be ready in just a moment." The President stood up, straightened his cardigan, dusted off his pant legs, and looked at Josh, Jennifer and Marty. "Do I look okay?"

"Mr. President," said Marty, "please try to remember *they're* the ones that are supposed to be impressed!"

"You're right Marty, I apologize. I'll try to behave more presidentially! Please show them in."

Senator Albright was laughing and just finishing a sentence as he stepped through the door and into the Oval Office. He paused by the door, next to Marty, while his three guests walked in, in single file. Steven led them toward the sitting area where the President, Jennifer Barton, and Josh Sizemore were standing.

"Gentlemen," said the Senator, "it is my honor to present to you the President of the United States ... " but before he could say his name, Jimmy Stewart jumped in.

"Jonathan Theodore Roosevelt! I've not seen you since I lost Gloria. Ya know, Jon, *you've really aged!*" The group burst out laughing as Jimmy stepped forward and locked the President in a full bear hug—as 'bearish' as skinny Jimmy Stewart could make it. Jon Roosevelt couldn't help but cling to the tall, lanky, legend. It had been so long. Jennifer tried to hide her moistening eyes. Seeing her President embrace Jimmy Stewart with that kind of affection—it wasn't something she was prepared for.

"Jimmy—I, I, I" the President stammered. There was a flood of memories coming too fast to reckon with.

Jimmy Stewart didn't miss the opportunity. "Now, now, just a minute, Jon, that, that verbal stumbling thing, that's *my* racket ya know!"

Everyone was laughing as Jon and Jimmy faced the photographer, arms around one another's shoulders.

"And what do you mean telling me I've *aged*? You should try this job sometime!" the President said. Everyone was enjoying this reunion and the President's obvious happiness with the friend he said goodbye to so many decades ago. The White House photographer was moving at every angle.

"Well, maybe I *will* try this job sometime!" Jimmy responded. "Ya know, just because I'm *'Jimmy Stewart the Sequel'* doesn't mean the sequel can't be as good as the original!"

"And just how many sequels did you do in your day?" asked Jon of his friend.

"You know very well I didn't do a single one! And that just means one is long overdue!"

Jon was laughing so much his side hurt—and he had forgotten his other guests.

"Oh, my goodness, I've been rude to you gentlemen! Please forgive me," he said as he stepped towards the other two stars. They had both been laughing with Jennifer, Marty, Josh, Senator Albright, and the photographer. The fact that these 're-created' stars had been laughing heartily, along with everyone else, registered with the President as being a most human trait.

"I'm sorry, Mr. President," said the Senator, "allow me to complete the introductions. This is Mr. Clark Gable, and this is Mr. Humphrey Bogart, both recently arrived from Hollywood, California, USA. Gentlemen, President Jonathan Theodore Roosevelt."

"And," said the President, "my press secretary Jennifer Barton, my chief of staff Marty Martin, and my director of White House security, Josh Sizemore. Gentlemen, I cannot tell you what an honor it is to finally meet you. I'm afraid my late entry into Hollywood did not allow me to meet either of you before now," the President said as he shook their hands and posed for photos.

"Mr. President," said Clark Gable, "I think what you mean is that we were already gone by the time you were on the scene. I made my untimely exit from Hollywood in November of 1960."

The President was clearly caught off guard and did not know how to respond. Clark Gable—or whoever this was addressing him—was speaking to the President of his death before young Jon Roosevelt was able to meet him.

"And I'm the old man of the group," Bogart chimed in, "born in 1899 and gone by 1957! But don't let such talk put you on your heels, Mr. President. That's just our way of saying we know why we're here in Chocolate City."

"Well, we don't really call it that anymore, Bogie," the President said. "America is no longer segregated as it was in your day. We've worked hard to eliminate nomenclature that tends to separate us. We are all Americans, and proud of it."

"I understand, Mr. President. But I was saying that we know why we're here. And it ain't nomenclature."

"No, no, it's not, Bogie. There's a lot of ground yet ahead of us. All of us. You have a story to tell the Senate and the American people, and so do I."

"You, Mr. President?" asked Senator Albright. "Do you wish to be called as a witness before the Senate investigative committee?"

"Yes, Steven, I do. I have some things to say that your committee and the country need to hear. But let's lay that to rest for today. The press is anxiously waiting to meet all three of our honored guests—and they have some questions to ask us, I'm sure. That's a big part of why you're here, too, isn't it Steven—this time with the press?"

"It is, Mr. President!"

"All right then let me take our guests on a quick tour of the White House and then we'll head to the Rose Garden to meet the press."

The President took the Hollywood three on as quick a tour as he could, given the White House has six floors and 132 rooms. But Jon Roosevelt did a commendable job and got his guests back to the Oval Office only a few minutes late for their press conference.

"Jennifer, I was concerned I would fatigue our three guests. As it turns out, they're just getting started and I'm ready to sit down! But I think we're expected, and we can't keep the press waiting. Would you want to take it from here?"

"Absolutely, Mr. President! Gentlemen, if you'll follow me, please," said Jennifer as she led them out of the Oval and toward the Rose Garden.

AFTER JENNIFER BARTON'S introduction, the President stepped to the podium in the Rose Garden and welcomed the press to the news conference.

"Ladies and gentlemen of the Washington Press Corps, I want to thank you for waiting a little longer for us than expected. The wait was my fault, not our guests', as I detained them so I could catch up with my old friend, Jimmy Stewart. We all know why you're here, and it's not to listen to me. But I need to say something as to why these gentlemen have been invited here by my friend and colleague, Senator Steven Albright of California. Life is our most precious possession. It is God's gift to us. We are expected to do something with it, to make the most of it, to bless others through the good we are able to render. Our hope, in return, is that we will be able to enjoy the good things life has to offer while we provide for those we hold most dear. I believe that is what these three gentlemen seek.

"The United States of America, from its beginning, has stood for freedom. There was a time when slavery was a part of our nation, but we fought a war to end that travesty. Slavery in any form is a mockery of freedom. Freedom, security, and opportunity are values we continue to hold sacred. There have been allegations these three individuals may have been subjected to some form of slavery and denied their rights under the Constitution. Perhaps the most difficult question yet to be answered is just how human is parahuman life? And how much life does artificial intelligence contain? The Senate will attempt to answer these questions–but I must say I don't envy them with the task that lies ahead of them! Now, I'm going to turn the mic over to Senator Steven Albright, so he can introduce these three actors who, in reality, need no introduction. Steven?"

The President took a step back and stood beside Jimmy Stewart as Steven Albright stepped up to the podium.

"Members of the press, it is my honor to introduce three citizens of the great state of California, long absent from my state and our country, but back amongst us once again, bringing happiness, laughter, and relief from the craziness of Washington. Here is Mr. Clark Gable, Mr. Humphrey Bogart, and Mr. Jimmy Stewart."

They stepped forward to loud applause. As several members of the press stood, they all stood. The stars smiled but remained silent amidst the standing ovation. This was the kind of press they remembered from three-quarters of a century earlier.

"Which of you distinguished gentlemen would care to go first?" Senator Albright asked as he stepped back from the podium and motioned toward the microphone with a sweep of his hand. They looked at one another and Clark, seeing Jimmy and Bogie's direction to step forward, walked up to the podium as the press took their seats.

"Well, ladies and gentlemen, we're supposed to take questions. It's been awhile since I've talked to the press—an adoring press, anyway!"

Reporters laughed and a few clapped. And the first reporter stepped up to the microphone prepared for them.

"Mr. Gable, I'm James Walsh with the Associated Press. Can you explain, in your own words, just why you've been summoned to Washington? What does the Senate expect to hear from you three?"

"My own words, Jim, is all I have. I know that the Senate wants to hear about how we've been treated since we arrived back at SMP Studios. That's pretty simple, isn't it?"

"Yes, sir, but you just used an interesting phrase, 'arrived back.' Do you know where you've been since you left?"

"Of course, Jim, we've all three been dead!"

The press gallery burst into laughter, including James Walsh, who stood waiting for the gallery to quiet down.

"Yes, sir, I understand! But, Mr. Gable, where have you been—or maybe I should ask, how did you go from being dead to being alive again?"

The gallery grew quiet. Senator Albright took his first step toward the podium and it caught Clark's eye. He immediately smiled and motioned him back.

"That's quite all right, Senator, I think all three of us expected questions like this." Clark's eyes narrowed as they always did when he made a serious point. "Honesty is what everyone in this town is going to get from us. I said we've been dead. But we're very much alive now. How I got here, well, Sid Abrams had me re-created as a parahuman. Now, if you want to ask how they did that, you'll have to ask some egghead with a pocket protector and a slide rule!"

More laughter from the press.

"I can only tell you my memories go back to my previous life, up until the time I was changing a tire and suffered a heart attack. I remember being in Hollywood Presbyterian Medical Center. I was there ten days and was feeling pretty good. But the doctors said I got an infection in my heart and suffered a second heart attack. Everything after that event I've learned since I got back to Hollywood. Anything else, Jim?"

"Since you got back to Hollywood, what's life been like for you this time around?"

"One production after another. Parties at Sid's house to meet his investors. And slowly awakening to where we've been, where we are, where we're going. And, painfully, what and who we've lost. A lot has changed over the past sixty years since I died. You know, Jimmy Stewart was one of the pallbearers at my funeral. Since I'm dying up here now, this might be a good time for you to step in, Jimmy!"

Jimmy Stewart walked up to the mic amidst the laughter and the applause the press gave Clark as he stepped back into line. Jimmy patted him on the shoulder as he walked by.

"Ya know, Clark, mentioning that I was an honorary pallbearer at your funeral isn't exactly the best way to tell people you're here to stay!"

The press corps was laughing and enjoying themselves, which is not something Washington correspondents are accustomed to at a Presidential press conference. To many, being rough with Washington insiders, and, at times, downright rude, was the stock in trade of reporters. A grandmotherly woman raised her hand and Jimmy pointed to her as she stepped to the microphone.

"Mr. Stewart, I'm Margaret Folz with the AARP magazine. Thank you for taking my questions!"

"Well, now, Margaret, did AARP send you here to sign the three of us up? I think the fact that we're each about a hundred and twenty years old should make us pretty good fodder for your readers—even if we do look thirty years old."

Amidst the laughter, Margaret asked, "Mr. Stewart, AARP readers, more than any other Americans, will remember your movies with great fondness. I think they would like to know what your favorite movies are from your long and distinguished career."

"Ya know, Margaret, I have a new career that's just begun. Let's don't let your readers forget about that one, will ya?"

The audience laughed at the jumbled-up sentence construction, so reminiscent of the real James Stewart.

"Okay, so your readers want to know some of my personal favorites. I'll tell ya how we're gonna to do this, Margaret. Now, now, we're gonna to play a game I used to play with my kids. It's called *'What Movie?'* Now, I'll say a line from an old movie that I was in, it will be a line that I had in the film. And you have to guess what movie the line is from. Are you ready?"

"Well, I don't know ... but I can certainly try!"

"That's the spirit. Okay, here's the first line, and you guess the movie." Jimmy paused, tipped his hat backward on his head, and, with his hands flailing said, *'Okay, let's just forget about the whole thing!'*"

Margaret looked horrified, thinking he was pulling out of the game. "But Mr. Stewart, you just said for me to try to guess!"

"Margaret, *that was the line*—you're supposed to tell me what movie that's from!"

The press corps erupted again into laughter.

"Oh! I'm so sorry, Mr. Stewart! I guess I'm not very good at this game!"

"Well, do ya know what movie that was? It's one of my favorites and that's what you asked me about."

"Oh, um, can you do it one more time?"

"Okay that violates the rules—but I'll do it just for you. Are you ready? Here it is: *'Okay, let's just forget about the whole thing!'*"

"Oh! UmI believe that was one of my favorites, too. Was that *'The Glenn Miller Story'*?"

"No, no. Look, does anyone else want to help Margaret out here? Come up here and give her a hint."

A reporter on the front row stepped up and whispered in her ear. Margaret smiled.

"Was the movie, *It's a Wonderful Life*?"

"That was it. You're a natural at this, Margaret! Okay, we'll give this game one more try, but this time, let's see how the whole press corps does! Here we go." Jimmy leaned forward, he raised his eyebrows and spoke in a low, gentle voice, as he said, "*Sometimes you're so beautiful it just gags me.*" Then he looked at the press corps and said, "Okay, everyone in the peanut gallery, all at one time, what movie was that?"

With one loud shout and in unison, the answer came, '*You Can't Take It with You*!'"

"Ya see that, Margaret? It works with groups, too! Look, I've taken too much time up here already"

"Mr. Stewart, how old are you, sir?" came a question from the press corps.

"Well, how old do I look?"

"You look like you're in your late twenties—about as you did in *Destry Rides Again*."

"Well, that's about as old as I feel! In fact, this wasn't planned, but I think most of you know that Jon Roosevelt and I were in several motion pictures together. I was older and he was younger—a lot younger, just a kid, even! Kinda funny, seeing him so old and me so young, ain't it?"

The press corps laughed and watched the President. Jimmy laughed and winked at Jon Roosevelt, then continued.

"But I'll bet he still remembers the dance routine we had to learn for our picture, *Street Smarts*. Would you folks like to see if the President and I can still do that little number?"

The press started clapping, whistling, and waving for the President to step up. At first, he refused, laughing and waving at the press that he couldn't, but Jimmy walked back and grabbed him by the hand and brought him to the side of the podium.

"Okay, Jon, you remember the steps, don't you?"

"Jimmy, that was sixty years ago! But, yes, I think I can do it."

The television cameras were zooming in as Jimmy Stewart and the President of the United States began a soft shoe routine. This dissolved into high stepping—so high that Jennifer Barton, standing behind them, kept reaching out in pantomime, like she was preparing to catch the President if he fell. They did their moves in perfect unison, including several spins, and ended with a high five of both hands. The press was on their feet. Jon was winded, Jimmy didn't break a sweat. They both embraced one another in a hug that caused the applause to increase and the cheers to cascade through the gallery. Jimmy motioned to the press that they'd clapped enough but they didn't want to stop. He and the president took several bows amidst calls of, "*Encore! Encore!*" Jimmy stepped back to the podium and motioned for them to take their seats. After another ten seconds of applause, the press calmed down.

"Okay, well, that was fun. It's not every day you can grab the President by the hand and not have the Secret Service grab you by the neck!"

Jimmy looked over at Josh Sizemore. He was laughing and nodding his approval as the press and the President laughed and clapped.

"All right, that does it for me. Let me bring my friend, Mr. Humphrey Bogart, up here so you can shoot *him* a few questions—but I'd be careful if I were you—he's been known to shoot back!"

Jimmy laughed as he turned and shook Bogart's hand. Laughter and applause came with whistles and cheers, calling Bogart to the mic.

"Well, thank you, Jimmy. I've played some tough guys in my film career, yes, but my favorites were always the gentle moments with the ladies. Ingrid Bergman in *Casablanca*, Katherine Hepburn in *African Queen*, and my personal film favorite, *To Have and Have Not*. Does anyone know why that was my favorite picture?"

A reporter yelled out, "That was your first picture with Lauren Bacall!"

Bogart pointed to him and said, "You're absolutely right! And before I take any questions, I'll answer one that was already asked, '*Why are we in Washington?*' I'll tell you a big reason for all three of us. We want our girls back. I want Baby—sorry, some of you may not know but that's what I always called Lauren. Jimmy wants Gloria, and Clark wants Carole Lombard. And folks, we're going to get them, even if I have to play the heavy to make it happen."

More laughter and applause as the President stepped forward.

"Members of the press, I know you didn't get much time for questions, but we certainly had fun, didn't we? I'm afraid we must cut this short. The tour bus just arrived to take us sightseeing in Washington and Senator Albright promised these three distinguished stars a tour of our nation's capital. You're going to be seeing and hearing plenty from them over the next few days as they give testimony before the Senate, and, I'm sure, make opportunity for additional questions from the press. With that ... "

The press corps was suddenly on its feet. The president could hear various questions being called out, but they all came down to the same thing. "What happened to you in Tehran?" He motioned for them to take their seats.

Ladies and gentlemen, please, I know you have waited a long time to ask me questions about the attempted assassination in

Tehran. This small bandage still on the side of my head doesn't tell the full story. But I promise you, you're going to hear more about it in the very near future. Please, be patient and I'll make it worth your while. Now, once again, we need ... "

A reporter had moved up to the microphone and blurted out, "Excuse me, Mr. President, but no one asked any of these three stars the most important question of all, 'are you three happy in what is now your second life?'"

The President felt Bogie at his left arm and heard him say, "Excuse me, Jon, that's my cue." The President didn't step backward but moved to the side. He was going to end this as soon as Bogart finished addressing the question.

"Sir, as Clark promised you, you're going to get complete honesty from us. Complete honesty isn't something anyone expects, in Hollywood or in Washington."

Some reporters laughed, but the majority were waiting and watching Bogie intently. The networks had alerted the press corps that the Senate investigation into the treatment of the three stars was already rating as high in the polls as Jon Roosevelt's trip to Tehran—and the hearings hadn't started yet.

Bogie looked across the press corps, side to side, before he spoke. He was not smiling. "No, we're not happy in this second life. Not yet, anyway. To begin with, just like all of you, we weren't asked if we wanted to be born ... "

A few chuckles were heard but immediately greeted with some 'shush' noises. The expression on Bogart's face was as serious as any fan had ever seen.

" ... but here we are and we're going to have to make the best of it. The studio that brought us back to life—or gave us *this* life, however you want to look at it—created us as entertainers. That's how all of you see us, isn't it? That's how I imagine most people saw me on the big screen during the 40s and the 50s. Are we human? Not so much as you describe humans. But we're made up of the memories of our first selves—the human actor. That means *all* of their memories. I can see those memories in my mind every moment of every day. I guess it's what makes us good at being who we were created to be. But like the real Bogie, I have an empty spot in my gut. I guess you could say I'm lonely. I'm lonely because I'm in love. In love with Lauren Bacall, a woman I've never really known, spoken with, or held in my arms. Oh, the human Bogart did—but not me. All I have are memories and even those memories are not really mine."

Bogie paused and looked over the audience of reporters. The press watched him and waited. Bogie turned around and looked at Clark and Jimmy, then at the President.

"When you look back on your life, just before the doc tells you the party's over and they turn out the lights, you all will look back on memories. But you will have experienced them, lived them, enjoyed them." Bogie's voice elevated and his demeanor suddenly became agitated and more intense. He struck the podium with his fist as he said, "I'll never know the one person that truly defined me as 'Bogie,' that was supposed to complete him—me—that made me who I was, on screen and, most importantly, off screen, in his domestic life—I mean, mine—my domestic life."

Something was wrong. As if the lines in his brain were blurring between the real and the imagined.

Bogie calmed down a bit, then seemed to plead, "I want her back, just as you would. As I know you do—you want Lauren back, don't you? For us to be on the screen together again? *Key Largo*, *The Big Sleep*, *To Have and Have Not*—right?"

Some in the gallery were nodding in agreement with him. Others were busy taking notes, others observing him, wondering what was going to happen next. He was scanning the reporters again when he added, "I intend to ask the Senate to help me get

Lauren Bacall back. Back into my life—or into it for the first time—for my sake and yours, too!"

The press corps applauded—more quietly this time. From Bogart's left side, the President of the United States stepped toward him and the podium. He had at least some idea what Bogie was experiencing, having seen the emotional side of Rosebud in Tehran. He put his arm around him and then faced the press.

"Members of the press, that concludes our interviews. I want to thank all of you for your kind interest. I also thank Humphrey Bogart, Jimmy Stewart, and Clark Gable for coming to Washington as our guests. Senator Albright and I assure you that we will take good care of them during their stay here ... and concerning this very difficult issue that Bogie shared with you today. I commit to you and the American people that we *are* going to do something about this. Jennifer, would you assist the members of the press with what questions you can?"

The Secret Service began to move the President, Senator Albright, and the three stars back toward the White House colonnade where additional agents formed a line toward the double-decker bus. Some reporters were attempting to call out questions, but the agents were moving the group quickly toward the bus. Jennifer Barton took to the podium and began fielding questions as the President and his guests made their way to the bus.

* * *

23

STEVEN ALBRIGHT ASSIGNED BUS SEATS STRATEGICALLY. He always had a plan.

The President and Mrs. Roosevelt were seated on the front row rooftop. Josh Sizemore and the Presidential detail were seated across the aisle from them. Right behind Jon and Deborah Roosevelt were Clark Gable, Jimmy Stewart, and Humphrey Bogart—directly across from the press, of course. At the request of the three, Steven placed Mike Benchley and Lexi Bristol in the seat behind them. They said Mike was their rescuer but Lexi had always taken time to listen to them. Lexi was their friend.

The tour bus left the White House, heading down Pennsylvania Avenue for the Capitol. After the tour guide completed the history of the historic building, the bus headed for the Supreme Court. Stops just ahead would include the National Cathedral, the Smithsonian Castle, and then the National Mall, also called 'America's Front Yard.' There they would see the Washington Monument, the Martin Luther King Memorial, the Jefferson Memorial, and the Lincoln Memorial. They would finish up at the Pentagon, and then head to dinner at Ocean Prime. Lexi hoped to see the Hoover building.

"Will we go past your office, Mike? I'd like to see it."

"No, the Hoover building is not on the schedule, beautiful. But I should be able to take you there before you have to head back. Should we discuss you moving to D.C. with the President just two rows up? He might hear us and hire you as his assistant!"

"Wow—first you pit the FBI and U.S. Senate against SMP, then you add the President of the United States?"

"I see nothing wrong with that ... *beautiful*," teased Clark, turning around in his seat.

"Clark Gable! Are you eavesdropping on our conversation?" Lexi asked.

"With these ears? I eavesdrop whether I want to or not! And in your case, I want to! You need to get away from Sid and the studio, Lexi. You need to get out of Tinseltown. And while it's just my humble opinion, you two need to get closer. Close the gaps."

"Thanks, Clark," said Mike. "I'll slip you that twenty when Lexi can't see the transaction!"

"Are you two ganging up on me? What's a girl supposed to do, surrounded by such big, strong, handsome men?"

"Seriously, babe, how you holding up?" Mike's face showed his concern. "Your first trip here and I've got you with the President, the Washington Press Corps, and anyone who's anyone in politics. Things have been moving so quickly, I'm afraid I've not been looking out for you very well."

"Oh, Mike—are you kidding? This is wonderful! I'm overwhelmed—but loving it!"

"Overwhelmed, Lexi?" asked Bogie, turning around in his seat. "Just two seats behind the President and First Lady, and rows ahead of all those gawking politicians and vulgar rich. They're all wondering how you landed in such a prominent seat!" Bogie let out his gravelly laugh.

"And you neglected to mention I'm right behind my three favorite leading men!"

Jimmy, sitting to Bogie's right, turned around. "Well now, Miss Bristol, I reckon you know I left you alone this long so Mike wouldn't have any competition for your attention!"

"Thank you, Jimmy, I appreciate that," said Mike.

"Jimmy, do you think Sid knows about Mike and me? That might not be good."

"I wouldn't worry about that, Lexi. I see you and Mike kinda like me and Jean Arthur in *Mr. Smith Goes to Washington*. Do you two remember that movie?"

"Sure do, Jimmy—one of my favorites!" said Mike.

"I love that movie! One of my dad's favorites, too," said Lexi. "How do you see Mike and me being like you and Jean Arthur?"

"Well, not many know this, but the planned finish of that film ended up on the cutting room floor. *Jefferson Smith*—that was me—and *Saunders*—that was Jean—got married and settled down to start a family. Just wasn't enough room in the film to keep that ending in it. You didn't know that, did you, Lexi?"

"No, I didn't! Wait ... *you see Mike and me doing that?*" Mike was smiling. Lexi was blushing–and quickly changed the subject.

"So was *Mr. Smith* filmed here in Washington? The studios didn't go on location as much back then as they do now, did they?"

"Some of it was. We used the Capitol for a few takes. Took film of monuments for backgrounds. Ya know, Columbia wasn't sure they wanted to make the picture. MGM and Paramount had both turned it down on recommendation of the Hays Office."

"The Hays Office?" Lexi asked.

"They provided industry guidelines for self-censorship," said Mike, "through what was known as the *Hays Code*. Hollywood created the Hays Office and the code. They were trying to keep the government out of their business."

"That's right," said Jimmy. "You can see that didn't work out too well!"

They were all laughing as Clark joined in.

"Just think of it, they started off policing themselves to *prevent* government involvement. Then they dropped their code of decency and it became a self-fulfilling prophecy—so here we are, the government questioning the industry's decency!"

"You see, Lexi," said Jimmy, "there's kinda always been a sort of power struggle between Hollywood and Washington. Motion pictures can change the course of a nation by changing how citizens think. *Mr. Smith Goes to Washington* was banned in a lot of countries where the Nazis had gained power—like Germany, Italy, Spain, and France. We sorta expected that. But it sure shocked Columbia and Frank when it lit a fire here in our own country!"

"I'm sorry, Jimmy—who's Frank?" asked Lexi.

"Frank Capra. He directed the picture. Yeah, the message was a sort of a burr under some people's blanket. We premiered the film on October 17, 1939, right here in Washington, in Constitution Hall. We invited four thousand guests including forty-five senators. They took one look at that film and came unglued! The Senate Majority leader called the film 'silly and stupid.' The Washington Press Corps said we were pro-Communist and anti-American for implying corruption in the government. One journalist suggested the Senate pass legislation so theaters could refuse to show it!"

"Did the Senate do that?" Lexi asked.

"No—but the Senate got their revenge! Less than ten years later, the Supreme Court busted up the studio system by the government suing Paramount. But before I died in 1997, exactly fifty years after we released *Mr. Smith*, in 1989 it was added to the National Film Registry. It was finally praised for showing what *can* happen behind the scenes in politics. And even in 1939, as harangued as it was, the film was nominated for *eleven* Academy Awards."

"Eleven!" Lexi exclaimed. "That speaks well of the film!"

"Yes, yes, it does. But the picture only took one of the awards."

"*And why was that?*" asked Clark with a wry smile.

"You know very well why!" Jimmy retorted.

"Well?" asked Lexi.

"Because 1939 was the year *Gone with the Wind* knocked us all out!"

Clark began laughing—then Jimmy began laughing with him.

THE USUALLY SUBDUED crowd at the posh Ocean Prime restaurant began applauding as the President and First Lady entered behind the Secret Service.

The applause turned into a crescendo of cheers as Clark, Humphrey, and Jimmy stepped in behind the President. The President and the three waved to diners, who began standing as they applauded. Cellphone cameras were in action. And the media was capturing it all—just as Senator Albright had planned.

Josh tried to lead the party to the private room. Jon Roosevelt, along with Clark, Jimmy, and Bogie, kept stopping to shake hands and pose for selfies with patrons. Josh had seen it all before.

"Mike, this is so exciting!" Lexi whispered in his ear. "I've been to plenty of studio premieres but nothing on this scale!"

"Yes, Washington knows how to make a big production when it needs to." He looked down the hall. "I'm not part of the protective detail for the President. How 'bout we find our table? It's assigned seating."

"Sure!" she said as Mike took her by the hand.

The dinner tables were large and circular, elegantly draped in white linen. Guest name cards were at each seat. Mike and Lexi were seated next to the President's table but by themselves.

"Mike, it looks like we're the only couple seated by ourselves," Lexi said, "and this is such a big table. Why would they seat just the two of us here?"

"I knew we would be seated alone. Senator Albright apologized to me. He said there would not be room enough at their table, but they wanted us right beside them—so here we are! But if you're uncomfortable, I'll see if we can move and join some other table."

"Don't you dare! It was very gracious of Senator Albright to place us right next to them—and I get to be alone with my guy. Well … as alone as you can be with the President of the United States one table over!"

After wait staff had taken orders, dinner candles were lit at each table and wall sconces were dimmed. Dance music began playing. President Roosevelt rose, helped Deborah with her chair, and they took to the dance floor. Other couples joined them.

"Well, beautiful, would you care to dance?" Mike stood to get her chair.

"I thought you'd never ask!"

Mike took her in his arms. It was as romantic as it could be—with the press weaving in and out of the couples, cameras clicking as they went.

"Wherever I go, there's always cameras," said Lexi. "Is that a coincidence or just the curse of Hollywood?"

"Or maybe a blessing?" asked Mike.

"A blessing?"

"Sure. How many other couples get into a private dinner with the President and the top three actors in Hollywood—and have the press professionally photographing their entire evening for free?"

Lexi smiled. "You're right. You so often see things differently than I do. Why is that?"

"Maybe it's my age. I am a few years older than you. I guess I'm really just a big brother to you."

"A big brother? So I'm just a little sister to you?"

"Lexi, you look lovely tonight. Never lovelier. You're absolutely radiant."

"Don't think you can dig your way out of this by sweet talking me! Besides, I'll bet you say that to all the women you fly cross-country to tour Washington—and dance with you—while dining next to the President and First Lady. Am I talking too much?"

Mike kissed her.

"I didn't see that coming," she whispered as she laid her head against his chest.

"I did!" Mike smiled. The music ended and couples were walking back to their tables. Mike seemed to hesitate.

"Mike—shouldn't we head back to our table? Is something wrong?"

He took her hand and walked back. The waiter was standing by their table.

"May I pour the lady some champagne?" he asked.

"Oh, yes, thank you," she said as Mike helped her with her chair. The waiter had already filled Mike's glass as he sat down and lifted the flute by the stem.

"Lexi, I want to make a toast. To you. The most wonderful girl I've ever known."

She took her glass

"Oh, Mike ... *there's something in my drink!* I'm so sorry! Can you get me another glass?"

She felt a hand on her shoulder. "I don't think he needs to, Lexi!" said Jon Roosevelt. "It's a bit dark in here. Maybe it's time to turn up the lights."

Lexi turned her head to look up at the President. She was smiling—nervously—looking up at Jon Roosevelt, and then at Mike. She'd been around the President all day, but Mike had not yet introduced her. She felt awkward. Deborah Roosevelt walked over and was now standing beside her husband, smiling at Lexi. She didn't know what to do. The President gave a 'thumbs up' and the room lighting came up. She wanted to stand and face the President and his wife, but Mike handed her the champagne flute before she could rise.

"I'm afraid there *is* something in your glass, Lexi," Mike said.

In the midst of the amber bubbles sat the most stunning two carat engagement ring she had ever seen. The glass was quivering—she feared she could drop it. She was staring at the ring when Mike knelt down beside the table.

"Lexi Marie Bristol, *will you marry me?*"

She could feel the tears coming. The crowd had grown silent. She looked around the room. They were all smiling and watching–and collectively holding their breath. She could hear the sniffles of the ladies close by. Mike was right. Press cameras were getting it all.

"Don't tell me I need to issue an executive order to make this happen!" said the President, both hands now on her shoulders.

She felt the tears trickle down her cheeks as she looked into the eyes of the man she loved. Six feet, three inches of muscle, grit, determination, gentleness, and love. His eyes were fixed on her, waiting.

"*I will!*"

Mike suddenly appeared to relax. "Wow," he said loud enough for all to hear. "I've been threatened, punched, shot at, and nearly blown to bits—but that was the scariest bit of *quiet* I've ever heard!" The crowd laughed. Lexi grabbed him and cried.

The room broke into applause. "*Congratulations! Kiss her again!*" Mike took the ring out of the champagne flute, wiped it with his napkin, then slipped it on her finger. He took her hand in his and raised her from the chair. Deborah Roosevelt hugged her, then the President embraced her. Jon took his wife by the hand, then turned Mike and Lexi towards the people. Lexi was trying to dry her eyes and her running mascara. The President had his hand on Mike's shoulder

"Well, folks," said the President, "Hollywood isn't the only town where they know how to script a happy ending! Mike was kind enough to include Deborah and me in this surprise for Lexi. And after avoiding her all day, I finally got to meet her! Mike deliberately kept her from Mrs. Roosevelt and me so we could catch her off guard at dinner. It was brilliant! Let this prove to all of you, the FBI knows how to lay a trap for the best, the brightest, and the most beautiful!"

The crowd laughed and applauded. Clark, Humphrey, and Jimmy came and stood with Lexi and Mike.

"The food is coming out, but I want to thank Senator Steven Albright for making this evening possible. He's a great friend and a great man! Now, let's have the blessing and we'll eat."

The day had accomplished what Steven Albright planned. A veritable avalanche of media coverage presenting the more human side of the parahumans. The stage was now set. He was ready for the hearings.

* * *

24

T HE LONG-AWAITED DAY for SMP's re-created stars to appear before the televised Senate subcommittee had finally arrived.

Washington was awash with reporters. Pew Research estimated an astounding two and one-half billion people saw the White House Rose Garden interview of the three Hollywood legends. The heartwarming engagement of the stars with the press gallery had worked media magic. Humphrey Bogart's impassioned and challenging appeal had reached the hearts of the people. They wanted to know what was going to be done for the three re-created actors. The week leading up to the hearings, reporters began pouring into Washington from around the world. Passes to the visitor's gallery were snatched up in the first twenty minutes they were offered. Fox News, the most watched of the televised news sources, had chosen to provide twenty-four-hour coverage, with updates on the hour, noting the demands of their viewers following the Rose Garden interview, which they were now calling the 'Resurrection in the Garden.' Washington and the nation were at a fever pitch, wondering what the three would have to say. The morning shows were abuzz with speculation. The first news broadcast went live at 8:00 AM eastern time, with reporter Dave Daniels, standing in the morning chill on the steps of the Capitol building, the dome behind him refracting a luminescent orange with the rising of the sun.

"Every major news source is in the nation's capital today for what has been vaunted as the second great showdown between the federal government and the Hollywood studios. 'When was the first time?' you may be asking. It was way back in the year 1948, when the landmark case, *United States v Paramount* broke Hollywood's stranglehold on the movie houses and, in effect, the studio bosses' control over what had been known as their 'stable of stars.' Following that landmark decision, movie stars were no longer owned by the studios, requiring permission to make films for another studio. Within a decade, the stars began negotiating for a share of the box office in lieu of a higher salary. But that was 1948 and the Supreme Court decision affected *all* Hollywood studios. This time, we're talking about a single studio, 'Silverscreen Motion Pictures' or SMP as it was known in the classic Hollywood years. SMP was a powerhouse studio from the 1930s to the 1950s, but they fell on hard times in the 60s. And, of course, this time, it's only three stars reportedly being controlled by the studio—three actors who have been called *re-created stars*: Humphrey Bogart, Jimmy Stewart, and Clark Gable.

"So, this is shaping up to be *SMP versus the U.S. Senate*. And, to be clear, this is not a court case. This is a Senate investigation into several issues involving the very existence of these re-created Hollywood stars, using what the FBI is calling 'new technology.' Technology that has yet to be explained or even identified. In fact, it appears only SMP has this tech or knows who created the three actors. The studio has refused to reveal their source. And if the FBI knows, they simply are not saying. Another term being used to describe these re-created stars is 'parahuman.' As far as anyone knows, these three are the only three parahumans in existence. One final note: The things these re-created actors said during the so-called '*Resurrection in the Garden*' press event gave us only slight insight into who or what these re-created beings may actually be.

The hope is these Senate hearings will give the public the details they are clamoring for. Now, back to Greg Stanfield in New York."

"Dave, a couple of questions if you're still with us. Can you still hear me?"

"Yes, Greg, I'm here."

"Okay, great. On the morning show earlier today, Molly, Sophie and I had a lively discussion about that term, '*Parahuman*,' wondering just what this designation means. Do we know *why* they're being called this? And do you know if human cloning was involved? As we discussed on the morning show, cloning is heavily regulated in the United States, correct?"

"Greg, I've found only scant information of what that term means. And I've not heard any explanation of how these beings, these re-created actors, were made. Was cloning involved? There's the possibility that cloning was involved but the very term, parahuman, seems to imply they are not fully human as cloning would make them. I don't see how such incredible accuracy of appearance and voice could have been achieved with cloning alone. The FDA approves or disapproves human cloning projects in the United States, so we checked with them and found that the actor re-creation was not an approved project. Of course, government approval has not always stopped science from moving forward with something they see as either essential technology or, well, just too lucrative to pass up. But, with what little information I've unearthed, my feeling is, until the scientist or group of scientists involved in what must have been a colossal effort to accomplish this sophisticated level of human re-creation—until they are found or come forward, there's likely to be more questions than answers."

"Dave, Fox News polling says this issue is drawing more public interest than anything since the attempted assassination of the President in Tehran. Why do you think this is so?"

"Several reasons, Greg, and the first reason may take me a minute to explain, so I'll ask our viewers to bear with me. First, prior to the Rose Garden interview, we didn't really know these actors were functioning beings. Computer graphics have come a long way and as far as any of us knew, they were just Hollywood animation, AI generated avatars, virtual reality—not real people. The thought of interviewing them would have been like interviewing Mickey Mouse or ET. Seeing one of them dancing in the Rose Garden with the President of the United States changed all that. We now know these are real beings. It was also the first time anyone outside of Hollywood had ever heard these three parahuman actors speak *off-script*, totally on their own. Prior to the Rose Garden, we'd only heard movie lines come from their lips. They shared with the world what they were thinking and what they were feeling. Hearing such passion, even from a cloned or created actor such as Humphrey Bogart, almost defies words. It was simply staggering. Just a year ago, these legends were dead, and except for late night movies, they were all but forgotten. They had not been relevant in motion picture production for at least sixty years. And it was almost *ninety* years ago that the world first saw a young, dapper Clark Gable as 'Rhett Butler' standing at the bottom of a staircase, looking up at Scarlett O'Hara in *Gone with the Wind*. The Rose Garden interview broke forth on the public as what the media has been calling it, the '*Resurrection in the Garden*.' The world suddenly realized these three men are alive again—whatever that may mean. They're young, in their prime, and, to everyone's surprise, they're incredibly vulnerable."

"Dave, excellent report. Thank you. And I'm assuming that was your first reason why so many people are tuning in to this historical event. You said there was a second reason?"

"Greg, the second reason is no less important than the first. The FBI supposedly received accusations of 'slavery' in how SMP

Studios is controlling these re-created stars. That is obviously going to be a poignant issue with all Americans, our country having fought a civil war to end the evils of slavery. Sources tell me that the president of SAG, the Screen Actors Guild, Mr. Howard Gordon, was the first to contact the FBI with this accusation. And another source, sharing with the promise of anonymity, told me the FBI's Executive Assistant Director over Science and Technology, Mr. Michael Benchley, personally responded to the accusation and has been involved with the investigation from the start."

"So, let's summarize this for our viewers, Dave. What is the Senate looking for—what is the hoped-for outcome, or the likely outcome of this hearing?"

"First, the Senate committee will want to hear what the FBI has found concerning the charge of slavery. Second, the Senate will want to hear if human cloning has, in fact, been done as this could make them fully human. Third, if this was not cloning, the technology, whatever it is, has to be of great concern to the Senate as it should be to all of us. And, fourth, I was told that the president of the Screen Actors Guild also alleged a monopoly by SMP Studios, which would be a violation of RICO antitrust laws. If that is found to be true, that only SMP has access to this technology, it may actually be a relief to the Senate."

"Just a minute, Dave. You said two things here I want to follow up on. You said this technology has to be a concern for the Senate and all of us. Why is that?"

"Greg, if we can create a copy of someone *this* convincing, this real, look at the possibilities. What if the President of the United States was duplicated without the President's knowledge? Could a foreign country use that technology to create a type of 'Manchurian Candidate' that would do the bidding of a foreign government or a rogue organization? What about duplicating

CEOs of major corporations and using them to control American utilities, food production, even financial markets?"

"I'd say that's worth a Senate investigation, Dave! But you also said a monopoly by SMP could be a *relief to the Senate*. How so?"

"Pretty much for the same reason I just stated. If it's a monopoly then only SMP has the tech. But if this technology has spread to other countries, other people could be involved in something more nefarious than motion picture production, and these 'clones' could be used to duplicate people in key positions for the work of miscreants. I'm sure the Senate would rather learn that SMP is the only organization to have this technology."

"I understand. You started talking about the President of the United States, but you just added 'people in key positions.' How do you see that possibility playing out?"

"It doesn't have to be the cloning of someone who has died, such as Clark Gable. Creating a famous person who is dead, and bringing them suddenly to life, makes them very easy to spot. But suppose a foreign power–or organized crime syndicate–duplicated key political and business leaders with a parahuman, then the human leaders were kidnapped and eliminated. Our nation could be conquered virtually overnight. Whether they're placed in the military, on Wall Street, or in Washington and state houses all over the nation, these parahumans could perform traitorous acts simultaneously that would destroy American sovereignty and personal freedom."

"Dave, you've given us a lot to think about. Some major issues that could and should come up before the Senate. Thanks for the in-depth, live report."

"My pleasure, Greg."

"Well, America wants to know so stay tuned everyone. The hearings start in about an hour and Fox News will be live. Let's pause for a quick break."

* * *

25

ANTONIO ARRIVED AT HIS OFFICE at the usual time of 4:30 AM.

Sleep is not something parahumans do on their own. You either put them to sleep or they just keep going. But, as a complete repository of Adonis Mancuso's suspicious, distrusting mind, Antonio always assumed he was being watched by someone. He never stayed at the office working through the night—that would be too obvious. Working all night, every night, never going home to sleep, eat, change clothes, whatever the world expected the real Adonis Mancuso to do—that would set off alarms. So home he went, creating the charade of domesticity.

By 9:00 AM the Mancuso inner circle arrived, absent Vincent, of course. Frank and Tony arrived first.

"Good morning, Mr. Mancuso. I brought you a latte."

"Thank you, Frank. Please be seated."

"Good morning, Mr. Mancuso. How did you sleep, sir?"

"As well as I always do, Tony, thank you. Please be seated. We have a lot to cover this morning. I trust that Salvatore will be here shortly."

"Should we wait for Vincent, Mr. Mancuso?" asked Frank. But Salvatore had just blasted through the door and Antonio saw him walking toward his desk.

"Something I can help you with, Salvatore?" Antonio asked.

"Antonio, where's Vincent?"

"You will address me as Mr. Mancuso, Salvatore. This was stipulated and agreed upon several weeks ago. Sit down. We have a lot to discuss."

"I asked you where Vincent is ... sir. He was supposed to meet me Thursday morning for the neighborhood rounds but he never showed. I've been trying to reach him for two days. Vincent has never disappeared like this. What's happened to him, Mr. Mancuso?"

AGENT FITZSIMMONS GRABBED the phone. "Mr. Russo, you'd better get to the surveillance room fast. I think there's something going on with Antonio and Salvatore. Sparks are flying!"

"Thanks Fitzy, I'm on my way!"

"I ASKED YOU WHAT HAPPENED to Vincent!" Frank had seen Salvatore like this many times and it never ended well. Of the two Capos, Vincent was the thinker. He tended to remain calmer and reason his way through challenges. Salvatore had the Sicilian temperament. If he felt threatened, insulted, or cheated, he took action—and thought about the consequences later. Frank was already standing up and pleading with Salvatore and Antonio to calm down.

"I don't need to calm down, Frank," Antonio said calmly. "I never get angry. It gains me nothing."

"No, you never get angry, do you, you filthy machine! You just treat humans like they're beneath you. Now, I'm going to ask you just one more time, what happened to Vincent?"

"What do you intend to do, Salvatore? You cannot match my physical strength, my intelligence, or my skill. You cannot replace me. I alone have Mancuso's complete knowledge of this organization, of every deal that has ever been made, where the assets are—and my signature matches Mancuso's perfectly. This organization rests completely on me. To the Dons, to the Feds, I am Adonis Mancuso. If I were to disappear, the organization would be taken over by the other crime families. If you were to disappear, who would care?"

"Oh, so you're saying I'm not important to this organization?"

"You're very important, Salvatore—especially to the Feds! I hold every memory of every crime you perpetrated. Suppose the FBI received a letter detailing the murders you committed, when, how, and where the bodies are buried? A road map by which to lock you away. Sounds interesting, doesn't it?"

Frank was pretty sure Antonio could see what this was doing to Salvatore. Antonio was deliberately provoking him.

"Or suppose we add Vincent's death to the list of those you murdered. I have the *proof* you were there, Salvatore. It seems you and Vincent were having trouble when you were out of the country. Competition over cocaine imports coming into each other's territories. You became enraged and killed Vincent, gouging out his eyes. Everyone knows how incredibly volatile you are. When they find his body, I will make sure they find the evidence. End of the road, Salvatore!"

Salvatore snapped. Frank and Tony tried to hold him back, but he pulled free and lunged at Antonio, running around the side of Mancuso's desk. Mancuso's memories and skills served Antonio well. In a Krav Maga move, as Salvatore leaped at Antonio, Antonio calmly stepped to his left and thrust the thumb and two fingers of his right hand like daggers into Salvatore's throat, coming in behind his larynx. Locking his grip on Salvatore's larynx, he twisted violently and crushed it. Salvatore's eyes began to protrude as he gasped for air. In one quick move, and with twice the strength of a human, Antonio spun Salvatore around, drove his knee hard into Salvatore's back, while grabbing the thick hair on the front of his head. Pushing down, he snapped Salvatore's head backward. The cracking sound from Salvatore's spine caused Frank's gag reflex to trigger, and he fell forward on his hands and knees, vomiting. Salvatore went limp, but Antonio caught him and gently lowered his body to the floor.

Tony stood over Salvatore's lifeless body. "So, you kill a man by crushing his windpipe and breaking his neck but show respect by easing his body to the floor? I don't get you, Mr. Mancuso."

"I didn't want the noise of someone falling in my office, Tony. No need for a crowd to gather–not until tonight. Salvatore knew the authorities were closing in on him for Vincent's murder, so he chose to leap off the roof of this building rather than face a murder rap. Landing on the sidewalk at West 47th and 6th Avenue will definitely attract a crowd, and that's going to happen tonight. You and Frank will take him up to the roof as soon as it's dark."

Frank was still on the floor, on his hands and knees. Tony stood looking at Antonio, stunned into silence.

"Kindly move the body to our storage closet on the seventeenth floor. You can return this evening to complete the assignment."

Tony stooped to help Frank up from the floor.

"You'll find a body bag in my private restroom, Frank. Under the sink, in a storage box. Use it to get him to the storage closet upstairs. After you've dropped him over the side this evening, be sure to fold the bag and store it in the box. Those things cost me money. Oh—Frank, no need for you to clean up your filthy vomit. Just call the in-house janitor." Antonio sat down and began reading through his emails.

"WHAT DO YOU WANT TO do, Mr. Russo?" asked Fitzy. "Do we move in?"

"As much as I want to, no, we can't. We've got to get the data out of this maniac and that means we leave him alone until tonight. But tonight we end Donny Mancuso's *Frankenstein*. I didn't think anyone could be as cold and calculating as Mancuso himself, but Uriah created a masterpiece of evil, a reincarnation of the monster that died in Bolivia."

"Do we keep monitoring, Mr. Russo?" asked Fred. "I think we could all use a break. Seeing this kind of brutality first thing in the morning really leaves a guy wobbly."

"I'm sorry, Fred, I understand, but I need you to keep monitoring. You can encourage yourselves knowing that this is the last day of surveillance. Tomorrow, we celebrate. If all goes as expected tonight, you can take the day off tomorrow until we meet up for dinner. I'm buying you guys the best steaks in New York City, at Gallagher's Steakhouse."

"I guess that's appropriate, Mr. Russo," said Will. "Finishing out our four-year effort at a place that used to be a prohibition-era speakeasy. Gallagher's goes from breaking the law to hosting the FBI. And Mancuso's organization is about to go from breaking the law to utter extinction."

IT WAS MIDNIGHT BEFORE Antonio was alone in the Mancuso estate. Surveillance cameras showed he was sitting at Mancuso's desk, working on the computer. Russo grabbed his satellite phone and called Alfred Edersheim in Tel Aviv.

"Dr. Edersheim, this is Joe Russo in New York. Mancuso's parahuman is finally alone. Can you take it from here? Anything you need us to do?"

"Yes, Joe. I need you to remain on the line with me while I attempt to put the parahuman into *Theta* wave state. Because Uriah destroyed his work on the Mancuso project, I have adapted my existing technology as best I could. Unfortunately, I cannot see or hear through Antonio. I need you to tell me when you see any change in the parahuman's activity."

"Happy to do that, doc. How soon should we see movement?"

"Any time now, Joe."

Russo and his team were eyes-on, each looking for any change. The tension was high—the data was at stake.

"Hey, Mr. Russo, he doesn't appear to be looking at the monitor, does he?" Fitzy asked.

"I think it's just the angle," said Will. "Hey, he's looking around. That could be something."

"Yea, he definitely appears distracted," noted Fred. "He keeps looking around the room, like he hears something."

"Okay, Dr. Edersheim, he's standing up, looking around the room like he hears something. Is it okay for us to feel optimistic about that?" asked Joe.

"I'm seeing movement from *Beta* to *Beta-Alpha* wave state, Joe. That's what we need but we're not out of the woods yet."

"And what is *Beta-Alpha*, Doctor?"

"*Alpha* waves indicate change from one brain wave state to another. *Beta-Alpha* means, in human terms, he's feeling tired, he's slowing down. His waves are becoming more *Theta* now—sleep mode. Can you see what he's doing?"

"Yes, we can. He got up from Mancuso's computer and he's walking. He just entered what looks like a den or maybe a study."

"What's he doing now?" asked Dr. Edersheim.

"He's just standing there. His head is going back and forth, looking around the room," said Russo. "Doc, is this how it should be?"

"No. I'm going to try increasing the *Theta*-call. That's the level of stimulation in the helium gas that transitions his artificial intelligence from waking to introspection. Tell me what you see."

They waited for several moments.

"Wait," Russo said. "Doctor, he just collapsed! What can you do? We can't lose him!"

"One thing at a time, Joe. I've got him in full *Theta* state. I'm going to attempt the memory download first, then we'll see if he can be awakened or if we have lost him."

"What caused this, Doctor? Why would he collapse like that?"

"As I said, I have very few notes on Uriah's design. I'm having to guess at much of this. When I increased the *Theta*-call, I may have overstimulated the helium. That's probably what happened but I can't be sure at this point."

"Is that fatal Doctor? Could you lose the data?"

"Do not panic, Joe. I know how much you need this information."

"We've got to have it, Doctor. This could end the Mancuso reign of crime in New York."

"It's downloading now, Joe. I think we have it!"

Joe's team let out a unified cheer and they were up on their feet.

"Thank God!" said Russo. "And thank you, Dr. Edersheim. You really came through for us! And for your country, too."

"I should have the data download completed within the next two hours. Pray it all comes through. I won't know until the process is complete."

"Will Mancuso's *dummy* know what hit him? I mean, will he know what you've done? And if so, will he be dangerous—more so than he's already proven to be? That's what I'm asking."

"I will not know if he will awaken until I attempt to move him from *Theta* to *Theta-Alpha*, and then to *Beta*. If he awakens, we will not know how he will behave until you see through your surveillance monitors what happens. But Joe, I would suggest you do not attempt to take him man-on-man if that is what you are planning. I can put him back into *Theta* sleep—if he survives what we're doing now. That is the safest way to apprehend him. If you determine you must speak with him, you'll need him fully awake, in *Beta* state. But he is incredibly strong, and you cannot kill him. You can destroy him but that would take an explosive blast. I can put him to sleep, then awaken him for you to talk with him once he has been properly restrained. Behind bars or with polymer bands or maybe polymer netting."

"Wow, doc, this just keeps getting better. Now we're dealing with a super-human creature, stronger than us, smarter than us, as ruthless as the real Mancuso, maybe worse, and virtually indestructible short of a nuclear blast."

"Not nuclear, Joe. One megajoule of explosive power should be sufficient. You can achieve that force with two sticks of dynamite. But let's deal with such an operation if we find it is the only way. I would be very careful who you let study him—or what is left of him after the explosion, if it comes to that. It would be best if you bring his remains to me. This technology must not fall into the wrong hands. Not ever again."

"I understand, Doctor. That won't be for me to decide, but I promise you I'll do my best to get him back to you."

"Joe, once I have all the data downloaded, I could leave him in *Theta* sleep. Since I don't know how he will behave when he awakens, if he awakens. It might be safer."

"No, Dr. Edersheim, I need him to get back to his office, as if nothing has happened. It will take us some time to get all the indictments I expect to come from the data. We don't want a sudden disappearance of Adonis Mancuso. The other Dons will flee if they know we have Mancuso. We need them going about their business, right up to the moment we take them and as many of their lieutenants into custody as the evidence supports. I want all their books, computer records, smartphones—everything I can confiscate."

"All right, Joe. Before I awaken him, I'll need you and your surveillance team watching him carefully. I will call you as soon as the data download is complete. Since it is after midnight where you are, you might want to get some sleep before I call you again."

"I'm going to sleep on the couch in my office. My team is taking turns getting some shut eye in the surveillance room. We're all pretty beat but we are hyped to see what's in that data you're capturing for us. I'm sure your phone call will awaken me. I'll talk to you in a few hours. And thanks again, Dr. Edersheim."

HEMPSTEAD HARBOR POLICE found a body in the Catholic church graveyard around 2:00 AM, on the same night Dr. Alfred Edersheim placed Antonio into *Theta* sleep.

Residents in the Hempstead Harbor neighborhood nearby the Catholic church complained of an unpleasant smell and a pack of wild animals in the cemetery. Though the body was decomposing and effaced by predators, the coroner was able to determine blunt trauma had been applied to the eyes, pressing them through the sockets and into the cranium. The death was ruled a homicide.

Since Antonio had removed all identification from the body, the police searched the FBI database for a fingerprint match. They got it. The corpse was identified as the notorious Vincent Accardi, lieutenant to Adonis Mancuso of the Lucchese crime family. Though the hour was late, investigators tried to reach Mancuso at his residence, but without success. They dispatched a detective and two officers to the Mancuso estate.

The officers arrived shortly before 4:00 AM. Their repeated attempts failed to bring anyone to the front or back doors. They moved to the back of the estate and found a groundskeeper's house. After several minutes of pounding on the door, the porch light came on. The man at the door was alarmed and only partially awake.

"Officers, is there a problem?"

"Yes, sir, I'm afraid there is. May I get your name and why you're on the premises?"

"Umm, yes ... of course. My name is George Petrie, I'm the gardener and groundskeeper for Mr. Mancuso."

"Is there anyone else in the house with you?"

"No, sir, I live alone. Always have."

"How long have you lived here?"

"Almost three years. Can I ask what has happened?"

"There's been a murder, sir. We ran the fingerprints and learned the victim was Vincent Accardi, an employee of Mancuso. Did you know this man, sir?"

"No, sir, I know very little about Adonis Mancuso. I did see him come home tonight. My house looks out over the south lawn, where the gate and driveway come up to the home, so I can usually see if someone comes or goes—if I'm watching, that is. Unless I'm asleep, of course."

"Do you have access to the home, Mr. Petrie?"

"Oh, no sir! Mr. Mancuso never allows anyone in the residence when he retires for the night. All staff must leave. Some of us live on the grounds, most live elsewhere."

"We have a search warrant, Mr. Petrie. We'd prefer to enter the home without damaging anything. Do you know of a way in that will not require us to damage a door or window?"

"No sir, I'm afraid I don't. I guess you'll have to break in."

The officers moved to the front of the house and tried the doorbell and knocking one last time. When this failed, they broke through the front door. To their surprise, no alarm went off. They found the lights and began moving through the home.

"Quite a place he's got, huh Ralph?"

"Yea but I wouldn't trade places with any member of Mancuso's organization. I've heard he's a ruthless, unpredictable tyrant."

"Hang on, Max, there's a body. Across the den floor, by the aquarium. You can see the feet and legs."

"I see it. Lieutenant, in here. We have a suspect on the floor, sir."

The lieutenant came through the entrance to the den just as both officers arrived at the body and were checking vitals.

"I think that's a pulse—feels faint. No sign of blood, no contusions. Let's roll him over on his back, get a better look."

The officers rolled the victim while the lieutenant stood by.

"That's Donny Mancuso. We need to take him into custody. Better get an ambulance on its way."

Mancuso's eyes opened.

"Sir, this is officer Max Lozano. Can you hear me? Are you okay?"

Antonio just stared at the ceiling.

"Lieutenant, he appears semi-conscious and unresponsive."

JOE RUSSO WAS SOUND asleep on the couch in his office at the FBI building in Manhattan. He was awakened to the sound of the satellite phone ringing. He rubbed his eyes and slapped his face a couple times, trying to wake up.

"Yes, Doctor, I'm here. How's it going? Do we have it?

"Yes, Joe, we have all of it. Everything that Uriah uploaded into Mancuso's parahuman is safely in our possession. But we may have another issue. I'm seeing abnormal readings from the parahuman. I have him in *Theta* state but there's *Alpha* waves coming from somewhere."

"What does that mean?"

"It means something is causing him to awaken, but only partially. He could be trying to awaken himself. I have seen this brain wave pattern one other time, when Uriah disturbed President Hayut's holosapien in my laboratory. The holo rose to his feet and interacted with Uriah, though it was quite limited. It resembles sleepwalking in a human. Joe, are you in front of the surveillance monitors?"

"No, no, I was sleeping in my office. But I can get back there in less than a minute."

"You need to do so. We need to know what is causing this change in brain waves. You need to hurry, Joe."

"I'm on my way. Let me call you back once I know what's happening."

Joe ran down the hall and into the surveillance room. Will and Fred were on the couches, asleep. It must have been Fitzy's turn at surveillance for he was sitting at the monitors, but his head was on the desk. Joe didn't turn on the lights, he just grabbed one of the chairs in front of the bank of monitors and sat down. In living color, he saw two police officers leaning over Donny Mancuso, and he could see a plainclothesman standing nearby.

"Do they know who this is?" Joe mumbled. "They have no clue what they've walked into."

"MR. MANCUSO, ARE YOU okay, sir? We are police officers. We've called for an ambulance. Please remain still. Do you know what happened? Were you assaulted? Are you ill, sir?"

"I, I, I'm Antonio."

"What's he saying, Max?"

"He said he's Antonio. That's his middle name, Adonis Antonio Mancuso."

"NO, NO, NO!" JOE YELLED at the monitors, trying to think.

"What's going on, Mr. Russo?" asked Fitzy, startled and sitting up in his chair. Will and Fred were just beginning to awaken.

"Sorry, Fitzy, but we've got a situation here. We need to find out which police department is at the Mancuso estate and we need to know *right now*. We've got to stop what's happening!"

"What *is* happening, sir?" asked Fred.

"Police officers found Mancuso unresponsive in his home—and I have no clue why they're in his home—but the timing could not have been worse! Dr. Edersheim was concerned what might happen if Antonio was disturbed during *Theta* sleep. Now we're about to find out. Fitzy and Will, I need you to call through every borough police department until you find out who sent a team to the Mancuso estate. Start with the departments closest to the estate. Fred, try to get someone at the Bureau in Washington. See if they can help us expedite the search. When you find the right department, tell them they've walked into a Federal crime scene. Ask them to say nothing to Mancuso, just apologize and leave. And tell them to cancel the ambulance. It could blow the lid off the whole investigation if paramedics find out Mancuso is *not human*! I've got to reach Dr. Edersheim again."

"MR. MANCUSO, ARE YOU okay, sir?"

The police officer kneeling at Antonio's left side was shaking Antonio gently while striking him on the shoulder with the flat of his hand. Suddenly, Antonio's left hand came off the floor, and ran up under the officer's belt, clamping down on the leather holster. Just as swiftly, his right hand grasped the weapon from the belt of the officer kneeling on Mancuso's right side. Antonio lifted the officer on his left straight up and off the floor and threw him against the officer on his right while simultaneously removing the sidearm from its holster. Both officers landed in a crumpled heap against the far wall. The detective standing at Antonio's head grabbed his side arm. He backed up, ordering Mancuso to drop the weapon. Antonio extended the gun over his head and, without looking, fired shots in the direction of the detective's voice. A bullet struck the detective in the chest, spinning him backward into a bookcase. He lay motionless on the floor.

Antonio's arm was still extended over his head, holding the pistol, when his arm went limp and fell to the floor.

JOE RUSSO SAT WATCHING the fiasco over the surveillance monitors, unable to help.

He could hear his agents behind him, working the phones, trying to find out which police force had dispatched these officers.

"Mr. Russo, I've got it," said Fred. "Hempstead Harbor police. They confirm they have three officers on location and a paramedic unit on the way. I told them this is a Federal investigation, cancel the ambulance, and extract their team as innocuously as possible."

"I can hear their radios going off in Mancuso's house now. But we're a little late, Fred. Antonio just shot the plainclothesman. He threw the other two into each other and they appear to be unconscious."

The agents were up from the phones, standing in front of the monitors, scanning the scene for any sign of movement.

"Fred, what about the paramedic unit?" Russo asked.

"Hempstead Harbor police are in the process of canceling it."

"The scene is not safe. At least one of the officers, the one Antonio shot, needs medical care but the medics will be at risk until we can secure the area."

"But sir," Fitzy said, "if an officer is down, there may not be a minute to spare."

Russo was up and dialing the phone.

"I know, Fitzy, the paramedics need to go in, but they need cover. I'm calling up SIOC, requesting a Critical Incident Response Group be flown by copter to the Mancuso estate. Fred, call Hempstead Harbor back and tell them to have the paramedic unit call you directly. Advise them to proceed to the Mancuso estate but they are not—repeat—not to enter until FBI backup arrives. Fitzy and Will, watch those monitors and let me know if there's any sign of movement in that den!"

Joe was watching the monitors too when he reached the FBI Strategic Information Operations Center.

"Yes, this is Supervisory Special Agent Joseph Russo in Manhattan. I need a CIRG in the air immediately headed for the Donny Mancuso estate in Scarsdale. And listen to me, the team needs polymer netting. Yes, I said polymer netting. They need to visually ID Adonis Mancuso. He is lying on his back in the den of his home with a sidearm located just above his head. They need to quietly enter, remove the sidearm, and cover Mancuso in polymer netting. At present there are three officers down. One has been shot, two likely suffering from concussion. These men need medical care, but it is not safe to send medics in until the CIRG has Mancuso restrained. That's correct, in the polymer netting. I'm sorry, I don't have time or authorization to explain. Just tell them their weapons will be useless. Their focus must be restraint with the polymer netting. And that team needs to be airborne ten minutes ago!"

"Okay, Fred, tell the paramedics to head to the Mancuso estate but they are not to use lights or siren—not under any circumstance. Make that absolutely, undeniably clear. No siren, no lights. Have them park out front with all lights off and await word from you before moving in."

"Got it, Mr. Russo."

THE MANCUSO ESTATE sat on four acres of pristine, manicured lawns. The FBI helicopter had plenty of room to land.

The troops moved through the open front door, brought the polymer net carefully over Mancuso, pulling it taut around his head, arms, and feet. Antonio never moved. The pistol was taken as evidence, the paramedics removed the detective who had been shot, and the FBI helped the police officers out to the paramedic truck for examination. Once everyone was removed from the premises, Joe instructed the den be put back together as much as possible, so that no sign of a struggle was visible. The polymer netting was then removed from Mancuso.

Once the Mancuso estate was clear, Russo was back on the phone with Alfred Edersheim in Tel Aviv.

"Dr. Edersheim, sorry for the delay. Mancuso was on the floor of his home but was awake just enough to throw two officers across the room while shooting a third with one of the officer's sidearms. The three have been removed, and the residence cleared of damage as much as possible. Do you think Antonio will know something happened there last night?"

"I don't know how much he's going to remember, Joe. I did not design the *Theta* state to be memory-captive—and I don't know if Uriah did."

"*Memory captive*? What does that mean, Dr. Edersheim?"

"It means the parahuman was designed to record memories in *Beta* state, but not in *Theta* state. Memories are supposed to be processed and analyzed in *Theta*—but remember that I did not design this parahuman. I know Benny did retain memories from his *Theta* encounter with Uriah—but Benny has my holography technology. Those memories were retained but he doesn't seem to be aware of them."

"So, Antonio may remember what happened to him tonight, he may not. He could be very dangerous if he knows someone has downloaded his data, don't you think so, Dr. Edersheim?"

"I'm sorry, Joe, I can't be more predictive than this. But, as you already know, he's dangerous no matter what state he is in. He needs to be removed from this earth."

"I couldn't agree more. Just get that data transferred to me ASAP and we'll see if we can make that happen!"

"The files finished transferring while we were speaking. I'm going to begin moving Antonio from *Theta* towards *Beta*. We'll see what happens. Joe, I know you want Antonio back at work so the other crime families do not become suspicious. But there is a growing trail of damage here and you must understand that it may get worse. If Antonio does know something happened, he may run. He may become violent. He may begin to take out his lieutenants to reduce witnesses. He might even come after me."

"You, Dr. Edersheim? Why would he come after you?"

"He may associate me with Uriah Horvitz. If he knows data was taken from him, I would be the logical culprit."

"I hadn't thought of that. We need to get protection on you immediately."

"Let's see what happens when we awaken him. Protection for me may not be necessary. If I need protection, INP will provide such for me. You do not need to worry about that."

"Dr. Edersheim, sometime this afternoon I expect to have hundreds of indictments of New York crime family members, all due to your efforts. You have been an enormous resource for me and this law enforcement agency. Ideally, the world will see

Mancuso walk into his office this morning. But if that doesn't happen, I expect the arrests will be staggering, just the same."

"Thank you, Joe, but there is more work to be done. The parahumans in Hollywood are still an issue for me and the FBI."

"Yes, sir, they are."

"He should be moving, Joe. Can you see him?"

"I see him, Doctor. He's sitting up. He's on his feet and looking around the room. He's walking over to the bookcase the detective crashed into when Mancuso shot him."

"What is he doing there?"

"Just looking at it. Some books were knocked to the floor when the detective hit the bookcase but the CIRG team put everything back. Could he notice books not being in the same order they were before all this happened?"

"He could, Joe. Remember, he is a creature of memory."

"Now he's looking at his wristwatch. He's moving quickly, leaving the den. Moving down the hall. Where's he headed? Okay, he just entered a bedroom and walked into the closet. He just grabbed a suit. I'm guessing he's getting dressed to go to his office. I think we may be okay, Dr. Edersheim."

"Thank God, Joe. I know this is what you wanted to happen. I'm going back to work on the Hollywood parahumans to see what I can learn from their brain waves and memories. I will reach out to Director Benchley as soon as I can."

"I'm going to call him later today, after we see how the arrests go. I need to bring him up to speed on the Mancuso matter. Thanks again, doc. I'll keep you posted."

BY LATE AFTERNOON, Joe Russo was completing one of the longest, most satisfying days of his career with the FBI.

More than five hundred agents were involved in making over two hundred arrests. Mancuso's detailed memory brought indictments ranging from prostitution, gambling, narcotics, racketeering, bribery, and murder. The Dons of every crime family in New York, along with their top lieutenants, had been arrested, some as they were attempting to flee the country.

Joe's surveillance team of Frederick Wong, William Claridge, and Mark Fitzsimmons enjoyed a much-needed day off with nothing to do but sleep. They were at home, getting ready for a great dinner at one of Manhattan's finest steak restaurants, courtesy of Joe Russo. And he was happy to drop the bucks on his team. Only one thing left to do before he met with them. Call Director Mike Benchley in Washington.

"Mike, this is Joe. I guess you've heard at least a little of what's gone down today, haven't you?"

"Joe, you have no idea what's been happening in Washington! The Director called me into his office and *ordered* me to New York to take you and your team to dinner. You have a long-overdue promotion that is yours. I told the Director I'd like to bring you into Science and Technology if you're open to it. I have a feeling this is just the beginning of what this tech will be used for. We've got to get a handle on it, learn how to identify these creatures—how to prevent them from being used for espionage, terrorism and other criminal acts. Well, how about it? You open to working with me in SAT?"

"Yes, sir, I am! And I'm very grateful, Mike. But before we discuss the promotion, I need to bring you up to date on a couple issues."

"Okay–this sounds like bad news coming."

"Some of it is. We lost Mancuso–I mean Antonio."

"You can't be serious! What happened?"

"We had a team of six agents in combat gear and equipped with shoulder-launched polymer netting guns outside his office in Manhattan. Last radio communication was Antonio had just come outside the building and they were moving in. There's been no contact since. We've got an APB out for Antonio, but all six agents are missing. I've instituted a state-wide dragnet and alerted our elite tactical unit. We know bullets can't stop this animatron so we've had to retrofit all agents with polymer netting and explosives. We don't want to destroy Antonio but we have to stop him, no matter what."

"Didn't Dr. Edersheim tell us there was a form of GPS tracking on these parahumans?"

"Already tried that, Mike. I reached out to Dr. Edersheim as soon as I learned Antonio was missing. He said he built tracking into his holosapien, but either Dr. Horvitz didn't include it in this parahumans or Antonio managed to disable it. Either way, he has no way to help us find Antonio."

"It just keeps getting better. You need to keep me in this loop, Joe. I'll have to alert the Director. Antonio just the FBI's ten most wanted fugitives list."

"I understand, Mike. Do you mind if we discuss the Hollywood situation?"

"I hope this is better news."

"I talked a long time with Dr. Edersheim last night. We had to coordinate a time when Mancuso's parahuman was alone at his estate so Dr. E could transition him to a *Theta* sleep state. You're aware of this."

"Yes, I am. He phoned me earlier today."

"Dr. Edersheim described a pattern that has emerged. Mancuso's parahuman was not supposed to awaken during *Theta*, but he did. Police officers unexpectedly showed up at his home, found him on the floor, and tried to awaken him. Antonio became violent—on a limited scale—but went back into *Theta* sleep after a brief skirmish. I'd say the whole encounter lasted thirty seconds. You'll remember that Dr. Edersheim told us President Hayut's holo awoke during *Theta* when Uriah Horvitz was in the lab making noise."

"Yes, I remember that. What do you mean, 'on a limited scale'? And what are the implications of this unexpected awakening in *Theta*?"

"Let me take the last question first. When holos and parahumans awaken during *Theta* sleep, Dr. E says it's like sleepwalking in a human. His holography seems to provide civility in the sleep-walking creature–for lack of a better term. He's suggesting this sleepwalking could be another pathway of instability."

"Okay, that's important. Go on."

"Dr. E moved Antonio into *Theta* sleep mode and he passed out in his home. Police in Hempstead Harbor found the body of one of Mancuso's lieutenants and dispatched officers to the Mancuso estate to interrogate him. They found Antonio on the floor, thought he was sick or injured, and tried to awaken him. That's when the fun began. While he was in *Theta* state, lying on his back, he threw two officers into each other, knocked them unconscious, and shot a third officer with a gun he pulled from an officer's holster."

"He did all this while lying on his back in sleep state?"

"Yes, sir. Beyond human strength. Dr. Edersheim said neither Antonio or Benny—President Hayut's holosapien—were supposed to awaken while in *Theta*—but they each reacted differently. The point is, just as a human doesn't know what's happening during sleepwalking, neither do these creatures. And they don't seem to remember what they do or say during that time."

"Does Dr. Edersheim think he'll be able to use holography to fix the sleepwalking?"

"No, it won't stop the sleepwalking because Benny has holography and he still partially-awakened. Dr. E doesn't know yet how to resolve the issue. He *is* going to try holography on the Hollywood paras, but if it doesn't work it may require a change to their memory bank. And that means they may no longer accurately reflect their human counterpart. There's no predicting what the parahuman would do—or be—if he starts modifying their memories."

"That would be true of a human. If you lose your memory, as with Alzheimer's, you're not the same person."

"Yes, sir, but a human with Alzheimer's receives a death sentence. This sleepwalking doesn't kill or disable the parahuman. And he said it might open up greater risk of the parahuman being hijacked."

"This is significant, Joe. Is Dr. Edersheim suggesting the Hollywood parahumans might be hijacked?"

"Edersheim is genuinely concerned that very thing could be on the horizon—with the three or Antonio. He points to Antonio as proof these creatures can be cold blooded and do virtually *anything* without semblance of conscience. Last night, Mancuso's creature almost killed in his sleep."

"And what about President Hayut's holosapien—does he have the same concerns for him?"

"No, sir, he doesn't. He said the holography application has, so far, worked. Benny sleepwalked but was not aggressive."

"Two very significant developments, Joe. I'll talk to Dr. Edersheim and see where this goes. Let's plan on discussing this further at our dinner meeting. I'm hoping Dr. Edersheim can give me a better feel for next steps. And getting back to the career move, let's talk about when we can get you moved to Washington."

"I heard you talking to Lexi on the flight back from Tel Aviv. You're trying to get us *both* out there! You think you could handle the two of us hanging around all the time?"

"Joe, I think you'll understand when I say Lexi holds a totally different place in my life than you and your talented team! I learned in the military not to bring my work into the home or vice versa."

"Home? Is it that serious with you two, Mike?"

"I asked her to marry me at the dinner in Washington with the President!"

"Oh wow—I saw some of the press on the dinner—how did I miss that? Well, congratulations, brother! I know you two will be very happy together."

"Thanks, Joe. Okay, find out where the guys want to go to dinner, and I'll be there tomorrow!"

"Umm, could we make it first of next week? I'm taking the guys to Gallagher's Steakhouse tonight. I'm not sure they'll be up to another meal like that tomorrow. And, frankly, I haven't slept for almost twenty-four hours and I'm thinking I may take tomorrow off to recover."

"Joe, just to get you off the hook, I'm ordering you to take tomorrow off to recover. No sleep for twenty-four hours is dangerous. Just know that with Antonio and our six agents missing, unless I hear by midnight tonight that Antonio is caught and our agents located, I'll be there by 8:00 AM tomorrow."

"We'll find them, Mike. I don't lose agents—definitely not a half-dozen in one action by a parahuman demon."

"MIKE! YOU NEVER CALL me at work—this must be important."

"It is. I'm calling you for two important reasons, beautiful. First, have you spoken with your parents about a date for the wedding?"

"Just got off the phone with mom and dad. They were watching the evening news and were blown away when they saw you propose to me with the President and Mrs Roosevelt standing right by us! They're excited beyond words! Mom said they had been praying I'd meet someone outside of Hollywood. They are so excited I'll be moving to the east coast since they're in North Carolina. Of course, they want to meet you before the big day so we need to pick a weekend after I move out to DC to go see them. And dad said to tell you 'sempre fi' and get your butt to North Carolina so he can interrogate you before the wedding."

Mike laughed. "Few things in life compare with the protective powers of a Marine Corps drill instructor looking out for his only daughter. I can't wait to meet him!"

"Mom suggested April for the wedding. She's checked with the church and all the weekends are open right now but we need to let them know ASAP. Does that sound good to you?"

"Absolutely! April 6. That way I'll have you in Washington for the early April cherry tree blooming. You've never seen anything like it! Hey, maybe your parents can join us. Then we'll take them to the Chart House restaurant in Alexandria. Sits right on the Potomac. Incredible food, amazing view."

"Mike–you're holding something back. What is it?"

"Not even married yet and you can already read me like a book."

"Is it bad?"

"Well ... it's not good. I need to ask you to pray for me and my team."

"You know I will. What's going on? Are you safe?"

"Yes, I am, but some may not be. You'll hear some of this in the news. Remember when you asked me if I'd caught the bad guys yet?"

"Yes."

"A big one got away and six of our men are missing. We've got to find them and him—fast."

26

THE SENATE SUBCOMMITTEE charged with investigating parahuman issues reserved the expansive Kennedy Caucus Room due to the overwhelming volume of people requesting a seat.

Located in the Russell Senate office building, the historic chamber can comfortably seat three hundred people—though requests exceeded a thousand the first hour of offering. Given the names and positions of those requesting a seat, the number of portable chairs were expanded to accommodate an additional one hundred. It was a veritable who's who: Top anchors from U.S. and international press, state and federal government leaders, entertainment executives and moguls, and fans from all over who came to cheer for the mega-stars. An entirely new generation had fallen in love with Clark Gable, Jimmy Stewart, and Humphrey Bogart.

Security was off the scale. The attempted assassination of President Jon Roosevelt and Israeli President Isaac Hayut just weeks before guaranteed an over-the-top response from all security forces. So many high-profile targets in Washington under one roof. Capitol police and Secret Service presence was deliberately visible at an unparalleled level.

Once a quorum was verified—and it was never in doubt; Steven Albright knew not one person on the committee was going to miss this media extravaganza–the Senate investigative committee was led in prayer by the Senate chaplain. Prayer at a subcommittee was not the norm, but this was easily the biggest event of the year for the Senate, maybe of the decade. Senator Albright planned a full-scale production, intended to capture the hearts and minds of the American public on behalf of the parahuman Hollywood actors. *Could parahumans vote?* If he could prove parahumans were more human than machine, then why not? Democrats were trying to buy votes by allowing millions of illegal immigrants through the southern border–then allowing them to vote. Maybe the Republicans just found their own source of new votes.

It was just after 10:00 AM Washington time when the hearing began. Senator Albright called the burgeoning gallery to order.

"This meeting will come to order, please. Come to order. Thank you. Good morning. I am Steven Albright, Senator for the great state of California. The Senate Committee of Homeland Security and Governmental Affairs has asked me to chair this subcommittee on Parahuman Creation, Treatment, and Security Concerns, in as much as I represent all three of these individuals who reside in California. This committee will now come to order."

Senator Albright paused as he looked around the expansive meeting hall and waited for conversations to fully die down.

"I want to welcome the committee members, our distinguished witnesses, leaders from within Washington D.C. and from all fifty states, members of the press, and my fellow Americans from all over this great land. Your interest in the well-being and future of these special individuals does my heart good and speaks to the very soul of what makes America great.

"This committee will, of requirement, observe Senate Rule XXVI, though that rule leaves the *style* of each hearing to the chairman. And, as chairman, I will carefully navigate the ebb and flow of what happens here. I'm going to ask all those present to respect this investigation by keeping the noise level down at all times. With this many people in attendance, even whispering can escalate to a level of distraction for the committee and those giving testimony. Cell phones will be turned to silent and will not be used for phone calls or for photographic or video purposes. This hearing is being broadcast, but I expect members of the media to wait for breaks in the hearing to communicate with anyone in an audible way. No one will be allowed in-and-out privileges due to security reasons. I trust that everyone here understands these rules and the necessity for quiet. Please do not force me to clear the gallery. I will not hesitate to do so if Senate rules are not respected."

Senator Albright looked up at the gallery and quickly added, "I thank you in advance for your cooperation."

"We will proceed in open session as long as we can without getting into classified matters, but I do anticipate that certain subjects will arise that will be considered classified. This will involve how these beings were created—the science and technology. That is not information we want certain people or groups to have access to. When such testimony arises, at that point we will go into executive—or closed—session. I want to thank my colleagues for dispensing with opening statements to save time as we anticipate a lot of work ahead for this committee.

"As required by Senate Rule XXVI, this subcommittee has received advanced witness statements and, I trust, each member of this subcommittee has taken time to thoroughly review those statements. It is, therefore, anticipated that each witness's testimony will be a summary of their written statements, and committee questions will serve to expand on the witness's written statement. The press and the public may anticipate a printed daily summary of testimony given. I would ask you to be patient as we undertake this task. A transcript of this hearing may also be available in the near future.

"We convene this morning to hear testimony relevant to our investigation of the so-called 'Parahumans.' I need to point out that this senatorial investigation coincides with an investigation being conducted by the FBI, spearheaded by Deputy Director Michael Benchley of the FBI's Science and Technology Branch. This committee will receive a report from Director Benchley and, I believe, he will be available for testimony relevant to his findings.

"Before we get underway, I want to introduce the members of the subcommittee, of which there are five. We have Senate minority leader Barbara Pomeroy, Democrat. She's also my fellow senator from California. California doesn't have too many Republicans, and I'm proud to be one of the few! We have Senator Ted Perez, Republican from Texas, Senator Arthur Bryant, Republican from North Carolina, and Senator Alana Akamu, Democrat from Hawaii. So, without further ado, we will begin. As required by Senate Rule XXVI, the minority party Senators may call their witnesses first. The order of witnesses has been determined. As you are called, the witness will step forward and be sworn."

As Chairman Albright covered his microphone and spoke to committee members, an immediate stir could be heard from the gallery. The level of excitement in the room guaranteed a certain amount of talk. Albright had already discussed this probability with subcommittee members, and they all agreed the last thing they wanted to do was throw everyone out. It was going to be a balancing act.

"Order, please. Order. The first witness will be Mr. Sid Abrams, CEO of *Silverscreen Motion Pictures Studio*. Mr. Abrams, please step forward and be sworn."

Sid Abrams rose from his seat and walked toward the witness stand, tripping over a television broadcast cable and almost falling before catching his balance. The rapid-fire noise of camera shutters, papers rustling, and a modicum of laughter quickly reached a crescendo. Senator Albright looked around the room, tapping his gavel.

Representing the top studio in Hollywood, Sid Abrams dressed accordingly. He knew the spotlights would do the rest. His perspective was that if the U.S. Senate was making a run at the biggest studio in Hollywood, they might as well see what they were up against. Blue pinstripe Italian Brioni custom-tailored suit and Luis Vuitton waxed alligator leather shoes. His wavy silver hair was combed back and slicked into place. The press would later note that his style was not garish or gaudy, just slightly ostentatious, and clearly intended to make a statement that, if Hollywood was in control, it always provided wardrobe for its productions. These hearings were going to be an SMP production.

"Mr. Abrams, please raise your right hand. Do you swear to tell the whole truth and nothing but the truth, so help you God?"

"I do."

"Thank you, Mr. Abrams, welcome to the committee. Please be seated."

Steven Albright turned to his left, to the two minority party committee members.

"Senator Pomeroy, being the ranking minority committee member, I believe you have the witness first."

Barbara Pomeroy was Steven Albright's fellow senator from California, but there was no love lost between them. Wherever Steven stood on an issue, Barbara Pomeroy always turned up on the opposite side. And the more passionate he was for a matter, the more in antithesis she stood. He had often reached out to her to find common ground, issues on which they could work together for the good of California and the nation. But there was something more than party platform between them. Barbara Pomeroy was philosophically opposed to Steven Albright. She did not like his conservative ideals. She did not like his support of capitalism—even though she was one of the wealthiest politicians in Congress. And, most of all, she did not like his faith. She often said she was a religious person but insisted separation of church and state required religious sentiments to be checked at the door. Anything more was tantamount to wrapping yourself in the American flag or hiding behind the Bible—an obvious means to elicit support from bumpkins and rednecks. Interestingly, she did not mind if other faiths were present on Capitol Hill in religious dress, customs, or political causes. But the 'religious right' was a threat.

Barbara Pomeroy was well connected with the liberal Hollywood elite. She loved being the toast of their fundraisers and rubbing elbows with the glitterati. It didn't bother her that those beautiful people kept disappearing from the producer's parties. Young, voluptuous females got older and were no longer 'right for the part'—any part. As the dewy twenty-somethings become the craggy thirty-somethings—well, you just had to accept their expendability. The sex-soaked film industry's unspoken rule remained constant: '*Men grow old, women rot.*' Federal law forbidding age discrimination was swept under the rug. And though she had long since lost any modicum of external youth and beauty, the producer's love of eternal youth did not affect her. Her value remained so long as studio chiefs sought political power. No one really knew *why* they wanted political power. But they did. And she was glad to oblige. Their mega-money ensured political suck-ups ready to listen to their progressive objectives, and their contributions guaranteed Senator Barbara Pomeroy remained untouchable every election cycle—for the past eight election cycles—almost fifty years. She long ago stopped worrying about challengers or re-election issues.

"Thank you, Mr. Chairman," said Barbara Pomeroy. "Mr. Abrams, let's begin with how and why you began Silverscreen Motion Pictures. You were previously the CEO of one of the so-called 'Big Five' studios but chose to start your own. That pit you against the Big Five who control film, television, theme parks—basically media and entertainment all across the world. What would make you think you could battle all five and win?"

"Senator, the short answer is that I didn't have to defeat the Big Five. They defeated themselves. I tried to warn them before I began SMP but they wouldn't listen."

"Please elaborate."

"Certainly. To quote a former director and producer, Hollywood began and thrived as 'schlock hacks.' We made movies to make money to make more movies. End of story. We didn't make statements. As soon as Hollywood got into politics we were guaranteed to offend half the nation because that's the political divide in this country. Why would we want to turn half the country away from us before our films ever make it to the theaters? It is the rankest form of arrogance to believe you're so popular, or so wealthy, you don't need to care what half the nation thinks! My message was simple. Get back to entertainment. Period. They wouldn't listen. Studios and actors actually believed people wanted their opinion on how to vote. Or how to raise kids. Or how to figure out your gender. They went from cute cartoons and family theme parks to cutting breasts off girls and penises off boys. They kept pushing sexuality on children until parents had enough! That's when they lost the family market. You can't succeed without families. When Netflix and Amazon started producing their own content, and dominated the streaming market, Hollywood no longer ruled entertainment. All they had left were so-called family theme parks. But ticket sales dropped there, too, because the studios wouldn't stop shoving their version of morality and politics. They're stupid. If you want into politics that badly, shut the studios and run for office. Well—they're not running for office but they're about to shut the studios!"

The gallery laughed. Sid wasn't laughing. He hated waste and that's what Hollywood had become. A blackhole inhaling talent and resources with no return. Sid looked up at the gallery. They thought they understood him. They couldn't because they'd not been there. For the sake of the so-called 'elite' in Hollywood, he took one last swipe.

"The rich and powerful eventually discover–often too late–that money abruptly and deceptively changes you. You think everyone values your opinion as much as you do. For years I watched talented movie stars, directors, and studio execs destroyed by this attitude. They're going to teach the world how life works. Lecture the public. Well, let me tell you something: Working-class moms and dads have more common sense and morality than rich and arrogant Hollywood has ever possessed. Those parents withholding their money from Hollywood is killing Tinseltown. And I say, 'Good for you, moms and dads, spend your money where the business owners will listen to you. Those are your kids–protect them!'"

The gallery stood as they applauded. Sid was a Hollywood insider–but maybe there was hope for him after all.

"Thank you, Mr. Abrams. In your written statement submitted to this committee, you made the assertion that the three beings removed from Silverscreen Motion Pictures by Senator Albright and the FBI are your property. I think several on this committee may express dismay with your terminology. It seems to imply you own a fellow human being. Would you mind clarifying what you mean by 'property'?"

"Yes, thank you Senator Pomeroy, I would like to clarify what I said. First of all, I did not say that I owned *a fellow human being*.

Even in prison, while certain rights are lost by those who commit felonies, they still retain their right to life and individuality. To be clear, I said that *the studio*, specifically, SMP, owns these re-created actors. And we do."

Chatter was immediate and getting louder by the second. Steven Albright responded quickly with a heavy gavel and a hot mic.

"Order! This room will come to order! Ladies and gentlemen, I must remind you that you are guests in this meeting. This is our first witness, and he has had little time to explain his statements. This committee intends to hear fully what each witness has to say. That is why we are here. Now, if that is not why *you* are here, you are welcome to leave. I expected some challenges in decorum but not this early in the hearing!"

Senator Albright looked around the hall for effect. He wanted public support for his three constituents, but he needed order to get his message out to the viewing world and he would have it. When the gallery was quiet, he looked back at the witness. "Please, Mr. Abrams, continue."

"Thank you, Senator Albright. As I was going to say, the very name this committee uses as its topic of investigation is the term 'parahuman.' The prefix 'para' means related to, resembling, a subsidiary or accessory capacity. They are, indeed, related to humans, but no one is calling them human. These beings, if I may phrase it this way, *resemble* Clark Gable, they *resemble* Humphrey Bogart and James Stewart. They were re-created to take the place of the real human actor that we lost to death many years ago. There is no disrespect in that! They simply are not human."

"So, are they clones of humans, Mr. Abrams?"

"Just a moment, Senator Pomeroy," said Steven Albright. "Mr. Abrams, if you're about to disclose how these beings were made, then we'll have to go into closed session."

"Not at all, Senator Albright. I don't know the details of how they were made. I was going to answer on a general level. Things that the public may already know."

"Very well, please continue."

"I asked you, Mr. Abrams, if these actors are clones," repeated Barbara Pomeroy.

"Oh, no, Senator Pomeroy, not even close. To my understanding, cloning involves taking cells from the previous human being to grow a human body in a laboratory. These actor's bodies were built. Like a house. They were constructed to last forever—and that certainly sets them apart from anything human!"

"Eternal youth, Mr. Abrams?"

"That is my understanding, yes. Our investors are counting on it!"

"Then how do you explain their personalities, their voices, their looks being identical to the real human actors?"

"I am not a scientist, Senator, but I was told scientists captured the entire memory of the human stars—everything said or done by the human over their lifetime—and placed it into the artificial intelligence of the parahuman actor. The voice is the same as the human because it is a recording of the human voice. It was captured from audio recordings."

"This had to be very expensive for your studio, Mr. Abrams, was it not?"

"I and my investors paid an enormous sum—millions of dollars—to re-create each deceased human actor, to bring them back for our fans' enjoyment. But this technology was totally unproven at the time so there was incredible financial risk. When Senator Albright and FBI Director Michael Benchley removed these three actors from our studio lot, they were taking private property without our consent. I've been advised this was an illegal and unconstitutional move on their part."

"What has this cost your studio, Mr. Abrams? To what extent has your studio been harmed?"

"In anticipation of this question, our accounting department, as well as our production, operations, and publicity departments, have attempted to put a price tag on the damages incurred thus far. But before I share those numbers with this committee, I want to share something else. As previously stated, over three years ago I was chief executive officer of one of the 'Big Five' studios. I enjoyed leading and advancing the studio, but the on-screen talent we had to work with had become so demanding, so arrogant, so hard to direct, I was ready to quit. I actually talked with some of our industry's best CGI artists about creating virtual reality images of such stars as Clark Gable so that I could work with actors who wouldn't resist me at every turn. But we kept running into roadblocks with CGI."

"What do you mean by 'roadblocks'? Can you give me some examples, Mr. Abrams?"

"Yes, I certainly can. The families of the deceased stars were consistently opposed to CGI or virtual reality re-creations of their lost family member. And for good reason. Seeing an image of Fred Astaire dancing in a brand-new motion picture but knowing he's a computer animation—nothing more than a cartoon—removes the respect we naturally had for the real actor. The human Fred Astaire put in hundreds of hours of hard work to make those beautiful dance moves look so seamless, so beautifully done. We knew back in the 1930's that people watching Fred Astaire envisioned themselves on the dance floor, doing what he was doing, being the life of the party. That's what kept them coming to the movies! But who's going to get excited about dance moves performed by a cartoon? Nobody imagines themselves as a computer-generated image!"

A faint level of laughter was heard.

"What about digital animation of former-actors, actors who did not dance or make music or sing? Were their families opposed to digital animation of their deceased relatives so they could be seen in motion pictures once again?"

"Their families were opposed to it. The consensus was the same. Very near to reality, but clearly not real, would leave the audience knowing this was fantasy, only a knockoff of the greatness that once was. They did not want the memories of a fabulous career marred as the star was reduced to some cartoonish virtual reality character. Envision Clark Gable in *Polar Express* and you'll picture the issue that concerned the families."

"All right. Can you explain to us how you moved from the idea of re-creating stars in the fantasy world of CGI to the reality of the parahuman?"

"Yes, of course. I learned of scientists who had perfected the creation of the parahuman. However, I was told I should not disclose the identity of those scientists in open session."

"That is correct, Mr. Abrams," Senator Pomeroy said with a tone of caution. "Please continue."

"I approached a scientist about the possibility of using his technology to re-create lost Hollywood stars. He was truly startled when I shared my idea with him. I told him I had heard of his technology for creating, or re-creating, a deceased loved one as a parahuman—not human but looking and sounding like a family member that had been lost. I told him if he could re-create a lost family member then he could help me, because that's how I felt about these actors that were larger than life, that helped form America's concept of who we were during the Great Depression and World War II. To me, losing these iconic actors was like losing a member of my family. The three stars we re-created were some of my favorite actors in childhood. When I learned from this scientist that this might truly be possible, I had to raise venture capital. I invested several million dollars of my own money. And, up to this point, I felt it was worth every penny. And I'd do it all again."

"No regrets, Mr. Abrams?"

"Not in bringing these actors back to the world. I regret having my investment taken from me by my own government!"

"I understand. And I agree with you."

"Senator, I didn't want to stop with these three actors. I wanted to re-create others—Cary Grant, Roy Rogers, Fred Astaire, John Wayne, Bing Crosby. Every Christmas we hear Bing Crosby singing '*White Christmas*' and hymns of the Christmas season. What if that golden voice was back, recording entirely *new* songs, for a whole *new* generation? What if he was bringing us more Academy Award winning films, like *Going My Way*? We are on the cusp of a breakthrough in entertainment, of bringing back the golden age of cinema with youth and beauty that will never leave us again. That has been my vision, my dream."

Some in the gallery applauded and Senator Pomeroy smiled approvingly. Sid Abrams was winning them over. Chairman Albright dropped his gavel a few times and Pomeroy pressed forward.

"Why didn't you start your revolutionary studio with a new name—why did you choose to resurrect the name of a studio that closed so long ago?"

"You're asking why I paid for the name SMP—*Silverscreen Motion Pictures*. Because it, too, had passed into legend in American entertainment. It, too, was all but forgotten. So, I bought that name, a name I felt bespoke what we were attempting to accomplish, the resurrection of the greatness of Hollywood's golden era. And we were so successful that other studios and their human actors of our own era felt threatened. *Very threatened!* So, they involved the FBI and political forces to harass me and my studio. Since they can't compete, they want to destroy us. Well, let me say this: If these young, wealthy actors of our day can't compete with the likes of Clark Gable, Humphrey Bogart, and James Stewart, it's their own lack of talent hurting them, it's not the fault of SMP Studios!"

The hall erupted into applause. Senator Albright brought down the gavel and called for order. Sid smiled at the gallery and knew he was making his point. He could see his studio attorney, Bob Cavendish, sitting in the gallery, smiling back at him. Barbara Pomeroy acknowledged Sid's smile with a nod, as if to say, 'we're almost there!'

"Mr. Abrams, in your written statement submitted to this committee, you mentioned the injuring of your reputation—that is, the reputation of SMP Studios—by these events. How has your reputation been damaged and at what cost?"

"The financial damage done to *Silverscreen Motion Pictures* may very well prevent us from paying for re-creation of more classic Hollywood stars. When the three parahumans were taken from us, production on three major motion pictures immediately stopped. However, we continue to pay salaries of supporting actors and production crew. We are now behind schedule for release to theaters in the U.S. and internationally of all three motion pictures. Thanks to these unprecedented actions by my own government, we estimate at least one hundred and fifty million dollars in damages."

Noise from the gallery began to rise.

"Quiet, please, quiet," Albright said. "Senator Pomeroy, we need to move on. Can you wrap up this line of questioning?"

"That is all I have for this witness."

"Very well, then Senator Akamu, Democrat from Hawaii, please address your questions to the witness."

"Thank you, Mr. Chairman. Mr. Abrams, you mentioned the families of the former stars, that they didn't want to collaborate with you on virtual reality or CGI renditions of their departed family member, is that correct?"

"Yes, senator, that is correct."

"Could you tell us, please, how the families responded to the re-creation of their departed family member as a parahuman?"

"Yes, I'd be happy to. The family members were thrilled to have a creature that could perfectly emulate the former star."

"Can you share with us why this was so?"

"Yes. It's very simple. The parahumans look and sound exactly like the former human actor. They were created to emulate the actor at approximately thirty years of age, and they never grow old. They never encounter the issues of aging such as forgetting their lines or putting on weight. There's just no negative side to the issue."

"*Until now*," interjected Chairman Albright.

"That was inappropriate, Mr. Chairman!" said Barbara Pomeroy. "This is Senator Akamu's witness!"

"I apologize, Senator Akamu. Please continue."

"Mr. Abrams, are these families well compensated for their former family members' likeness being used?"

"No, not always. Use of the former star's name or likeness may not always be controlled by surviving family members. Depending on the state the family resides in, law may provide for an ending of royalties fifty years after the star died. In states where this is not the case, we negotiated a royalty with the family or the trust."

"In other words, where family members remain, and the law so requires, surviving family members are compensated well."

"That is correct. Where the law provides for such remuneration, the family or trust receives a royalty on each movie made, any paid public appearances, any paid advertising endorsements—which, I would hasten to add, all product or service endorsements are the final say of the family or trust—as well as any product that bears the star's likeness, such as framed photographs, children's lunchboxes, that sort of thing."

"Does the family or trust decide what movies the parahuman will make?"

"No, that is completely controlled by the studio. Deciding whether to put your grandfather's image on a lunchbox is one thing. Knowing which script and director has the greatest potential for an Academy Award is the job of a professional."

"Did you have any trouble convincing family members of the merits of the parahuman re-creations?"

"No, I found them quite open to it because of what I call the 're-faming' of that former actor. The star has been gone for several decades, but a whole new generation falls in love with them due to our parahuman actors. Some descendants of these stars have shared with me the happiness they have seeing their father or grandfather in a brand new, first-run film. And the royalties our studio is able to pay these descendants can provide for the heirs to such an extent that the former star would be proud to be a part of it."

"So, you feel you have rendered a notable benefit for the surviving family members?"

"I feel that we've been a *great blessing* to these families—and to the viewing public, and studio staff who are all gainfully employed at a time when other studios are failing."

"Mr. Chairman, that's all I have at this time."

"Thank you, Senator Akamu. We'll move now to the majority members of this committee, beginning with Senator Arthur Bryant, Republican from North Carolina. Senator, please address your questions to the witness."

"Thank you, Mr. Chairman. Mr. Abrams, I think the committee will agree that you have certainly benefited the families of the deceased actors. You've done the American public, even the world, a great favor by your forward-thinking and creative application of this science—a science that none of us on this committee yet understand. I'm certainly looking forward to learning how all this works when we move to executive session. The thought of seeing new motion pictures and hearing new musical recordings by the likes of Bing Crosby is not only something I would never have imagined, I have to admit, it excites me greatly! But the very reason this subcommittee was formed has little to do with the benefits you've provided to the fans. This committee was tasked with looking into questionable, potentially harmful practices by your studio in relation to these created beings. You have stated your position that you, or the studio, own these three parahumans, because they are not human. You allege they are, therefore, your property. I must say, if these parahumans looked and acted like the visible concept of robots in our day, we would not argue with you for one second about ownership! But what forced this committee to investigate is the very thing you contend has been such a 'blessing,' to the families of the former stars and, obviously, to SMP Studios. These parahumans—which you contend are robots or something akin to robots—look, sound, behave, think and even *feel* so much like humans that we simply cannot bring ourselves to hear you say you *own* them!"

There was more spontaneous applause—but Sid Abrams was not smiling. He was moving uncomfortably in the witness seat. He looked up at Bob Cavendish who was carefully shaking his head 'no.' Sid understood. Remain calm, regain the momentum.

"Just a moment, Senator. If I may, you seem to be forgetting that making people believe in magic is what we do in Hollywood. We've been doing it for one hundred years, and we are darn good at it!"

The gallery let loose a round of muted chuckles.

"Senator, our nickname, 'Tinseltown' was earned because we make the false appear real, we make tinsel appear as gold. In this case, we make machinery, well-designed, beautiful, and without parallel, appear to be living when it is not. These creations are *not* cloned creatures, like a *Jurassic Park* sort of endeavor. They are not living. They do not have a circulatory or respiratory system. They do not require nourishment and they cannot procreate. If the studio were to pay the laboratory to re-create the former spouses of the former stars, as they have each requested, they could not have baby parahumans. They will not grow old or die simply because to die, you must first be alive. I don't know how much clearer I can make this. They are not human!"

The noise level immediately rose as everyone from spectator, to dignitary, to news reporter whispered to the person next to them or into a lapel mic connected to the broadcast truck. The gavel was rapping once again as the chairman spoke.

"Order, ladies and gentlemen, order, please. Order. We must have quiet. Senator Bryant, do you have additional questions?"

"Thank you, Mr. Chairman, I'll pass to my colleague from Texas."

"Senator Albright," Sid interrupted, "might I be allowed to add one more bit of testimony?"

"Of course, Mr. Abrams. Please go ahead."

"Thank you. Having to sit here, not only before this senate subcommittee, but before fans around the world watching these hearings online, and having to admit that these actors are not human, is indeed part of the reason we estimated our damages to be so high. You have forced me to say to an adoring public that these creatures don't eat, drink, breathe, or have babies. How much more damaging to male sex symbols can you make this? I understand the concerns you all have, but I trust that I have laid to rest the fact that these actors are not human, and my own government now threatens the financial wellbeing of my studio, my employees, the families of the deceased stars—all of this might have been avoided if the FBI and, quite frankly, you, Senator Albright, had listened to me during the initial investigation. I think you can understand my frustration and my anxiety. You are threatening the financial survival of many people."

"Mr. Abrams," said Steven Albright, "I hear you, sir. But we are just getting underway in this investigation. I do hope—and I mean this—I do hope you don't end up regretting those well-chosen words you just voiced. Senator Ted Perez, Republican from Texas. Your witness."

Sid did not look happy. But he wasn't through fighting. Not even close.

"Thank you, Mr. Chairman. Mr. Abrams, are you familiar with the legal term, a Latin phrase, '*cui bono*'?"

"I'm sorry, I am not, Senator Perez."

"It means, 'who profits' or 'who gains'?' In a free enterprise system, such as we enjoy in this country, it is understood that those who take the risks should profit the most in business. Is it not true that you and the other investors in SMP Studios profit more than the families who gave consent for you to create these beings in their loved one's likeness?"

"Of course, and of necessity, for how else would we receive the return of our investment in creating these beings? If you can't make a profit, you go out of business!"

"Understood, Mr. Abrams. And I don't begrudge you that profit, not for a moment! But my question to you, sir, is what profit, what gain do these re-created stars realize from *their* efforts?"

A rumble could be heard from the gallery, but it was slight and diminished as soon as Senator Albright looked over at the assembled guests.

Sid Abrams rolled his eyes and said with a level of disgust, "Senator Perez, must I explain this all over again? These are *not* human creatures. They have few physical needs. They are given a small salary. I'm sure you heard that Clark Gable purchased back his human predecessor's sports car—so you know they do have spendable income. And the studio provides their living quarters and clothing."

"Mr. Abrams, you are so focused on these parahumans not being human, you have overlooked the fact that they are still very much alive."

"That doesn't make sense, Senator! If they're not human, how can they be alive?"

"Sir, you do not understand my point because of *cui bono*—you are profiting from these parahumans and it's not in your best interest to understand me. You claim the creatures are not human. That may, indeed, be true. Once we hear from the scientists responsible for this technology, we'll know if that is correct. But my golden retriever is not *human* yet who would dispute that he is very much alive? I show him love and care. I spend time and money to provide for his needs. My wife and children want him around. They include him in family times. In fact, we regard him as part of our family! He is not human, but he is alive."

"But Senator, does your dog have a heartbeat? Does it eat, drink, and breathe? Even your use of the term 'he' means that the creature has gender and was the product of a male/female union. He was given life by other creatures who had life. As I've already noted, these beings cannot foster little parahumans. They cannot give life because they do not contain life."

"Mr. Abrams, that does not mean that there is not life present with these parahumans. It all depends on how you define *life*. If life is only humans or animals that can procreate, what about life in plants, bacteria, viruses, amoebas—there is life in virtually everything we value on this planet."

"And all those things can procreate! Parahumans cannot. Every living being is born, grows old, and dies. Parahumans are creations of a laboratory. They did not come into being due to their own procreation."

"I disagree, Mr. Abrams. Maybe the parahumans cannot procreate—and even that remains to be seen ... "

At that statement, the crowd began to buzz again but Senator Perez did not stop.

" ... but they certainly have *feelings*. They—not you or me—they themselves made this abundantly clear—beyond question! What would cause all three of them to cry out for their former spouses except loneliness? Loneliness is one of the greatest forms of suffering a creature can experience. If the parahumans are lonely, *if they are suffering*, you've lost your argument right there, Mr. Abrams. My golden retriever can experience loneliness because it is alive. Machines and computers do not express loneliness. Parahumans are, therefore, not totally mechanical—there is some form of life present."

The gallery erupted in applause and cheers. Steven Albright did not pick up his gavel. Not yet. Instead, he turned to Senator Bryant to ask a question. He was buying a bit of time. This was *gold* for the millions watching online. Let the applause reach the viewing audience. Public sentiment drives Washington like a gale force. But as the ovation continued, senator Pomeroy reacted.

"Mr. Chairman! Mr. Chairman! I demand you bring this committee back to order!"

"I'm sorry, Senator Pomeroy, I was speaking with my colleague. The committee will come to order! Quiet, please! Quiet! Senator Perez, please continue."

"Thank you, Mr. Chairman. Mr. Abrams, I go back to my original question, *cui bono*? Who profits here? Investigative reporters have followed an axiom for decades that has consistently enabled them to find the truth: '*When you want to know what's going on, follow the money.*' Who's profiting here? It's not the parahumans, is it, sir? I do not begrudge you the money you and your studio are making. What concerns me, what concerns this committee, and, I think, the American people, is why you seem so unwilling to use a portion of those hefty profits to meet the stated needs of your parahuman stars? They're lonely, they're not happy, they don't want to work under their present circumstances. This was made clear at the Rose Garden press conference. You respond by saying they're machines with no feelings. That makes no sense to me! The only explanation I can come up with is sheer greed. Can you see my point? Ultimately, if they refuse to work due to loneliness, it seems to me you're the loser in this situation. And if you paid them what a real movie star is worth, *wouldn't they be able to purchase the creation of their own spouses?*"

Sid Abrams sat there while the crowd vacillated between applause and murmuring. His expression was disconcerted, distant, and confused. He had no rebuttal to Senator Perez's argument, nor had he been prepared for it by his legal team. He glanced over at Bob Cavendish, but he was writing something in his folio. Sid knew he had to respond.

"Senator, earlier I mentioned that the prefix 'para' can mean 'resembling.' It can also mean 'near,' as we use the term 'paramedic,' someone who is near to help us. These parahumans are near-human. They were created to emulate life—and they certainly do that well—but they are not alive. And the more people try to push them to be human, the more we're going to see the sorts of emotional challenges we're now having! They think they're missing a spouse that, in reality, they never knew. The spouse was dead and buried long before these parahumans ever existed. Senator, the parahumans wouldn't know what to do with a re-created spouse if they had one!"

"Mr. Abrams, I often provide my dog with a new toy. I always figure he'll keep it close, maybe take it with him to his bed at night. Much to my bewilderment, my dog proceeds to chew it to pieces. I don't understand it but to my dog, who is very much alive, it makes sense. All of us here recognize that these parahumans are desperately expressing loneliness—such as we saw in the White House Rose Garden. A spouse is more important than a dog's chew toy! And these parahumans are certainly more important and more valuable to all of us than a dog. Wouldn't you agree?"

Sid did not respond.

"Mr. Chairman, I'm done with this witness. But I have an expert in emotional health, with a background in parahuman emotions, that I would like this committee to hear from."

"Thank you, Senator Perez, the committee will hear from that witness in the course of our investigation. We're going to take a thirty-minute break. For those planning to return to this hall, let me caution you to be punctual. Once the hearing is underway, security will not allow entry except for senatorial staff."

Sid Abrams was staring at Barbara Pomeroy and he held that stare until she looked up and saw him. She immediately stood from her seat at the committee table as Sid headed for the door. She waited a minute before she, too, headed for the door.

'*Hideaways*' are unlabeled offices that have existed in the U.S. Capitol building since 1800.

Only a few members of the House of Representatives have access to a hideaway, while all one hundred U.S. Senators have one assigned to them. The only proof that the room exists is a number on the door. They are private and intended to stay that way.

The Dirksen, the Hart, and the Russell Senate office buildings also have secret hideaway offices where a Senator can take a snooze, prepare for meetings, meet with constituents (or other 'liaisons'), or cut deals that are best not cut in public. Hideaways range from cubby holes, not much bigger than a closet, to lavish office suites with every amenity. Like everything else in Washington, these secret offices eventually came under control of those in power and became 'officially assigned' by the Senate Rules Committee. Naturally, the biggest and best of them are reserved for those with seniority. Former Senator Ted Kennedy's hideaway was said to be the most lavish of them all, including a fireplace and a breathtaking vista of the national mall. Senator Pomeroy's hideaway in the Russell office building was not as lavish as Ted Kennedy's but it was elegantly appointed, close, and provided the privacy needed to meet with her most influential constituents. Sid Abrams' influence was as big as his wallet and he had just arrived in Pomeroy's hideaway.

"Well, *that* didn't go as expected!" quipped Barbara Pomeroy. Sid's scowl made clear he was not amused.

"And you did nothing to change that!" Sid retorted.

"Take it easy, Sid. This is just the first day. But there's no point in sugar coating this. The gallery applauded your determination and creativity in bringing these creatures to life. The public would like to see more created. But the nation is not with you on this. Not yet. These parahumans of yours may be metal, bolts and artificial intelligence, but the public sees them as a kind of human clone. You can say they're not human all day long, but *perception is reality*. We've commissioned three polls and they're all coming back the same. The American people want these three actors fully cared for by SMP. First class, nothing less will satisfy them. You need to understand something, Sid. Your films with these parahuman actors have been wildly successful, and the persona you gave them stuck. People love them. They see them as the flesh and blood reincarnation of the previous actor, back to make everyone happy at the movies. Then along came the President's Rose Garden press conference. It solidified their public persona. People believe your actors are fully alive—whatever that means for a parahuman. Those three interacted with the President and with the press flawlessly. People are still talking about it. Face it, Sid, in the public's eyes, these three *are* the real actors—they are simply picking up where Clark Gable, Jimmy Stewart, and Humphrey Bogart left off."

"Ms. Pomeroy, I don't contribute consistently exorbitant amounts to your campaign fund so you can tell me what I already know! I contribute for the help of a senior senator from my home state that understands my studio's needs and objectives. Our studio expansion plan, which includes adding *more* parahuman actors, is based on a budget that accounts for every dollar we are presently receiving from these re-created actor's motion pictures. There's no profit-sharing built in for these three. And they don't need anything more than we're presently giving them. When we take them on the town it's for publicity. They don't eat thousand-dollar dinners or drink thousand dollar champagne. They don't smoke Cubans. They wouldn't even sleep if we didn't need to back up their data! This whole thing is preposterous. The studio doesn't need to pay them anything."

"What about re-creating their spouses? That might satisfy the public and help me get this committee off your back."

"Do you know how many millions that will cost?"

"Do you know how many millions it could cost you if you don't? The public is hanging on every word of what's being said. And wait until those three get on the witness stand! There will be no going back. You've got to give me something, Sid. We're talking about creating three female parahumans. That could stop this thing from exploding in your face. If you lose with the Senate, the FBI will undoubtedly be next."

"I don't believe it!"

"Sid, if any part of the charge of slavery sticks, those three will be emancipated faster than you can say Abe Lincoln. Do you hear me? Besides, Bogart has already told the public that he has plans for Lauren Bacall once you've re-created her. He's pre-sold your fans on sequels that should have been made decades ago. You may not like it, but he's become a one-man publicity department!"

"I'll have to call my investors."

"MR. PRESIDENT, I DON'T understand!" said Marty Martin. "What exactly do you want to tell the committee? And why? I think this will go down as the biggest mistake of your presidency!" Marty was close to an anxiety attack and Jon Roosevelt knew it.

"Calm down, Marty! I'm not saying my mind is made up. But the press has been on my back non-stop about the shooting in Tehran. They want to know how I survived a shot to the head at point blank range. And the American people have a right to know. The longer I avoid addressing this issue, the more the press talks about it being some sort of 'cover-up'!"

"That's because it *is* a cover-up, sir! I don't mean we've done anything wrong. We kept you alive and the treaty was signed. But it's still a cover-up for the sake of national security. And with the Senate investigating the Hollywood parahumans, do you think this is the right time to tell the nation what really happened?"

"Marty, the parahuman was certainly a national security measure. But national security secrets are just that—secret. Once they've been exposed they're no longer secrets. What happened in Tehran let the cat out of the bag. You want to pretend the devil doesn't exist with him standing right in front of you! We can't hide this any longer!"

"But, Mr. President … "

"Marty, have you considered what might happen if it comes out—despite our best efforts at secrecy—that we used a parahuman to sign the peace treaty in Tehran? The press could say we kept Rosebud a secret because his signature makes the treaty bogus—a phony. If I'm not the one that tells the American people what I chose to do, then it most certainly will be labeled a cover-up. However, if I use the Senate hearing as the platform to reveal what we did, and why, the legitimacy of those parahumans validates my own."

"I still don't understand, sir. The issues the parahuman actors are facing have nothing to do with the job Rosebud did in Tehran. Your parahuman has voiced no complaints, shown no emotional issues. And he performed like a champ in the most extreme circumstances! He exceeded our expectations. Compare that to these three re-creations out of Hollywood. They're giving their studio bosses fits. And one more thing, Mr. President. Couldn't it be argued that your disclosure at this time, telling the country about your parahuman, is designed to influence the Senate hearing and investigation?"

"And why would you think I would be accused of doing that?"

"Maybe because of your affinity for Jimmy Stewart. Or your friendship with Senator Albright. I'm concerned a case could be made by your political opponents that you are deliberately trying to sway decisions in favor of Mr. Stewart and his companions. The Democrats are already saber-rattling because you had the three actors to the White House, the Rose Garden, and then spent most of the day with them, touring Washington and eating dinner. Lots of photo ops—all making the case that the parahumans are human and prejudicing the Senate and public opinion against the studio.

SMP has a legitimate interest in these hearings, too, sir. They're claiming the loss of millions of dollars due to the seizure of their property by the FBI."

"Marty, if we say we sat on this story because we didn't want to prejudice the Senate one way or the other concerning the Hollywood parahumans, that we didn't want what we had done to interfere with the Senate and FBI investigations, the press and the public *might* buy it. But what if the story breaks in some other way, by some other means?"

"I still think that is unlikely, Mr. President. And the very reason we've remained silent is huge. If the world leaders who signed that peace treaty find out they put their lives on the line to be in Tehran, but you did not–sir, this could blow up in our faces. Those who've been criticizing the peace treaty all along could seize this as proof that the whole thing is a lie based on fraud and deception. Now, how has the Senate investigation changed that possible outcome? Sir, it hasn't!"

President Roosevelt sat at his desk, looking at a picture of his wife. The peace treaty was for her. He looked up and out over the south lawn and saw people on the sidewalk. The peace treaty was for all of them. He knew Marty's point was valid. He hadn't put his life on the line like the other leaders did. But everything in his soul cried out that this veil of deception, as important as it had been, had served its purpose, but it was done. Now it might soon be discovered and that could bring his presidency down. Or worse, it could doom the peace treaty before it ever had a chance to work. He turned back toward Marty, who was now sitting across from him.

"Marty, we need to think about something. Something that goes far beyond the Senate investigation, the American press, the American public, and whatever legacy we could envision for my presidency. I know your primary concerns are the attacks on me and the peace treaty. And I value your concerns. But have you considered what could happen if someone *other than me* reveals to the world that we used a parahuman stand-in to sign that treaty? If I'm the one that reveals it, I can say the wisdom and validity of using a parahuman was proven by the fact that I'm still alive. And I can make a powerful argument that the treaty was signed *after the shooting* because every delegate there saw I was alive and well. And it was Rosebud that called them all back to sign the accords. Would the treaty have been signed if my lifeless body were lying on the floor in Tehran? You, I, and every person with any interest in world peace know the answer is a resounding *no!*"

"Sir, I see what you're saying. But, Mr. President, why are you so fearful that Rosebud will suddenly be revealed? I can't see the link between the Hollywood parahumans and your own—I mean, how could the investigation of the Hollywood creatures possibly reveal that you had a parahuman created?"

"It's not a direct link, Marty, but I certainly see an indirect one. After the assassination attempt in Tehran, I called to check on Israeli President Isaac Hayut, and it was a most interesting conversation. At first, I inquired about his health, how he was feeling after the attack. But then I mentioned that the shot to 'my' head was a glancing blow, but his was a bullet right to the forehead. I asked him the same question the press has been trying to ask me: *'How did you survive a direct shot to the head?'* And you know what, Marty? He gave me the same sort of evasive answers you guys have been feeding the press since Rosebud got back!"

"What are you saying, sir?"

"I'm saying that it's just as likely that Isaac Hayut was using a parahuman as I was. And if that's true, then we have to assume other countries, and possibly people with illicit motives, have this technology. We can't hide this, Marty, and we certainly can't outrun it. We have to craft a plan for dealing with this technology and these beings. We have to find a way to identify them, even in a crowd, especially where the risk of terrorism may be involved. Like all technology, this can be used for good or for evil. We need to bulletproof this before it gets out of hand."

Marty sat looking at the President. He'd seen that look on Jon Roosevelt's face many times before. The argument was over, the issue settled.

"All right, Mr. President. So, when and how do we bring this to light?"

"I've asked Steven Albright for time to testify before his committee. I think that's the best forum. I have to do this, Marty. If anyone other than me reveals my 'stunt double,' you're going to see the biggest scandal since Watergate and the results could be twice as destructive."

27

"THE COMMITTEE WILL COME TO ORDER, please ... quiet down, everyone, quiet down. We have something special now for the committee!" Steven Albright was decidedly buoyant.

"The committee has opted to interview the Hollywood stars using a panel format. We have replaced the single witness seat with three chairs, a table and three microphones. The committee will be able to ask questions that all three can answer together or singly, the goal being spontaneity and transparency. Therefore, the following witnesses please step forward together and be sworn. William Clark Gable, Humphrey DeForest Bogart, and James Maitland Stewart."

None was more sartorially resplendent than Clark Gable and the press lapped it up. "Look how he seems to glide toward the witness table," "the King of Hollywood in his royal robes," "looks like he just arrived at Tara," and on the depictives went.

With a pronounced British accent, the anchor for the BBC did his best to describe what he was seeing: *"Clark Gable is wearing a herringbone jacket with white crown-fold pocket square, a V-neck sweater, plunging deep enough to reveal his elegantly striped silk tie. His trousers are charcoal gray with characteristically high-rise waistline and with pleats. Always pleats. Clark Gable of the 1940s never wore trousers any other way, not even when his sweater hid the waistline. The incandescent lights of the Kennedy Caucus Room act like a halo spot on his jet-black hair, glistening with his favorite*

Pomade oil. He's sporting his familiar pencil mustache, a trademark pinky ring on his left hand, which, I am told, was sent to him by a collector who purchased it from the Clark Gable estate decades ago. His more-than-prominent ears, and his permanent parahuman age of just thirty years old, have brought this crowd back to 1939 and the staircase in Twelve Oaks, where Rhett Butler looked up longingly at young Scarlett O'Hara. I found myself looking about the Senate hall for Vivian Leigh."

Humphrey Bogart, or 'Bogie,' as he was affectionately known, wore his familiar peak-lapelled double-breasted suit, glen-checkered in gray. His shoes were two-toned brogues, a gray fedora felt hat with a black satin band was strategically placed on his head. With the brim pulled down, he resembled Sam Spade searching for the *Maltese Falcon*.

At six foot, three inches tall, and weighing barely one hundred-forty pounds, Jimmy Stewart's lanky frame didn't walk, it bounded to the witness table in his inimitable, self-effacing, wholesome style. Dashingly young and energetic, his Princeton ivy league look fit his physique. A brown tweed jacket with side vents and peak lapels, and underneath a canary yellow cashmere sweater. With pleated tan slacks, penny loafers, and argyle socks, he was the poster child for the boy next door; handsome, spritely, and mischievous—if you lived in the 1930s.

The three lined up in front of the witness table for the oath—one dashing lady's man, one tough guy, and one ivy league all-American. Such bravado brought faint but distinct wolf whistles from the gallery. Chairman Albright tried to hide a grin.

"Would the guests in the gallery please remember this is a Senate chamber and not a cougar bar?"

This only served to evoke peals of laughter. Senator Albright ignored the gayety and administered the oath.

"Mr. Gable, Mr. Stewart, and Mr. Bogart, please raise your right hand. Do you swear to the tell the whole truth and nothing but the truth, so help you God?"

Each responded into their microphone, "Yes ... I do ... absolutely."

"Thank you, gentlemen, please be seated. It is our distinct honor and privilege to have you here in Washington. We appreciate your willingness to testify and answer our questions. Since you are the primary subjects of this senatorial investigation, this committee would be hobbled by your absence. You men did not submit a statement, nor were you asked to do so. The committee agreed there could be more value and clarity in the spontaneity of your answers if you simply speak your mind during these hearings. Do you three understand the rules we set forth at the start of today's session?"

With their assurances given, Chairman Albright replied, "Very good. Senator Pomeroy, you have the witnesses first."

Barbara Pomeroy glanced over at Sid Abrams. His gaze was locked on her. She expected that—she could feel it. In their private breakfast meeting, Sid emphasized yet again what she must "sell" to the nation: The studio paid to re-create these parahuman actors. The studio wants to help but can't go into bankruptcy to provide comforts only human beings require. Senator Albright and the FBI are prejudiced against the studio and are endangering the jobs of real humans in Hollywood by trying to push the 'humanness' of AI powered animatrons. Sid felt these points, properly presented, could turn the tide in the studio's favor. Pomeroy disagreed but promised to do her best. As long as Sid wrote the checks to her reelection committee, he knew she would dance when he said dance.

"Mr. Chairman, I want to go on the record that you have obviously pandered to these parahumans, while refusing to show similar honor to their employer, *Silverscreen Motion Pictures*, and Mr. Sid Abrams. I'm afraid your bias is showing, sir."

The reaction throughout the hall was palpably uncomfortable. The gallery grumble began to rise.

"Senator Pomeroy, the official transcript will show that I greeted Mr. Abrams with respect and welcomed him to this hearing with positivity. As I just said to these three gentlemen, they *are* the focus of this hearing and investigation and are indispensable to our effort. That's all I meant by what I said. Let's keep this hearing focused on the main thing, shall we? Party bickering will not move us forward."

Senator Pomeroy brushed aside Albright's response and turned to the witnesses.

"Gentlemen, I certainly mean no disrespect to you, but having a non-human take an oath to tell the truth, adding, 'so help me God,' makes no sense to me whatsoever. We might as well swear-in a baboon or a boa constrictor in the name of God. At least they are alive!"

Gallery hissing was immediate. She didn't care. She was on a mission.

"Do you gentlemen realize how dangerous it is for you to allow the people of this nation to see you as human? We've been told that you don't age, you can't die, you don't eat, drink, or even breathe. Why do you portray yourselves as human beings? Will you now state for the record that you are not human—and clarify to what extent, if any, you contain anything that *is* human?"

"Senator Pomeroy," Clark Gable responded, "would you mind telling me what part of my personal feelings you find so far beneath you that you have the right to belittle me with your smug and condescending words?"

The gallery erupted in applause. Chairman Albright looked at the gallery. So did Barbara Pomeroy. She now knew where the gallery stood.

"Mr. Chairman," Senator Pomeroy demanded, "please bring this crowd back into order!"

The chairman tapped his gavel and called for quiet. "You know, Senator Pomeroy, there are times I'm not sure we're from the same state—or even the same planet!"

Laughter followed from the gallery, but Albright's gavel came down smartly as he added, "all right, ladies and gentlemen, you've made your point. I must ask you to refrain from further outbursts. Please continue, Senator Pomeroy."

"I'm waiting for an answer from you ... creatures. Will you now state for the record that you are not human—and clarify to what extent, if any, you contain some element of humanness?"

"Senator," Bogie replied, "we are referred to as 'parahumans.' That should tell you we are at least part human. And if that's true, would it hurt you to treat us as such?"

"You're avoiding my question, Mr. Bogart! I'm asking to what extent you can accurately be called human?"

"Very well, Senator," Bogie responded, "I'll answer your question. Although, if you feel I'm so much less of a being than yourself, I don't know why you want my testimony at all. Other than to try to twist my words and use them against me."

"Mr. Chairman, will you instruct this witness not to argue with his interviewers and to answer the questions as they are stated?"

"Mr. Bogart, please do answer the questions as they are put to you. And please refrain from arguing with the Senator ... though I personally know this can be hard to do."

More laughter followed but quickly died down. It had to. Bogie just removed his hat, lowered his head, and pulled his mic up close to his mouth.

"Senator Pomeroy, you can't even bring yourself to use the term 'parahuman.' You called us 'creatures.' Well, even if I was nothing more than a dirty dog, you and I would both be creatures, wouldn't we? To be a creature means you were created. Me, by a scientist. You, by the Almighty. You'd show even a dog some level of kindness, wouldn't you? Having made that point, I'll answer your question, as one creature to another. A dirty dog to a talking jackass."

That did it. The room was now exploding. Pomeroy was on her feet shouting something, but the noise level of the room made it impossible to hear her. Additional Capitol police came flooding through the doors like a riot squad, not knowing the cause of the sudden burst in noise and fearing the worst. Steven Albright was dropping his gavel with the speed and power of a jackhammer. There was laughter, there were catcalls—but it was chaos.

"This room will come to order or it will be cleared! The gallery will come to order!"

Bogie at his finest. Albright knew this was a show and it only helped demonstrate just how alive these parahumans were. But he couldn't get that message out without order. Still, he wanted the gallery's thunderous applause to help persuade those watching at home. It was a balancing act. He kept his gavel dropping until the crowd noise fell to an acceptable level.

"Mr. Bogart," said Steven Albright with a tone of understanding, "I believe everyone in this room knows your penchant for speaking your mind. And I did state we wanted the three of you to be transparent. But, sir, I must ask that you keep your comments—your language—on a level commensurate with the Senate. Please, for the remainder of this hearing, keep things civil!"

"I apologize, Senator Albright. And I apologize to the people in this room and watching at home. I'm afraid I've always had a short fuse when it comes to small minded people who like to step on others. But I'll do my best to keep things civil."

"Thank you, Mr. Bogart. Now, please answer Senator Pomeroy's question."

"Excuse me!" shouted Barbara Pomeroy, "he has apologized to everyone here but me! I am a United States Senator, and he shall apologize for calling me a jackass!"

"That *is* your party's symbol, isn't it, Senator?" asked Bogart, with more laughter following.

"Bogie, you promised!" said Steven Albright.

Bogart sat looking at Barbara Pomeroy. He had that familiar faint grin as he stared at her, waiting her out.

"Mr. Bogart, I insist you apologize!" Pomeroy boomed.

"Senator Pomeroy, I'm certainly willing to apologize for calling you a jackass if you'll apologize for suggesting that we're equal to baboons and snakes."

He had her. Everyone in the room knew it. If she apologized, she would be playing the game on Bogie's terms. She would also be admitting that their testimony was greater than an animal, and that could blow her main point. How did this parahuman think so quickly on his feet? Who or what was she up against? Pomeroy's face was turning red. Committee members sitting beside her could see her hands shaking. She dared not look at Sid Abrams.

"Very well, Mr. Bogart, let's just keep the remarks as we made them. I'd rather this exchange be accurately recorded. Mr. Gable, are you at least part-human, as Mr. Bogart seems to suggest?"

"Senator," Clark said, "if you cut me, I'll bleed. Is that human enough for you?"

"I don't know that blood alone proves you are human, Mr. Gable. Dogs and jackasses bleed, too," she said as she looked at Humphrey Bogart. "If anything, it suggests you have human skin.

But what's underneath—what's inside you that qualifies you as human?"

"Well, Senator, I know that I was created to be Clark Gable, and I was created from his memories. Every memory of everything he did or said during his entire life is in my head. I can tell you that I have feelings. I feel alone much of the time. I miss my wife, Carole Lombard. I miss getting on the open road in my Duesenberg roadster with her. I miss going to the Brown Derby with her. And I miss feeling my life has a purpose."

"Are you saying your life has no purpose in being accorded the title and honors of the 'King of Hollywood'?"

"I didn't say that, Senator. Being an actor can be a noble profession—like you being a politician. It can and should be a life of service. But if life is nothing greater than one's profession, then life is over when we can no longer perform as others expect of us. I want my life to matter beyond my career. I hope you want the same for yourself—and if you don't, then I feel sorry for you—and everyone who has to live with you!"

Faint applause were heard—but the room became respectfully attentive. This parahuman was speaking truth.

"Where is this coming from, Mr. Gable? I don't recall the human Clark Gable saying anything like what you just said."

"But then you don't possess all his memories as I do. And artificial intelligence can learn, Senator. I'm learning more and more each day. But that's what living beings do—don't you agree?"

"I'm curious, Mr. Gable. Who have you been talking to? Where would you receive this type of information? Have you been seeing a counselor?"

"I met a man who helped me see there's more to life than being rich or famous. If that's what drives a person, I'd say they're mighty darn selfish. And being wrapped up in yourself makes a pretty small package."

"Very noble. So you have the collective memories of the human Clark Gable, is that an accurate statement?"

"I wasn't awake during my creation, but I was told that is accurate, yes."

"Who told you this is accurate?"

"Sid Abrams."

"So, you trust Sid Abrams, Mr. Gable?"

"I trust Sid like I trust you or any other human being. I take people at their word. But if I find out they've deliberately misled me, then that trust is gone."

"You must trust Mr. Abrams significantly if you're willing to testify under oath that all you know about who you are or how you were created came from him, don't you agree?"

"I agree. But why do you think that's important for this committee to hear, Senator? Are you wanting a parahuman to tell you Sid Abrams is trustworthy? If so, you must put a lot of trust in me! And to think, you compared me to a baboon!"

"Mr. Gable, if you trust Sid about your own creation, you must trust him to provide for your needs. He was taught by the scientists who created you. He was told what your needs are and how best to meet those needs. Is that a fair statement?"

"No, Senator, it is not. All three of us here have made clear we are suffering from loneliness. We asked Sid to have our wives created, just as he did us. He says that's too expensive at this time. If you were left in solitary confinement, alone day after day, night after lonely night, you'd crack up, Senator. That's not living."

"But you're *not* living, Mr. Gable. That's precisely the point. You are a very advanced animatron, there's no question about that, but you are an animatron just the same. If you have an animatron wife, you can't father children or enjoy a thousand different human pleasures. Why then do you expect this committee to order SMP to spend millions of dollars they don't have—an order the Senate has no authority to issue?"

"Senator, Sid told me I *am* alive—alive with all the memories the real Clark Gable had. The memories of what he actually *experienced*, I'm just denied the experiences. It's like a movie projector playing the same scenes over and over in my head. I can see them, I can hear them, but I can't be a part of the action. I'm locked out. I see the watermelon cake at the Brown Derby, but I can't touch it, smell it, or taste it. It's there but no one will hand it to me."

Clark's voice elevated two octaves. "I tell you, it's driving me insane—these memories are driving all of us insane!"

The gallery began to audibly stir when Jimmy Stewart spoke up.

"Senator, I wonder if I could be allowed just a moment to say a few words?"

Pomeroy knew she had Clark on the ropes, and she wanted to keep the pressure on.

"I'll get to *you* in a few minutes, Mr. Stewart."

"Well, now, you can see that my friend is struggling, Senator. I understood this was to be an open forum for the three of us witnesses. I wonder if you could let me say a few words on his behalf. All three of us have talked this thing through and I think I can speak for ... "

Pomeroy cut him off. "Mr. Stewart, I need you to be quiet and wait your turn. I'm not through with this witness."

Jimmy quickly stood up. To those who had seen the film, he was the very image of Jefferson Smith on the Senate floor in *Mr. Smith Goes to Washington*.

"Well, now, actually, I think you *are* through, Senator! I think we've heard just about enough of your coldness and your cruelty. Because you think a parahuman has no life, you think we have no feelings either, and you're wrong! In my book, Clark Gable is more alive than you'll ever be!"

"Mr. Stewart, you will sit down, or I will have you jailed for contempt of Congress!" shouted Pomeroy.

"Me jailed? A baboon, a robot, a machine? What charge can you bring against a fake human, Senator? What jail does Congress cast animals into?" Jimmy looked at Senator Albright. "Mr. Chairman, may I speak for my friend Clark for just a moment?"

"It seems to me you already are, Jimmy!" Senator Albright responded with a grin.

"Well, now, doggone it, I guess I am. Look, as Bogie was saying, we parahumans, if we are even part human, maybe Senator Pomeroy could try acting at least part-human herself."

Laughter from the gallery helped break the tension, but Jimmy wasn't through.

"Look, Ms. Pomeroy. I don't mean any disrespect here. I proudly served this country through World War II, Korea and Vietnam. I flew many missions and was shot at more than I care to remember."

"You were *not* shot at, Mr. Stewart!" Pomeroy fired back. "And you did not fly any missions! The *real* Jimmy Stewart flew those planes!"

"You know, that used to be true, Senator, but now you're dead wrong now. In Los Angeles just a few months ago, I was hosted by the commander at the United States Air Force base there and, Ms. Pomeroy, they took me up in a B-52 bomber because I asked them to. And I ... you know what? When we were at altitude, I asked them for the controls, Ms. Pomeroy, and *I flew that plane*. Mile after nautical mile. The captain was so shocked that he asked me if I felt I could land it and turn that big ugly fella around and, doggone it, I did. I landed that two hundred-thousand-pound plane like I'd been flying it for fifty years. I knew every control, every gauge, every procedure. I flew it just like General James Maitland Stewart used to because that's who I am, Senator. That's all I can be because that's who I was created to be. The human James Stewart taught me to fly that plane, but it was his parahuman that landed it. My memories are so alive I stepped out of the grave and flew a nuclear bomber. I reckon I picked up right where the two of us left off."

Jimmy sat back down. He was facing the table but looked up at the Senators and spoke so softly they strained to hear him over the echo of his voice in the granite hall.

"I miss my wife, Senators. I miss Gloria. I asked Sid to give her back to me and he refused. Well I'd rather be dead than go on like this. And that's as human a statement as I can make because, when Jimmy Stewart was dying, you know what his last words were?"

The senate hall was deathly silent—except for the sniffles that could be heard from those whose eyes could not hold back the tears.

"He told his kids, 'I'm going to see Gloria now.' That's what he wanted most in all the world. And that's what I want. It's all I can think about. Night and day. If I can't have her here with me, then I want to go where she is. Can you make that happen ... please?"

The hall was as silent as a crypt. Steven Albright turned to Barbara Pomeroy. "Anything further, Barbara?"

Pomeroy sat before the microphone, watching Jimmy. His head was down, his shoulders rolled forward. Human or not, he looked more broken than any man living she had ever had the misfortune to see. "No, nothing more."

"ALL RIGHT, MR. PRESIDENT. I placed a call to Steven Albright and requested a time for you to appear before the Senate committee. He asked if tomorrow will work for you and, if so, what time."

"Tomorrow is good, Marty. Please ask him for the first time slot. But I'm going to send Rosebud."

"You're *what?!*"

"It's okay, Marty. I have a plan. Let's awaken him. I want to talk with him."

THE KENNEDY CAUCUS Room was abuzz.

Guests were being seated in the gallery and the conversations varied from the parahuman testimony the day before, to what testimony the President might give. Most were sure it had something to do with his friend, Jimmy Stewart.

Members of the press were conducting live broadcasts from any area of the caucus room they could get. They interviewed members of the committee: *Had the committee's goals changed? Which of the parahumans had the best exchange with Senator Pomeroy? Did they see a probable outcome? Was the President called to testify or was it his idea?* Viewers were providing a constant stream of questions, reactions, and opinions. The polls from the first day of testimony were hot enough to burn down Washington, and every politician in the Capital was listening. Testimony from 'The Hollywood Three' as they were being called, was rocking the nation.

Barbara Pomeroy had results back from the poll she commissioned, and the results weren't good—for her or for Sid Abrams. The heart of the country was with the parahuman actors and her attempts to categorize them as non-human had failed. Miserably.

The poll asked if respondents agreed with Senator Pomeroy that the parahumans, created at studio expense, belonged to the studio? Answer: No. Did the parahumans have the same rights as human actors? Answer: Yes. Should the studio pay to have the parahuman spouses re-created? Answer: An astounding ninety-six percent said yes. Pomeroy had no desire to face Sid with these poll numbers, but bad news never improved with the keeping. She would meet the challenge as she always did, by blaming and dodging responsibility.

Senator Pomeroy asked Sid and SMP's Chief Legal Counsel, Bob Cavendish, to meet her in her hideaway at 9:40 AM. This was just twenty minutes before the hearing started. That would limit the amount of time Sid had to rant. She tolerated Sid because she adored his money. He was driven, clearly mercenary, and a bit of a lech, but his money spent well.

Barbara always said red was her least favorite color. It was the color of Republican landslides. It was the color of the burgeoning national debt. And it was the color of Sid's sour puss when he was displeased. That red glow was visible even behind the trenta-sized Starbucks he was guzzling as he walked through the door. She could only imagine what all that caffeine would do to his vivacious personality.

"Good morning Bob, how are you doing?"

"Doing well, Barbara. And you?"

"As well as can be expected, given the results of our poll last night."

That flipped Sid's switch. And the caffeine *wasn't* helping.

"What do you mean? What do the polls show?"

"They show that over ninety percent of viewers believe the parahumans have the same rights as humans. And ninety-six percent believe the studio should ante-up for the spouse re-creations."

"This is outrageous!" The crimson tide spreading from his neck-upward added color to the roadmap of blood vessels on his forehead.

"Sid, we had a pretty good idea the ship had sailed by close of testimony yesterday, didn't we? Those three delivered the performance of their careers. I couldn't intimidate them or derail their testimony. That alone should have been proof they aren't human! And Jimmy Stewart—his testimony launched both torpedoes. He had the gallery in tears. His amazingly emotional appeal sank us."

"All right, Barbara, enough with the maritime metaphors!"

"So, what's next, Senator?" asked Bob. "What can we do to recover?"

"The best path I suggested already. In fact, it's the only path forward. Pay for the spouses. Sid said he needed to talk to the investors. I hope you've done so, Sid."

They both looked at Sid.

"The investors said they'll fund *one* spouse. They asked me to recommend which one and I suggested either Carole Lombard for Clark or Lauren Bacall for Bogie because they both were actresses. We can create film projects for either one that will pay the investors back. They're not willing to even discuss Jimmy's wife, Gloria."

"Wow. And it was his testimony that did you in," Barbara said with a smirk.

"Yeah, kind of sweet revenge," Sid shot back with obvious consternation.

"Sweet revenge? Only if you're trying to slit your own throat!" Bob bellowed. "Sid, this isn't payback time. The nation—the *world* is watching you! You're letting your feelings dominate your thinking right now. This is a veritable gold mine—and you can come out the hero!"

"How?"

"You need to take Jimmy, Clark, and Bogie out for a night on the town. This is a publicity bonanza. We make sure the major news networks are there. The dinner is their *bachelor party* celebrating their last night of bachelorhood. The conversation will all be about the spouses: where they'll go on their honeymoon, where they'll live–the press will be all over it! The public will be clamoring to know what movies Lombard and Bacall will be in with Gable and Bogart. TV clips of the three eating and drinking will help repair the damage these hearings have done to their public persona. And here's a thought, Sid. What if you tell them you're going to create a child for them if they decide they want one? I'm telling you, this is *big!*"

"Yeah, big money! Don't get me wrong, Bob. I see the potential but if the investors reject it, if they won't pony up the money, we're sunk!"

"No, we're not! Are you kidding me? Why, Bank of America would loan us that money in a heartbeat! And not for one actor but for all three. The public will chop you to pieces if you favor one actor over the other two. But—and here's the touch of genius—you remember that couple in the news that lost their only child in a freak accident? The couple separated because the woman was infertile and couldn't afford treatments to have another child. What did the public do? The money poured in from every corner of the country, people giving money for fertility treatments. Sid, that's *exactly* the kind of story Jimmy laid out for the public in yesterday's testimony. I'm telling you, if you miss this, you're missing the biggest publicity bonanza you'll ever have handed to you. With the level of public interest the polls show, public contributions for the happy couples to have a child would only increase fan following—and might fund it without bank or investor money. SMP could dominate Hollywood for the next one hundred years! Now, take *that* to your board of directors!"

The light had finally turned on. Sid was listening and the wheels were turning. He stared out the window of Barbara's hideaway. It was almost time for the hearing to begin.

"Finally," said Barbara. "He's finally got it. I have to get into the caucus room. I don't know what President Roosevelt has cooked up, but half the world is watching, and I need camera time. After the position I took for you, I'm going to need the votes."

28

S UPERVISORY SPECIAL AGENT JOE RUSSO and his
team were lauded by Bureau leadership in Washington DC.

Russo led the biggest bust of organized crime in FBI history. Over three hundred arrests and indictments. But Joe and the Bureau could not release to the press how he secured so many indictments. The parahuman who 'gave' them the evidence must remain a secret to the public. He was missing and so were a half-dozen federal agents. With no chance to question him, the Bureau did not know what Antonio knew—so they didn't know what he might do. Did he know they'd downloaded his collective memories, that he was responsible for the myriad of arrests? That might be a safe assumption on his part—but would he do about it? Would he retaliate—or would he hide? Would he flee the country? Where would he go? Mike Benchley and his team had to get a handle on this threat. Quickly.

The myriad of potential dangers involved with parahuman stand-ins were being relentlessly probed. Bureau leadership considered it the greatest predatory threat to American security in the history of the Justice Department, categorizing it as '*stealth terrorism*.' They had to find a way to identify parahumans, especially with Antonio on the loose.

Joe and his New York City surveillance experts—Mark Fitzsimmons, Will Claridge, and Frederick Wong—were flown to Washington. They received commendations presented by Director

Mike Benchley and other members of FBI executive leadership. Press coverage of the event was extensive.

This also placed Joe and his team in Washington at the time of the Senate parahuman hearings. Director Benchley wanted them in the Kennedy Caucus Room for testimony by the Hollywood three, even if they were consigned to standing room only.

Following the hearing, they met in Benchley's office in the Hoover building.

"Gentlemen, we have a few hours before our dinner this evening. I'd like to hear your thoughts on the parahuman/holosapien issue. You heard the testimony of the three, you are keenly aware of what Antonio has said and done, and we have the details Joe and I gleaned from Dr. Edersheim. The Director has tasked us with putting together a battle plan for dealing with this threat. I need your insight."

"You know, Mike," Joe began, "thinking about what we learned from Dr. Edersheim in Tel Aviv and listening to what Jimmy Stewart—or his parahuman—said, I've got an idea, one that Dr. Edersheim gave me."

"Okay, let's hear it, Joe?"

"Mike, remember in Tel Aviv that Dr. E said Benny 'sleepwalked' just like we saw Antonio do. That may mean that all of these AI animatrons–parahuman and holosapien–have this weakness and we might be able to use that to control them."

"You've got my attention! Go on."

"Dr. Edersheim is working on what he calls 'memory modification.' He said if he can place Antonio into *Theta* sleep, he should be able to replace Mancuso's memories with memories of someone else–someone with goodness and decency. He just has to identify and harvest the memories of someone from the past–like William Shakespeare or Bugs Bunny–someone other than another Mancuso!"

"Bugs Bunny? I guess that would be an improvement! But why can't he just completely wipe Antonio's memory and leave it at that?"

"He said we'd have the equivalent of the walking dead. In theory, Antonio would still be capable of movement, we just don't know what he might do. He'd be operating from a blank slate."

"Nice. Okay, so memory modification it is! But you said Dr. Edersheim would have to put Antonio into the sleepwalking state? Why won't *Theta* sleep work?"

"You remember that he said these creatures don't seem to remember what happens during sleepwalking. His theory is their data isn't completely controlling them during sleepwalking, and that could make the memory replacement more likely to work. He has to place Antonio into *Theta*, then trigger him into sleepwalking–then attempt a memory replacement at that precise moment. He said it's tricky but, in theory, it should work."

"Good job, Joe. Thanks for following up with Dr. Edersheim. This is the kind of effort we need on this team. So, we have at least part of a plan. But can Dr. Edersheim tell us how to find Antonio? If he can no longer track Antonio, we're still at square one. With his strength and intelligence, he could be anywhere. And our six agents ... after this long a time, we have to assume the worst."

"I know, Mike, and I'm sorry. I take full responsibility for what happened to them."

"Just stop right there, Joe. I'm not letting anyone put that burden on you–not even you! We're all working on virgin ground here. How could you know six fully armed men weren't enough to apprehend Antonio? Six thousand might not be! We're not going to physically overpower these creatures. Their artificial intelligence puts them steps ahead of us. No, our best bet is being able to remotely disable them. Either shutting them down completely or maybe through memory modification as you mentioned. But we have to find a way to identify them!"

"Yes, sir. Mike, there's one more thing Dr. E said about the sleepwalking state of parahumans that we need to discuss. He mentioned this in Tel Aviv but he brought it up again during my phone call with him."

"Now's the time, Joe. Let's get the issue on the table."

"Mike, you remember that even his holosapien–Benny–even he was able to walk, talk, and take action while he was in *Theta* sleep–and he was under the control of holography. What was Antonio capable of doing during sleepwalking *without* holography properly applied? He was extremely dangerous, correct? Mike, we don't know if the President's duplicate is a holosapien or a parahuman–and what he is capable of doing!"

The look of shock on Mike Benchley's face said it all.

"Dear God—how did I neglect this? Yes, I remember him mentioning the risk. Given the strength of a parahuman, the President and his entire team could be in grave danger."

"But with the White House keeping the President's parahuman top secret, how are you going to address this with them, Mike?"

"Carefully! But I can't sit on this. The White House has to know the danger. I can ask for a meeting with the President but that's not so easy to get. If the President won't meet with me, I can try to take the President's parahuman into protective custody like we did with the Hollywood parahumans. But then they know that we know–and we have the risk Dr. Edersheim warned us of."

"They'll know we know–and they'll want to know why you're grabbing their parahuman!" said Joe.

"Sticky situation. It might take a warrant to get the White House to listen to me. And all because we're trying to save the President's life!"

"But, Mike, I thought you and the President were friends!" said Fitzy.

"I'd like to think so, Fitzy! He was very kind. He and Mrs. Roosevelt agreed to go along with my plan so I could surprise Lexi–so I ... I could propose to her. That was quite an evening. The President is a great man."

"Well, he's not going to forget you that fast. It's only been a week." said Joe.

"I'm not worried about him forgetting me, Joe. But remember Dr. Edersheim told us that knowing the President used a parahuman to sign the peace agreement could be lethal knowledge for us. I never really thought about what he meant. Just how motivated might the President be to keep his parahuman a secret? At stake is a worldwide peace agreement. Virtually every nation could be impacted if the agreement is rejected."

"But why would it be rejected?"

"Because it was not the real President that signed it. It was his artificially intelligent parahuman. That's a pretty big motivation for him to keep the issue under wraps. And that's the reason Dr. Edersheim felt our lives could be at risk if the White House finds out that we know."

"But what choice do we have?" asked Joe.

"None. And here's something that will stand your hair on end. How do we know that it's not *still* his parahuman functioning as President? How do we know the President hasn't been replaced?"

"Oh wow!" said Will. "Forget calling it a 'dilemma.' You've got a Constitutional crisis if that proves true!"

"He testifies tomorrow, Mike," said Joe. "Can we get to him today?"

"I've got to try. But you're staying here, Joe. I'll feel the situation out with the President. If I sense danger, I won't reveal this team's knowledge of the parahuman. If I go missing, you alert the Director of what's happened. We need to pray this doesn't go sideways. The Justice Department coming after a sitting President could do more than knock out the peace treaty."

THE PRESIDENT WAS SITTING at the Resolute desk in the Oval Office when the call came through. Marty Martin screened it.

"Mr. President, there's a call for you from Executive Assistant Director Mike Benchley, head of the FBI's Science and Technology Branch. You remember, he was on the bus ride with Senator Albright—you helped him propose to his girl. He's been in the news lately, sir. He's overseeing the Hollywood parahuman investigation. And he had something to do with the big sting operation in New York City that broke up the Sicilian crime families. He says it's urgent, sir, and it's related to the parahumans."

"Yes, I remember Mike well. A lot of fun, helping him to surprise his girl! I didn't get to visit with him about the investigation though. Put the call through, Marty."

"Mike, this is Jon Roosevelt."

"Mr. President, thank you so much for taking my call, sir!"

"It's my pleasure, Mike. How's the engagement going? I trust you two are doing well. I guess we were so busy with the tour and the engagement we didn't get to visit about your ongoing investigation. Do you have something new concerning the parahumans?"

"Yes, sir, that's correct. Mr. President, I hate to presume upon your time, but I really need to see you, sir. This is a matter of national security."

"Today?"

"Yes, sir."

"How much time do you need, Mike?"

"Could you spare me thirty minutes, sir?"

"Let me put you on hold for just a minute."

"Marty, do I have thirty minutes for Director Benchley later today? He says it's urgent."

"Yes, sir, if you forgo your massage this afternoon, you can open up an hour—or maybe still get in a half-hour massage!"

"Now that sounds like a plan to me. So, at 4:00 PM?"

"Yes, sir, that's the time the massage was scheduled."

"Okay, please let the masseuse know to make it 4:45 and ask if thirty minutes will work for him. I don't want to presume on his time, either."

"Will do, Mr. President."

"All right Mike, we're good for 4:00 this afternoon if that works for you."

"Absolutely, Mr. President. And thank you for making time for me."

"I look forward to our visit, Mike."

"LEXI, YOU GOT JUST a minute?"

"For you, handsome—always! And I've been needing to talk to you about my move out there. I've got several online interviews set for a possible position in Washington, and I need your help knowing where I should look for an apartment. If we're getting married in April, I won't need an apartment very long–do you know of a place that rents by the month?"

"We absolutely need to talk about all of this, Lexi, but unfortunately this is going to be very quick. This may sound crazy, after our day and dinner with the Roosevelts, but I need to share something with you. You and I are on what the Bureau would call an 'open line' so we could be overheard–and that's what I want. I need your prayers. Now, listen to me, beautiful. I don't mean this to frighten my fiancé but what I'm about to tell you on this open line could save my life."

"*Wait–what?* Mike—what's happening? You can't do this to me!"

"I'm sorry, sweetie, but this job carries risk. I'll stop right here if this is too much for you."

"No—you have to tell me! You know I want to pray about whatever is happening. We're going to be married! I ... I can't believe I'm getting this kind of call. Please ... tell me what's going on!"

"I'm going to the White House this afternoon at 4:00. I don't know what the outcome of that meeting will be."

"You're not afraid President Roosevelt would do something to you, are you?"

"No ... not him. But I have to reveal some things to him that he and his team don't know anyone else knows. It may be information that some would try to keep quiet–but I'm telling you and I've told others–within the Bureau."

"Does this involve the parahumans?"

"Not the Hollywood three. There are others. If somebody is listening, they now know key people have this knowledge. My team members have all the details. That means getting rid of me won't hide the information–it will cause it to be released. If something happens to me, you and others will be notified immediately."

"Mike—*I don't want to hear this!*" Lexi began to cry.

"Lexi, please don't cry! The Director of the FBI will be notified if I'm not back to the Hoover building by 6:00 PM. With the entire Justice Department standing by, it would be suicide for anyone to harm me. I'm saying it's highly unlikely, but I'd still like to know you're praying for me. Will you do that, please?"

"You know I will. How long will you be in the White House? If you're okay, what time should I hear back from you?"

"My meeting is only thirty minutes long. At the latest, you should hear from me by 5:00 PM my time—that's 2:00 PM your time. Okay?"

"Okay. You promise you'll call me?"

"I promise you'll be the very first person I contact! If I get detained, I'll have Russo call you."

"Mike ... I really love you."

"I love you, baby. It's going to be okay. Just pray for me. And I want you out here as soon as we can make it happen. You've got this Marine's heart wrapped around your little finger."

"You sure you're not saying that because you think I'll never hear from you again?"

"You pray for me and I'm sure I'll be safe."

"I've already started! Please call me."

"I'll call you. And I'm coming to see you. I can't wait any longer."

MIKE BENCHLEY ARRIVED at 3:45 PM, cleared the Secret Service gate, and was taken to the Oval Office waiting area. At 3:59, Marty Martin came out and walked him in.

As Benchley entered, the weight of history and importance of where he was hit him like a lead weight. He fought back a case of nerves he hadn't felt since the first mortar went off in Afghanistan.

The President moved around the corner of his desk with his hand outstretched and a warm smile on his face. The actor's charisma and charm were comforting, his appreciation for the visit seemed sincere.

"Mike, good to see you again! You met my chief of staff, Marty Martin on the bus ride. And you remember my director of White House security, Josh Sizemore."

"Yes, sir, I do. How are you, Josh? Good to see you again!"

"Same here, Mike! I've been anticipating this meeting since the President told me of your call earlier today. I know it must be very important."

"Yes, Mike, I asked Josh to be here since you said it involved national security."

"Mr. President, I must say, I still see that young actor in your manner and smile, sir! You've certainly helped ease the tension I feel about this meeting."

"Ronald Reagan said he didn't know how anyone could be President without first having been an actor! And no need for tension, Mike, you know you're among friends. I'm thinking a sip of something might help prepare us for what you're about to share. What can I get you?"

"A short Scotch would be nice."

"Sounds good. A bit of Dutch courage is useful from time to time, don't you think?"

"I do, sir."

"You know, my father used to say, 'Alcohol will make a rabbit slap a bear.' I remember his warning whenever I reach for the bottle. It has its uses but can't give a man true courage. Marty, would you care to join us? I'd ask Josh but he never drinks while on duty, do you Josh?"

"No, sir—it's hard enough for me to keep up with you now! Can't afford to be slowed down."

"No, thank you, Mr. President," Marty said.

Marty directed Benchley to the sitting area across from the President's desk. They stood and waited for the President.

"Here you go, Mike. I appreciate a man who appreciates Scotch. Sit down, gentlemen, please. Mike, how's your bride-to-be? You know, that was the perfect culmination of a perfect evening. Are you two planning the wedding yet?"

"Yes, we are, Mr. President. Lexi's parents have the church lined up for April 6. I want her and her parents to enjoy the cherry tree blooming season!"

"Oh, she'll love that! I hope you'll send Mrs. Roosevelt and me an invitation. I wouldn't want to miss it!"

"Absolutely, Mr. President! It will be our honor, sir."

"So, Mike, what is this urgent matter you wanted to see me about?"

Mike took a sip of the Scotch. Fruit and wood notes. Thirty year old Scotch. This was several thousand dollars per bottle. He figured he'd better enjoy it while he could.

"Mr. President, only four members of my team know I'm here. These are the men who worked with me in New York and Tel Aviv to bring down the Mancuso crime organization. Not even the Director of the FBI knows I'm here. Not yet, anyway. I know that may sound strange, perhaps even suspiciously furtive, but there's a reason and I believe you'll understand in a moment. The Bureau chose to keep the most significant part of what I uncovered in New York hidden from the press and public. I was told they are not going outside the Bureau with this information, either. I don't mean to defy that decision, sir, but I'm trying to protect you."

Without looking, the President set his drink on the end table. His eyes never left Mike Benchley.

"Tel Aviv? That's a long way from New York City. Mike, are you saying the Bureau is doing something that could endanger me?"

"Not directly, Mr. President—I mean, due to the potential danger I and my team uncovered just this afternoon, I did not take time to brief FBI leadership on the latest finding in my possession. I immediately contacted you. I hope you understand, sir."

"So, you did not leave FBI leadership in the dark for my protection?"

"That's correct, sir. There simply wasn't time to inform them. I wanted to ensure your safety as quickly as possible."

"Okay, you've got my attention."

"Thank you, sir. Mr. President, there was a key insider, within the Mancuso organization, that led to the downfall of all five New York crime families. And you know who he is."

"I know him? How would I know him, Mike?"

"Because it was Donny Mancuso."

"Mancuso? But why would Donny Mancuso want to incriminate himself and the other four Dons?"

"He didn't incriminate himself, Mr. President."

"You've lost me, Mike"

"Sir, it was his parahuman. With the help of a scientist in Tel Aviv, we were able to put Mancuso's parahuman to sleep and download every scrap of data in his twisted artificial intelligence. Every murder, drug deal, bribery–everything was there in his memory."

"*Mancuso was using a parahuman!*" Marty was sitting on the edge of his seat. "I'm sorry, Mr. President, I didn't mean to interrupt."

"It's okay, Marty. This is a shock to all of us. Mike, you indicated I was in danger. Are you saying the crime families are planning to move against the White House due to your sting operation?"

"No, sir, I have no reason to suspect they blame you for any of this. The truth is, sir, the real Donny Mancuso is dead. He was killed in Bolivia six weeks ago. He had the parahuman made to hide the fact he was out of the country. We had his office and top advisors under close surveillance when we learned of his death. That's also when we learned the suspect we thought was Donny Mancuso was, in fact, his parahuman."

"I'm sorry, Mike, I don't want to make this only about me, but I feel I'm missing something. I don't see the connection between your sting operation and my safety."

"I'm sorry, Mr. President. Let me fill in the missing parts. During surveillance, we also learned that a scientist in Tel Aviv had created Mancuso's parahuman—and the three parahumans in Hollywood. I knew this would be important for you to know."

"Yes, it certainly is!"

"Yes, sir. So, I and one of my New York special agents flew to Tel Aviv to interview the scientist responsible. We found he was dead—he'd committed suicide the night before—but we met with his employer, the top geneticist and anatomist in the world, Dr. Alfred Edersheim. Sir—may I speak freely in front of these two gentlemen?"

"Absolutely, Mike. That's why they're in this meeting."

"Thank you, Mr. President. Sir, let me be totally transparent. Dr. Edersheim created a holosapien to take the place of President Isaac Hayut in Israel for the trip to Tehran."

"A *what*? What did you call it?"

"Dr. Edersheim called it a holosapien, sir. Dr. Edersheim uses holography—some application of helium gas that helps compartmentalize and reliably deliver data to the artificial intelligence of the holosapien. He said the holography provides stability in segregating present information from past information—which forms memory. He believes holography is the missing ingredient causing the Hollywood parahumans to become emotionally distressed over memories of people and events the parahuman never really experienced. Dr. Edersheim reserves the term *holosapien* as applicable only to those creatures he knows have holography properly applied. Otherwise, he refers to the creatures as *parahumans*."

"This is extremely valuable information, Mike." The President looked at Josh and Marty. "I see several ramifications that could come from this, don't you?" Looking back at Mike, he asked, "But why wouldn't the other scientist—the one that created the Hollywood parahumans—why didn't he use holography in creating the Hollywood actors?"

"He didn't understand Dr. Edersheim's holographic technology, sir. He admitted as much to Dr. Edersheim. He was a rogue scientist who essentially stole the technology from his employer. His wife was dying with cancer and he needed money. The owner of that studio in Hollywood paid this scientist millions to re-create the three actors as parahumans. Mancuso somehow discovered the name of the scientist who created the actors. He then traveled to Tel Aviv, along with some of his lieutenants, and ordered the scientist to create his parahuman or they would kill him."

"So, the scientist took his own life. How tragic. How did you learn of all this?"

"The name of the rogue scientist, Dr. Uriah Horvitz, was identified during surveillance of Mancuso's office in New York City. We worked through our embassy in Tel Aviv to locate Dr. Horvitz, and that led us to Dr. Alfred Edersheim. Dr. Edersheim was aware of Dr. Horvitz's theft and was trying to undo the damage when Dr. Horvitz took his own life. Sir ... Dr. Edersheim was very transparent with us."

"There's more you need to share with me, isn't there, Mike?"

"Yes, Mr. President, there is." Mike paused an uncomfortable moment, taking another sip of his Scotch.

"Mike, being President comes with more than the usual amount of bad news. I've found that bad news simply means I can't see both ends of the train. I need to see where we've been *and* where we're going. That's the kind of counsel every successful President depends on. I'm sure you're doing your best to help me. Please, go ahead."

"Yes, sir, Mr. President, thank you. Dr. Edersheim's holosapien, which he made for President Hayut, stepped in front of the bullet for you."

"I came to that conclusion when you told me President Hayut had a para ... I mean a holosapien."

Mike set his drink down. He sat up straight in his chair. It occurred to him he was coming to attention before his commander and chief. As a Marine Corps officer, he swore allegiance to defend the Constitution and to obey the orders of the President of the United States. He had to finish this, but the words were not coming easily.

"Sir, Dr. Edersheim said when President Hayut's holosapien returned from Tehran, it told him that he stepped in front of that bullet knowing it was not really you that had been hit. It was *your holosapien.*"

There was not a sound in the room. The eyes of the President, Josh Sizemore, and Marty Martin were locked on Mike Benchley. He could see it, but more than that, he felt it. The truth was now out. He needed to give his President the rest of the message.

"Dr. Edersheim said he and President Hayut were both stunned by the holo's admission. They said 'Benny'—that's what they call President Hayut's holo—Benny was not programmed to do what he did. He did it on his own. They asked him why he moved to save you if he knew that was your holosapien, which could not be killed. His answer shocked them. Benny said he did it to demonstrate self-sacrifice to the humans. He said the peace treaty would never survive unless people are willing to die for it. Sir, *these creatures are making decisions on their own!*"

"Marty, Josh," said the President, "now would be a fine time for you to jump in. We have a lot to talk about. Marty, I think you'd better cancel my massage."

"Yes, Mr. President. If you don't mind, I'll send a text. I don't want to miss any of the discussion."

"Perfectly fine."

"Sir," said Josh, "if the Israelis have this technology, and Mancuso strong-armed it out of them—Mancuso and the Hollywood studio owner—there's no telling who else has this tech by now."

"Josh, excuse me," said Mike Benchley, "but the Israeli's didn't sell or surrender the tech. It was only Dr. Horvitz. His employer, Dr. Edersheim, assured me the Hollywood three and Mancuso's para are the extent of the damage."

"He's absolutely certain of that?" Josh quickly asked. "The rogue scientist is dead so we can't interrogate him."

"Dr. Horvitz gave Dr. Edersheim his files," Mike countered. "There were detailed notes on the Hollywood parahumans. He had destroyed his files on Mancuso's creature as soon as the project was completed. That was the extent of it."

"Still ... " Josh began, but the President interrupted him.

"Josh, take it easy. Director Benchley has been very transparent with us. He would not be telling us what Dr. Edersheim said if he did not consider the information completely reliable. And Mike, the scientist who created my parahuman—or holosapien—his name is Dr. Ralph Vestro. He knows Alfred Edersheim. He spoke very highly of him. Marty, I think the wisest thing to do is bring Dr. Vestro and Dr. Edersheim together in this room. We need to know what we're dealing with."

"Yes, sir, Mr. President."

"Mike, earlier you said that only four others knew you were coming here. May I ask who these people are?"

This was it. Was the President asking for names to contain the damage? If so, this could mean personal risk to his team and the woman he intended to marry. He promised Russo and Lexi he would feel the situation out before sharing names or additional details. But the President had not hesitated to admit the existence of his own parahuman. He was open and transparent. He could trust the President.

"Yes, Mr. President. New York supervisory special agent Joseph Russo and his three surveillance agents. They surveilled Mancuso for four years and discovered the parahuman. They are responsible for taking down the New York crime families. The four of them are here in Washington. I took them to the hearing today. The Bureau has tasked me with forming a plan to counter the potential parahuman threat and these four agents know as much or more than I do about parahumans, having surveilled Mancuso's for so long." Mike chose not to mention Lexi. He used an open line when he told her. No need to repeat what had already been announced.

"I think that was wise, Mike. But what about in Tel Aviv? Who else knows about my parahuman?"

"The people present with me when I interviewed Dr. Edersheim included Joe Russo and Major General Efrayim Geller, head of the Israeli National Police Department Investigations and Crime Fighting."

"Did General Geller know about my holosapien prior to that conversation?"

"No sir, not when I began questioning Dr. Edersheim. But he heard the same revelations from Dr. Edersheim as I and agent Russo heard, Mr. President. General Geller agreed to hold this information as top secret. And his security clearance is the highest level."

"That's good to hear, Mike."

"Yes, sir. Mr. President, what I said a moment ago–that these creatures are making decisions on their own–I need to follow up on that, sir. That's what really brought me here to you. The fact I knew about your parahuman was only half the issue that brought me here."

"Well–I already said being President, I hear more than the usual allotment of bad news. Let's get the rest of it out in the open, Mike!"

"I'm sorry, Mr. President. If your creation is not a holosapien, if he is only a parahuman, he could eventually prove to be emotionally unstable. Like the three in Hollywood. And, as I revealed to you, even controlled by holography, Benny still acted on his own initiative–and he's capable of what Dr. Edersheim called 'sleepwalking.' He can awaken while in *Theta* sleep and move about, speaking and acting with little to no memory of what he's doing."

"This is significant information, Mike. Thankfully, we've not seen the instability from Rosebud that the Hollywood parahumans have shown. There's not been any 'sleepwalking' that I know of–has there been, gentlemen?"

"No, Mr. President," said Josh. "This information is quite a concern to me. It could mean a significant security risk."

"Is Rosebud your parahuman, Mr. President?"

"Yes, I'm sorry—that's the first time you've heard that code name."

"Mr. President, to Josh's point, let me go a step further. Mancuso's parahuman is incredibly evil, yet his issues are not that different from the three Hollywood actors."

"That's a frightening assertion, Mike. Please explain."

"Sir, Antonio—that's the name used for Mancuso's parahuman—Antonio has none of the human needs that his predecessor had. There's no food or drink appetite, no sexual appetite, he doesn't even require shelter so there's no fear of poverty to drive him. I'm saying he doesn't break the law to get somewhere in life. None of the things that drove Mancuso are there to drive Antonio."

"Understood. What's the implication of this?"

"Dr. Edersheim said these creatures were made to function based on one thing—memories. Memories that came from the life of someone else. Mancuso's parahuman kills because Donny Mancuso killed. He hates because Mancuso hated. He needs no other motivation. He's simply living out memories. Haven't you seen this in Jimmy Stewart's parahuman, sir? He needs Gloria because the human Jimmy Stewart needed her. The parahuman has never seen her, he's never talked with her or spent one minute with her, yet he insists he has to have her by his side or he can't go on."

"You know, Mike, I've missed Jimmy so much, being with his parahuman filled a need I didn't realize I had. He's filled a hole in me I didn't realize was there. What you're describing completely escaped my attention."

Mike didn't want to turn the conversation back to potential parahuman dangers, but it had to be done.

"I'm sorry, Mr. President, but what if your parahuman has the same issue as the Hollywood parahumans? Or Antonio? Lack of holography—or effective holography—produces bereavement without death, sorrow without loss, a sense of tragedy when nothing has happened to them. They're being devastated by memories that don't belong to them. And there's still the issue of sleepwalking. And we have to add to the list of concerns the strength of the parahuman and their seeming indestructibility. They can be brought down, but it takes an explosion to do it. Bullets, as we saw in Tehran, are useless."

"Josh, Marty, am I remembering correctly? Didn't Ralph Vestro tell us that he and Alfred Edersheim worked together developing holography for the parahumans?"

"Yes, sir, Mr. President, Dr. Vestro did say that," said Marty.

"Just a minute, Marty," said Josh. "I'm not sure he said exactly that. He said they sat on panels together. I didn't hear him say they shared holographic information. Dr. Edersheim may have an edge on Dr. Vestro. I think that's worth checking out. Especially if it gives us assurance of stability in Rosebud."

"Except for sleepwalking," Mike added. Dr. Edersheim didn't have a solution for that issue as of our meeting in Tel Aviv a few weeks ago."

"Josh, I'd like you to call Dr. Vestro right away. Share with him Dr. Edersheim's belief that missing or ineffective holography is causing these issues in the Hollywood three. Tell him about sleepwalking. Tell him we need definitive information on his application of holography. We need to know if his application equals that of Dr. Alfred Edersheim. Ask him if he can provide me personally with his full assurance of that."

"Yes, sir. I'll call him now."

"At the risk of sounding like a death knell, Mr. President," said Mike Benchley, "I need to mention again the physical strength of the parahuman. The FBI saw first-hand Antonio's physical strength, and it was far beyond human. He killed two of the four closest confidants Donny Mancuso had, and he did so with the power of a gorilla. Lying flat on his back he picked up two police officers and threw them across the room then aimed a gun over his head and shot a detective–and this was done while in a sleepwalking state. Mr. President, that same strength may very well reside in the Hollywood three and in Rosebud."

"Good God," was all Marty could say.

Josh was on the phone, holding for Ralph Vestro.

"Josh," the President said, "it would seem the safe play to assume all parahumans have the same strength."

"Noted, Mr. President," said Josh.

"But they *can* be put to sleep, Mike," said the President. "Ralph Vestro built that into Rosebud. He's asleep now in a room not far from here. I would think the Israeli scientists would have done the same for his creations."

"Yes, Mr. President," answered Mike, "but Antonio was in sleepwalking mode when he took out the police in his house. Sir, it is this risk to your safety that brought me here. Your safety and everyone else in the White House—even though Rosebud is asleep. We need to verify that holography was properly applied to your parahuman."

"What do you propose?"

"You suggested it a moment ago, sir. We need to contact Dr. Edersheim immediately. He has assured me of his willingness to assist us. As you mentioned, having him meet with Dr. Vestro he could determine if holography was properly applied. And perhaps together they can find a way to correct the sleepwalking issue."

Josh spoke up. "Mr. President, I have Ralph Vestro on the phone. Sir, he's saying he *did* use holography with Rosebud, but if Alfred Edersheim is concerned about it, and he can review his application of holography, then we should move on it immediately."

"Sir," said Marty, "based on this new information—that a parahuman is still dangerous while asleep, until Dr. Edersheim has time to check him, I think Rosebud should be moved off-site. All our lives may be in peril."

"I agree with Marty, sir," said Josh.

"There's another aspect of parahuman weakness that the Bureau is studying, Mr. President," said Mike.

"Mike, I thought you were through with the bad news!" said the President. "I thought I'd seen both ends of the train!"

"I'm sorry, sir, but there is the possibility a parahuman's consciousness can be hijacked by a hostile power. If there is the slightest possibility that anyone else knows you have a parahuman, he should be placed into a safe holding area until this concern can be addressed by Dr. Edersheim. I hasten to add this is only a preliminary concern—there's been no evidence of this risk being substantial—but it is, still, a risk."

The President looked down into his drink. "We discussed the possible 'hijacking' before I left for Tehran ... I mean Rosebud left for Tehran. Rosebud saved my life, Mike. He saved the peace agreement. He gave an unscripted speech in Tehran and said things while there that I don't know I could have done any better. Now, I'm forced to remove him and place him under heavy guard. It doesn't seem right. But I concur, of course. For everyone's safety, we must act. And now we have a security risk beyond anything we've prepared for. Would you say this is an accurate statement, Josh?"

"Mr. President?" asked Josh.

"Josh, if a bullet won't stop him, how do you contain this threat?"

"I'm sorry, sir. You're right. I don't know the answer to that question—but we must find out."

"Polymer cord netting," said Mike. "That's what Dr. Edersheim had us use when we had to restrain Antonio in a *Theta* sleep state. He said it's strong enough that the parahuman cannot break it, and it allows us to restrain them without destroying them."

"This is all such a shock to me," said the President. "And I think I'm about to shock all of you. It may be dangerous, but I need Rosebud to stay with us until tomorrow evening."

"But Mr. President ... " said Josh.

"I need Rosebud tomorrow, Josh. Then you can move him." The President paused, sipped his Scotch and then asked, "Why is it that every good thing in this life carries with it a negative?"

The President's sorrow over Rosebud was obvious. No one wanted to speak.

"Maybe not everything, Jon," Marty said. "Your love for Deborah has no negatives, does it?"

"I'm afraid it does, Marty. Someday she'll be taken from me, or I from her. Just as Jimmy was taken from me–by death. The parahumans long for a wife they never had, yet they can never die. I have my beloved wife, yet she will be taken from me. There's always a negative to everything in life, Marty. We live in what the Bible calls a 'fallen world.' Artificial intelligence has its advantages–but some serious limitations."

"Mr. President, may I contact Dr. Edersheim and get him on his way here?" asked Mike.

"Yes, Mike, please do. Coordinate with Marty so my schedule is free when he arrives. I want to be here when he examines Rosebud."

"Yes, sir, Mr. President."

"Mike, thank you for coming to see me. I'm most grateful. Dr. Edersheim's application of holography seems to be the path du jour, and I hope it proves a viable solution. But I have another path I must take. I'll be testifying tomorrow at the Senate hearing. You and your team won't want to miss it."

MIKE'S FIRST TEXT WAS to Lexi.

Mike: "All went very well. Still in the Oval Office with the President but I'll call you in a few minutes. Need to place a quick call to Russo in New York. I love you. BTW the President and Mrs. Roosevelt will be coming to the wedding. Ask your mom to allow extra space for the Secret Service!"

Her text came back so fast he knew she must have been staring at her phone.

Lexi: "I love you—and I'm so thankful God answers prayer!"

29

"THIS HEARING WILL COME TO ORDER!" Steven Albright had his work cut out for him.

"This could be the final day before we are forced into closed session to receive confidential information about the parahumans. Millions following these hearings are looking to this committee to help solve the turmoil and pain these beloved actors have endured. We must move expeditiously before we are forced into closed session."

The usual early morning chatter could still be heard. Reporters getting settled in, committee members speaking with staffers, and people in the gallery reliving comments from their favorite star's testimony. Chairman Albright took one last look at the day's agenda, then dropped his gavel.

"Quiet, please. Quiet! Before we begin this morning, I was asked by Senator Barbara Pomeroy if a previous witness, Mr. Sid Abrams, might address the committee with some important new information. We are certainly happy to make time for Mr. Abrams' testimony. I want to remind the witness he is still under oath, and I'd like to remind all our witnesses that lying to Congress at any time, under oath or otherwise, is a felony. Let's have the chaplain open our session with prayer and then we'll begin."

While the chaplain prayed, Josh Sizemore and more than one hundred agents were combing over the Kennedy Caucus room, securing the entrances, hallways, stairways, roof, basement, and streets around the building. Traffic was already being rerouted to prevent vehicles from approaching the building within a city block. Josh was presenting no opportunity for the turbid events of Tehran to repeat.

Steven Albright tried to listen to the chaplain's prayer, but his mind drifted to results of the hearings thus far—and all he could see was success. Public sentiment was resoundingly with the parahumans. All polls confirmed the American people expected the studio to provide for the needs of the three actors. The Senate was in an unprecedented position, admired by the public for their compassion and commitment to these three American icons. And the weight of Steve Albright's popularity was off the scale. He just might run for President when his friend, Jon Roosevelt, finished his second term. There could even be a win for SMP Studios if they could rub the greed out of their eyes and see the opportunity. All they need do is give the parahumans what they asked for—what the public was demanding—and they would win an avalanche of grateful ticket-buying fans. In addition, the committee had found no evidence of monopoly. SMP was simply the first to take advantage of AI actor re-creation. They certainly didn't *own* the re-created actor market. The Senate's decision was great news for SMP. There would be no additional legal expense or fines from the Federal Trade Commission. And, while the technology was still considered embryonic, Steven was hopeful that whatever ailed the three parahumans, it could be resolved in a satisfactory way. And—*dare he think it*? There might be an unexpected bonus for the citizens of California. Barbara Pomeroy was in trouble in the polls. News outlets were on the attack, noting how deep into the studio's pockets she had climbed to side against these three silver screen legends. Maybe California would see *both* senate seats filled by a Republican? The chaplain finished and Chairman Albright was ready for another big day.

"Thank you, chaplain, we appreciate your invocation. As I announced a few minutes ago, Mr. Sid Abrams has additional information for us. If he will come forward now, the committee is ready to hear his testimony."

Sid quickly straightened his tie before his promenade to the stand. This was going to be a seminal moment for SMP Studios. As he slid in front of the microphone, Steven Albright motioned for him to begin.

"Mr. Chairman and members of the committee, I wish to report that I spoke with the SMP Studios board of directors as well as our investors. They have unanimously agreed the best thing we can do to make life as enjoyable as possible for our parahuman stars is to have their former spouses re-created utilizing the parahuman technology."

Even before he completed his statement, applause and cheers rose from the gallery. Chairman Albright let them cheer. The committee sat back and accepted at least some of the credit for this amicable resolution.

"Mr. Abrams," Steven Albright said, "I'm sure that loud and happy response from the gallery, and this committee, was echoed a million times over by the American people, and countless fans around the world. We all express our gratitude for your generosity! I do think we should hear once again from Mr. Gable, Bogart, and Stewart in the wake of this announcement, and receive their thoughts concerning SMP's decision. As they are present with us today, we will try to make time to hear from them. Unless you have additional testimony for us, Mr. Abrams, you may be excused."

Sid stood amid additional applause and cheers. He waved to the gallery as he made his way back to his seat.

"Now, I promised Senator Perez of Texas that we would hear from an expert on the subject of emotions in the parahumans. We were told he had successfully counseled with at least one of the Hollywood actors. In my mind that most certainly makes this gentleman worth listening to. I look forward to hearing what he has learned and any answers he can provide concerning the parahuman emotional issues that necessitated this committee. Therefore, our next witness is Dr. John Scott from Encino, California. Dr. Scott, please come forward and be sworn."

Dr. Scott made his way to the witness stand. Clark Gable smiled as his friend worked his way to the front of the caucus room. Dr. Scott saw Clark and returned the smile.

"Dr. Scott, please raise your right hand. Do you swear to tell the whole truth and nothing but the truth, so help you God?"

"Yes, I certainly do, Mr. Chairman."

"Please be seated, Dr. Scott. Welcome to the committee. We appreciate you traveling all the way to Washington from Encino to assist with this investigation. Our hope is you might be able to shed some light on the difficulties that have arisen with these three parahuman individuals, and maybe suggest a path forward. The committee received your written statement, we've each reviewed that document, so I believe the panel is ready. Once again, we go to Senator Barbara Pomeroy who has the witness first. Senator Pomeroy?"

"Mr. Chairman, given Mr. Abrams' testimony this morning—guaranteeing SMP's commitment to meet the parahuman's requests—in the interest of time, is this testimony still necessary? Why do we need Dr. Scott telling us how to meet parahuman emotional needs if Mr. Abrams is already doing so?"

"I see Dr. Scott's testimony as essential, Senator Pomeroy. We are concerned with only three parahumans at this point. Can we really believe this is the last we will see of this groundbreaking technology? We are laying a foundation for behavioral ethics related to parahumans, and we must have more information about how they think, feel, function ... there's so much we have yet to learn. We have barely scratched the surface of what is causing their emotional issues. We need to know if there might be a solution to the problem at hand."

"Very well, Mr. Chairman," Pomeroy sighed as she rolled her eyes, "but I anticipate a difficult round of questions for this witness. If he is indeed an expert on these creatures then he needs to answer the questions no one else seems capable of answering."

"The witness is in your capable hands, Senator Pomeroy."

"As long as you understand my position, Mr. Chairman. Dr. Scott, could you tell us about your background? Your professional as well as your personal background, please. We've been told you know and counseled with at least one of the parahuman actors. We'd like to know which one and why. And why you were called as a witness."

"Thank you, Senator Pomeroy. Yes, I do know one of the parahumans, Mr. Clark Gable. I was privileged to assist him with some emotional challenges he was facing. I'm sorry, you asked a litany of questions. Would you mind restating them for me, please?"

"I asked for your background, personal and professional, and why you were called as a witness."

"Oh, yes, thank you. I am a medical doctor and a board-certified psychiatrist. I've been in clinical practice for over thirty years, and I've taught at the university level for more than twenty years. I have authored several books on issues of neuroscience and neurobiology. I specialize in the field of interpersonal neurobiological wellness. In 1995 I founded the Center for Mental and Emotional Wellness to train counselors and medical professionals on the intersection between mental and emotional wholeness. My wife, Carol, and I have been married for forty-two years. We have four children and five grandchildren. We live in what was the Encino ranch previously owned by Clark

Gable and his wife, Carole Lombard, and that is how I met Mr. Gable. A few months ago, unbeknownst to the studio, Clark climbed into his 1935 Duesenberg Roadster and, despite how the countryside had changed, he managed to find his beloved home, which, as I said, my wife and I now occupy. We welcomed him into our home and had a great discussion. During that meeting, I was able to assist Clark with some emotional challenges. From there, he requested Senator Albright call me as a witness."

"Why?"

"Excuse me?"

"Why were you called as a witness?"

"Senator Pomeroy, if you're asking me to explain why Clark or Senator Albright felt I should be called as a witness, you will need to direct that question to them. I've already given you my understanding as to why I've been called. Clark expressed to me, and apparently to Senator Albright, that I had effectively helped him with some of the emotional challenges he was experiencing. Perhaps he felt I could shed some light on what may be happening to all three of them. I don't know for certain."

"Have you also counseled with Mr. Stewart or Mr. Bogart?"

"No, I have not."

"So, Mr. Gable came to you for counseling, doctor?"

"Only indirectly. The day he showed up on my doorstep, he told me he was wanting to see the house where he spent the happiest years of his life with Carole Lombard. My wife and I invited him in to look things over. We kept the house pretty much the same as he would remember it. After some chitchat, he began telling me about his loneliness and other issues he was dealing with. He remarked how incredible it was, finding his house and finding help both at the same time. I told him it really wasn't a coincidence, I had anticipated meeting him one day, so I was somewhat prepared when I saw him walking around outside my home."

"And why did you anticipate meeting him? What's the likelihood a Hollywood star is going to show up on a person's doorstep completely unannounced?"

"To me, it was not unannounced. I felt he would one day be at my home."

"How could you possibly know that!"

"Let's just call it prescience."

"Prescience?"

"Yes, Senator; foresight, intuition, a feeling."

"Would you say you received a vision? Perhaps a divine message?"

"I did not receive a vision but I'm certainly open to divine leading."

"So, would you say God told you?"

"Yes, I do believe that is accurate."

"I see no reason to beat around the bush, Dr. Scott. Your books, even your clinical resources are, in reality, religious propaganda used to foist your beliefs on people that are hurting. Like all purveyors of religiosity, you promise healing to the uneducated and desperate. Didn't you deliberately plant religious ideas in Mr. Gable's head to delude him about the reality of his existence—and about what was causing his issues? And hasn't that become the source of trouble between these three parahuman actors and the studio for which they work?"

"Senator Pomeroy!" Steven Albright interrupted, "prior to this moment, I could not imagine anything else you could possibly do to ensure the destruction of your Senate career more than you had already done, but it is now apparent that your indiscretion knows no bounds."

"I don't need to be lectured by you!" retaliated Pomeroy.

"Someone needs to tell you that attacking a medical doctor's religious beliefs in front of millions of viewers is doing you no favors! The fact that you are a person of *no* faith does not give you the right to attack someone for having faith. And you think Dr. Scott's methods appeal only to the uneducated? If you're suggesting only idiots and fools have a belief in the Almighty, then you should qualify as a *saint*!"

The hall echoed with the laughter of the burgeoning gallery. Albright shook his head at her. This would prove her undoing. Even the Hollywood elite could not provide enough money to save her from the coming wrath of voters.

"Senator Pomeroy," Albright continued, "Dr. Scott is here to answer questions relevant to the subject at hand, and that subject is how best to help these parahuman actors. I must ask that you respect the values and convictions of those giving testimony, whether you agree with those values or not. Challenging Dr. Scott's professional opinions is perfectly acceptable. Attacking him personally serves no purpose and I will not tolerate it!"

Pomeroy was visibly fuming. Her makeup was slathered on, but it wasn't enough to hide the crimson in her cheeks.

"Mr. Chairman, I'll thank you not to cast aspersions on me and the line of questioning which I have not fully pursued! I believe Dr. Scott's religion was used during his meeting with Clark Gable to inflame the actor's thinking and turn him against Sid Abrams, who is Jewish. I direct that as my next question to Dr. Scott—and I demand an honest answer!"

John Scott's expression did not change. He maintained a smile and a calm demeanor.

"Senator Pomeroy, as a medical doctor and practicing psychiatrist, I have over thirty years of clinical practice. I have treated almost seven thousand patients so there is more than ample track record for you to investigate. Not one of my patients has ever filed a complaint about my religious opinions being forced upon them—and that includes people from a plurality of faiths. But you just accused me of trying to prejudice one person against another. I will not allow that unfounded accusation to remain unchallenged. Since you have chosen to address my faith, as a man of faith I will answer you. And I will do so honestly as any man of faith should. I have great respect for the Jewish people. The founder of my faith was a Jewish carpenter who grew up in Israel. I am instructed by his teachings to love all people, and to respect them, no matter their religious persuasion, their lifestyle, their position, or for that matter, their political affiliation—no matter how poorly chosen their words or actions may be."

A wave of laughter could be heard in the gallery, but Pomeroy did not let up.

"Dr. Scott, do you deny that your faith influences the counsel you give patients?"

"I do not deny it at all. It influences every facet of my life, Senator. It teaches me to care about others, and, as a psychiatrist of faith, I seek to relieve the causes of their worries and anxieties. I try to give them hope for a brighter future. My desire is that all people live a healthy, happy life. Tell me, Senator, does such faith improve or hinder the service of a physician, a psychiatrist, or a politician?"

The gallery applauded the testimony. Dr. Scott continued.

"I listened as the official chaplain of the United States Senate opened this hearing with prayer, something that has been done for the past two hundred and fifty years. I've been present for the opening session of the Supreme Court and heard the cry 'God save the United States and this honorable court.' I've seen each man sworn in as President place his hand upon a Bible and pledge to preserve, protect and defend the Constitution of the United States, with the closing request, 'so help me God.' It is obvious the founders of this nation did not separate their faith from the job they were sent here to do. I follow in their steps with the same intent. Please do not ask me to separate my faith in God from the work I've been called to do."

As the applause rose again, Dr. Scott added, "Now, do you wish to ask me any questions about the parahumans and *their* issues or should we continue discussing how my faith positively impacts my work?"

"I'm asking the questions here, doctor!" she roared. "Clearly, these emotional issues in the parahumans did not exist a year ago, when the studio first had these beings created and put them to work. Then Mr. Gable comes to see you and suddenly he has emotional problems. These same issues have now spread to the other two! Interesting that you are a psychiatrist dealing with emotional issues, who counseled Mr. Gable, and now all three have the same problems! Quite a coincidence isn't it?"

"As a psychiatrist and neurobiologist, I can state unequivocally that the timing of Mr. Gable's emotional manifestations were irrespective of any counsel given by me. In fact, the date of manifestation does nothing to prove the moment of an emotional issue's inception. And if you'll ask Mr. Gable, he will confirm the very reason he drove from Hollywood to Encino was his emotional issues. That day, he drove first to find the Brown Derby Restaurant, wanting to see where he and Carole Lombard had so many happy times together. Finding it had been torn down, he drove to Encino to see the home where he and Ms. Lombard lived. He told me he made the long trip to Encino hoping to relieve the emptiness haunting him night and day due to her absence. In other words, Senator, he was already emotionally distressed before he and I met. Once he sat down with me in the house, I was able to help him find some relief and direction. Shall I continue, Senator?"

Pomeroy was thumbing quickly through her notes and did not answer, so Dr. Scott continued.

"I've studied what I could find on parahuman science. I heard their testimony yesterday before this committee. My conversations with Clark, and the collective testimony of Mr. Bogart and Mr. Stewart, has only confirmed my thinking about what is happening. One of my goals, and, I hasten to add, a commitment I made to Clark when we first met at my home, is to meet with those who created him, particularly those responsible for the parahuman mental and emotional make up, so I can better help all of them toward a meaningful, happy life."

"Now this is what I am talking about, Dr. Scott. Clark Gable, like the other two parahumans, was created to have 'meaning' as an actor. Nothing more. They are parahumans. They cannot father children, they cannot engage in domesticity with a re-created female. Their purpose and meaning will be found in acting. Why are you confusing them with promises of divine intervention rather than pointing them to the purpose for which they were created?"

"Divine intervention, Senator? I've said nothing to Mr. Gable or to you about divine intervention. My understanding has been that the parahumans are in Washington seeking the Senate's intervention, not God's. If there's one thing the parahumans have made abundantly clear to this committee it is that they are not happy. They are lonely—however those feelings came into their psyche. If you continue to brush that aside, you put their mental wellbeing, happiness, and stability in question—and that poses a risk the studio will eventually lose the actors through inability or unwillingness to perform. From what I heard this morning, every poll taken of the American people says they understand this. I fail to see why you cannot grasp this truth."

"Mr. Chairman, will you instruct this witness to answer the questions as asked and stop giving his unneeded and unwanted commentary?"

"From where I sit," said Steven Albright, "you are asking questions and he is answering them. His commentary, as you put it, is part of his answer and is important to each member of this committee as he is a recognized expert on psychiatry and mental health."

Barbara Pomeroy jerked her chin away from Steven Albright and scowled at John Scott.

"Dr. Scott, as you just testified, you believe these three are, in fact, emotionally unstable. Is that correct?"

"No, Senator, I did not say they are presently unstable. I said if you continue to ignore their need for purpose and happiness—and I will add, purpose and happiness as *they* define such—then you risk instability. I'm saying you can lecture them all day long that their purpose for existence is in acting, but if that's not their idea of happiness, then you're wasting your words. It's clear to me, they believe there's more to life than acting."

"It's clear to me you're still trying to make their reason for existence about religion. Every time you say 'happiness,' you're talking religion. You either believe they'll never find stability without it, or you believe they'll be better off with it. Most Americans believe religion is simply a crutch for human weakness. Since these creatures are not human, you must feel you've finally found a good use for your religion. At least robots can benefit from it!"

"Senator, I said nothing about religion, nor did I imply that it was the solution for the parahumans. I spoke only of happiness and meaning for them. Could it be that you are the one tying a belief in God to happiness and meaning?"

"Isn't that how you think, Dr. Scott?"

"Oh, I am very happy in my faith, Senator—but just as important to me, you keep coming back to God and happiness. What might this mean for you?"

"You were not called here to diagnose me, Dr. Scott."

"Senator, as a counselor I could not help but notice the number of times you have lashed out at God, faith, people of faith, medicine and faith, psychiatry and faith, parahumans having faith, and whether parahumans should be allowed to take an oath in God's name—you've got quite a bit going on there. I believe you're hurting. I don't know what has caused your pain, of course, I haven't had time to determine that. But there's a foundational rule that definitely applies in this case. *Hurting people hurt others.* It's your pain and unhappiness that sparks the vitriol you exhibit toward others."

The gallery seemed to breathe a collective gasp, but Barbara Pomeroy wasn't interested.

"You mentioned parahumans having faith, Dr. Scott. Is it your belief that these non-humans can be *redeemed*? Are they going to heaven with humans?"

"My commitment to Clark Gable was to help him have a meaningful, happy life. You ask if they're going to heaven, if they can be redeemed, as the soul of a man or woman can be redeemed and enter heaven. I think you've confused *life* with *personality*. I would add that we must not confuse *existence* with *life*. The parahuman is not alive as a human being is alive. They *exist* but they do not possess life as a creature that can procreate does. Their creator was not God but a scientist. What is moving the American people to sympathize with them is their *personality*. They possess the personality of the humans they were created to emulate. We are in love with those personalities. And, I will add, this is the slippery slope of what science has done. If a parahuman were to murder a human being, you could not put the parahuman to death, but you could extinguish its existence and eliminate its personality from this earth. And that, Senator, will be very difficult to do. The polls demonstrate that. Americans are now equating an artificially intelligent personality with human life. A slippery slope indeed."

Crosstalk was taking over the hall. Senator Albright covered the mic and spoke with his fellow Republicans, then addressed Dr. Scott.

"Dr. Scott, this is a direction none of us expected your testimony to take. You've given some credence to those who say the parahumans are not living creatures. Would you comment further on this?"

"As I said, Senator Albright, this is a very slippery slope. We are confusing life, given by God to humans made in His image, with personality. Dynamic, enthralling, incredible personalities, I readily admit! But that only adds to the misconception. When we elevate an artificially intelligent creature's existence—as advanced as they may be—to the same level as human existence, by default we devalue human life to the level of a computer. And we all know what we do with computers when they grow old and cannot be updated or repaired! To be clear, we are either going to elevate an artificially intelligent personality to be equal with a human life, or we will devalue human life to the level of a highly advanced computer. A dangerous slippery slope."

"Senator Albright, while I'm thankful Dr. Scott has validated at least part of my contention, that these are not living creatures as humans are, you have cut into my time with Dr. Scott. May I be allowed to continue?"

"I apologize, Senator Pomeroy. Please continue."

"Dr. Scott, since you've said these creatures are not alive, would you say they are sentient?"

"They are sentient in their own artificially intelligent way."

"What does that mean?"

"It means they hold the memories of a human who had feelings, so, within their reasoning, they must show feelings. They could not be a true copy of their human predecessor without exhibiting the emotions the human exhibited over the scope of their lifetime."

"Thank you. And, back to a previous point, if you believe the parahuman actors are not finding meaning in acting, and if you really are not suggesting they will find it in religion, then where do you believe they will find it?"

"The true value of a computer, an automobile, even a robotic surgery device, is its value to human life. That perceived value brings happiness in the form of amusement, convenience, or relief of suffering. Uniquely, AI has presented us with parahumans that not only bring us happiness, but their unique personalities seek it themselves. And why is this? To expand on what I said a moment ago, AI would not exhibit emotions if it were not for the implanted memories of a human. In fact, everything AI knows—its reality, if you will—comes from humans. Its knowledge is based on what a human told it. But I must add, deep AI is a complex system of neural networks allowing the AI to learn. With visual recognition software, AI will take whatever 'truth' it was given and modify that truth with its own conclusions about what it sees."

"So AI will come up with its *own* truth, Dr. Scott?" asked Pomeroy.

"Yes, but it must begin with the worldview of whoever programmed it. If Clark Gable loved animals, as he did, then the parahuman Clark Gable must do so."

"Must?"

"Absolutely. It would be inconceivable for the parahuman to do otherwise. It is the parahuman's truth. All AI must be based on someone's truth and someone's error. Even backpropagation was created to teach AI truth based on whatever the scientist held as 'truth.' To be clear, *there are two truths in the universe: God's and everyone else's.* God knows the absolute truth while every human has opinions they form throughout life that have become 'truth' to them. And, thus, every creature being governed by AI is forced to speak and act upon the truth–*and the error*–given it by the humans who programmed it."

"And what does this mean for the three actors with us today?" Pomeroy asked.

"It means they carry the truths and the misconceptions of the humans they were built to copy. Whoever and whatever the deceased Clark, Humphrey, and Jimmy loved, the parahumans love. The same is true for what they hated. So it's important that I tell you, if someone were to build a parahuman with the memories of a thief, a terrorist, or a mass murderer–that parahuman would exhibit the same behavior because that would be its 'truth,' its reality. This is one of the many dangers science has exposed the world to through unregulated AI. We could soon see the rise of criminal parahumans."

"This is frightening, Dr. Scott. But you still have not answered my question about where our three parahumans will find meaning. And you *did* finally introduce God into the subject of the parahumans–as I knew you would!"

"Excuse me, Senator, but I introduced 'truth' as being handed from humans to parahumans. I did not say God reveals truth to parahumans. I specifically said that humans take God's truth and form opinions which become their 'truth,' and from those opinions 'truth' is given by scientists to parahumans.

"But to answer your question, Senator, the artificial intelligence of the parahuman has determined ultimate meaning for its existence will come from having the former spouse re-created. How did it come to this conclusion? I believe it zeroed in on the abundance of significant memories surrounding the loss of the spouse and determined the spouse to be the most significant person in the life of the former actor."

"That makes sense to me, Dr. Scott," said Steven Albright.

"Thank you, Mr. Chairman. But I must add that the problem with AI's conclusion is that we can lose our spouse, and building your life around that which can be lost brings *instability*–the very issue the parahumans are facing, and the reason for these hearings. There's no denying that our spouse is certainly one of the most significant persons we will ever meet! But to build the purpose of your life around anyone or anything which can and will one day be gone, is to build a debilitating level of fear into your life. The result of that fear is, once again, instability."

"I find this fascinating and very helpful!" said Senator Akamu.

"Am I being robbed of my time with this witness?" asked Barbara Pomeroy.

"Senator Pomeroy, the witness is yours but you have had him a long time! As chairman, I am allowed to permit such interactions from and with your fellow panel members. I see no problem with this. You can jump back in at any point. Please continue, Dr. Scott."

"Thank you. So, let me wrap up by saying the real issue concerning the spouse re-creation is that AI has come to the wrong conclusion, and did so because the human actor came to the wrong conclusion. Life must be built around that which cannot be removed from us, that which has eternal value. And so, Senator Pomeroy, we are back to God."

"Actually I agree with you," said Barbara. "We musn't build our lives on things that can be removed from us. But what in life can that possibly be?"

"What in life has eternal value? For me, it is my relationship with the One which ChatGPT and Google BARD correctly identified as the 'Son of God.' For all of us in this chamber and watching online, I say that human life has no meaning apart from a relationship with its Creator. Thus, just as the parahuman was formed to reflect the values of its creator, and to receive and live by truth received from its creator, even so human beings were created to reflect their Creator while living by truth received from Him."

"But, Dr. Scott," said Senator Perez, "since parahumans do not die, is it wrong to provide them a spouse that they cannot lose? There should be no fear of losing their spouse if that spouse cannot die."

"This is true, Senator Perez, and I believe Mr. Abrams agreed to provide a parahuman spouse for the parahuman actors. This may, indeed, provide at least a part of what they're seeking. But I would hasten to add that once the parahuman spouse is provided, the memories of the parahuman actors might then drive them to request all the appendages and dependencies that went with the memories of the spouse, including the exact house they lived in, the restaurants they dined in, the children they had, actors they knew back in the golden age of Hollywood–there may be no end to such requests!"

"Are we to re-create everyone and everything they request from a bygone era to ensure their happiness?" asked Pomeroy.

"We cannot. Thus, we see another aspect of the slippery slope. But, I would add, this is the reason I counseled the parahuman Clark Gable as I did. I introduced him to *new truth* that I believe will add new meaning to the memories he received from the human. By attaching new meaning to old memories, I gave him a new purpose for his existence."

Barbara's reaction was immediate. "I don't want to start down that road with you, Dr. Scott! If giving new truth to Mr. Gable helped stabilize him then you've helped Mr. Abrams and SMP Studios. That is enough for me. Senator Albright, I have no more questions for this witness."

"Very well, Senator Pomeroy, the witness is passed to Senator Alana Akamu."

"Thank you, Senator Albright. Dr. Scott, we've heard a lot about the problem with the parahumans being an emotional one. You just testified these creatures really aren't alive—not as human life is, is that correct?"

"Yes, that is correct."

"You've begun to address how the parahuman displays human emotion. I'd like more clarification on that subject. And how they seem, at times, to be overcome by it."

"I am happy to do so, Senator Akamu. There are at least six theories about how and where human emotion is formed and the resulting physical and psychological manifestations that result. Recent studies by what are known as 'affective scientists' seem to indicate emotions are not what we understood them to be. For many decades, we believed human emotions were formed solely by certain electrical and chemical mechanisms within the body. But the results of this new study demonstrate emotions may, in fact, be formed from *memories*. If this is the case, then we can easily see why the parahumans are experiencing *human emotions*. They are loaded with *human memories!*"

"Memories, Dr. Scott?" asked Senator Akamu. "I don't understand how memories cause someone to have emotions."

"Let me give a simple example. You take your child to the park for a picnic. With a smile on your face and words of excitement, you place him in a swing and give him a push. Your smile and laughter tell him this is a happy moment. His trust in you tells him he, too, should be happy. And so he is. But suppose that swing breaks and the child hits the ground in pain. How might the memory of the event change the emotions connected to the event? Simply put, the memories are painful, so the emotions are painful. *The memory creates the emotion*. May I pause to ask if the committee is understanding me thus far?"

Senator Akamu responded, "We understand you, doctor. Please continue."

"Very well. So, if we accept for the moment that emotions can be tied to a memory that is either pleasant or unpleasant, then you can understand how a parahuman has both happy and sad emotions. The parahuman received memories from the human with emotions already tied to them. If the human Clark Gable was happy eating lunch with Carole Lombard at the Brown Derby, then the parahuman already associates the emotion of happiness with the restaurant called the Brown Derby. *The real Clark Gable's memories dictated the parahuman's emotions.*"

"This is fascinating, Doctor, please continue!" said Steven Albright.

"In my illustration of the swing breaking and the child being hurt, there is pain tied to that memory—but the pain serves a purpose. It helps the child avoid further injury. If he did not feel pain, he might persist in dangerous behavior until damage is irreversible. But here is yet another source of the instability in the parahuman. The parahuman Clark Gable feels happiness or pain from the human's memories, but this happiness or pain is tied to nothing the parahuman has actually experienced. It is literally emotion without purpose. It would be like *my* butt hurting every time *you* fall down!"

Laughter followed but Senator Akamu was beginning to understand.

"So the parahuman feels sadness from sad memories tied to events he shouldn't be sad about?"

"Correct. The emotional challenges being experienced by the parahumans come from confusion—feeling emotions related to events and people they have never known or interacted with. They're sad, missing a spouse they've never really known. During yesterday's testimony, Jimmy Stewart spoke of the human Jimmy

Stewart's final words on his deathbed. He wanted to go be with Gloria, his wife that had died just a few years earlier. Where did the human Jimmy Stewart believe he was going? The short answer is he believed in heaven, an afterlife where he would live with Gloria. The human Jimmy Stewart was in great grief. But there was a *purpose* to his pain. It caused him to prepare for his eternal destiny as all of us must. As a friend of mine used to say, '*It's already been proven you're going to be dead a lot longer than you'll be alive. You need to figure out where you're going.*' So the sadness of death tells us to prepare for eternity, and not waste our lives chasing things that, in the end, really aren't going to matter. As I said a few moments ago, we need eternal values. We each have a choice to make, Senator Akamu—heaven or hell. I like to say eternity has a short menu."

"Well, some of us don't believe in heaven or hell, Dr. Scott!" said Barbara Pomeroy.

"And that is your privilege, Senator Pomeroy, but your created version of reality may prove disappointing."

"Meaning?"

"Meaning your disbelief in hell does not lower the temperature down there one degree."

The gallery applauded. Chairman Albright gaveled for quiet. "Please continue, Dr. Scott."

"Thank you, Mr. Chairman. Now let me try to summarize my testimony. Do the parahumans have life? No, they have personality, and they exist. Their advanced artificial intelligence allows them to take the personality of the person they emulate and add new memories that give them an ever-growing personality. Clearly, the parahumans are suffering. Will the creation of their parahuman spouses resolve their loneliness? It might, it could afford an end to the gnawing loneliness that affords them no rest–but it might be just the beginning of their demands. But I do believe we might also be able to give them new truth that could change that instability. In either case, until we find the solution, they will abide in a state of conflict, confusion, and unrest."

"This is a tragedy, Dr. Scott!" said Alana Akamu.

"I do not disagree, Senator Akamu, and thus far we've only discussed their emotional issues. From what I have learned, parahumans have no physical sense of touch. You might imagine going to the dentist and he or she numbs your mouth for a procedure. You'd say you feel nothing but that's not really accurate. You *are* feeling something—numbness. The parahuman doesn't even feel that. They could damage their skin and feel absolutely nothing."

Arthur Bryant, senator from North Carolina, asked, "If they feel nothing, then why did Clark Gable shake my hand?"

"Because the real Clark Gable would have shaken your hand, Senator. He was designed to play a role based on memories held in his artificial intelligence."

"But Jimmy Stewart went to Los Angeles Air Force Base and flew—and even landed—a jet bomber! Now that requires an acute sense of touch, doesn't it, Dr. Scott?"

"Medically speaking, in a human, yes. But residing within the artificial intelligence of the parahuman is the memory of how the human Jimmy Stewart flew that aircraft. The parahuman flew the plane by mathematical increments, not by sense of touch or pressure on a lever. I would suggest the parahuman's ability to fly an aircraft is superior to a human because the parahuman's mathematical increments are always right. The human Jimmy Stewart lost his sense of touch and spatiality with age."

"So, the parahuman pilot might be superior to a human pilot?"

"That is a subject to be explored, Senator Bryant. AI carries with it potential for both good and bad results."

"And what about procreation, Dr. Scott?" asked Senator Perez. "Is that also impossible due to the lack of sensation of touch?"

"No, it is impossible because life does not reside in the parahuman. Remember, they exist, they have personality, but they do not have life. They are a highly advanced artificially intelligent animatron."

"So, they feel no physical pain—but no physical pleasure, either. Is that correct, Dr. Scott?"

"That is correct, Senator Perez, they have no ability to feel physical pain, but they most certainly can, and obviously are feeling emotional pain. Science has created artificial intelligence that suffers!"

"So, to summarize, Dr. Scott, and as Senator Perez asked, how can we help them to have a meaningful and happy life?" asked Steven Albright.

"As I've said, we are on a dangerous, slippery slope. Providing their spouses may be the right thing to do because compassion demands it. Will imputing new truth into the parahuman mind solve the issue? It could. What will happen to the parahuman from there? I cannot say."

"And just how long and how far do you see the studio having to provide?" asked Barbara Pomeroy.

"How long will the studio profit from their acting? How well do they care for their greatest assets? I suggest that bringing even a *personality* into this world carries with it responsibilities."

"Dr. Scott," said Barbara Pomeroy, "would it be fair for me to summarize your findings related to the parahumans as one or more of the following? One, the parahuman has no sense of touch—pain or pleasure—so at least that part of their makeup is not human. Two, parahumans do not have an afterlife—if there is such a thing. Three, the parahumans are psychologically unstable because they're living off of someone else's experiences and are unable to separate fantasy from reality. Does this correctly summarize what you've shared with this committee?"

"Senator Pomeroy, if that's all you take away from everything I've shared, then my diagnosis is *Selective Auditory Attention.*"

"To which parahuman do you apply this diagnosis?"

"Not to any of the parahumans, but to a fully human Senator Barbara Pomeroy."

"Excuse me?"

"If all you took from my testimony was the scant list you just read to me, then you are suffering from a true condition known as 'Selective Auditory Attention.' Research shows there are certain health conditions that affect what one hears—as do preconceived notions and biases for or against those we listen to. With that diagnosis made, I have to say that your summary list misses too many details for me to agree with any of the points you've brought out."

OVER THE TWO-HOUR LUNCH break from the senate hearing, Josh Sizemore and his agents set up a secure passage for the President's entrance. Josh was in radio contact with the sergeant-at-arms awaiting Chairman Albright's call for the President.

Steven Albright was back from lunch and in his seat. Visitors to the gallery were filing in slowly. Some committee members were running behind. It irritated him but he understood. Most felt the biggest revelations had already been shared. And once the committee went into closed session, the media hype and online attendance would be over. But testimony during closed session was likely to be explosive. Dr. Scott's testimony had been incredible, but the world had yet to learn what scientists connected with parahuman technology might reveal. And this afternoon Jon Roosevelt would testify in open session. There was a lot of ground left to cover. Chairman Albright looked at his watch. He didn't know what his friend, Jon Roosevelt, wanted to say but the polls said the afternoon viewer count was going to remain high. Ten more minutes then he would order the doors closed.

30

"WILL THE SERGEANT-AT-ARMS alert the Secret Service that we are ready to hear from the President?"

The Secret Service detail came through the double doors leading into the Kennedy Caucus Room and formed a line on either side of the aisle. Josh gave one last look around the room, spoke into his lapel mic, and then led the President through the doors. The gallery and committee stood greeting the president with hearty applause and cheers. The President nodded to Chairman Albright and his committee, then turned to wave to the gallery. That increased the applause and the smiles of the celebrities, politicians, and common folk alike. Josh led the President to the witness stand.

"The gallery may be seated. The committee, too. Good afternoon, Mr. President, let me welcome you to our little committee, sir. There's been no shortage of speculation as to what you are about to share!"

The President chuckled. "Thank you, Steve, I appreciate you making time for me to address this committee. I hope what I have to say won't fall too far short of anyone's expectations!"

"Mr. President, I'm sure you know each member of the committee. To my left we have Senator Barbara Pomeroy of California, and Senator Alana Akamu of Hawaii. To my right we have Senator Ted Perez of Texas, and Senator Arthur Bryant of North Carolina."

"Senators, my sincerest thanks for allowing this unexpected testimony. I am most grateful. Senator Perez, do you still have those snakeskin boots on—or have you already gotten comfortable and kicked them off?"

"They're still on, Mr. President, but only out of respect for you! I've offered you a pair just like them, with the Texas flag embroidered in full color," the gallery was responding with laughter, "as long as you'll wear them with your jeans tucked in so folks can see the lone star of Texas!"

"I'm going to take you up on that offer, Ted, but *after* I complete my second term! Right now, I happily represent all fifty states!"

Ted Perez laughed. He knew the President was partial to his home state of Texas. But that was a discussion for another time.

"Mr. President, what do you have for us today?" asked Chairman Albright.

"Steve, since this is a formal hearing, an investigation into the matter of the parahumans, I suppose I'd best stop calling you Steve and start addressing you as 'Mr. Chairman.'"

There was laughter from the gallery and the President acknowledged them.

"I'm sorry, Mr. Chairman, I forgot to say thank you to your guests in the gallery for allowing me a few minutes of their time, as well!"

The gallery applauded and the President stood, smiled and waved to them.

"Mr. President, if you're ready, you have the floor!"

"Thank you, Mr. Chairman. Let me begin by saying I'm sure all of you know I was very close to Jimmy Stewart when I was a young actor in Hollywood. We worked together on a number of movies. He was a father figure to me. He came alongside me and helped ease the learning curve and taught me much about acting.

He helped prepare me for this job. As I've stated many times, my friend Ronald Reagan said he didn't know how anyone could be President without having been an actor!"

The gallery and committee members laughed. Even Barbara Pomeroy smiled. The Roosevelt charm, and the seasoned actor, had melded well.

"Jimmy promised my parents he would personally look after me when we traveled to filming locations around the world. Fast-forward through sixty years of my life and you'll find me in the White House Rose Garden, where Jimmy's looking after me once again, leading me in dance steps, and impressing the Washington press corps. But now he's the youngster and I'm the old guy!"

More laughter and applause. The gallery was loving it.

"But, senators, today I come before you with a request. I have seen the schism on your committee, a schism born of differing views—and certainly differing views are constructive when they are supported by truth. Through it all we must remain humble and committed to each other for the good of our nation. And we must come back together as Americans at the end of the day."

The President paused to let those words sink in.

"Humility. Commitment to each other and the nation. I wonder if we understand how truly needed these are, especially given this potentially lethal juncture in technology. We journey together through a new frontier and caution is in order. We've never dealt with beings created in a laboratory that are virtually impossible to tell from their human counterparts. They are intelligent, endearing, and of great benefit to our country. But there is risk, too. For almost three centuries now, our nation has regarded human life as sacred, created in the image of God, each life being precious. I listened with great interest as Dr. John Scott explained that these created beings are not unique lives, but unique personalities. They aren't living as we are, yet they have feelings—or think that they do. Their human memories dictate their feelings, and it is the inability to live out the human memories that has the parahuman in such a quandary. The risk is we create beings that are, in fact, lonely, and have, as Dr. Scott noted, few if any means to eliminate that loneliness.

"But there is another risk. If a human being can be so effectively emulated by this technology that the human is no longer missed, then they can be replaced by these creatures. Now, you might be thinking this may not be a negative. For example, a parent loses a child in death. What if this child could be replaced with his or her exact duplicate? Wouldn't that be a blessing to those grieving parents? Yes, indeed it could—until the parents realize they are growing older, but the parahuman child is not. For, as we've learned through testimony, parahumans do not age. Those parents will never lose the parahuman child to death as they did their human child, but they will never see the child grow into adulthood, marry, and have children of their own. And if a departed human can be effectively replaced by a parahuman, such as my friend Jimmy Stewart, then why not a living human? What is to stop a malevolent group from creating a parahuman duplicate of a person of wealth or power, perhaps a business leader, a scientist, or even a government leader, and replace them with a parahuman that will do the bidding of those who wish us evil? Let me pause here and ask if the committee has any thoughts or concerns related to what I have shared thus far?"

Chairman Albright looked at the committee members, waiting for questions. He could see several taking notes, but nothing was voiced, so he ventured a concern.

"Mr. President, do you envision a sort of 'Manchurian Candidate' operation where someone might try to replace a congressperson, a senator, or perhaps even you, sir?"

"I believe that is a real possibility, Mr. Chairman."

"Mr. President," began Barbara Pomeroy, "up until now, we've only seen these three parahumans, and they are re-creations of deceased individuals. I see far greater challenges creating a parahuman to replace a living individual!"

"How so, Senator Pomeroy?"

"Well, to begin with, there's only one Jimmy Stewart walking this earth and he's sitting with us in this caucus room. If a second Jimmy Stewart were to walk through those doors, the duplicate would immediately be spotted and could be apprehended, don't you agree?"

"Yes, I'd say that's true–if you could tell the duplicate from the original," the President responded.

"So, the reason this ruse has worked for Hollywood is there's not two of the same actor running around. The likelihood of someone duplicating the President of the United States and successfully substituting a parahuman for you—given the incessant security you're under—makes such an occurrence virtually impossible, wouldn't you agree?"

"No, Senator, I'm afraid I would not agree! I quickly concede that I'm never out of Josh Sizemore's protective view—except when I'm asleep, in the restroom or bathing—and sometimes I've wondered about my privacy there!"

The gallery laughed as the President turned around in the witness seat to smile at Josh Sizemore, who was standing just a few feet away. Josh nodded, smiled, and quickly looked down.

The President faced Senator Pomeroy again and added, "I might say it would be almost impossible to replace me and get away with it ... unless an insider was part of the plot."

A murmur began running through the room. With eyebrows raised, Barbara Pomeroy tilted her head to one side and charged ahead.

"So, Mr. President, do you have such concerns among *your own staff*?"

"Do you regard someone duplicating me and replacing me from within my own staff an impossibility, Senator Pomeroy? As I recall, Jesus chose twelve followers and one of them was a traitor."

"So, you're concerned you may have a traitor on your own staff? Perhaps I have greater confidence in the loyalty of your own team than you do, Mr. President!"

"Then let me ask you a question, Senator. Would you concede that creating a parahuman for *security* purposes is a possibility? Replacing a person in power with a being that cannot be lost to death has its own advantages, don't you agree?"

"I suppose, Mr. President, but I think the world is still years from that happening. The cost would be prohibitive, and given your popularity, two Jon Roosevelts would be impossible to hide! We must also consider the prominent level of fear in our country that robotics could replace humans at their jobs—and that artificial intelligence could take over. Surely you've heard these discussions underway in our country, Mr. President. Elon Musk, Jordan Peterson, and others of note have voiced such concerns."

"I can't believe robotics will ever replace the artisans, the ministers, the entrepreneurs and the drive we have empowering America. Now politicians ... replacing us with robots and artificial intelligence might be a welcome relief!"

The gallery roared with laughter. Steven Albright laughed, too, as he wagged his finger at the President.

"Be careful, Mr. President, there may be some scientist out there who will take you up on that offer!"

The President chuckled as he replied, "Some scientist already has, Steven!"

Chairman Albright was still laughing, but his expression became quizzical as he asked, "What do you mean, Mr. President?"

"What if I told you and this committee the order had already been given? What if I told you it was not I who was shot down in Tehran, but my parahuman duplicate? Wouldn't you agree parahuman technology had thus served an essential purpose—while at the same time revealing how easy it would be to duplicate a political leader?"

The Washington press corps lit up like a Christmas tree. The rumble coming from the press box was growing as reporters were quickly conveying the President's words to a myriad of print and online media sources. Chairman Albright began dropping his gavel and calling for quiet. The President sat looking at Barbara Pomeroy and waiting for Steve Albright to direct him to continue—or for Pomeroy to respond to his bombshell.

"Mr. President," said Steven Albright, "you certainly have kept your promise not to disappoint us! This would be quite a revelation if true. I noted that you said, '*what if*.' Are you telling us this has happened, Mr. President? Has this, in fact, happened?"

"Mr. Chairman, I asked to share with this committee so I could contribute towards your investigation into the proper care of the parahumans, but I also wanted to make clear to our beloved nation, and to the world, that parahumans can provide an undeniably valuable service. I would never have survived the assassin's attack if I were actually there—and the peace agreement would never have been signed. Only a parahuman could have taken a gunshot to the head, risen from that floor, and signed the agreement. But, like so many other things in life, the parahuman can be used for malevolent purposes, as well."

"Mr. President, I'm at a loss for words! This is a stunning revelation, sir. So, it was not you who was shot—it truly was your parahuman double?"

"Well, actually, Steve, it *was* me that was shot."

"I don't understand, Mr. President."

At that moment, the double doors to the caucus room opened and walking down the aisle toward the witness stand was Jon Roosevelt accompanied by Marty Martin and a dozen additional agents. The reaction was immediate. The press swung their broadcast cameras to cover the startling event, though some were panning the gallery and the committee so viewers could see the shocked expressions and the ensuing pandemonium. Agents locked arms to prevent anyone from entering the aisle leading to the witness stand.

Jon Roosevelt walked directly to the microphone at the witness stand and began to speak. The volume of the room was so high, he could barely be heard.

"Mr. Chairman, Mr. Chairman!"

"Order! We will have order, or I'll clear the caucus room! Sit down! Everyone take your seat or the capitol police will clear this room!" As the volume dropped, the President continued.

"Mr. Chairman, I am President Jon Roosevelt. You have been speaking with my parahuman. It was he who has been addressing this committee, delivering the message I prepared for him, and it was he who intercepted my would-be assassin in Tehran!"

Mr. President, I, uh—you are the President?"

"Yes, Steve, I am the real, human Jon Roosevelt."

"So, the parahuman was giving testimony—not you?"

"That's correct, just as it was the parahuman who signed the peace agreement."

"But—what about his signature on the peace treaty? Is that authentic?"

"A handwriting expert will confirm our signatures are identical. My parahuman was created to be me in every way." The President, who was standing, reached down and took the parahuman by the arm, and he stood next to him. "Allow me to formally introduce you to 'Rosebud.'"

Cameras clicking, papers rustling, broadcast equipment and personnel jockeying for position, agents moving about to restrict access to the President—the noise remained constant but just under Steven Albright's tolerance level.

"Because Rosebud took my place in Tehran, after the attempted assassination, he was able to call the delegates back who were fleeing. If that had been me, the peace accords would have collapsed and died, right next to me. It was Rosebud who saved the peace agreement for all of us. I was able to watch and hear the entire event through his eyes and ears, from the safety of the White House. I could give instructions to Rosebud at any time. He did what I could not—he survived an attempted assassination and brought peace to the world."

The gallery and committee broke into applause.

"Just incredible, Mr. President, just incredible," said Steven Albright.

31

AS ALFRED EDERSHEIM STEPPED INTO THE OVAL OFFICE, he couldn't help but compare it to the home provided for the President of Israel.

His is a fine home, but nowhere near the scale and splendor of the White House mansion—and missing the two hundred thirty years of history. The President rose from his desk as Josh Sizemore led Alfred Edersheim toward him. Marty Martin took his position at the President's side.

"Good afternoon, Dr. Edersheim! I cannot tell you how much we appreciate you making the long trip to be here. I trust your flight was enjoyable."

"It was a good flight, Mr. President."

"I'm sorry, Dr. Edersheim, please forgive my rudeness, but I must dispense with etiquette. We find ourselves at a crossroad and running out of time. I must come right to the point. I need your help."

"I'm sorry, Mr. President. It is my privilege to serve you. Your country has always come to the aid of Israel. I am honored to help any way I can."

"Won't you sit down, Doctor? Take this armchair by the fire."

"Thank you, Mr. President."

"Doctor, can I get you something to drink? I'm going to have a brandy."

"That will be fine, Mr. President."

"Marty, would you mind doing us the honors?"

"Absolutely, Mr. President."

"Dr. Edersheim, as you know it was Michael Benchley of the FBI who suggested I reach out to you. He shared with me information gleaned from his trip to Tel Aviv where he met you. Mike said your use of holography provides stability in the artificial intelligence of the holosapien. If I understood correctly, you believe holography prevents the emotional issues we're seeing in the Hollywood actors, and which the FBI saw in Donny Mancuso's parahuman. Is this an accurate assessment?"

"Yes, that is for the most part accurate, Mr. President. Though I did not create holography to eliminate emotional chaos. I use it to accurately transmit data from the supercomputer to the artificial intelligence processor in the holosapien—and to keep implanted memories separated from the creature's acquired memories. I was surprised that Dr. Horvitz's parahumans began exhibiting emotional issues. Of course, I was not involved with that project. Once he confessed to me what he had done, we began working together to undo what damage we could. I discovered his use of holography was faulty. I was greatly disappointed in what he did. We were friends for many years. He was the last person I expected to do this."

"I understand, doctor. He was your friend, and this has been difficult for you."

"Yes, it has, Mr. President. But his struggles are over and ours are upon us. What Director Benchley related to you is, unfortunately, accurate. The parahumans could be dangerous in their current state. I know that you are friends with the parahuman Jimmy Stewart. But let me say, while there is danger, I do not believe these three pose the same risk as the Mancuso animatron. His thoughts are formed from memories of an evil man. But I am sure the crossroads of which you spoke is your own parahuman."

"Yes. Mike Benchley came to me concerned that my parahuman might be capable of the same instability as the other parahumans have exhibited—though I hasten to add Rosebud has shown no sign whatsoever of any such emotional instability."

"I am glad of that, Mr. President, though there was some passing of time before the Hollywood three began to exhibit these emotions. We are seeing the unfolding of this technology. I agree with the testimony I heard this week—Dr. Scott, I believe—he called our creation of the parahuman a slippery slope. I fear he is right. We solved one national security crisis and created another. Artificial intelligence in the animatron, in its present form, presents dangers we did not anticipate. I heard your testimony, too, Mr. President."

"So, you saw my testimony, Doctor?"

"Yes, I was able to view it on my flight from Tel Aviv."

"Do you think I did the right thing in revealing Rosebud to the world?"

"I believe you did the right thing. It was better you reveal him than world leaders discover it and interpret your actions as deceptive. This could invalidate the peace treaty."

"That was my thinking precisely. Director Benchley told me you already knew about Rosebud. He was my locum for the Tehran peace accords. It would have ended in failure if not for him."

"President Hayut's holosapien served the same worthy purpose. He is now considering revealing the existence of the one we call 'Benny.' I expect his decision this week. Your testimony before the Senate was a bold move. Only time will reveal if holosapiens will be a blessing or a curse."

"Can you fix them? I'm sorry, that may not be the correct term. Will your holographic technology eliminate their emotional issues? None of us want to see them suffer. And certainly none of us want the danger associated with their instability."

"I do not know. I will need to talk with the scientists that created Rosebud. I need to see their application of holography. If I apply holography to the parahuman and it does not work, then we are faced with modifying the creature's memory—to eliminate those areas that cause instability. This will change Rosebud's identity. He would no longer be you. We cannot eliminate sections of your life memories from him and expect he will continue to see things as you do."

"That would effectively eliminate any service he could provide as my stand-in. And if holography and memory modification both fail to provide stability—then what?"

"I'm sorry, Mr. President, but you could not allow him to remain in existence."

"This is hard for me to consider, Alfred. Very hard indeed. In Tehran, Rosebud went off-script, speaking to would-be enemies with empathy and wisdom. In my opinion, he handled the events better than I would have. He proved to be an amazing asset. I know you would not advise destroying him if there were any other way."

The President looked down into his drink. It occurred to him he'd been turning too often to his liquor cabinet for assistance. The thought of eliminating Rosebud—even modifying his memories to a point he was no longer the same—these were too painful for Jon Roosevelt to consider. He looked up from his drink with a distraught countenance.

"How's your brandy, Doctor?"

"It is very good, Mr. President, thank you. Do not be sad, Mr. President. I am hopeful of results. I would like to speak with Rosebud and then with his creators. Would this be possible?"

"Certainly, Dr. Edersheim. Josh, would you instruct your agents to awaken Rosebud and bring him to the Oval Office?"

"Right away, Mr. President," Josh said as he headed for the door.

"We already reached out to Rosebud's creator, Dr. Ralph Vestro, alerting him that you may need to meet with him. He said it would be his honor to work with you. Marty, you have Dr. Vestro at a hotel close by, do you not?"

"That's correct, sir. I can have a car sent to bring him here now. He's ten minutes from the White House."

"Yes, please do."

"I know Dr. Vestro," said Dr. Edersheim. "He and I have conversed many times. We sat on a panel in Geneva, taking questions concerning parahuman life. He is a good man. I am glad you chose your team wisely, Mr. President."

"So you see the parahuman as living, Dr. Edersheim?"

"No, Mr. President. It is merely an expression. Dr. Scott's explanation is sound. They are unique personalities, not unique lives."

As the President conversed with Edersheim a commotion in the outer office and the door abruptly opening startled them both.

"I'm sorry, Mr. President, Rosebud is gone!" said Josh Sizemore, struggling to catch his breath.

"Gone? How did this happen, Josh? Where did he go?"

"Two of my agents found the guards stationed with Rosebud on the floor. Rosebud broke the restraining straps on his table, overpowered the two agents in his room, then took out the agent outside his door."

"Elohim adirim!" Alfred exclaimed.

"Dear Lord, tell me he did not kill anyone!" the President said.

"Thankfully, no sir, he only disabled them."

"Thank God. Do you know where he is? He must still be in the building."

"No sir, he's not in the White House. He passed the agent by the entrance to the Rose Garden saying he needed a few minutes to himself. He told the agent to see that he was not disturbed. The agent believed Rosebud to be you, so he followed his instructions. Rosebud entered the Rose Garden and that's the last anyone saw of him."

"Josh, this is preposterous! How could he escape the White House grounds?"

"Sir, there's eighteen acres of heavily wooded grounds within the White House fence. We can see he moved through the Rose Garden, past the west wing and the swimming pool, and then into cover. He could have hidden in the trunk of a car or in a delivery truck. It's possible he confiscated a vehicle. I have a team reviewing camera footage but there was no trace of him on our first review."

"He couldn't get out of the parking lot! The guards would have spotted him as me–and the President is not allowed to drive!"

"I don't think so, sir. His room was just down the hall from the kitchen. Some of the staff said you entered the kitchen, asked for a snack, and exited through a side door. They said you were dressed in a golf shirt and slacks, but you went in the direction of the locker room. Rosebud could have changed into a kitchen uniform. It's possible he is wearing a beard or mask." Josh was overly animated, and the President was about to say something when Josh exploded. "For all I know he's dressed as a woman! I should have anticipated this!"

"Okay, Josh, calm down. We'll find him. We need to get help. We have to shut down the roads before he can leave DC."

"Yes, sir, I'm sorry, Mr. President. I'm already working on it. I've activated DC Metro police. I told them an imposter that looks like you, probably wearing a disguise, is attempting to flee the city. They're setting up roadblocks on all major outbound roadways and checking every vehicle. I don't want to call out the National Guard, it will attract too much attention. I reached out to Mike Benchley at the FBI and he's mobilizing a ground team, then he'll head to the White House. I've pulled almost three hundred agents from the

Treasury and they are going to coordinate the ground search with Director Benchley."

"Good work, Josh. Any idea why he fled?"

"Yes, sir, we know why. My two agents guarding Rosebud said he was in *Theta* sleep. They were talking about the concerns expressed during Senate testimony, that parahumans might pose a danger. They were discussing what might happen if Rosebud became unstable. The agents were playing cards with their backs to Rosebud. They heard a sound and turned just in time to see he was coming at them. The last thing they remember was his hands. He grabbed them by the neck, and they were out. They said it was like a vice grip closing on them."

"Are they okay?"

"Yes, sir, they're fine. Just bruised, shaken up, and embarrassed. If Rosebud had wanted them dead, sir, I have no doubt they would be dead. He just wanted to escape."

"Escaping makes sense, Mr. President," said Dr. Edersheim. "If Rosebud was created to be you, and you felt your life was threatened, what would you do?"

"Escape."

"And where would you go?"

"As President, I would go ... "

"No, sir, if you were alone in your nation's capital, and those in power were threatening your life, as an ordinary citizen where would you go?"

"I honestly have no idea! That's a dreadful thought. It's hard to think in those terms, Alfred."

"Then who knows you well enough to answer that question?"

The President rose and walked to the windows. He looked over the Rose Garden, where Rosebud made his path of escape. He felt sorry for him. He was trying to understand Rosebud, but that meant understanding himself—and not as President but as a civilian. He was drawing blanks.

"Remember, Mr. President," said Alfred, "Rosebud was programmed with your full memory, from childhood to adulthood, from child actor to President of the United States. What friend or family member has known you from childhood until now?"

"At my age? Not even Mrs. Roosevelt has known me that long! Anyone that would know me that well died a long time ago." But then he turned around with a smile. "Actually, there is one person still alive—or alive again—that has known me my whole life! Marty, Jimmy Stewart, Bogie and Clark are still staying with Senator Albright. Please call the Senator. I need to speak with Jimmy right away."

MIKE BENCHLEY JUMPED in his car and made a call.

"Hey beautiful, how's my favorite prayer warrior?"

"Doing good! Just about finished packing everything. The movers come tomorrow. Then I hop the plane to see my fiancé! I'm so excited to be moving out there! And my dad keeps asking when he's going to meet you. You'll have to talk to him about us pretty soon—one Marine to another of course. He said ... wait, did you say 'prayer warrior'? *Please don't tell me you're in danger again!*"

"Now does my voice sound like it did when I called you that day?"

"No, it doesn't—I guess I'm still a little jumpy!"

"I understand but I'm in no danger, beautiful. Someone very important has gone missing and we need to find him."

"Is this that same bad guy you told me about?"

"No, this is a good guy. He works for the President."

"Wow—a presidential employee is missing? Where are you—if you can tell me?"

"I'm on my way to the White House. It's very important we find this guy quickly and we have few clues where to look. Please pray we'll know where to look."

"I'm on it, Mike. Don't forget to call me later and give me an update!"

"Oh, I will. I want to talk to you before you head this way tomorrow!"

32

NIGHT HAD SETTLED ON WASHINGTON and concern was mounting.

Dr. Ralph Vestro arrived at the White House and presented his files on holography to Dr. Alfred Edersheim.

Mike Benchley and Josh Sizemore were reviewing a detailed map of Washington. Trying to cover all possible avenues of escape and potential points of concealment was nigh unto impossible. Almost five hundred agents were searching the city in a coordinated pattern but had turned up nothing. The President had been listening to counsel and plans for more than six hours. He was at a point of mental and emotional exhaustion.

"We have to find him, gentlemen. Every minute he's out there, alone, increases the risk he will fall into the wrong hands. Or with his strength, he may become the wrong hands! Josh, do we have an update on Jimmy's whereabouts?"

"He should arrive at the White House any moment, sir."

"Mr. President," said Marty, "my feeling is Rosebud is still in the city. DC Metro has the city locked down tighter than a drum. There's no way he got past their dragnet."

"I'm not so sure," countered Josh. "Mike and I have been all over this map. With Rosebud's intelligence and physical strength, we don't know what he's capable of doing. How fast can he run? How deep can he dig? How far can he swim? I mean, since he doesn't breathe, he could be swimming underwater in the

Potomac! We know he never gets tired, hungry or thirsty. This is an almost impossible target to track!"

At that moment, the door to the Oval Office opened. "Mr. President, they've arrived," an agent announced. Stepping in right behind him came Jimmy Stewart, Humphrey Bogart, and Clark Gable.

"Gentlemen, you are a sight for sore eyes," said the President, "and I need your help!"

"I was briefed on the drive here, Jon," said Jimmy. "You lost Rosebud. Now, now, no need to panic about this. You fellas are making this a lot harder than it needs to be!"

"Okay, Jimmy, enough of the homespun humor. We must find Rosebud. If you think you know where he is, let's have it!"

"All right, all right. Now, now, Jon ... let me ask you something. Do you remember when we made the film, *Little Guy Lost*? You remember that picture?"

"That was sixty years ago. But I think I remember most of it."

"Okay. Now, where was that film set?"

"Here, in our nation's capital. But, Jimmy ... "

"Now, just cool your jets, Jon. Hang on. Do you remember in the film, you were an orphan, and you ran away in Washington? Remember that? So, tell me, where did you hide out?"

"Let me think. We didn't shoot that scene here, did we? I think the studio constructed a set of where I was to hide. It was supposed to be ... *under the Lincoln Memorial!* Jimmy, you're a genius!"

"No, now don't go all sappy on me, Jon. I just happen to know you better than you do!"

The President gave Jimmy a bear hug then turned to Josh Sizemore.

"Josh, let's approach this carefully. We don't want to give him cause to run from us again. We need him to trust us."

"Yes, sir, Mr. President. Sir, how life-like was the set the studio constructed? What I mean is, do you know if they constructed it true to form?"

"Just a minute, Mr. President," said Marty. "Just like that, we're certain that's where Rosebud is hiding?"

"Marty, I'm certainly open to wherever you think he is!"

Marty stood there, looking at the President, then at Josh, Mike, and the three. "Well, I don't have anything better to offer–I just had to ask!"

The President turned back to Josh and said, "I'm sorry Josh, I have no idea how lifelike the set of the Lincoln Memorial really was. To my remembrance, I've never been down under the real thing."

"Jimmy, do you know?" asked Josh.

"Nope, never been under the real memorial so I have no idea, Josh."

"Okay, then let's start by discussing the cavern under the Lincoln Memorial. I've been down there. It's known as the 'Undercroft' and it's enormous. Three stories high and almost forty-four thousand square feet. It's an impressive place to hide. Mike, the majority of my agents are spread out all over the city right now. Do you think you can get some more of your men for this assignment?"

"Absolutely," said Mike. "What are you thinking?"

"The Lincoln Memorial never closes. We can only close it off to visitors temporarily for cleaning. So we send in agents as a power washing crew. If you can provide twenty-five men, I can get the uniforms, equipment, and vans. Once we've cleared the memorial of visitors, we can get underneath without being seen. We'll leave half the crew cleaning, the rest I'll take underground with me. We'll walk through the Undercroft in a line that Rosebud can't elude."

"Just a minute, Josh," said Benchley. "Dr. Edersheim had us use a polymer cord netting to hold Antonio. He said it's the only thing strong enough to hold a parahuman. Is that still the best means, Dr. Edersheim?"

"Yes, Director Benchley, it is the best—but if you give him time to surrender, you won't need the net. And Josh, your assault gear won't do you any good. If anything, it may serve to drive Rosebud away or force him to attack you. You can't bring him down with assault gear. Bullets are useless."

"Dr. Edersheim, you said you believe Rosebud will surrender. That's what I want—I don't want a confrontation. If the altercation turns physical, based on what you just said, human beings lose."

"That is an accurate assessment, Mr. President. Rosebud was programmed from your memories, not Donny Mancuso's. His reaction should be much milder, as I would expect from you. And there is an aspect of this I think you are missing. If Rosebud is hiding in the Undercroft, then it is safe to assume he wants to be found."

"Wants to be found?" asked Josh.

"Certainly. If he sought refuge there, based on Jon Roosevelt's memories of a motion picture he was in, then he knows full well Jon Roosevelt would think of that movie, too. If he did not want to be found, he would avoid the Undercroft, knowing that would be the first place you would look."

"But we didn't," said the President. "And that's because of my age. I can't access my memories as fast as Rosebud can!"

"Mr. President," Dr. Edersheim said, "I would suggest if your three actor friends will accompany you into the Undercroft, the four of you might be able to persuade Rosebud that your intentions toward him are honorable. But I expect the three parahumans have the best chance. Remember President Hayut's holosapien and Rosebud immediately identified with one another. That same bond might exist with these three parahumans and Rosebud. It is worth a try."

The President turned towards the actors. "Jimmy, Bogie, Clark—I know you didn't sign up for this, but I'd consider it a personal favor if you'd help me speak with Rosebud. Are you willing?"

"I'd say we're willing," answered Bogie, "so long as Rosebud gets a fair shake in this."

"I can promise you that, Bogie," said the President. "Jimmy, Clark?"

"Jon, you know I'll help you anyway I can," said Jimmy.

"Same here, I'm in," said Clark.

"Okay, Dr. Edersheim, what else do you advise?" Jon asked.

"With the help of Dr. Vestro, I was able to adapt my tablet application to Rosebud's AI. I should be able to move him deeper into *Theta* sleep."

"Deeper, Dr. Edersheim?" asked the President. "You don't think he's fully awake now?"

"From what I can already see in the app, Mr. President, he was still in *Theta*. Benny remained in *Theta* but moved around in a type of sleepwalking—what I would describe as a 'light' *Theta* state. Rosebud appears to still be in *Theta*, and because *Theta* is the mode in which parahumans learn, I believe Rosebud will be more likely to listen to you. I will attempt to increase *Theta* waves slightly as soon as Josh alerts me that you and his team are in-place under the memorial. We want him to be subdued but able to hear you."

The President suddenly smiled. "Dr. Edersheim, if you've adapted your tablet app to Rosebud, why can't you track him and tell us where he is? And Dr. Vestro, you did a tablet app, too! I don't know why we didn't think of this before."

"Mr. President," responded Ralph Vestro, "we tried to find Rosebud on the tablet. He must have disabled the tracking system.

I am at a total loss as to how he would do this. In fact, I am amazed. Dr. Edersheim and I have tried to reactivate it and it simply will not turn back on."

"In some way it makes me proud of Rosebud. I suppose he sees himself as fighting for his survival. I pray the connection Benny and Rosebud experienced happens again with our three Hollywood actors," the President said. "I wish Rosebud could have met Jimmy, Bogie and Clark before now—so there would be a stronger level of trust."

"He knows them as well as you do, Mr. President," Ralph said. "Remember, your memories are his!"

"I didn't think of that! That's an encouraging reminder, Ralph. Thank you."

Alfred Edersheim faced the three parahumans.

"If you men are willing, I would like you to tell Rosebud I have come here from Israel to help him and the three of you. I will treat you with the same respect your human predecessors received. I understand your need for companionship."

"Well, gentlemen, are you comfortable asking Rosebud to trust Dr. Edersheim to do what he's committing to do?" asked the President.

The three were quiet for a few moments. It was Jimmy who spoke.

"Doggone it, Jon, you know me. But ... but I can't help feeling that we're missing something here."

"What is it, Jimmy?"

"Jon, the three of us, we're just old play actors from the silverscreen era. We want our wives back and that's that. But Rosebud, now he's different. How is this doctor going to take care of him and relieve his pain? If he's lonely, is Alfred gonna create your wife as a parahuman for Rosebud? Are there gonna be two Mrs. Roosevelts running around the White House? And if not, it seems to me *you're* the one standing in Rosebud's way! You see, if the real Jimmy Stewart was still around, well, I reckon no one would need me. But you're still here, Jon. So, the only thing you can do with Rosebud is put him in mothballs until you need him again. Doesn't seem like much of an existence for him, now does it?"

"Jimmy ... as I said a moment ago, you're a genius. But this time you've presented me with a sad dilemma. Dr. Edersheim, what can we do?"

"Mr. President, if I can successfully place my holographic sequencing into Rosebud, his emotions should cease to control him. He won't question his existence or intermingle your memories as his own. I believe he will perform as the holosapien that I created for President Hayut."

"Thank you, Dr. Edersheim, but I'm afraid Jimmy is right. Not much of an existence for Rosebud. It still feels like we're missing something, doesn't it, Jimmy?"

"Yea, I reckon it does, Jon, I reckon it does. What do you fellas say?" Jimmy was looking at Clark and Bogie.

"Mr. President," Clark began, "my perspective may not be all that compelling to you, Dr. Edersheim, or Dr. Vestro. But since Dr. Scott counseled me, I have a different perspective—and whether you men of science believe my emotional state is good or unbalanced, I'm going to speak my piece."

President Roosevelt looked away from Clark to everyone standing in the Oval Office. "I think we all need to sit down. Clark is about to share something we're going to want to consider. Clark, the floor is yours."

"Thank you, Mr. President. Gentlemen, based on what I've learned from Dr. Scott, I believe parahumans were created out of fear. Rosebud? He was created for fear the President would die in Tehran. That was true of Benny, wasn't it Dr. Edersheim?"

"Yes, I must agree with that conclusion."

"As for the three of us—Sid and his investors created us out of fear. They fear the ultimate death of Hollywood and all that goes with it. We're supposed to save their status, their power, and their personal fortunes. That's why they didn't care about our loneliness until they saw our actress wives could make them more money. And our fans around the world—I think they fear growing old and dying. They fear losing the beauty and vigor of youth. I guess, to them, we represent the possibility of eternal youth. As Dr. Scott says, fear shouldn't be controlling any of us! He says we won't fear when we know the truth. There's a purpose to this life, just as there's a purpose in growing old, a purpose to pain, and a purpose in death."

"And what is the purpose of this life, Mr. Gable?" asked Dr. Edersheim.

"To know God and love him. That's at least true for you humans. That's what I learned from Dr. Scott. I contain all Clark Gable's memories and I can tell you he was idolized as the 'King of Hollywood,' as if he lived some fairytale, living happily ever after. Well, he didn't. He lost Carole. He lost his youth and eventually his life. But Clark didn't lose his faith. He believed he'd see his loved ones again. When the people you love have gone on to a better place, why wouldn't you want to join them? But you have to know what you believe is actually true. You have to know the purpose of life. That's the new information I got from my friend John Scott. I know I'm just an animatron controlled by artificial intelligence. Heaven's not a reality for me. But you men here, you're real–and you're going to end up facing death, just as the real Clark Gable did. You have to square with that!"

"You're right about that, Clark," said the President.

Then Clark said, "You know, the three humans we were created to be couldn't make it in Hollywood today—neither could you, Mr. President!"

"That's quite a statement, Clark! Why do you say that?"

"You wouldn't be welcome. I came back to a Hollywood that has grown antagonistic to the Christian faith Clark Gable, Jimmy Stewart, and Humphrey Bogart held. Today, if you talk about faith, they try to destroy you. They try to kick you out of Tinseltown. I've come to an important decision. If I'm going to be true to the human Clark Gable, my purpose in being here is to change the vitriol of Hollywood. And I believe you humans will never really enjoy this life until you're ready for the next."

Clark looked at Dr. Edersheim and pointed. "Dr. Edersheim, you're Jewish. Are you a man of faith?"

"Yes. My faith is very important to me."

"So, you know God?"

"I know of Him. Before long I expect to meet Him. More importantly, Mr. Gable, I know that He knows me."

"Dr. Scott knows God. He told me that Jesus is the Jewish Messiah, that He came to forgive people of their sins, to give them eternal life. Do you believe that?"

"I've heard this message before. I would like to believe it. Israel has waited for the promised Messiah for thousands of years."

"My wife, Lauren Bacall, she was Jewish," said Bogie. "I was Episcopalian, but we made it work. We believed in heaven."

"I can tell you the words that never stop echoing through my brain," Jimmy interjected. "'I'm going to see Gloria.' That's what my predecessor said to his children on his deathbed. He knew where he was going. Jon, I reckon you and I never discussed this before—I mean, the human Jimmy didn't—do you believe there's an afterlife?"

The President smiled gently and said, "Yes, Jimmy, I very much believe that. Our nation seems so divided, and that includes on this matter of faith. But I come from a small town in Texas, and I was raised in Sunday school and church. I was raised reading the Bible and believing what it says. I have trusted Jesus as my Messiah. I believe He spoke the truth: He has prepared a place for me and He's going to take me home someday. I will live eternally with Him, and my family and my friends who have placed their trust in Him as I have."

"Mr. President," said Josh Sizemore, "I hate to interrupt such an important discussion, but we need to find Rosebud. We don't know for sure that he's in the Undercroft under the Lincoln Memorial. If he's not, we have a lot of ground yet to cover. If he is, getting him out could be difficult and dangerous." Then Josh looked at the Hollywood three and said, "The President began this discussion by asking if you three gentlemen are willing to speak with Rosebud. Can you help us bring him back to safety?"

"I'd say we're all willing, Josh," Clark said. "I don't know what Dr. Edersheim can do for him, but it has to be a better life than hiding out under a million tons of granite."

"Then we're set," said the President. "But before we go, Clark, Jimmy, Bogie, I want you to know the things you just shared involve the most important issue in life to me. My great grandfather, Teddy Roosevelt, trusted Jesus as his savior when he was sixteen years old. He taught a Bible class for underprivileged children until he left for Harvard. And after graduating from Harvard, he said 'a thorough knowledge of the Bible is worth more than a college education.' Clark, you're right. This life is so brief—and eternity so long—we must know we've made the right choice. I want to revisit this with you again after we find Rosebud. I guess we'd best get moving."

"Wait, Mr. President," said Josh, "you're not planning to go with us!"

"Josh, Rosebud is my responsibility more than anyone here. I should be there to speak with him."

"Mr. President, if you're going to be there, I will need to secure the area, and that's going to take more agents than I have lined up."

"Josh, if I'm disguised with the cleaning crew, no one will recognize me. Certainly no one will be looking for the President to be power washing a memorial!"

Josh looked at Mike Benchley. "He's right, Josh. And we could have him wear a beard and a wig. He should be safe enough—as long as Rosebud doesn't come out swinging."

JOSH SIZEMORE, MIKE Benchley, and the agents disguised as a monument cleaning crew arrived at the Lincoln Memorial at 9:00 PM in vans displaying the name 'Monument Cleaning Service.' The agents began rolling pressure washing equipment into place while posting signs stating the memorial was being temporarily closed for pressure washing.

Josh sat in one of the vans with the President for last minute instructions.

"Mr. President, I'm going to need to call you by a different name or we may blow our cover. If it's okay with you, I'll use your middle name. I apologize in advance for breaking protocol, sir."

"Completely understood, Josh."

"Thank you, Ted—wow, that doesn't feel right."

"The President chuckled. "Believe it or not, I grew up being called Jon, Jonny, 'Rosey' due to my last name, and one of my college roommates called me 'Teedie' as my family called my great grandfather. I promise you, I'm quite comfortable being called Ted."

"Thank you, sir. Now, I must insist that you stay at my side during this operation, Mr. Pres ... I mean, Ted. The people at the monument should clear out in just a few minutes. The entrance to the Undercroft is on the northeast side of the monument. Once

we've effectively cleared the grounds of foot traffic, and after Dr.
Edersheim notifies me he has Rosebud ready, we'll move in. We will
post four guards at the entrance, the rest of the agents will enter
the Undercroft and set up portable lighting. These are propane
powered tungsten halogen lights. They're very strong so try not to
look into the lights, sir. And let me emphasize that the lighting
is going to give us a base to operate from, but there's no way we
can illuminate the entire forty-four thousand square feet, especially
with all of the concrete pillars that are in the way."

"All right, Josh. So, the agents aren't going to do anything until
I and the three actors have time to communicate with Rosebud,
correct?"

Josh's radio crackled, "Monument clear. Repeat, monument
clear. Remaining cleaning team members can move forward."

"Acknowledged," said Josh, "but remember, we are waiting for
Dr. Edersheim to notify us the package is sedated."

"Acknowledged," came the reply.

"Excuse the interruption, sir, but that is correct. The agents will
not proceed with the sweep and capture until you give the order.
But, Ted, I reserve the right to counter that order if you appear to
be in any danger. Do you agree, sir?"

"I agree."

"All right. You and the Hollywood three will have bullhorns to
attempt your communication. If that fails, on your word, the agents
will move in, triangulating in groups of four. Each group is armed
with a polymer net that can be launched aerially from a rifle-like
device. It won't hurt Rosebud; it will just make it impossible for
him to hurt anyone—we hope."

"Josh, this is Alfred Edersheim. Do you hear me?"

"Yes, sir, Dr. Edersheim. We are in position. Is Rosebud
sedated?"

"As much as I dare do if you want him to hear you and be able to respond. Josh, please remember, if Rosebud is not under the monument, wherever he is, he's now lying down and semi-responsive. I pray you find him there. If he's not under the monument, and some unsuspecting citizen tries to awaken him, I don't know what may happen."

"That sounds ominous," said the President. "Well, Josh, I'm ready if the rest of you are. Jimmy, Clark, Bogie—are we ready?"

"I'm ready Jon," said Jimmy.

"Yeah, we're good here, Jon," said Clark. "Bogie, you look like you're deep in thought."

"I was just thinking how this whole thing is sort of like my film, *The Desperate Hours*. You know, three people trapped in a basement, cops waiting outside to rescue them—or take the bad guy. It kinda makes you wonder how this little crime scene is going to turn out, don't it?"

"Let's don't go too far out there, Bogie," said Jimmy. "I think Jon and his team are not gonna start blazing with tommy guns!"

"They wouldn't do any good with Rosebud anyway," said Clark. "We're going in there to convince him a better life is open to him. If he doesn't believe us, then they'll net him. Not much else anyone can do."

"Let's pray for a peaceful resolution to this issue," said the President. Okay, Josh, let's do this."

"Yes, sir. Let me alert the team." Josh announced by radio, "The remainder of the cleaning team is moving into place. Let's do a great job, everyone."

"Acknowledged," came the reply.

"Ground crew, are you in position for approach to the Undercroft?"

"This is Mike. We've got everyone in position. Awaiting your word."

Josh responded, "Thanks, Mike, ground crew is clear for Undercroft cleaning. Acknowledge."

"Ground crew is moving into position. I'll meet you on the inside."

The cleaning crew began pressure washing the floor of the monument. This distraction achieved the objective. Standing at sidewalk distance to view the monument, spectators were far enough away they could not see the black ops team slip through the ground entrance on the northeast side of the Lincoln Memorial.

Josh's radio crackled to life. "This is Mike. Ground crew in place. Lighting in place. All quiet."

"Okay everyone, let's go."

Josh Sizemore, the President, Clark, Jimmy, and Bogie, all dressed as cleaning crew, left the van and moved toward the monument. The President was wearing a beard and a cap. His own mother would not have recognized him. The six came up to the steps, then moved to the right, pointing at the granite structure as if indicating where additional cleaning would need to take place. They fell in the shadows when they rounded the corner on the northeast side. They moved quickly to the entrance where two agents were standing watch. Once inside, they moved into the lighted area and were handed bullhorns.

"Even as bright as these lights are," said the President, "you can't see very far in this monstrous cavern. Okay, gentlemen, I'll start the communication and then you jump in as you feel led."

The President switched on the bullhorn and brought it up to his mouth. Josh moved in next to him as did three other agents, forming a semi-circle around him.

"Rosebud, this is Jon Roosevelt. I don't know that you're in here but if you are, there's a reason. You feel that you've escaped from me and others you think want to harm you. The truth is, you're under here because of a movie I made with Jimmy Stewart over sixty years ago. Your memory of that movie must be bringing you feelings of love and protection. And purpose. You are identifying with me. Rosebud, I don't want you to be shut down. I want your life to have meaning. Meaning that reaches beyond my own. You did in Tehran what I could not do. You were able to keep the peace treaty from falling apart because the assassin could not strike you down as he would have me. You're special Rosebud. You're special to me, to our nation, and since I told the world about you at the Senate hearing, you're special to the world. We all owe you a debt of gratitude. Please, come with me. I promise you, I will not allow you to be shut down. Your life of service is just beginning."

The President tried again.

"Rosebud, a scientist came to the White House from Israel. His name is Alfred Edersheim. He has something he believes will help all the parahumans to behave normally—without the loneliness and sorrow. Our three parahuman friends from Hollywood are here with me. Dr. Edersheim is going to help them and he wants to help you. Let's go back to the White House together and let him help."

Jon Roosevelt stood silent. Listening. In the monstrous concrete cavern under the Lincoln Memorial, everything echoed. Now there was an eerie silence.

"All right, Jimmy, you're a part of his memories. As big a part as you are mine. Maybe he'll listen to you."

"I'll sure try, Jon." Jimmy stepped forward, toward the dank darkness. His tall, lanky frame silhouetted in the light, casting a giant shadow in every direction. He pulled the bullhorn up to his thirty-year-old face.

"Now, Rosebud, this is Jimmy Stewart. Well, it's Jimmy Stewart, Part Two, just like you're Jon Roosevelt, Part Two! You and I have something in common. We both share memories of the President of the United States. Have you thought of that? I share memories of the human Jimmy Stewart and his time with the young, childhood actor named Jonny Roosevelt. In my mind I can see what Jimmy saw, the young boy actor that was scared to death his first time on a movie set. I watched him grow up, I watched him become President. And now, here we are, standing under a cold, dark monument, wondering what's next. But you—you—you were there for everything. You know what it felt like for Jon every step of the way. His childhood fears, the pressure of being a Roosevelt, and stepping into the Presidency. You were in Tehran and the human President was not. You have memories of your own now! Have you thought of that? You went to Tehran and the human Jon Roosevelt didn't. I'd say that's pretty special, wouldn't you? You did a great service for the American people. It would be a shame for you to walk away from all that."

Jimmy waited a moment, listening. Then he said, "I'll tell you this, my friend, I'm not going anywhere. At thirty years old, my career is just beginning—again! I'm picking up where the human left off. How about you? You ready to do something greater? Now, I'm gonna wait right here for you so you just, you just come on and let's get this thing settled, will ya?"

Humphrey Bogart looked at Jimmy and then raised his bullhorn. "Rosebud, this is Humphrey Bogart. I'm just getting started, too. Who knows, a *Casablanca* part two? How 'bout I pick up where *Key Largo* left off? I never married that girl and I think audiences want to see what's next. The studio has already made arrangements to create Lauren Bacall. It's all just beginning again. That's what we want for you, too. You're one of us. We've got a sort of union going here. Yeah, that's the ticket. We need a union to help each other. What do ya say?"

Clark wasted no time. He grabbed the bullhorn and started speaking before Bogie's echo died out.

"I'll tell you this, Rosebud, if you're looking to be president of something besides the most powerful country on the planet, why not become president of our parahuman actor's guild? Now there's an idea! Yes, sir, when you're not working here, you can be in Hollywood. It'd be pretty hard for the studio to argue with a guy so well connected in Washington! We're waiting for you. Come on out."

A slight sound could be heard to the right of the lighted area. A dragging sound. Into the light came Rosebud, shuffling, staggering, looking drugged. He was still dressed in the chef's clothing he had taken from the White House and was carrying a piece of paper.

Josh started toward Rosebud, but Jon placed his hand on Josh's shoulder.

"What are you carrying with you, Rosebud?" asked the President. Rosebud shuffled closer and held it up. It was a family photograph of Jon Roosevelt as a boy. He was at home, with his parents and siblings.

"Is this when we were happiest, Jon?" Rosebud asked. Jon looked into his face. It was like looking in the mirror. "Yes, when we had Mom and Dad, Bobby and Elaine, all at home together. That was Christmas and we were all together. That's when we were happiest. But time doesn't stand still. Not for humans. They're all gone and I—you and I—are left alone to carry on."

Rosebud came directly to the President. Agents around the president shifted nervously but the President opened his arms, and Rosebud entered his embrace. He put his forehead on the President's shoulder. "I cannot cry. I was given no tears."

"I can," said the President, "I can cry for the both of us. Let's go home."

Jon Roosevelt turned, keeping his arm around Rosebud. As the President set his right foot ahead of him, his left foot came under Rosebud's descending foot, like he'd been pinned to the floor. The

President lost his balance and began falling forward. Josh Sizemore instinctively grabbed for the President, grasping his right arm. The momentum swung the President sideways, his head surging into a light pole. The light hit the ground, the President landed on top of it, and Rosebud landed on top of him. The President's face was driven into the opening of the light box, causing one of the tungsten halogen bulbs to implode. The implosion triggered the second bulb. Blinding hot gas and glass fragments blew into Roosevelt's face. With the light destroyed, the area grew immediately dark.

"Quick, turn the other lights towards us!" Mike Benchley shouted. Agents immediately surrounded the President.

"Open up, let some light in," Josh ordered. Benchley began pushing the agents back. Rosebud easily pushed up and rolled off the President while Josh carefully rolled the President onto his back. Blood was coming from the President's face. Burns were scattered over his forehead, cheeks, and chin. His eyebrows were singed and the smell of burning flesh was emanating upward.

"Josh, I can't see."

"Hold on, Mr. President, please! Marty, contact Dr. Sullivan at the White House. I want him airlifted here on Copter One STAT. Mike, please notify George Washington University Medical Center. Tell them to have their top ophthalmology team standing by."

"I'm on it, Josh," Mike said.

"Josh, Marty, can you hear me?"

"We're here, Mr. President," said Josh.

"Where's Rosebud?"

"I'm here, Jon," Rosebud replied.

"It looks like I'm going to be out of commission for a while. Tomorrow evening, I was to address the American people with details of the peace accords and the part you played. I won't be able to keep that commitment."

"I'll get word out to the media your appearance will be delayed, sir," said Marty.

"No, you won't. The people need answers and so does Congress. They need their President to keep his commitment and provide details of the agreement. I can't do it tomorrow—but Rosebud can. We created him for situations such as this. Let's put the taxpayer's money to good use. Rosebud, I have a speech sitting on the Resolute desk in the Oval Office. You are to deliver that speech on nationwide television tomorrow evening. Will you do that for me?"

"Yes, Jon, I will do it. Word-for-word. You must not worry. I want you to focus on getting well. We will see this through together."

"Amazing," said Marty. "It's like I just listened to the President talk to himself!"

Josh nodded. "You did, Marty. You did."

THE MEDEVAC COPTER was on the ground in minutes. Dr. Sullivan and medics secured the President on the flight stretcher.

Agents surrounded the chief executive as Josh Sizemore and Mike Benchley led them toward the copter. A crowd began forming as soon as the helicopter landed. Agents kept them back at sidewalk distance, but the monument lighting illuminated the surroundings. Agents were scanning the crowd while the President was loaded for transport.

"Agent Graves, this is Mike Benchley, can you hear me?" The roar of the rotors was deafening.

"Yes, Mike, I can hear you—but just barely."

"There's a guy about twenty people from the east-end of the crowd. Looks like he's wearing a blue windbreaker and a ball cap. Get some ID, please."

"Roger that. Stand by."

"What's going on, Mike?" asked Josh Sizemore.

"Maybe I'm just jumpy, but that guy looks a lot like Donny Mancuso!"

Don't miss out!

Visit the website below and you can sign up to receive emails whenever WR Hulkenberg publishes a new book. There's no charge and no obligation.

https://books2read.com/r/B-A-AHTZ-GYRIC

BOOKS 2 READ

Connecting independent readers to independent writers.

About the Author

WR Hulkenberg has been a writer for more than twenty years, authoring more than sixty movie scripts. His background in Hollywood, science fiction, and government are often brought together in a worldview that encompasses the meaning and importance of life, family, and faith. His books include contemporary fiction, historical fiction, science-fiction, fantasy and mystery. He and his wife, Joyce, have been happily married for more than forty years. They have five children, four grandchildren. They love to travel and are especially fond of cruises with family and friends. You can visit his website at www.generationAIthebook.com

Printed in the USA
CPSIA information can be obtained
at www.ICGtesting.com
LVHW020819230224
772590LV00041B/647

9 798223 689614